"*You are everything to me.*

"Wh[...]
ing bu[...]
I . . . I[...]
if I wa[...]
strong[...] with you. I'm going to do that now. I promise. Because I simply cannot imagine choosing a life without you in it."

She barely managed to speak the last words before he was kissing her, pulling her closer, his arms tight about her waist and shoulders, too impatient to wait a moment longer to embrace her softness and taste her sweetness.

She reciprocated with an eagerness that wrought a groan from his throat, her desperation for closeness equal to his. Fingers splayed across his back, she matched his movements, following his lead as he deepened the kiss, exploring and sharing an unspoken wave of emotion.

By Sophie Barnes

Novels

A MOST UNLIKELY DUKE
HIS SCANDALOUS KISS
THE EARL'S COMPLETE SURRENDER
LADY SARAH'S SINFUL DESIRES
THE DANGER IN TEMPTING AN EARL
THE SCANDAL IN KISSING AN HEIR
THE TROUBLE WITH BEING A DUKE
THE SECRET LIFE OF LADY LUCINDA
THERE'S SOMETHING ABOUT LADY MARY
LADY ALEXANDRA'S EXCELLENT ADVENTURE
HOW MISS RUTHERFORD GOT HER GROOVE BACK

Coming Soon

THE DUKE OF HER DESIRE

Novellas

MISTLETOE MAGIC (from *Five Golden Rings:
A Christmas Collection*)

SOPHIE BARNES

A Most Unlikely Duke

Diamonds in the Rough

AVONBOOKS

An Imprint of HarperCollinsPublishers

HarperCollins
PUBLISHERS
Since 1817

A MOST UNLIKELY DUKE. Copyright © 2017 by Sophie Barnes. All rights reserved. Printed in the United States of America. No part of this book may be used or reproduced in any manner whatsoever without written permission except in the case of brief quotations embodied in critical articles and reviews. For information, address HarperCollins Publishers, 195 Broadway, New York, NY 10007.

First Avon Books mass market printing: July 2017

Print Edition ISBN: 978-0-06-256678-2
Digital Edition ISBN: 978-0-06-256681-2

FIRST EDITION

17 18 19 20 21 QGM 10 9 8 7 6 5 4 3 2 1

To the underdogs of the world
And to George Bernard Shaw for offering inspiration

Chapter 1

London, 1818

Thick clouds darkened to shades of gray as they rolled across the London sky. Beneath them, standing in the middle of the Black Swan courtyard, Raphe Matthews drew back his fist, his muscles bunching tightly together—just long enough for him to assess the angle and speed with which to release all that power. Instinct made it a brief calculation. Less than a second, and then he sent his fist flying.

The punch snapped his opponent's face sideways, producing a spray of spit and blood that painted the air with specks of crimson. A cheer erupted from those who'd come to witness the fight—a motley selection of hardened individuals. This place was not for the weak or the wealthy. It reeked of filth and the daily struggle to survive. This was St. Giles, but it might as well have been the bowels of hell for all the difference it made.

"Come on!" someone shouted.

Raphe's other fist met a hard chest with a *crunch*. His knuckles ached, the force of the punch vibrating through him.

"Matthews, Matthews, Matthews . . ." The chant shook the air while Raphe shifted his footing, regaining his balance just in time to accept the blows that followed. He didn't mind, for it only revealed his opponent's sudden desperation.

Raising his fists to block the attack, Raphe bobbed to the side, turning away, just out of reach. And yet, he was close—so close he could smell the sweat on the other man's skin, see the fear that shone in his eyes, the beads of moisture clinging to his hair that dripped onto his brow.

More shouts flooded the air, drowning him in a cacophony of unintelligible noise. The wave of encouragement shifted, alerting him that support had changed—no longer in his favor.

Forcing it into the background, Raphe focused on the man he was meant to beat. Today his name was Calvin Butler. Raphe launched himself forward, surrendering to the rage, and let the punches fly, beating back pain and anger until Calvin Butler lay stretched out on the ground, hands covering his face in surrender. A fleeting second of silence passed, just long enough to be sure of the outcome, and then the spectators sent up a roar in response to Raphe's victory.

Exhausted, he stumbled back, a light drizzle dampening his skin. A coat was draped over his shoulders while Butler was helped to his feet—a sorry sight, with his blackened eye and swollen lip distorting an otherwise handsome face.

Turning away, Raphe pushed his way in the direction of the taproom. All he wanted right now was a drink.

Fast.

"Butler ain't lookin' too good," Raphe's friend, Benjamin Thompson, said as he came up beside him. A couple of inches shorter than Raphe, his green eyes were a handsome complement to his ginger hair and freckles. He was without a doubt the kindest and most dependable person Raphe knew, besides his own sisters. Together, they made their way to the bar, where Ben promptly called for a server. "Give us a couple o' pints."

Resting his elbows on the counter, Raphe grunted his response to Ben's question. "He knew what 'e was in fer."

Ben nodded. The beer arrived, and both men took a healthy swig. "Ye could 'ave been gentler, though. The man was done. No need to keep beatin' at him like that."

Stilling, Raphe slid his gaze toward his friend. "I couldn't 'elp it." The rage had burned its way through him, driving him forward and filling his mind with one singular purpose: The need to win. "I don't know 'ow to fight any other way."

"I know," Ben said softly.

No, you don't. You have no bloody idea.

In this, he'd never been completely honest, not even with Ben. "In any case, the blunt's pretty good—lets me keep a roof over me sisters' heads."

"Aye, an' a decent one at that."

Raphe couldn't argue. He'd visited Ben's home once—an overcrowded single room that he shared with his parents and five siblings. By comparison, Raphe and his sisters lived like royalty. "Have ye ever thought of gettin' out of this place? Out of St. Giles?"

Ben shrugged his shoulders. "An' go where?"

"Somewhere better. Christ, Ben, anywhere's better than this. Ye're a likeable man. Ye could probably snatch up a job at one of 'em fancy 'ouses in Mayfair."

His friend snorted. "An' 'ave some nob lookin' down on me, demandin' I polish 'is boots—or worse, empty 'is chamber pot? I'd rather stay by the docks, thank ye very much. At least there I can take some pride in me work."

"Understood. But the pay there's never goin' to afford ye with yer own home. Don't ye wish to marry one day?"

"Sure. But there's a limit to what I'm willing to do for a bit of blunt, Raphe." He took another sip of his beer. "I'll not lose me dignity by workin' for a class o' people I can't abide, nor by lowerin' meself to doin' demeanin' work."

The words speared Raphe to his soul, filling him with shame. "I know," he muttered with admiration. If only he could be more like him, not wanting anything beyond what life had tossed his way. Perhaps, if he didn't have his sisters to consider, he wouldn't care so much.

"Ye fought well today, lad," a man's voice suddenly spoke from directly behind him.

Bristling, Raphe set down his beer on the counter and turned to face his handler, whose attire—a purple velvet jacket and matching top hat—lent an air of flamboyance unmatched by anyone else. And yet, in spite of the fine clothes, there was nothing cultured about this man, a scoundrel who'd gained his wealth through illicit deals and by taking advantage of others. His origins were questionable, but rumor had it he'd killed more than once in pursuit of power. Raphe didn't know what to believe. All he knew was that in spite of his own prejudices, crime in St. Giles had decreased since Carlton Guthrie's arrival eighteen years earlier. Or so he'd been told.

"Mr. Guthrie. Good to see ye." A blatant lie, if ever there was one.

Guthrie's moustache twitched. "Likewise." He

sounded jovial, but only a fool would mistake that for
kindness. Least of all when his henchman, a scarred
boulder of a Scotsman by the name of MacNeil,
stood at his right shoulder. Guthrie nodded toward
Ben, who returned the salutation.

"Come. Share a drink with me," Guthrie said, addressing Raphe. "We've much to discuss, you 'n' I."

"And Thompson?" Raphe asked, not wanting to
abandon his friend.

"I'm sure he'll be willin' to wait for ye till ye get
back." Reaching into his pocket, he pulled out a gold
coin and dropped it in front of Ben. "For yer trouble.
What I 'ave to say to Matthews 'ere doesn't concern
ye. Understand?"

Raphe glared at Guthrie for a moment before
looking at Ben. "I'm sorry. I—"

"No worries," Ben said, pocketing the coin that
would keep his family fed for the next few days. "I'll
see ye tomorrow at work, aye?"

Nodding, Raphe watched him go.

"Well?" Guthrie's voice drew Raphe's attention
back to him. "'Ow about that drink then?"

Eyeing first Guthrie and then MacNeil, Raphe
gave a curt nod. "By all means."

Guthrie's eyes sparkled. "Excellent." His lips
stretched into a smile. "Follow me." Turning away,
he led Raphe through the taproom, where tobacco
smoke mingled with the smell of roasting meat and
beer. Dice rolled across one table in a game of hazard.
A hand touched his thigh, inappropriately stroking
upward until he pushed it away.

"No' in the mood, luv?" the woman to whom it
belonged asked. She was sitting down, her legs spread
across the lap of a man who was busily burying his
face between her half-exposed breasts.

Pitying the life she'd been dealt, he told her gently, "I've not the time."

"La'er then?" she called as he strode away, not answering her question. Blessedly, his sisters had managed to avoid such a fate.

"'Ave a seat," Guthrie said moments later as they stepped inside a private room at the end of a hallway. It was sparsely furnished, with just a plain wooden table and four chairs. On top of the table stood a pitcher and a couple of mugs. "Some ale for me champion?" Guthrie asked, indicating the pitcher.

Grabbing a chair, Raphe dropped down onto it and poured himself a drink, while Guthrie claimed the other chair with more finesse. "Will ye 'ave some?" Raphe asked, indicating the same pitcher.

Guthrie beamed. "Don't mind if I do." He waited for Raphe to pour before reaching for the mug and raising it. "To yer victory today."

"To me victory," Raphe muttered, downing the bitter resentment he felt with a brew to match.

"I've 'igh 'opes for ye," Guthrie said, tapping a finger against his nose. "Unbeaten for the fifteenth time. That's unprecedented, tha' is."

Raphe saw the spark that lit his eyes, like the promise of treasure or some such thing. "Wha' do ye want, Guthrie?"

"So cynical, Matthews." Guthrie's upper lip drew back, revealing his teeth. "Must a man always want some'in? Can't 'e simply enjoy a drink wi' an old friend?"

Old friend?

Hardly.

"Not when 'e's got 'im by the bollocks."

Guthrie's mouth tightened, his eyes darkening just enough to offer a glimpse of his true nature. "Is tha' 'ow ye see our relationship, laddy?"

His demeaning tone made Raphe's muscles flex. He glanced at MacNeil, who stood by the door, running his thumb along the edge of a wicked blade, and was instantly reminded of the punishment he'd suffered the one time when he'd been foolish enough to try and thwart Guthrie's wishes. Shoulders tensing, Raphe returned his gaze to the man who owned him. "'Ow else should I see it? I'm yer puppet, ain't I?"

Guthrie nodded. "Aye, but ye're me favorite one. Which is why I'd like to offer ye a deal."

Raphe stiffened. "What sor' of deal?"

"The sor' that could set ye free, laddy."

A tempting notion, but surely too good to be true. Still, he couldn't help but ask. "What do ye have in mind?"

Leaning forward, Guthrie placed his elbows on the table, the fingers of his right hand reaching up to stroke his chin. "Ye see, there's goin' to be an opportunity soon—a grand one, at that."

Raphe crossed his arms. "Ye don't say."

The corner of Guthrie's eye flinched. "No need to get cocky, now." Snapping his fingers, he drew MacNeil closer. "Give the laddy 'is earnin's." There was a pause, and then a pouch dropped onto the table with a jangling *thump*. "Naturally, we've kept our share."

A fat 90 percent.

"Naturally," Raphe echoed. He didn't bother to hide his displeasure.

"But . . ." Guthrie took another sip of his ale. "Word 'as it, the Bull will be comin' to town in a month or so." Raphe straightened in his chair, while Guthrie wiped his mouth with the back of his hand, removing a line of foam. "If ye figh' 'im and ye win, ye'll be debt-free. The winnings are gonna be that huge."

Raphe didn't doubt it. The Bull was, after all, the

bare-knuckle boxing world champion—undefeated since beating Tobias Flannigan several years earlier. Since then, he'd crippled several of his opponents. The man was a legend. "I'll do it," Raphe said without blinking.

"But if ye lose . . ."

"I won't," Raphe assured him.

"But if ye do . . ."

Grabbing the pouch that still sat on the table, Raphe pocketed his money. "I know the risk, Guthrie, an' I'm willin' to take it."

It was past eleven o'clock in the evening by the time Raphe returned home, his knuckles tender and his body still sore from the fight. Glad to get out of the cold, he closed the door on the rain that now poured from a thunderous sky, shrugged out of his coat and hung it on a hook behind the door just as his sister Amelia entered from an adjoining room that served as a small parlor.

"Good evenin'." She yawned, leaning against the door frame.

Squinting through the darkness, Raphe echoed her salutation. "I thought ye would be asleep by now." Stepping past her, he entered their tiny kitchen and snatched up the tinder box.

"I was," Amelia said, following him into the chilly room.

A threadbare shawl was draped across her shoulders, and as she pulled it tighter with pale and trembling fingers, Raphe felt his heart lurch. This wasn't right. His sister did not deserve to live like this. None of them did.

Pushing aside such fruitless ponderings, he found

a candle, struck a flint and held it to the wick until a flame began to bloom, driving the darkness toward the walls where it struggled against the light.

"If it makes any difference, Juliette's safely tucked into bed." Amelia said, referring to their younger sister, whose weaker disposition was a constant cause for unease. When Raphe lifted the lid of a nearby pot and peered inside, Amelia added, "I made soup for dinner."

"Smells delicious," he dutifully told her.

"We both know 'ow untrue that is, bu' I appreciate yer optimism."

Meeting her gaze, Raphe made a deliberate effort to smile. "Per'aps I can manage some meat for us tomorrow." It would certainly be a welcome change from the potatoes and turnips they'd been eating for what seemed like forever. Christ, he was so tired of having a sore belly all the time, and his sisters . . . they never complained, but he knew they needed better nourishment than what they were getting.

"That'd be nice," Amelia said. Her tone, however, suggested that she doubted his ability to manage such a feat.

Bothered by her lack of faith in him, he grabbed a chunk of bread and tore off a large piece. "A chicken ought to be possible. If we make it last a few days."

Amelia simply nodded. Grabbing a cup, she filled it with water and placed it before him. "I miss the smell of a bustlin' kitchen."

The comment threw him for a second. "Wha'?"

"Meat roastin' on the fire, bread bakin' in the oven." She shook her head wistfully. "It's funny. I can't picture Mama, but I remember Cook—plump cheeks an' a kind smile. I remember bein' 'appy in the kitchen back 'ome."

The sentimental thought made Raphe weary. He didn't bother to point out that she'd only been seven when they'd lost their parents and there'd been nothing left for Raphe to do but turn his back on the house in which they'd spent the early years of their childhoods and walk away, taking his siblings with him. He'd been no more than eight years old and with a mighty burden weighing on his shoulders. "I know this isn't the sor' of life that any of us ever imagined." Feeling his temper begin to rise at the memory of what their parents had done to them all, he added, "Hopefully, in time, things'll get better."

"I'm sure ye're right." *Could she possibly sound any more unconvinced?*

He ate a spoonful of soup, the bland flavor just a touch better than plain hot water. Amelia took a step forward. "The reason I didn't retire with Juliette earlier is 'cause of this letter." She waved a piece of paper in his direction. "It arrived for ye today while ye were out."

Frowning, Raphe stared at her. "Do ye know who sent it?" He couldn't even recall the last time he'd received a letter. Nobody ever wrote to him or his sisters.

"The sender's name's smudged. So's the address. It's a miracle it arrived here at all." Handing the letter to Raphe, she watched as he turned it over and studied the penmanship. Sure enough, the only legible part of the address, which even appeared to have been altered once or twice, was his name: Mister Raphael Matthews.

Curious, he set down his spoon and tore open the seal.

"What's it say?" Amelia eagerly asked.

Reading it slowly to ensure he understood it correctly, Raphe sucked in a breath. He looked up at his sister, blinked, then bowed his head and read the letter again. Silence settled. Amelia's feet shifted, conveying her impatience. It seemed impossible, yet there it was—an extraordinary pronouncement staring him right in the face. Raising his gaze, he leaned back in his seat, the letter rustling between his fingers. "According to this . . ." He shook his head, unable to fathom the absurdity of it. "I'm the new Duke of Huntley."

The silence that followed was acute. Amelia stared at him, eyes wide with a strange blend of surprise, uncertainty and hope. She looked like she wanted to believe him, and yet . . . "Really?"

"If what this says is true, then yes."

"But as far as I know, Papa 'ad no title, so I don't— I don't understand."

"I know. It seems inconceivable. Preposterous. But . . ." He handed her the letter and watched while she read. "Do ye think it might be a hoax?"

Amelia shook her head. "I daren't suppose such a thing. It looks authentic enough with this seal right 'ere and a stamp at the bottom." Squinting, she read the small print that Raphe had missed in his surprise. "Mr. Rupert Etheridge, Solicitor to the Duke of Huntley." Amelia drew a deep breath. Expelled it again. "Bloody hell!"

Raphe quietly nodded. "It's the damnedest thing, don't ye think?" He stared up at Amelia, still trying to process the news.

"Yes. It is. In fact, I wouldn't 'ave thought it possible at all. Not ever."

"Me neither." Amelia handed the letter back to Raphe, He set it on the table next to his bowl of soup and jabbed it with his finger. "But our great grandfather *was* the Sixth Duke of Huntley."

"I'm aware of that. But when 'e died, the title

passed to our great uncle an' split off from our side of the family." She hesitated, as if trying to understand. "I thought succession 'ad to be lineal—that it 'ad to go from son to son. So 'ow can it possibly jump to ye?"

"That's just it. Says 'ere that—" leaning forward, he carefully read what had to be the most significant part, "the letters patent generally include a limitation pertainin' to the heirs of the body, but in this instance it 'as been left out. With this taken into consideration, we've looked fer the late duke's nearest kin, and ye, Mr. Matthews, appear to be it."

"Ye're *it*?" Amelia's eyebrows were raised, her lips parted with dumbfounded surprise.

"Apparently so."

"Bloody hell," she said again as she slumped down onto another chair with a dazed expression. "I can't believe 'e 'ad no sons. Don't aristocrats always 'ave an heir an' a spare for these situations?"

"Yes, but accordin' to this, the Eighth Duke of Huntley's sons perished at sea a couple o' months ago. The shock of it was apparently too much for their father. It killed 'im."

"God." Amelia paused for a moment before saying, "So there's nobody else but ye to fill 'is shoes."

"No. Only problem is, I ain't so sure I'll be able to manage it. It's been fifteen years since . . ." His shoulders stiffened and his chest tightened. He couldn't speak of the event that had plunged them all into destitution. Refused to do so—refused to open the door to the darkness.

Thankfully, Amelia spoke, filling the silence. "Ye can ignore the letter if the thought of being a duke disagrees with ye."

"True." He considered the ramifications of showing up at Huntley House. And then the door to the darkness creaked open, quite unexpectedly, and he was faced with the faith that Bethany had placed in him. She'd believed in his ability to save her. He'd been her older brother, and she'd looked to him for help. Except he'd failed her, and now she was dead.

He slammed the door to the darkness and stared at Amelia. This was it. The chance to do what he wished he could have done for Bethany—a chance to get his surviving sisters out of St. Giles and back to the world where they belonged. "I can't ignore this opportunity. I can't deny ye the things ye deserve." *I can't take the risk of losing you because of my own apprehensions and prejudices.* "Think of it, Amelia. No more 'ungry bellies, or worryin' about money. No more scrapin' to get by."

"No more Mr. Guthrie," she murmured.

The uplifting thought spilled through him, immediately halted by another. "Ye know, we'll never fit in." They'd spent too long amidst the lower classes—could barely recall what it meant to live in a fine house and to have servants. Fox Grove Manor, where they'd grown up, had not been overly large, and most of the servants had been gone at the end, but he had a vague recollection of tin soldiers and the sound of piano music playing while Molly dusted the china. It seemed so peculiar now, the thought of hiring someone to do the simplest task.

He shook his head at the absurdity of it all and wondered if he would be capable of becoming such a person after growing accustomed to the working-class ways. And that was just the beginning. It did not take into account the ridicule they were bound to face with every misstep they made. Because if there was one thing he knew about the aristocracy, it was their cold, hard censure of those who didn't belong.

"Here at least we 'ave friends." He thought of what Ben had told him earlier. Of Ben, in general. He'd never understand the decision Raphe now considered making. Worse than that, Raphe knew in his gut that claiming the Huntley title would destroy that friendship—that in order for him and his sisters to stand any chance at all of making a life for themselves in Mayfair, they'd have to sever all ties to St. Giles.

"True. There·are surely people I'll miss—people who've been kind to us over the years, like Mary-Ellen's family an' the 'aroldsons." She reached for Raphe's hand and squeezed it tight. "But we also 'ave no future 'ere. At least none that I can see."

"I know. It's me greatest regret."

"It's not yer fault."

"No, but I 'ave the chance to change things now." Mind made up, he said, "I'll claim the title an' make things right fer both of ye."

She pressed her lips together and nodded agreement. "It'll be an easier life than the one we 'ave now."

Even though he knew she underestimated the task that stood before them, he didn't argue, happy with the knowledge that his sisters would soon be living the lives to which they'd both been born. But the truth of it was that they faced a daunting struggle—one in which their pride and dignity would be tested at every turn. Steeling himself for the battle ahead, Raphe bid his sister a good night, aware that the dawn would bring turbulence with it.

Chapter 2

Lady Gabriella Radcliffe sat in the parlor of her family home, regarding the man who was sitting opposite her. His name was Simon Nugent, otherwise known as the Earl of Fielding, and more furtively referred to as the most eligible bachelor on the marriage mart. On either side of her sat two of Society's most esteemed women: Gabriella's mother, Portia, the Countess of Warwick, and Gabriella's paternal aunt, Caroline, the Dowager Countess of Everly. Forced from her home by her late husband's detestable nephew, she'd accepted her brother's invitation to come and live at Warwick House two years earlier, much to Portia's aggravation. For although they did their best to be cordial and polite, the two women were so opposite that they collided at almost every opportunity.

"How often do you hunt?" Gabriella's mother inquired of Fielding. Reaching forward, she picked up the plate of biscuits that sat on the table and offered it to him.

He declined with a subtle hand gesture, then simply said, "I do not."

Gabriella's aunt shifted in her seat. The sofa was not very wide, which made Gabriella wonder why they had to sit in such a silly way, like three judges quizzing a plaintiff. Stopping a chuckle that threatened to rise up her throat, she made a choking sound and was rewarded with an elbow in the ribs by her mother.

"I thought all gentlemen hunted," Aunt Caroline remarked.

Brushing something invisible from his knee, Fielding shook his head. "It's a dirty business. I much prefer fishing when I'm in the country."

Gabriella quietly sipped her tea, her concentration fixed on holding the cup correctly. *Crook this finger and point the other.* "Perhaps we can do it together sometime?"

"What? Fish?" Raising an eyebrow, Fielding looked at her incredulously.

"You're slouching," her mother whispered.

Straightening her back, Gabriella silently cursed the day her sister had gone away. Victoria should have been the one sitting here right now. Marrying well had been *her* destiny. Heck, she'd been courted by a marquess—a very determined one at that. Everyone had been thrilled by it. Until she'd thrown it all away in favor of something that no one approved of and forced all attention on Gabriella—the awkward one who wasn't expected to do better than marry someone desperate enough to overlook her flaws.

What a depressing thought.

Another jab in the ribs made Gabriella flinch. She quickly nodded, realizing that she'd abandoned the conversation and that everyone was staring at her. "I—"

"She jests," her mother cut in.

"I don't believe she does," Aunt Caroline said.

Fielding looked from one to the other before pinning Gabriella with a most serious expression. "You are a refined woman, Lady Gabriella. Fishing—well, it's rather a chore, in a way—work that you ought not be engaging in. And then of course there are all the insects to consider."

"I actually rather like them," Gabriella confessed. She'd found a bit of loose trim on her gown and couldn't quite stop herself from picking at it.

Fielding tilted his head. "I beg your pardon?"

"Insects," Gabriella clarified. "I find them rather intriguing."

"She has a collection," Aunt Caroline said.

"Perhaps you would care to see it one day?" Gabriella suggested. "The spiders are especial—"

"She says such silly things, my lord," her mother interrupted with a nervous chuckling sound. "Gabriella does not engage in such . . . such . . ." she waved her hands about as though hoping to catch the appropriate word, "*wild* activity."

"I'm relieved to hear it," Fielding murmured, looking not the least bit convinced as he eyed Gabriella with censorious aloofness. He hesitated a moment as though reflecting on something, and then his eyes suddenly widened. "Was it you who once defended a bumblebee?"

"A childish lapse in judgment that you mustn't hold against her," Gabriella's mother hastened to say before Gabriella could respond. "She's completely transformed now. And her dowry is rather impressive. One mustn't forget about that."

"Of course," Fielding said, allowing a smile. He seemed to relax a bit before saying, "Still, I would suggest that you give up on fishing and entomology. Neither is a very ladylike hobby."

"Indeed," Lady Everly said dryly, "God forbid she gets bit by a mosquito."

Although Fielding's comment grated, Gabriella had to force back a chuckle. On her other side, she could feel her mother's disapproval of her sister-in-law's sarcastic sense of humor radiating off of her.

"An unsightly blemish that you would do well to avoid," Fielding remarked.

"Oh, indeed," Gabriella's mother breathed with unfeigned appreciation of the man's insightfulness. "Perhaps admiring nature from a respectable distance would be best."

Gabriella bit her lip, fighting the urge to argue, since doing so would be considered highly disagreeable. After all, *men do not care for confrontational women*, as her mother had so often told her. To her left, she distinctly heard her aunt say, "Oh, for heaven's sake. It's not as though she's asking to ride in the races."

Fielding paled, his bone-china cup clattering against its saucer to further convey his shock. "I should hope not!"

Gabriella winced, a little embarrassed by her aunt's outspokenness, even though it was one of the traits Gabriella admired most about her.

"Please forgive my sister-in-law," Gabriella's mother grit out. "She has the uncanny ability to say the most nonsensical things."

Though her aunt did not respond, Gabriella could sense her annoyance, as though it were a ball of heat expanding beside her, just waiting to explode. Gabriella would never have the courage to tell Fielding he was wrong about something, or to thwart his wishes herself. To do so would go against her parents' wishes and the duty that weighed on her shoulders since Victoria's scandalous departure from Society. And since Gabriella *had* had the fortune of attracting Fielding's attention—albeit with the help of her dowry—she would try not to do anything to upset the delicate balance of their courtship, lest she ruin everything by sending him running in the opposite direction.

So, rather than adding fuel to the proverbial fire, she prayed for the mood in the parlor to change for the better, while keeping her mouth firmly shut. She turned her attention to admiring Fielding's attire instead—a gold waistcoat, embroidered with pale blue flowers beneath a navy blue jacket. He was celebrated by the *Mayfair Chronicle* as the most fashionable man in London. She briefly wondered how much of his time he must spend with his tailor, valet, and mirror.

"Gabriella!"

Gabriella blinked. "I beg your pardon?"

"Pay attention," her mother hissed in her ear.

"I was just complimenting your beauty." Fielding spoke gently, his voice no doubt capable of capturing any number of hearts. "May I say that you look particularly pretty today?" With his hands elegantly folded upon his lap, back straight and feet precisely placed at just the right angles, he sat as he always did—as though he were posing for a portrait. "The rose-colored hue of your gown agrees with your fair complexion in a very pleasing way."

Dipping her head, Gabriella responded with a discreet smile that she hoped would reflect her pleasure without distorting her features. As her mother always said, one must not smile with exaggeration. *Teeth are for eating, not for displaying.*

"You are too kind, my lord," Gabriella murmured.

"Not at all." Carefully, he picked up his teacup, took a sip and returned it to its saucer. The biscuits on the plate in the center of the table remained untouched. Fielding would not eat in front of any of them, and because he wouldn't, neither would they. He glanced toward the window before looking back at her. "It is a pleasant day today."

Gabriella nodded. "Did you walk here, or ride?"

"I drove my curricle." He paused for a second as if considering something. "Perhaps you would like to try it? We could take it for a drive in the park. With your mother's permission, of course."

"What a generous offer," Gabriella's mother said. "I see no reason why you cannot go."

Setting down her teacup, Lady Everly said, "It will be your first public appearance together, will it not?" Her aunt's implication was clear. She meant to caution Gabriella that if she accepted this offer, people would see her with Fielding, thus making their courtship official.

Gabriella hesitated, torn between duty and her lukewarm feelings for the man her parents had selected for her. Was marrying Fielding what she truly wanted? No. It wasn't. Not in the least. But with the scandal of Victoria first ending her engagement to the Marquess of Bellmore and then marrying into the working class still looming, Gabriella was keenly aware that her family depended on her to save them. And besides, there was no one else whom she liked better than Fielding. Whether she married him or one of the other earls or viscounts who'd shown an interest made little difference. In the grander scheme of things, he was better than nothing, she supposed.

And she certainly had no illusions about marrying for love. It simply wasn't the way of her world—a world in which all that really mattered was one's reputation, fortune and pedigree. So rather than decline, as her aunt no doubt hoped she would since she couldn't abide Fielding herself, Gabriella chose to please her parents instead by saying, "Certainly, my lord. I think I should like that a great deal." At any rate, it would give them something to do beyond drinking tea and discussing trivialities. "Allow me to fetch my bonnet and shawl."

As she rose, so did he. Offering her his hand, he guided her carefully around the furniture, releasing her when no more obstacles stood in her path. "I would recommend a blue one," he said as they bid her family adieu and exited the parlor.

"I beg your pardon?"

"The shawl," he said. "A blue one will match your eyes, as well as my jacket."

"Of course." Thankfully, she managed a smile—one that hid her inclination to hit him.

They set out ten minutes later at an easy trot, the horse's hooves clopping against the cobbled street while their tails swayed happily from side to side in perfect synchrony. Hesitantly, Gabriella cast a look in Fielding's direction. Too often, his pomposity detracted from his physical appearance, which was, Gabriella decided, quite pleasing to the eye. Oh, her aunt spoke of some great passion and how important it was for Gabriella to find that in order to be truly happy, but she disagreed. Right now she was only concerned with convincing him to let her continue with her entomology.

Biting her lip, she considered the task. Perhaps they could live apart? What a pleasant thought. She could spend her days cataloguing butterflies and playing with their children. She instinctively cringed at the idea of how such children might be produced, but she supposed she would simply endure the ordeal with eyes closed and good cheer while pondering . . .

something else. But to fantasize about making a love match . . . well, she was not disillusioned enough to allow such fanciful ideas to distract her from her duty.

Determined to earn his good favor, lest his thoughts still lingered on her less agreeable attributes, Gabriella indicated his horses with a wave of her hand. "They are a magnificent pair," she remarked as Fielding navigated his way along Piccadilly to where Hyde Park began.

"Thank you," he said, sounding genuinely pleased. "As you know, I take my horses quite seriously. When I saw these two beauties at Tattersall's last week, I simply knew I had to have them. Quite a blow to the Earl of Bromwell, who was eager to buy them as well."

"Perhaps you will allow him to borrow them one day?"

Fielding turned then, the shock on his face conveying his astonishment, and perhaps his outrage too, at what she'd just suggested. "I think not." Returning his attention to the reins, he added, "I am not the sort of man who enjoys sharing."

Gripping the seat iron at her side, Gabriella did her best to hide her emotions. She knew he was both competitive and possessive, that he loved nothing better than winning—it was what he lived for, the knowledge that he outdid all others in every pursuit that interested him. Which was why he always bought the year's most fashionable carriages, the best bred horses and the latest innovations, including a private rail and locomotive for his country estate. It also explained his reason for coming to call on her in the first place.

Glancing aside as they entered the park, the cool May air infused with warm rays of sunshine blushing her cheeks, she knew the attention she'd garnered after her father had added Victoria's dowry to her own was the only thing that had piqued Fielding's interest. He wanted her fortune, she sensed, just as he'd wanted the horses last week, and just as he'd want another silk waistcoat tomorrow.

But, she reflected, she ought not complain. After all, she would be gaining a countess's title and would live a life of comfort. Her parents would be pleased, and the whole of Society would be impressed, while she would have her children and her insects. She glanced at Fielding once more. Perhaps she ought to make her continued practice of entomology a prerequisite for marriage. Yes, that was the answer. She'd speak to her father and make the request and then cross her fingers and toes in the hope that he wouldn't deny her.

"Ah, look," Fielding said, the horses slowing to a gentle walk. "Here come the Marquess and Marchioness of Wilmington." He tipped his hat while Gabriella waved, their curricle passing the Wilmington phaeton as it rolled in the opposite direction.

She was keenly aware that Fielding had refrained from mentioning Lord Wilmington's friend, the notorious Mr. Lowell, who'd also been present in the carriage—a wealthy club owner whose fondness for opera singers, ballerinas and other men's unhappy wives, if the rumors were to be believed, had labeled him something of a lothario.

But Gabriella knew that it was more than that alone—that it was Lowell's constant criticism of the nobility that grated on Fielding's nerves. As if to underscore this thought, he suddenly said, "I cannot abide that man. He completely lacks the elegance and poise that sets our class apart from the rest." There was no doubt to whom he was referring, for she'd heard him say it before. "The aristocracy can only survive if we keep ourselves raised above the masses. All will be lost once we dip our toes into the pool of commonality, and frankly, there is nothing more common than Mr. Lowell, if you ask me. If you knew of the places he is said to frequent—" Fielding shuddered. "He is without a doubt bad company, my lady. *That* is an unavoidable fact."

She would not argue.

"Your mother has invited me to join her book club," she said instead, deliberately changing the subject. "I received a letter from her yesterday afternoon."

"She likes you a great deal, you know, which is something of an accomplishment on your part." He glanced at her briefly before turning the curricle onto a tree-lined path. "Mama detests silly girls, and I quite agree with her. Most of the debutantes these days are far too bold and—daring."

"But I am not," Gabriella found herself saying as they passed a trio of young ladies who were out enjoying a stroll. She recognized all of them, and so she waved. They returned the gesture with disingenuous politeness.

"Heavens no. You, my lady, are the very picture of propriety."

The remark almost made Gabriella laugh. If he only knew how boisterous and carefree she'd been until a year ago when her parents had realized that everything depended on *her* ability to comport herself. She'd been pulled and squeezed ever since until she'd finally fit the box they intended for her.

"You would never say something untoward or do anything scandalous," he added, her bumblebee

rescue completely forgotten. "Your perfect upbringing would simply disallow it. Indeed, your code of
conduct is, in my experience, so thoroughly ingrained
in you that it would be impossible for anyone to find
fault with your character."

Gabriella stared at him. Fielding was describing
the sort of lady she'd been trying to be since making her debut one month earlier—the attributes that
her mother had assured her would secure an ideal
husband—even though it was always forced. Now
it was making her feel horribly dull and uninterest-
ing too. She couldn't help herself from sighing. "My
sister, Victoria, is very different."

"Yes," he agreed, his tone significantly tighter
than before. "I would advise you not to speak of her
if you can avoid doing so since distancing yourself
from the scandal she caused last year should be your
greatest priority."

"I suppose so," Gabriella agreed. She regretted
bringing it up.

"Not to worry though. Keeping my company
ought to be of great advantage to you, and once we
marry, your sister's mistakes will simply fade into the
background. You shall see, my lady. As the Countess
of Fielding, people's eagerness to earn your favor will
make them forget what happened."

Gabriella cringed at the superficiality with which
Fielding described their peers. As for her sister . . .
she still had a hard time coming to terms with her
hasty decision to marry, and her sudden departure
from England. The wedding had taken place by special license, so swiftly that Gabriella had not found
out about it until it was over. Which could only mean
one thing. *Couldn't it?*

An awful report in the *Mayfair Chronicle*, describing the broken engagement with Bellmore and Victoria's apparent elopement with Mr. Connolly, an ironworks owner from New York, had followed. In response to which Gabriella's mother and father had sat Gabriella down and told her of her duty and how she alone would have to save them from ruin.

A year of unrelenting tutoring had followed, for it was no family secret that Gabriella was the difficult child on whom little hope had been placed before. It had been awful, but she had also understood her parents' despair. Losing Victoria to such a fate had been both surprising and devastating, though Gabriella supposed that the choice her sister had made to marry for love was something to be admired. In fact, she knew that she ought to be happy for Victoria, yet, she simply couldn't help resenting her for not confiding her feelings for Connolly in her. After all, they'd always been close, the two-year age difference between them completely insignificant.

Just a note. That was all that Victoria had left her in parting. And that had been almost a year ago. She'd yet to receive a letter with news of her life in America.

Disliking the mood their subject of conversation had brought on, Gabriella said, "I don't believe I have commented on your gloves yet, my lord. I must confess that I find that shade of brown extremely fetching. Your taste in clothes as a whole is quite impeccable."

He immediately rewarded her compliment with a pleasant smile that almost reached his eyes. She did not love him and she did not think that he would ever love her, but that didn't really matter, did it? In the end they would both be perfectly content, and with her sister in mind, Gabriella was determined not to stray from her obligations, even though the thought of praising her husband's ego until the day one of them expired did seem rather taxing.

No. She would definitely have to arrange for them to live apart. Perhaps that ought to be stipulated as well? She would have her children, her insects and perhaps a dog—a small one that could curl up in her lap—while Fielding would have his horses and her dowry and the heir he needed while avoiding the trials and tribulations that invariably came with marriage. Really, the suggestion would no doubt thrill him. He could remain in town while she enjoyed the country. It was the perfect solution, though one that probably ought to be discussed during a later visit when she'd had a little more time to consider the correct way in which to broach the topic.

But considering what she knew of Fielding and his keen determination to get his hands on her hundred thousand pounds, she was fairly confident that he would agree to a great many concessions.

With this in mind and her spirits greatly lifted, she spoke with her soon-to-be fiancé about the people they saw and the beautiful weather—inane topics, but pleasantly safe. And although she disagreed with him on several points, she refrained from voicing her opinion, since she knew that it wouldn't matter one way or another. Indeed, it would serve no purpose at all, other than to irritate him, which was the last thing she wanted now that she sought his compliance.

By the time they returned to St. James Street, where her home was located, she'd learned nothing new about him, and he'd learned nothing new about her. Which meant that all was as expected—their courtship nothing more than a practical arrangement for both parties.

But as they neared Warwick House, they saw that a carriage—indeed, a common hackney—had pulled to a stop in front of the neighboring house where the late Duke of Huntley had resided until his sudden demise two months earlier. Rumor had it that he had not been able to bear the loss of his sons, who'd died just a couple of weeks prior to him in a tragic boating accident. Since then, there had been much speculation about the continuation of the Huntley title, for the duke had been an only child, and his sons had not yet married.

As the curricle came to a halt, Gabriella considered the hackney now blocking the street and delaying their progress. She couldn't help but frown. More so when she saw two girls descending from it with hops and bounces, almost stumbling to the ground in a most inelegant fashion. Clearly, they were not accustomed to anything other than walking. And their clothes . . . well, they looked as though they belonged to street urchins.

"Are they not aware that the servants' entrance is at the back?" Fielding asked, his harsh tone startling Gabriella out of her own ponderings.

"Apparently not," she said as she watched the girls, who appeared to be older than she'd initially thought—around her own age, it seemed. They certainly looked like servants, with their rumpled attire taken into account, but why on earth were they there? Pierson, the Huntley butler, did not have reason to hire more staff. *Unless* . . . The door to Huntley House swung open and a footman strode out, approaching the girls without pause. Gasping, Gabriella placed her hand on Fielding's arm. "Do you suppose that an heir has been found?"

"I don't know. Perhaps—"

His words were cut short by the *thud* of a bag being tossed from the carriage. A man's head appeared next, his profile drawing attention to his unshaven jaw and the stray locks of dark hair falling against his brow. Gabriella stared as he leapt from the carriage, straightened himself to an astonishing height and stepped onto the pavement, where he extended his hand to the footman, who paused for an uncomfortable moment before awkwardly accepting the gesture.

Another figure began to descend from the carriage. "How odd," Gabriella remarked as she recognized Pierson. "Don't butlers usually conduct interviews at the house?"

"Mine does," Fielding said. "Fetching the servants himself, by common hack, seems highly irregular."

The scruffy-looking fellow suddenly turned toward the driver. "That'll be all," he called, his voice carrying the uncultured tone of someone who had no business standing on the pavement of St. James Street in the middle of Mayfair.

"Most irregular indeed," Fielding murmured.

Gabriella had to agree. She watched with growing curiosity as the footman struggled to pick up the bag that had been dropped from the carriage earlier, while its owner seemed quite unwilling to part with it. A strange tug-of-war ensued with Pierson looking on in exasperation.

"Forgive me, my lady," Fielding said as he tied the reins securely to the front rail of the curricle, "but this situation demands some clarification. Just give me a moment. I will be right back." And then he was gone, leaving Gabriella to watch as he approached the group, his affected tone halting all action with impressive efficiency.

Ignoring the tableau was not an option. Not when she found her curiosity piqued for the first time in as long as she could remember. Annoyingly, she couldn't hear the exchange that was now taking place several yards away, save for the occasional word.

But, at least she could see the expressions of the would-be servants and Pierson as they faced Fielding—a distraction that allowed the footman to take control of the bag and go back inside the house. As far as Gabriella could tell, none of the newcomers appeared to be the least bit bothered by Fielding's arrival, though Pierson did seem uncharacteristically flustered. Curiously, it looked as though he didn't know how to respond to the argument that was presently brewing between the scruffy-looking man and Fielding. And they *were* arguing. Or at least the man was. Indeed, he'd pushed the girls behind him and stepped toward Fielding, confronting him with his much larger size while Pierson stood to one side with a perplexed look on his face.

Which was when Gabriella decided that she simply *had* to interfere. Clearly, the servant lacked manners, while Fielding would likely get himself hurt.

So she hoisted herself down, smoothed her skirts so she looked presentable, pasted her practiced Society smile on her face and strolled forward, realizing belatedly that she'd made a tactical error as soon as she met the gaze of the man with whom Fielding was quarrelling. He must have sensed her approach, for his eyes flicked to hers with unashamed interest.

A second passed, but it was enough—enough for Gabriella's footsteps to falter beneath the perusal of those dark, unyielding eyes. His appearance was rough and rugged, his hair a mass of stray locks just begging to be tamed, while his mouth . . . Gabriella swallowed, determined not to let her momentary slip in composure show. He was not of her social class, and yet, with one look, he'd sent heat rushing to her cheeks. It was a reaction unlike any she'd ever experienced before. And in that moment, she hated how weak and susceptible she was to the pleasure of this man's forthright admiration. For it was surely this sort of feeling that had led her sister astray.

His mouth curved with the sort of confidence that could only be owned by those who cared very little about the opinion of others. And as he turned back to Fielding, Gabriella realized that the man had assessed her, found her wanting and promptly dismissed her. "Ye're all the same," he said to Fielding. "Makin' assumptions."

Pierson sputtered as if in protest. "You—"

"I beg your pardon, sir," Fielding said, "but are you telling me that you are *not* hired help?" He punctuated the question with a glare that made Gabriella cringe.

"My lord," Pierson managed as though choking on bread crumbs. "This is—"

"Nobody of consequence," the man finished.

Fielding held his ground. "Have some respect, man. Pierson is a butler, above you in every conceivable way and hardly deserving of being interrupted by the likes of you."

"Is that so?" The scruffy man asked as he took a step closer.

"My apologies," Gabriella said, deciding to act before the man, whoever he might be, decided that this piece of pavement was somehow worth fighting over. "My friend here merely wished to discover if the next Duke of Huntley has been found, since it does appear as though Pierson is hiring new servants. We could think of no other reason and were simply curious to know who he might be and when we might have a chance of making his acquaintance."

She'd caught his attention again, and not without some degree of discomfort. She was a lady, after all, and Fielding was an earl. How could this man possibly find them wanting? And yet, the evidence that he did was plain to see in his critical expression.

For the longest moment, the man simply stood there staring at her while the two young girls—women, really—peeked out from behind him with narrowed eyes. Dressed in a plain white shirt, brown trousers and a jacket to match, he wore no hat, waistcoat, or cravat. Gabriella watched in fascination as he swallowed, the movement so subtle and yet so utterly perfect.

"Madam?"

Her eyes shot to his, the indignation of realizing that her perusal had been observed flipping her stomach inside out and setting her off balance. The feeling was swiftly followed by no small degree of irritation. "*My lady*, if you please," she told him tartly. Tipping her nose up a little, she did her best to feign unaffected aloofness.

To her consternation, he reached out, snatched up her hand and bowed over it, brushing her glove with his lips. And yet, in spite of the barrier between them, she felt the heat of that kiss all the way to the depth of her soul. *Ridiculous*. She straightened her back and prepared to give the presumptuous man a piece of her mind just as Fielding jumped in, pushing the man away from her while Pierson made an odd sound of protest.

"How dare you take such liberties?" Fielding demanded.

The other man raised an eyebrow. "I wasn't aware that I was doin' any such thing." And then he shrugged before turning about and addressing Pierson and his two companions, who stood wide-eyed and gaping. "Shall we go inside then?"

"Yes," Pierson exclaimed, already leading the way up the front steps while the three raggedly clad individuals paraded after him.

"Well. I never," Fielding muttered, looking rather as if he might stomp his foot in protest at any moment.

Gabriella paid him no mind. She watched until the front door of Huntley House closed behind them, more curious than ever about what had just transpired.

Chapter 3

When Raphe woke the morning after arriving at Huntley House, the first thing he noticed was how comfortable he felt, his body completely relaxed in a liquid state of bliss made possible by the luxurious mattress on which he lay. And the delicious beef stew he'd had for dinner. That alone had been worth coming here for. Stretching his body, he opened his eyes and looked up, admiring the velvet canopy of the four-poster bed he presently occupied. It was his now: the bed, whatever furniture stood beyond it, the other rooms, the house itself . . .

What a peculiar thought!

He sat up and glanced about, his eyes shifting from the marble-topped bedside table to a footstool upholstered in a very expensive-looking fabric, to a crystal vase filled with porcelain flowers. He blinked. *Why the hell would anyone want porcelain flowers?* An absurd extravagance, to be sure.

Swinging his legs over the side of the bed, Raphe stood up and crossed to the wardrobe. It squeaked open to reveal the few clothes he'd brought with him, all neatly hanging to one side. He straightened himself and selected a clean shirt and a pair of fresh trousers. Not the fashionable look expected from a duke, but it would have to do for now, as there was nothing else available.

A knock sounded, and before he could utter a word, the bedroom door swung open and his valet marched in. Raphe had forgotten about him. "Good morning, Your Grace. I trust you slept well?" the man asked.

"Err . . ." Raphe scratched his head. Christ, he sounded daft. Not to mention that he was naked—a fact that didn't appear to faze his valet in the least. Raphe stepped behind the still open wardrobe door and put on his trousers. "What's yer name again?"

"Humphreys, Your Grace. Max Humphreys." Raphe pulled the shirt he'd selected over his head. "Right. Well I shan't be needin' ye, Humphreys. Now, if ye don't mind . . ."

"But—"

"I've been dressin' meself since I was a lad, Humphreys. T'would be bloody strange to let another man manage it fer me now."

Humphreys stared at him for a fraction of a second as though he were some rare artifact one might discover on an anthropological dig. "Of course." He didn't budge.

Running both hands through his hair, Raphe let out a strenuous sigh. It wasn't Humphreys's fault that his new master was undeserving of his title—that he'd likely embarrass the Huntley name and everyone associated with it. It wasn't his fault that Raphe felt more comfortable talking to washerwomen and laborers than with ladies and gentlemen.

The unbidden image of pale blue eyes framed by long dark lashes floated to the front of his mind. She'd been stunning, the lady he'd met on the street outside his new home yesterday, even if she had tipped her

arrogant nose at him. But she hadn't been quite as in-
sufferable as her friend, whom Raphe had been sorely
tempted to punch.

Instead, he'd enjoyed the sport of unsettling the
lady, which in turn had riled the gentleman most ef-
fectively. He could still envision her creamy skin and
her golden curls—the flushed lips that had somehow
reminded him of the strawberries he'd once enjoyed
as a child. Best of all, they'd had no idea who he was.
That bit made him laugh.

"Your Grace?"

Collecting himself, Raphe focused his eyes on
Humphreys, who still hadn't moved. "I'm sorry. I
didn't mean to be rude to ye just now. All of this—it's
still quite fresh, an' . . ."

"Frustrating?" Humphreys prompted when Raphe
failed to finish his sentence.

"Quite."

A pause followed. Humphreys gave a curt nod.
"If that will be all, Your Grace, I would like to ask
your secretary to make arrangements for a tailor to
be brought round, along with a seamstress for your
sisters."

"Speakin' of which," Raphe said as he slid his foot
inside one of the woolen socks that Amelia had knit-
ted, "Have ye seen them yet today?"

"No, Your Grace, but—"

"Do me a favor an stop callin' me that. Me name's
Raphe. Matthews if ye prefer to be more formal."

"I . . . I'm afraid I cannot call you that, Your
Grace. It wouldn't be seemly." He averted his gaze
and Raphe decided to drop the issue since the man
was looking horribly uncomfortable. "As for your
sisters, I do believe they are presently having their
breakfast in the dining room."

"Well then," Raphe said as he put on the other sock and his shoes, "Ye'd better lead me to 'em." He was eager to see them both, to talk to them about the drastic change in their lifestyle and to hear their impressions. He also wanted to get on with the day, mostly because he was bothered by the way in which he'd left things with Guthrie. In order to have a clear conscience, he would have to ensure that the one hundred and fifty pounds he still owed the man on account of his father's poor judgment was paid off as soon as possible—with an additional sum to compensate for walking away from the deal they'd struck regarding the fight. It was imperative that Guthrie found the amount large enough to forgive him the slight.

"Are you quite certain that it is wise of us to come here at this hour?" Gabriella asked her mother as they made their way up the front steps of Huntley House together with Gabriella's aunt. "According to Anna," she added, in reference to her maid, "the duke only just arrived yesterday. Should we not allow him more time in which to get settled before requesting he see us?"

"Nonsense, Gabriella. He will know to expect callers, and as his neighbor, I should like to see him first."

"What your mother means is that she'd like to sate her own curiosity before Lady Hammersmith has the opportunity to do so," Aunt Caroline remarked, while Gabriella's mother gave the knocker a solid rap. "Gossip is, after all, such a valuable commodity."

Gabriella's mother huffed. "Must you be so dramatic all the time, Caro? All I want to do is issue a dinner invitation."

"What you want," Aunt Caroline countered, "is to show off the duke as though his presence here reflects directly on you."

"I am merely trying to be polite." The front door opened and Gabriella's mother immediately produced a brilliant smile. "Pierson! How lovely it is to see you again."

Gabriella found her mother's over-joyous demeanor a trifle too sugary. Perhaps Pierson did too, for he did not look the least bit pleased. "Lady Warwick," he said. "What can I do for you?"

"I hear the new duke has arrived." Gabriella's mother craned her neck as though hoping to find the man hiding behind Pierson. "Frankly, I was a little disappointed to discover it from my maid, since I would have thought that you would have had the courtesy to send me a note yourself. No matter, though, since we are now here. Please show us in."

Pierson looked as though he might choke. "I . . . er—that is . . ."

"Good heavens," Aunt Caroline said. "You look unwell, Pierson. Whatever is the matter?"

"Nothing!" He stared at them stiffly, his body firmly wedged between them and the foyer, as though he was facing a tidal wave that he was intent on holding back.

From behind him came the sound of approaching voices. *Men's* voices. Pierson closed his eyes for a brief second, as though willing the sound away. "Ladies, this really isn't a good time." He moved with the distinct intention of closing the door on them.

"Our apologies," Gabriella said. Coming here had clearly been a mistake. She turned to her mother. "Come, Mama. We can return at a more opportune time."

"Very well." Lady Warwick sniffed. The approaching voices grew louder. Pierson's face went stark.

"I think that may be him right now," Aunt Caroline remarked.

Gabriella's mother craned her neck again and rose up onto her toes. "Oh yes. I think you may be right."

"Lady Warwick," Pierson clipped. The man seemed to grow in height. "Please step away from the door so that I may close it."

Gabriella groaned. He really wasn't acquainted with her mother's tenacity when it came to satisfying her curiosity. A fact immediately made clear when the lady in question turned swiftly about and appeared to lose her footing. One moment she was standing elegantly at Gabriella's side. The next, she was complaining about the pain of a supposedly sprained ankle. All so that she could be the first to tell her friends about the new duke. Gabriella dropped her gaze. She wished she'd stayed home and away from all the drama.

"Would you like me to send a footman to inform your husband of your mishap?" Pierson asked.

Gabriella couldn't help but admire the man's unwillingness to bow to her mother's machinations. He'd obviously seen right through her.

"No," her mother said. "What I would like is a chair on which to sit and rest for a while."

Pierson frowned. He studied her. Assessed her. Appeared to be on the verge of denying her request, when a tall, broad-shouldered man stepped up behind him, his eyes as dark and unyielding as they'd been the day before when Gabriella had met him in the street. "What's all the fuss about?" His gaze swept over them, and Gabriella felt her heart tremble a little when it paused on her before moving on to her aunt.

"Your—*ahem*, that is . . ." Pierson looked thoroughly out of sorts. He drew a breath, then cleared his throat. "These ladies have come to call on the duke."

A second passed. The man tilted his head. Gabriella tried not to stare. He looked just as imposing as he had done yesterday. He had to be a servant, just as she and Fielding had surmised, considering his clothing. But why on earth would a servant be interfering with Pierson's duties? A thought struck her. He must have been in the new duke's employ before arriving here—perhaps at some smaller country estate—and had simply arrived ahead of his master. *Yes. That explained it!*

"Well then . . ." The man's gaze returned to Gabriella. The edge of his mouth tilted, not quite enough to form a smile, but enough to do silly things to her knees. She looked away, annoyed that someone like him should have any effect on someone like her. "Let's show 'em to the library."

Pierson's head whipped around to stare at the man. "But—but . . . you cannot possibly—"

"Do it," the man said before turning away. "And 'ave some tea brought in," he shouted before disappearing down a hallway.

Gabriella had no idea what to make of such an encounter. Neither did her mother, it seemed, for she just stood there, blinking as though the world she knew had just come to a screeching halt.

Aunt Caroline, however, allowed a faint chuckle as they started forward. "I do believe this is turning out to be one of the most memorable visits I've had the pleasure of enjoying in a long time. Thank you for suggesting it, Portia."

"I must confess that I am wondering if it was wise

of me to be quite so insistent," Gabriella's mother muttered as they followed Pierson toward the back of the house.

"As the saying goes, curiosity did kill the cat," Aunt Caroline murmured.

"Let's hope it doesn't kill *us*," Gabriella's mother said. "That servant who granted us entry looked positively savage, with that bronzed skin of his and those ill-fitting clothes. One would think he was more at home in a mine than in a duke's employ. Really, I cannot believe such a . . . a . . . *filthy* man is living right next door to us."

"He did not look *filthy*, Mama," Gabriella couldn't help but say. She was feeling a little bad about all the criticism the poor man was getting, first from herself and Fielding and now from her mother. Even though he really should make more of an effort if he meant to live in this part of town. A haircut and a shave would certainly be a good start.

"Here we are," Pierson said, arriving at a large oak door. He knocked once, waited for permission to enter and then opened the door wide so the ladies could file into the room beyond.

Gabriella glanced around the impressive space, where books lined shelves from floor to ceiling, row upon row. It was a while since she'd been inside it last, for she and her family had usually been admitted to one of the parlors or the dining room whenever they'd come to call. But a few years ago, while having tea with the duke and his sons, the Marquess of Shirring and Lord John, the conversation had turned to Gabriella's interest in entomology and Lord John had kindly offered to show her the Huntley collection on the subject. He'd never judged her for it and neither had his brother, perhaps because they'd been childhood friends, their difference in age not too great to stop them from playing catch with each other in the garden. It seemed so strange to be here now when they were all dead—a horrible intrusion that sent a shudder down Gabriella's spine.

Shaking off the depressing sensation, Gabriella looked around in search of the duke, wondering if he would be young or old. Perhaps he'd be married? She really had no idea.

"I don't see him," her mother whispered. "Do you?"

"Not yet," Aunt Caroline said.

"Try lookin' behind ye." The deep rumble, so close that Gabriella felt the air shift as he spoke, made her spin on her heels. Her lips parted at the sight of the man she'd now seen twice before, and air rushed into her lungs, expanding her chest against her thrumming heart. She shook her head, determined to hide her surprise.

It was just like the time when her father had told her that her sister was gone. And she knew now, just as she had then, that things weren't as they should be, and that somehow, in spite of all her efforts to the contrary, her life had become more complicated than it had been before. "*You?*" She tried to look past him. "I don't understand. Where is he? Where is the duke?"

The edge of his mouth tilted, and then he simply stepped around Gabriella, her mother and her aunt, and went to the sideboard. To Gabriella's astonishment, he calmly poured himself a drink. "I'd forgotten how blind the nobility can be," he said, eyeing them as though they were gnats he wouldn't mind swatting. "Ye're a superficial lot." He sipped his brandy. "Ye care only for facades and monetary worth."

"I beg your pardon?" Gabriella's mother asked in the same superior tone that had made many servants wither. It seemed to have no effect on the man she was presently addressing—a man who appeared surprisingly at ease in the duke's library, sampling his liquor.

Gabriella frowned.

No.

She shook her head.

Surely not.

It just couldn't be. *Could it?*

"The worth of a title," he was saying, "yer property . . . yer appearance . . . yer daughter's dowry." His gaze flicked to Gabriella without hesitation. "Yer daughter's ability to elevate yer social status by marryin' well."

Gabriella's mother gasped. "Now see here—"

"Mama," Gabriella hissed, her hand going to her mother's elbow in an urgent attempt to stop her from saying another word.

"I will not allow you to—" Gabriella's mother was saying just as a maid entered carrying a tray.

"The tea, as you requested, Your Grace," the maid said, confirming Gabriella's suspicions.

The silence that followed was so acute, it reminded Gabriella of a still winter's day in the country—fields blanketed by thick snow, muting all audible sound. And then the duke moved, the heel of his shoe scraping the floor as he stepped away from the side table. The effect was a piercing reminder of both time and place, producing a sputtering sound from Gabriella's mother and a light chuckle from Aunt Caroline who seemed to be the only one in the room who found the situation amusing.

The maid departed, barely managing to close the door behind her before it swung open again and two young women tumbled into the room—the same young women whom Gabriella had seen in the duke's company the day before. She eyed them both with interest, watching as they became aware of their guests. Their eyes widened to the size of saucers. "Blimey," one of them said smoothing her gown while the other one made a funny movement that might have been an attempt at a curtsy. "Ye look mighty fine." And then her gaze drifted past Gabriella and her mouth dropped open. "Bloody 'ell! Would ye look at the size of this place?" Gabriella heard her mother take a sharp breath and couldn't help but sympathize. Such unrefined manners must be terribly taxing on her nerves.

"Me sisters," the duke explained. "Amelia an' Juliette."

"Pleasure to meet you," Gabriella said. She couldn't help but feel slightly sorry for the pair, who would now have to interact with her mother over tea with no apparent training to help them. It would not be the least bit enjoyable for them, not to mention the work that lay before them if they were ever to stand a chance of fitting in. She was just about to introduce herself to the women when her mother leaned a bit closer to her and whispered in her ear, "This is a disaster. We ought to leave at once."

But then the duke strode forward and gave them each a hard glare as he waved in the direction of a seating arrangement. "Will ye sit?" he asked.

Chapter 4

Forcing a stoic expression, Raphe waited for the ladies to make their decision. It had taken a great deal of effort not to laugh in response to their wide-eyed dismay when he'd told them who he was. But he'd refrained. Even *he* knew better than to try and ease the mood with a touch of humor. *No.* Against these three Society women, intimidation would be his best ally.

Hesitantly, one of them stepped forward. "I don't believe we were formally introduced." Her cool gaze assessed and considered him in a manner that might have forced a lesser man to retreat. Raphe stared straight back at her without flinching. "I am Lady Warwick," she continued, "And this here is my sister-in-law, the Dowager Countess of Everly." She then waved her hand toward the youngest of the three— the woman whose face had haunted his mind since he'd first laid eyes on her the day before. "My daughter, Lady Gabriella." The three then dipped into graceful curtsies while Amelia and Juliette stood gaping in awe.

Tilting his head, Raphe considered the trio, their perfect posture and elegance. It must have taken years of training to achieve such fluidity of movement. But to what avail? What did they really gain by it? Admiration, perhaps? *What an inane notion.*

Which was why he chose to ignore their efforts by arching a brow, crossing to the sofa and taking a seat. Leaning back, he crossed his legs and nodded to the other available spaces. "Well?"

Lady Warwick's face appeared to turn a shade of green. Clearly, she was not accustomed to such ill treatment. After all, a gentleman did not sit while a lady remained standing. He was perfectly aware. But then again, Raphe mused, he was not a gentleman. Not by any stretch of the imagination. And his sisters . . . well, they were bound to cause a stir, he mused, as they plopped down next to him.

His gaze flicked to Lady Gabriella again. Rather than looking alarmed or angry, as he'd expected her to in response to his poor manners, she looked intrigued and . . . pensive. It was almost as though she considered him a puzzle—one that she was presently trying to solve. The thought did not agree with him in the least. He shifted in his seat, aware that he was probably scowling now.

"Thank you," Lady Everly said, her voice jostling the momentary silence enough for it to shatter. Smiling as though nothing were amiss, she crossed to an armchair and lowered herself into it. "Tea would be lovely right now. Shall I pour?"

The question propelled Lady Warwick and Lady Gabriella forward, both claiming a seat upon the sofa opposite where Raphe and his sisters were sitting. Absently, he watched while Lady Everly served the tea. "Ye live next door. Right?" Raphe found himself saying.

"Yes," Lady Everly replied. She wore a secretive smile that Raphe didn't care for.

"My husband is the Earl of Warwick," Lady Warwick said with pride, as though the title meant that she had made some great accomplishment in life, when all she'd done was agree to marry a man who'd inherited his wealth from his father. Who'd inherited it from *his* father, and so on.

"I see," Raphe said. "How fortunate for ye."

Gabriella coughed, the sound interrupting Lady Warwick's assurance that it was most fortunate indeed. Raphe allowed a bare hint of a smile at the sight of tea spilling from Lady Gabriella's plush lips. There was something so satisfying in unsettling these women who believed themselves to be above mere mortals in every conceivable way. One thing was for certain, however. Lady Gabriella was not an idiot. She'd recognized his insult, as veiled as it had been, with immediate precision. And it had shocked her.

Enjoying himself far too much for his own good, he therefore couldn't help but say, "I suppose it's equally fortunate for ye, Lady Gabriella, that ye've caught the eye of an earl."

"I err . . . ahem . . ." Lady Gabriella set her cup down.

"How do you know that?" Lady Warwick asked as she leaned forward in her seat. She shot a look at her daughter. "How does he know that?"

Apparently, Lady Gabriella had made no mention of her encounter with him on the pavement the previous day. Allowing his head to fall back against the chair, Raphe stretched out his legs and briefly wondered about her reasoning. Had she thought their verbal exchange so insignificant that there had been no reason to speak of it? Or did he detect something else? Studying her closely, he realized that she appeared more rigid than her mother and aunt, and that her hands were tightly clasped in her lap, as though by keeping them so, she would stop herself from succumbing to some dreaded fate.

But then her eyes met his, strong as steel, and full of courage and determination. "Fielding and I were returning from our drive in the park when we happened upon His Grace," she said, her sweet voice carrying not a hint of the turbulence that Raphe had just seen.

"They were so welcoming," he murmured. Narrowing his eyes, he watched as a splash of pink flooded Lady Gabriella's pale skin.

Denting her lower lip with her teeth, she averted her gaze. "We did not know who you were."

"Oh dear," Lady Everly said, clearly discerning what must have transpired.

"Well, if you looked like *that*," Lady Warwick said, her hand fluttering in Raphe's general direction, "one really can't blame her."

"Mama!" The note of indignation in Lady Gabriella's voice was startling.

Raphe stilled, his glass of brandy hovering an inch away from his mouth. "Yer mother is right," he said. Lowering the glass, he set it aside rather than take another sip. "I'm aware I don't look the part."

Smiling tightly, Lady Warwick sipped her tea. "Might I ask where you have come from? Your—manner of speech has me at a loss."

The prim innocence with which she spoke did little to hide the malevolent intent of her words. For a second, Raphe was tempted to tell her the truth, just to watch her expire from shock. Instead, he thought of his sisters. If word of their previous residency got out, of Raphe's work as a laborer, not to mention the sport in which he'd frequently engaged and his connection to Guthrie, they wouldn't stand a chance.

So he did what he knew had to be done and said, "After our parents died . . ." Sensing that Amelia was about to comment, he gave her a slight pinch.

She squeaked.

All eyes shifted to her. "Are you all right?" Gabriella asked.

"Oh . . . err . . ." Amelia moved in her seat.

"She's fine." Raphe paused for a second before continuing his explanation. "So, we went to live with a distant relation close to the Scottish border. That's why it took so long fer news of the duke's death to arrive."

"I see," Lady Warwick said. She'd tilted her head back so that she was now staring down her nose at him. *Awful woman.*

"Did they not feed you very well?" Gabriella asked.

Lady Warwick gave her an indiscreet nudge but Lady Gabriella pressed on, her tone slightly lower as though she hoped Juliette and Amelia wouldn't hear her. "Your sisters look very pale and thin." She eyed them each in turn before pushing a plate of biscuits in their direction. Leaning back, she folded her hands neatly in her lap, a satisfied smile spreading across her lips as his sisters reached for the biscuits with eager fingers.

Raphe stared at Lady Gabriella. "I believe most women would take that as a compliment."

Lady Everly almost spat out her tea in response to that comment, her ensuing cough a thankful distraction from Raphe and his sisters. "Right," he said while Lady Everly gathered her wits. "Well, if that will be all—" He'd had enough of his guests' inquisitiveness and of putting himself on display. The sooner he got rid of them, the better. "I've things to do."

Lady Warwick gave him the affronted look of a cat who'd just been given a bath. "Well, it was certainly interesting, making your acquaintance, Your Grace," she told him tightly as she got to her feet. Lady Gabriella and Lady Everly rose as well, while Juliette and Amelia tried to control the crumbs that were falling into their laps.

"Likewise," Raphe said. If only he'd had enough sense to let Pierson send them away. Judging from Lady Gabriella's narrowed gaze and the gentle puckering of her brow, she was having some trouble making sense of his story.

She looked at Amelia and then Juliette. "Perhaps we can have tea together again soon? Would you like that?"

Both girls nodded with enthusiasm. "Oh yes," Juliette answered softly as she wiped her mouth with the back of her hand. "That'd be splendid, that would."

"Very well then," Gabriella said, her smile broadening into something so dazzling that Raphe found himself wishing that it were directed at him rather than at his sisters. Halting next to the sofa on which he sat, she addressed him directly and with a far more serious expression. "I'm sorry for whatever hardship you had to endure before coming here, but now that you are here, I hope that you will see to getting your sisters some proper nourishment."

Touched by her genuine concern, Raphe felt his initial opinion of her as a snob begin to crumble. "Ye needn't worry, me lady. Cook 'as been advised to show us 'er talents."

"Come along, dear," Lady Warwick called from the doorway. "We must not keep His Grace from his busy schedule."

"Of course not," Lady Gabriella said. Bidding them each a hasty farewell she thanked them for the tea and then followed her mother from the room.

"Well done," Lady Everly said with a wink as she went in pursuit of her sister-in-law and niece. "I look forward to watching you take the *ton* by storm, as you no doubt will."

And then the three of them were finally gone, leaving the library alarmingly quiet.

Expelling a deep breath, Raphe leaned back, belatedly realizing that he probably should have stood when they'd departed.

"Lady Gabriella seems nice," Juliette said, breaking the silence.

"It's 'ard to believe she's got such an awful mother," Amelia remarked. Scooting down in her seat, she stretched out her legs and placed her feet on the table.

"Unfortunately, I think the *ton* will prove to be more like Lady Warwick than 'er daughter," Raphe muttered. "Very aloof an' fastidious. I didn't care for 'er at all."

"What about Lady Everly then?" Amelia asked.

Raphe shrugged. "I'm not sure. I couldn't quite tell if she was 'avin' a laugh at our expense or if she genuinely enjoyed our company." He expelled a deep breath, more aware than ever before of the challenges lying ahead. A knock sounded and Raphe looked up to find his secretary, Mr. Richardson, standing in the doorway together with Humphreys. "May we come in?" Humphreys asked.

"Yes, yes." Raphe waved them forward. "If ye'd like a drink, please 'elp yerselves."

"No. Thank you," Richardson said. He pointed to one of the recently vacated seats. "May I?"

"Of course," Raphe told him, a little surprised that he'd ask for permission.

Both men sat. A moment of silence passed, and

then, "How did it go?" Humphreys asked, his gaze shifting from Amelia and Juliette before returning to Raphe.

"Terribly, I suspect," Raphe told them honestly.

"Lady Warwick really didn't like us," Amelia added.

"But we didn't like 'er much either, did we, Raphe?" Juliette said. She got to her feet and crossed to the door. "Come on, Amelia, let's explore the rest of the 'ouse while the men talk." They left with haste, almost skidding in their excitement.

Heavy sighs escaped both servants. "You ought to have waited," Humphreys said.

"Taking on Lady Warwick is a difficult task for the most accomplished gentleman," Richardson explained. "She views everyone as her inferior, and every man as a threat to her daughter's virtue." He shook his head. "Humphreys is right. You ought to have waited."

"Precisely what I advised him." Came Pierson's incriminating voice from the doorway. "But there is only so much we can do. At the end of the day, His Grace's word is law in this house. If he wishes to speak with someone, there is little we can do to stop him."

"I'm still 'ere, Pierson," Raphe shot back. "In case ye didn't realize."

The butler gave him a condescending glare that made Raphe's insides churn. "You have two sisters of marriageable age who are yet to make an introduction to Society. To admit the likes of Lady Warwick—the greatest gossip and most critical judge of character that London has ever seen—to this house, was exceedingly poor judgment."

"Good God," Raphe spoke. "Are ye allowed to speak to me like that?" He turned to Richardson. "Is 'e allowed to speak to me like that?"

"When it's in your best interest," Pierson said, "I would rather speak plainly than mince words, Your Grace. I find it to be far more efficient."

"An' admirable," Raphe added.

"Thank you, Your Grace." Pierson spoke without the slightest hint of pleasure. Apparently a good night's rest had restored the butler's composure from the shaken state it had been in yesterday when he'd first made Raphe's acquaintance.

"At any rate, this cannot happen again," Humphreys said. "Naturally, as Pierson has already mentioned, you have your sisters' reputations to protect. Without that, they will stand no chance of securing good matches for themselves, regardless of what your title may be. But, aside from your sisters, it is also imperative that you consider your own position."

"*My* position?" Raphe shook his head. "If ye think I plan on paradin' about on account of me new title, then ye must've mistaken me for another sor' of man."

"What Humphreys means," Richardson cut in, "is that aside from you, there are no other heirs to the title, which means that you now have quite the responsibility toward the continuation of it."

Raphe blinked. "Are ye speakin' of procreation?"

"I err—*ahem*. That is to say . . ."

"Yes," Pierson said. "That is precisely what he's talking about. And to that end, you shall require a wife. And in case you're wondering, no lady of noble birth will agree to marry you unless you can come up to scratch."

Richardson nodded. "Which is why we would like to—"

"I'm not marryin' some nob. Not now, not ever," Raphe ground out with a deadly edge to his words. "Got that?"

"But—" Humphreys looked to Pierson, as though praying he'd work a miracle.

"It's your duty to do so," Pierson calmly responded.

"No!" Raphe fairly spat the word. "I refuse to consider it. The only reason I'm 'ere . . . is to offer me sisters a better opportunity."

"Very well then," Pierson said, to which Humphreys and Richardson both sputtered as though they were being strangled. Pierson served them each a quelling look. "If His Grace is not the marrying sort, then he is not the marrying sort. We can hardly force him—simply advise. However," he added, "since your sisters will be requiring your assistance, I would suggest that you make every effort to improve upon your appearance as well as theirs. Which brings us to what Richardson was going to propose earlier."

"We should like to help you," Richardson said, with the eagerness of a schoolboy thinking up his first prank.

"How?" Raphe asked. As much as he hated the thought of subjecting himself to their ministrations, he saw their point. Juliette and Amelia would have to look and sound the part of sophisticated young ladies if they were going to marry as well as he hoped. Which meant that he would have to improve upon himself, as well.

"For starters, I have taken the liberty of sending for a tailor," Richardson said, "which means that you ought to have some new clothes within a few days. Similarly, a seamstress has been summoned to tend to your sisters' needs."

"And then of course there's your speech," Humphreys muttered with downcast eyes. "We think you can do with some proper pronunciation lessons."

"There's nothin' wrong with me pronunciation," Raphe clipped.

"No," Pierson agreed. "Not if you wish to sound as though you belong in a cotton mill."

"Since when was earnin' an honest livin' frowned upon?" Raphe asked.

"A little too close to home?" Pierson asked. "Tell us, what were you doing before you arrived here?"

Narrowing his gaze beneath a deep frown, Raphe glanced at each of the men in turn—his employees. "I was a dockyard worker."

Humphreys and Richardson stared at him as though he'd just dropped from the sky. "Bloody hell!" they exclaimed in unison.

Pierson showed no emotion. "And the *ton* will see that as soon as you open your mouth. Which is why you ought to accept our assistance."

Raphe said nothing for a moment. Eventually he tossed back the remainder of his drink, set the glass aside and nodded. "Perhaps ye're right." Keeping up appearances would be a necessity if they were going to benefit from his title. It didn't take a genius to figure that out. "As it is, I told the ladies that me sisters an' me—"

"*My* sisters and *I*," Humphreys supplied.

Grumbling a little, Raphe raised both eyebrows, drew a breath and said, "*Myyyy* sisters and *I*."

"I say," Humphreys exclaimed as he clapped his hands together. "That was splendidly done. Don't you agree?" He turned an expectant eye on Richardson and Pierson.

Raphe groaned. He hated the pomposity with which he was now required to behave. It reminded him too much of a past he'd rather forget.

"*My* parents were gentry." *Christ.* It was like being

forced to speak a foreign language he hadn't used in years. "They taught us correct diction, but—once they were gone an' me—" Catching Richardson's eye he quickly amended, "*My* sisters *and* I moved, we adjusted to our new surround*ings*." Exasperated with the effort of trying to pronounce each word properly, he allowed himself to slip back into his usual dialect. "Wouldn't 'ave done us an ounce of good usin' hoity-toity speech in St. Giles. Been fifteen years now. Changin' us won't be too easy, what with force of 'abit an' all."

"Agreed," Pierson muttered, "but that doesn't mean you're incapable. If anything, you've just demonstrated that you are indeed quite capable of change, if you put your mind to it. The trick will be altering what comes naturally to you."

"What were you going to tell us before?" Humphreys asked. "Something about the ladies?"

Leaning forward, Raphe propped his elbows on his knees. "Lady Warwick inquired abou' our previous place of residence—on account of the way I talk. I told 'er that me sisters an' I went to live with a distant relative close to the Scottish border after we lost our parents."

"Do you think she believed you?" Pierson asked.

"I do," Raphe said, though he had his doubts about Lady Gabriella.

"That's good," Richardson muttered. "Knowing her ladyship, she only asked because she's looking for something salacious."

"Why?" Raphe asked.

"Because gossip is one of Society's highest commodities. It's nothing personal, Your Grace. She just wants the attention that she'd undoubtedly acquire if it became known that she has damning information on you."

Raphe frowned. "She could resort to blackmail."

"Blackmail?" Richardson shook his head. "That's not her style. Lady Warwick prides herself on three things: her appearance, her wealth and other people's reactions to those two things."

"And her daughter?" Raphe couldn't help but ask. Even though he knew he shouldn't.

"Lady Gabriella?" Humphreys said. "She used to visit quite often when your predecessor and his sons were still alive. With her sister and her parents, of course."

"She 'as a sister?"

Richardson gave Humphreys an odd look before saying, "Lady Victoria broke her engagement with a marquess in order to marry an American tradesman. The Warwicks are still recovering from the scandal."

So, not as perfect as they pretended to be, Raphe mused.

"Which is why Lady Gabriella has formed an attachment with the Earl of Fielding," Humphreys added. "Once the two are married the *ton* will be quick to forgive and forget any wrongdoing on her sister's part."

Raphe frowned. "So let me get this straight. Lady Gabriella is gonna sacrifice 'erself because of a mistake that wasn't 'er own, just so 'er family can save face?"

"Well . . ." Humphreys said, "When you put it like that—"

"It's the most idiotic thing I've ever 'eard! Does she realize that marriage is fer life? That there's no gettin' out of it unless she or Fielding dies?"

"I believe she is aware, Your Grace," Pierson said dryly, "but such is the way of the aristocracy, as unfortunate as it may sometimes be. Duty before all else."

"Even common sense?" Raphe asked.

Pierson didn't respond, leaving Raphe to draw his own conclusion.

"There is no denying that they will make a fine couple," Richardson said.

"I'm sure they shall," Raphe said, detesting that thought. *Why?* He couldn't say. After all, he didn't know Lady Gabriella at all, and from their brief interaction with each other, he had no reason to care about whom she married.

And yet . . . he couldn't tear his mind away from her pretty eyes and rosy lips. He shook his head. *What basis was that for developing an interest?* It was a physical attraction, nothing more. And with his sisters' welfare in mind, the arduous work that lay ahead of them all and his disinclination to marry, there was no point at all in considering anything more than a polite acquaintance with his neighbor.

To do otherwise would be not only mad, but a complete departure from all of his principles. It would never work. Which was why he decided to push all thoughts of Lady Gabriella from his mind by focusing on his own affairs. A plan that seemed very promising indeed, until Richardson said, "And since only a lady who has already made her debut is allowed to vouch for another, I would recommend asking Lady Gabriella to assist with Lady Juliette's and Lady Amelia's presentations at court. Her mother will likely refuse, but as it stands, you have no one else to turn to and nothing left to lose."

Chapter 5

Standing by her bedroom window, Gabriella glanced out at the street below, her gaze lingering on the pavement where she and Fielding had encountered Huntley three days earlier. She pressed the palm of her hand to the cool glass, thankful for the peace and quiet that her solitude offered.

Not a second had passed after leaving Huntley House before her mother had sharply remarked, "The nerve of that man! Who on earth does he think he is?"

To which her aunt had calmly replied, "The Duke of Huntley, I suspect."

Gabriella had done her best not to smile.

"He's a disgrace to the title," her mother had said, "A mushroom, and an imposter."

"I don't see how that can be possible, Mama," Gabriella had murmured. "He would not have been brought to Huntley House unless he was the legitimate heir. The solicitors would have made certain of that."

Her mother had responded with a cutting scowl. "You're not to speak to him again. Is that understood?"

"What if I pass him on the street?"

"Then you must cross to the other side."

"That would be terribly rude," Aunt Caroline had said, "and would probably reflect poorly on Gabriella."

Gabriella's mother had stopped for a moment, as if frozen. Eventually, she'd given a curt nod and resumed walking. "You are correct." She'd looked at her daughter, her eyes narrowing as if she were able to look inside her head. "Just don't speak to him then."

Arriving home they'd handed over their gloves and bonnets to their butler, Mr. Simmons, before proceeding out onto the terrace, where a pergola covered in roses offered a shady retreat.

"And what if he speaks to me? What if he wishes me a good day in passing? Am I to ignore him?"

"You may acknowledge his greeting with a nod," her mother had said.

"Mama," Gabriella had said, barely managing not to roll her eyes, "I do believe you are exaggerating."

"Exaggerating?" Her mother had squeaked as she'd dropped down onto a wicker chair and proceeded to fan herself with a handkerchief. "Did you not *see* what he looked like? Did you not *hear* how he spoke?"

"Yes, Mama. I both saw and heard."

"And his sisters!" she'd continued. "They looked like they belonged in a hovel. Did you happen to notice their hands? They were red and calloused, with cracking nails and—"

"Mama," Gabriella had cut in. "The fact that they have had a difficult life was plain to see. But that does not warrant our condemnation, surely."

"I agree," Aunt Caroline had said. She'd taken the seat facing her sister-in-law. "It would be unkind of us to treat them too harshly."

"Perhaps if they were servants I would agree, but he is a *duke*, Caro. A *duke*!" She'd waved her handkerchief with greater enthusiasm. "And we are his neighbors. The Warwicks and the Huntleys have always been close—our titles securely linked both socially and politically. Oh heavens, whatever will people think?"

"I suppose that depends on what they see," Gabriella had said, her attention drawn to a peacock butterfly that had been showing great interest in a potted marigold.

"Whatever do you mean?" her mother had asked.

Bracing herself for the argument that would surely follow, Gabriella had looked straight at her and said, "Simply, that I think we should help them."

Her mother's mouth had dropped open. "I beg your pardon?"

"Any improvement on their part can only serve to reflect well on us."

"Gabriella does have a point," Aunt Caroline had said.

"Of *course* she has a point," Gabriella's mother had hissed. "But that does not make her suggestion any more appropriate. And considering what a chore it was for *her* to prepare for her own debut, I hardly think she's in any position to make such propositions." She'd given her daughter a dubious look. "Have you any idea of the amount of work that would have to be done in order to turn that man into a gentleman or his sisters into ladies?"

Heat had risen to the nape of Gabriella's neck. "I know it won't be easy, but I should like to try." Having spent a lifetime in her sister's shadow only to find herself suddenly tossed into the center of attention with expectations that were difficult to meet,

Gabriella felt a deep need to help her neighbors adjust to their new way of life. She knew how it felt to be whispered about and teased, her interests so different from those of other young ladies that she'd never managed to secure close friendships with any of them. Until Fielding had started showing an interest, her existence had scarcely been acknowledged.

"I don't like the idea of you keeping their company," her mother had complained. "What if they bring you down to their level instead of you raising them up?"

Gabriella had sighed.

Adhering to her mother's guidance, of practicing the perfect curtsy and the perfect smile in front of her mirror, were beginning to grate. Perhaps because of their recent encounter with Huntley? It had certainly brought out a side of her mother that Gabriella found she could not approve of. Because although she conceded that Huntley did not appear to be eligible for his title, the man did not deserve to be insulted because of it. And although she'd always known that her mother was somewhat high in the instep, she would never have supposed that she would treat another peer, let alone another person, with such complete and utter scorn. Least of all when she felt he deserved their sympathy rather than their censure.

"Well, I think it's a marvelous idea," Aunt Caroline had said.

"Of course you would," Gabriella's mother had muttered.

"And you have always placed great import on participating in charitable work." Gabriella had given her mother a sweet smile. "Surely you would not have us turn our backs on someone in need when we are in a position to help?"

"Well . . . I . . ." Her mother had frowned. "I really don't have the time, Gabriella. You know how busy I am raising money for the hospital and advocating on its behalf."

"Of course. I wasn't suggesting that you take on this task but rather that I do," Gabriella had said. "And besides," she'd added before her mother could voice a protest, "it will give me something different to do besides studying insects."

That remark had apparently settled it, although her mother had still been concerned about Fielding's opinion on the matter. Eventually she'd said, "I will have to ask your father for guidance in this matter."

Which had resulted in another conversation filled with questions and explanations, at the end of which Gabriella's father had said, "If what you say is true and the Duke of Huntley and his sisters are as unprepared for their new positions as you claim, then something must indeed be done to rectify the situation. But," he'd added with a pointed look at Gabriella over the rims of his spectacles, "I am not convinced that your helping them as you suggest would be the right approach."

"My thoughts exactly," Gabriella's mother had said.

Flattening his mouth, Gabriella's father had given his wife a quelling look before adding, "Your sister brought disgrace upon this family, Gabriella. We cannot risk a single mistake. I'm sorry."

"But—"

"The answer is no."

And that had been the end of that, but it had not put a damper on Gabriella's determination to help Lady Juliette and Lady Amelia. She simply could not bear the thought of them going through what she had once had to endure. A shudder went through her as she recalled how the other young ladies of her acquaintance had reacted when she was a child and they'd seen her pick up a spider. It had been during a party in celebration of the eighth birthday of Penbrook's youngest daughter, Lady Charlotte. The children had been gathered in the parlor and Gabriella had spotted the tiny creature crawling on one of the roses in a nearby vase.

"That's disgusting," Lady Charlotte had squealed as Gabriella had stood with the spider crawling around her hand.

"*You're* disgusting," Lady Rowena had said while scrunching her nose.

"Only boys would touch an insect," Lady Hyacinth had told her with mocking disdain.

Gabriella hadn't spoken to any of those girls since, but she had been keenly aware of their critical gazes and hurtful snickers whenever their paths crossed over the years that followed.

Now, with the eventuality of Lady Juliette and Lady Amelia enduring a similar painful experience, Gabriella could not stand by and do nothing. Her moral compass simply wouldn't allow it. Which meant that she would have to find a different way—one that meant thwarting her parents' wishes.

A knock sounded at the door, pulling Gabriella away from her thoughts and back into the present. "Come in!"

One of the maids entered. "My lady, the Earl of Fielding has come to call on you. Shall I tell Simmons to show him into the parlor?"

With a sigh, Gabriella nodded. "Yes. Tell him that I will be down in just a moment."

The maid departed with a bit of a bob, the door gently closing behind her.

Marry well.

The mantra that had been repeated in the Radcliffe household since she'd been a child reverberated in her head like a bell. It had become even more constant since her sister's marriage. Gabriella winced. Victoria had summoned the courage to determine her own future—one apart from the *ton*. *But at what cost?* She'd left behind her family and all of her friends, travelling to the far side of the world for the sake of one man. It seemed incomprehensible.

Glancing down at the vanity table, Gabriella's gaze fell on the mother-of-pearl comb that had been her sister's. Victoria had pressed it into her hand one day, shortly before her departure, and said, *"No matter what happens, I'll always love you. Don't ever doubt that."*

But if that was true, then why hadn't she written?

Angered by her sister's betrayal, Gabriella turned from the vanity table and headed for the door.

Arriving in the parlor a few minutes later, she had to admit that Fielding did look rather dashing in his navy blue jacket and beige trousers—certainly more fashionable than Huntley. She cast the thought aside and went to greet Fielding, not liking the fact that she'd just compared her almost-fiancé to another man.

"You look as lovely as always," Fielding told her as he came to place a kiss upon her outstretched hand. It was elegantly done—much more so than Huntley's awkward effort.

Stop it!

She forced a smile. "Thank you, my lord. You are exceptionally kind."

"It's not kindness, my lady. I merely speak the truth." He gestured toward the sofa. "Shall we sit for a while?"

"Of course."

Passing him, Gabriella lowered herself to the plush silk brocade and swept her legs to one side, a position that would ensure a perfect drape of her gown. She then folded her hands in her lap and waited for Fielding to sit down next to her, albeit with an arm's length between them.

"I hear that the heir to the Huntley title has been found," Fielding said.

He maintained the same pose as usual—a glaring contrast to the way in which Huntley had casually lounged in his chair when he'd welcomed her for tea in his library. And then of course there were the physical differences to consider. Fielding was slim and roughly the same height as she, while Huntley . . . his bearing spoke of pure strength and power. And when he stood, he forced her to look up at him. There was something about that gesture that demanded respect, even if he was rough around the edges and spoke as though he'd just climbed out of a coal mine.

"My lady?"

Startled by Fielding's voice, Gabriella blinked. "I beg your pardon." She could feel her cheeks grow warm beneath his gaze. The flush of a guilty woman. "Yes. Yes, it would seem that he has."

"Well? Have you met him yet? I would love to hear your impression."

Swallowing, Gabriella instinctively glanced at the clock. It appeared to be moving with infernal slowness. "I—err . . ." She couldn't lie, could she? *Probably not.* "Do you recall the man we met on the pavement the other day when we were returning from our drive?"

His frown deepened. "The servant?"

"Yes—well," she steeled herself, "as it turns out, *that* was the duke."

The silence that followed could only be described as *loud*—so loud it seemed to fill every corner of the room, burrowing its way beneath tables and chairs and climbing the walls until it dripped from the ceiling.

"Surely, you jest," Fielding finally murmured. He shook his head. "That man was a peasant. The way he spoke—it cannot be. It simply cannot!"

"And yet it is. Quite so."

Rising, he began to pace. "Do you have any idea what a mess this is?"

"Some."

He came to a halt before her. "No, you do not seem to understand. Mother has invited him for dinner next Friday at Fielding House. The invitations have already been sent out."

"Then . . . then you must call it off," Gabriella insisted. "Find an excuse. Any excuse. *Please.*"

"But—" He met her gaze, and Gabriella's heart sank. "Several peers have already accepted. Cancelling is out of the question."

"Right." Her mind began to whirl with ideas. "Perhaps I can talk to the duke then. I'll advise him to decline."

Fielding remained silent for a moment as though considering such a solution. "No," he eventually said. "Let him make his own decision."

"But—"

"If he's not up to it, then he's not up to it. But Society deserves to know who the new Duke of Huntley is, don't you think?"

"What I think, is that he ought to be prepared for what to expect. A dinner at Fielding House is no small matter."

"Precisely. And as the new Duke of Huntley, he must be capable of keeping proper company. If he's not, then perhaps he ought to return to wherever it is he came from."

Gabriella stiffened. "That's rather harsh."

"Perhaps." Returning to his seat, he enfolded her hand with his. "But there is a difference of class for a reason. In my opinion, people ought to stay where they belong, rather than try to break rank. It helps ensure a certain order, which in turn keeps the world spinning in the right direction." Giving her a bland smile, he stood up again. "Now, if you will excuse me, I really must be off. Mother will be beside herself when she hears this news. The least I can do is to help her prepare."

"Right. Yes, of course." Ignoring the numbness that filled every limb, Gabriella rose to her feet, bid Fielding a good day and then stood for a long moment after, reflecting on their conversation.

The chiming of a clock eventually jolted her into action. "Simmons," she called, addressing the butler as she snatched her spencer off a hook on the hallway wall, "if anyone asks, you may tell them that I have gone out."

One minute later, she was standing at the servants' entrance of Huntley House, with Anna by her side. "I need to speak to His Grace at once," she told a maid, who hastened away to convey her message.

"My lady," Anna implored for what had to be the fifth time at least, "You really shouldn't be here."

That sentiment was echoed by Pierson, who arrived soon after with a brisk step. "Lady Gabriella. Would it not be more seemly to use the front door? This is highly irregular."

"I am aware of that, Pierson, but I would like to keep this visit discreet—especially since my parents are unaware of my coming here." She gave him a meaningful look that would hopefully do the trick and then said, "Now, will you please let me in?"

Staring down at her, Pierson stepped back and waved her through, closing the door behind her. "Right this way," he said, striding off through a hallway that led past the kitchen and onward to the servants' stairs, by which they were able to reach the foyer. "Please wait here a moment," Pierson said as he closed the stairwell door behind them. Turning about, he then strode away to deliver the news of her arrival.

Gabriella glanced about. She considered the bench against the wall. Perhaps she ought to sit? *No*. She was much too agitated for that. Instead, she began to pace while Anna watched with increasing unease. Surely the duke's secretary would have advised him against accepting the invitation from Lady Fielding. She clasped her hands to still her trembling fingers. *This was bad. Really, really bad.*

"My lady?"

She spun about to find Pierson standing behind her. Inclining his head, he indicated the hallway to his left. "His Grace will see you now. If you'll please follow me."

Chapter 6

Nodding, Gabriella told Anna to have a seat on the bench while she waited and then followed the butler, his leisurely pace provoking her nerves until they finally reached a door where Pierson paused to knock.

"Come in!"

The door was pushed open. "Lady Gabriella to see you, Your Grace," Pierson intoned. He then stepped aside so she could enter, her eyes falling first on Mr. Richardson, who was standing the closest. He bowed his head in greeting, while she offered a smile in return. She then turned more fully toward the other person in the room—the man whom she'd come to see.

Her breath caught.

Standing behind a massive desk was Huntley, except he bore no resemblance whatsoever to the man whom she'd sat down to tea with a couple of days earlier. Gone were the plain, working-class clothes. Instead, he wore a crisp white shirt with a brown waistcoat, a dark green jacket and beige trousers. His coffee-colored hair had been trimmed around his ears and at the nape of his neck. His jawline, which appeared freshly shaved, accentuated the angular shape of his face. She noticed for the first time that his eyes were dark brown with tiny flecks of amber, and that his nose was elegantly shaped—a feature she'd initially missed when she'd been distracted by his unpolished looks.

"Lady Gabriella." His voice held a raspy texture that somehow, quite inexplicably, managed to tickle her senses.

Swallowing, she tried to ignore the sudden flutter in her belly. "Your Grace—you appear quite transformed."

The edge of his mouth twitched. "Do y—*you* approve?"

His attempt at proper speech went straight to her heart, accelerating its pace like a piece of music approaching a crescendo. Unsettled by the sensation, Gabriella deliberately straightened her spine. She forced herself not to stare at the slight dip between his collarbones. "Yes. But a cravat would not have hurt."

His eyes remained on her, unblinking. "I disagree."

Unsure of how to respond, Gabriella looked to Richardson. He'd been with the previous duke for the last five years or so, so Gabriella was well enough acquainted with him to feel comfortable in his presence. He glanced toward the duke, who hesitated a moment before waving at a chair. "Will ye-ou have a seat . . . my lady?"

"Thank you." Gabriella lowered herself onto the chair, her skin pricking at the realization that Huntley was following her every move. Sucking in a breath, she expelled it slowly in an effort to calm herself.

He cleared his throat, the sound immediately drawing her gaze to his by reflex. "I err . . ." He scratched the back of his head with a boyish restlessness that forced a smile to Gabriella's lips.

There was something so endearing about the uncertainty of a large and powerful man that very nearly melted her heart. "Would y—" Huntley caught himself again. "*You*, care for some tea, Lady Gabriella?"

"I would love some. Thank you."

Her positive response seemed to ease the tension in Huntley's posture. He went to the bell pull and gave it a tug before returning to his chair and sitting back down.

"If that will be all, Your Grace," Richardson began.

Gabriella instinctively froze. Huntley looked at her, his brown eyes warming with understanding. "Stay," he said, addressing Richardson, before adding a gentler, "please."

"If you wish," the secretary replied.

Gabriella breathed a sigh of relief. The thought of being alone with Huntley tightened her nerves. Perhaps it was silly, but there was just something about him . . . something that urged her to keep her wits about her when in his presence. She licked her lips, moistening them before gathering her courage and meeting those dark brown eyes of his with determination. "I have come to warn you."

He raised an eyebrow. "About what?"

"The Dowager Countess of—"

A knock sounded, and a maid entered. "We'd like some tea, please," Huntley told her.

The maid nodded. "Shall I bring some cake as well?"

The duke stiffened. "Well—err . . ." His eyes darted from Gabriella to Richardson and back to Gabriella again. "Cake?" he asked, as though it were much too complicated a matter to contemplate.

Taking pity on him, Gabriella leaned forward in her seat. "A small plate with a slice for each of us," she whispered.

The duke nodded before returning his attention to the maid. "Per'aps a small plate, with a slice fer each of us?"

Gabriella's heart clenched at the sound of his unschooled speech. She'd never heard anyone slaughter the English language with such lack of remorse before.

Very good," the maid said before disappearing once more.

The duke relaxed against his chair. "Ye were—" He closed his eyes briefly and expelled a deep breath. Opening his eyes again, he spoke with deliberation. "*You* were saying?"

Gabriella nodded, impressed by his effort to speak correctly. "The Dowager Countess of Fielding is having a dinner party next Friday. She has sent you an invitation in the hope that you will attend since she would like to be the first to show you off."

"The invitation arrived earlier today," Richardson said. "I have advised His Grace to decline."

"Oh good," Gabriella murmured. "Indeed, that is my reason for calling on you. Lady Fielding is very partial to propriety and etiquette. She prides herself on the company she keeps."

"Like yer—*your* mother," Huntley said, his eyes narrowing slightly.

"Yes, I suppose the two are rather similar in that regard," Gabriella confessed.

"In other words, she's a snob."

Huntley spoke the words not as a question, but as though he'd assessed both women at great length and concluded that this was the most fitting word for them. And for some reason, even though Gabriella knew that there was some truth to it, his censure bothered her. "They are of a certain class, Your Grace, and they have never been accustomed to anything else. You cannot simply expect them to accept . . ." *Oh dear.* She'd no idea how to finish that sentence without causing offense.

"Yes?" he inquired.

She dropped her gaze. Perhaps coming here had been a mistake.

"I cannot expect 'em to accept *what*?" Huntley prompted. Although he spoke softly, his tone cautioned her to choose her words carefully.

Swallowing, she tried to think of a polite way of stating the obvious. She glanced at Richardson, whose expression had grown somewhat tight around the edges. Realizing she'd get no help from him, she forced her gaze back to Huntley and braced herself for his response. "To accept a peer with a questionable background."

Huntley stared at her, his gaze burrowing its way straight through her until she felt herself tremble. "In other words, I'm not worthy to sit at the same table as yer noble self."

"I—I . . . No, that is not what I meant to say."

Leaning forward, his gaze caged her until she found it difficult to breathe. When he spoke again, it was with controlled crispness. "Then by all means, yer ladyship, tell me what ye meant by insultin' me in me own home."

Shrinking back, Gabriella felt her heart drop. This wasn't going anywhere near as well as she'd initially hoped, and she hadn't even suggested helping his sisters yet. "I just meant to warn you of what to expect. These people—"

Another knock at the door brought the maid back. She entered on Huntley's command, bustling in to set a tray on the table before departing once more.

Thankful for the momentary reprieve, Gabriella nodded toward the teapot. "Shall I pour?"

Huntley hesitated a moment before eventually giving her a curt nod. Gabriella edged forward in her seat, her entire body aware of his direct perusal. Not once did he avert his gaze, the effect sending a trail of heat along her limbs, flushing her skin and tightening her belly. Disturbed by it, she tried to focus on other things, like the tea that she was supposed to serve if she could only stop her hands from trembling.

Taking a deep breath, she strengthened her hold on the teapot and filled three cups. "Milk or sugar?" she asked, her eyes going first to Richardson before sliding across to where Huntley was sitting. Her heart skipped. There was something about his gaze . . . something dark and dangerous and terribly unnerving. She didn't understand it any more than she understood her reaction to it. Because, although it frightened her, it also intrigued her in a way she'd never been intrigued before. It was a new awareness—the sort that only a woman would feel in the presence of a man who . . .

"Neither," he said, the word scattering her thoughts.

Jolting slightly, she turned to Richardson. "And for you?"

He gave her a quizzical look, akin to the sort one might offer a person who'd forgotten to comb their hair before leaving the house. "A drop of milk and a spoonful of sugar, please."

Completing her task, she picked up her own cup and took a lengthy sip. *Good lord!* She hadn't felt this muddled since her lessons in the "secret" language of fans, and all because of a duke who neither looked nor behaved anything like a duke ought to look and behave.

"You were saying?" Huntley prompted after a couple of seconds.

"Hmm?" *What had she been saying?* She searched her mind for the answer and almost groaned when she recalled what they'd been discussing prior to the tea's arrival. "Oh, yes. These people—the *ton*, that is—will assess you and judge you. They will not forgive the way in which you—" She hesitated a moment before saying, "express yourself, on account of being a duke. On the contrary, they will likely condemn you even more *because* of your title."

"Why?" Huntley asked.

Studying him—the glint in his eyes, and the firm lines of his jaw—she realized that he probably knew the answer already. So she decided to be completely honest. "Because you will not live up to their expectations. Instead, you will come across as an undeserving intruder—a man who, if I may make an educated guess, never attended a commendable school, who lacks proficiency in simple etiquette and who takes no issue with getting dressed without putting on a cravat."

His lips parted slightly, his expression one of complete astonishment. "You dare to speak to a duke like that?" There was something about his eyes that suggested he might be a little impressed by her courage.

The thought made her straighten her spine. "No. Of course not. But your situation is different from the norm. You must learn what it means to have such an impressive title, and until you do, you won't earn the respect or the status you require in order to see your sisters properly settled, as I imagine you wish to do."

"You seem to share me . . . *my* . . . servants' opinion." His eyes shifted to Richardson before returning to Gabriella. "They want me to take all sorts of lessons. An' you'll be 'appy to know that I've agreed."

"Oh." Gabriella was pleased by how simple her suggestion now seemed. "Well, that is excellent news." She took a deep breath before adding, "I would like to offer my assistance. If you like."

His mouth dropped open. He darted another look at Richardson, stared at Gabriella for a fraction of a second and finally leaned forward in his seat. "Your ladyship wants to teach me 'ow to be a gentleman? Ain't that a bit inappropriate?"

Good Lord!

"That is *not* what I was proposing," Gabriella managed to say while heat rushed from the top of her head all the way to the tips of her toes. "I was offering to help your sisters."

"I see." He drummed his fingers on the desk. "And yer parents approve of this idea, do they?"

Gabriella bit her lip. "No. They've forbidden me from socializing with all of you."

Richardson made a groaning sound that suddenly made Gabriella doubt her resolve. If her parents ever found out about this . . . She'd rather not think of how they'd react.

"Then why did ye come? Why do ye—*you*—care so much about me an' me sisters that ye'd risk yer parents' wrath?"

Glancing at him, she saw that he looked genuinely curious, as though he'd never before encountered someone who might be kind toward him or his sisters for no other reason than to simply be kind. And in that instant Gabriella knew that the chance she was taking would be worth it.

"Because I know how challenging it can be to satisfy Society's many demands."

He scoffed at that. "I find that very 'ard to believe."

Rising to his feet, he left her no choice but to look up at him. The force of his masculinity was overpowering in its straightforwardness—the strength of his body so skillfully harnessed beneath his perfectly tailored clothes, crowding her until she felt like shrinking away into nothingness. It was overwhelming . . . frightening . . . and unlike anything else she'd ever experienced before. Because, in spite of everything, she felt an inexplicable urge to move toward him, rather than to flee.

"Well, it is the truth." She forced the words out past the thickening of her throat, disturbed by the gentle quiver in her voice.

Huntley frowned. He seemed to assess her once more with uncanny precision, until she was certain that every inch of her was permanently branded in his mind. "I've decided to accept the Fielding invitation."

Gabriella blinked. "What?"

"It's not in me nature to run away with me tail between me legs."

"*My*," she said, pronouncing the word with deliberate emphasis on the '*y*.'

For a moment, he looked a bit baffled, but then he collected himself and said, "Right." He then repeated the word just as she had spoken it. "*My*."

She couldn't help but smile, which, if she wasn't mistaken, made the edge of his mouth twitch. The reflex sent a wave of warmth through her, like a welcome fire on a cold winter's day.

"I mean to prepare *my*self instead. The servants 'ave offered to 'elp, but if ye . . . *ou're* truly willing to assist *my* sisters, I'd be mighty grateful."

The distinct discomfort with which he spoke made it clear to her that he was pushing aside his pride for his sisters' sake, and Gabriella couldn't help but admire him for it.

"They will have to be presented at court," she said.

"I have already put in a request," Richardson told her. "Given the length of time it can take for an invitation to arrive, I thought it prudent to start right away."

"Very good," Gabriella agreed. Rising, she forced herself to meet Huntley's gaze directly. "You may tell your sisters to expect me tomorrow morning at ten. And speak to your servants too. Their discretion is vital to our success since one whispered word about my coming here will put an abrupt end to your sisters' lessons."

"I understand."

"Good," she told him, relying on the rigidity of her spine to distract her from the charming dimples that appeared at the edge of his mouth whenever he smiled. "Then I'll thank you for the tea and bid you a good day." She moved toward the door.

"Just one more thing," he said, his voice a touch lower than before—more intimate somehow.

The effect made her nerves shiver. She glanced back at him over her shoulder. "Yes?"

"Do ye like dancing, Lady Gabriella?"

Chapter 7

Raphe could tell by her sharp intake of breath, the hesitant look in her eyes and the flush creeping into her cheeks that Lady Gabriella found the question unnerving. He'd suspected she would, which had only tempted him even more since the way she responded confirmed the suspicion he'd started having from the moment she'd entered his study a half hour earlier. Against her better judgment, no doubt, Lady Gabriella was attracted to him. And that thought alone—that a man like him might stir an unwelcome desire in a woman like her—filled him with an undeniably primal sense of victory.

The edge of his mouth quirked with amusement. He watched as she followed the movement with her eyes, her chest quivering slightly on a tremulous inhalation. He felt his body grow taught. *No*, he warned the devil within. She was destined to marry Fielding. *Pompous arse.* And yet . . . he couldn't help but imagine . . . after all, she was here in his home against all common sense . . .

"Dance?"

Her question halted his increasingly scandalous thoughts. Which was just as well. "Yes. Richardson has arranged for me sisters an' I to take lessons. I'll be needin' a partner."

"Then I would suggest you ask your sisters."

"They won't know the steps."

"Well." She stood completely still for a moment as if she might actually be considering his proposal. But then she said, "It wouldn't be proper. I am to marry the Earl of Fielding, a man who insisted I stay away from you, and that I give you no warning about the dinner his mother is hosting, because he believes Society ought to know the truth about you."

"And yet it seems as though you thwarted those wishes," Raphe said.

A sigh of exasperation drifted past her lips. "In regards to your sisters, Your Grace. But where you are concerned, I do believe we ought to keep all contact to a minimum."

"Why? Are ye afraid I might tempt ye away from Fielding?" She was looking so delightfully flustered that he couldn't help but tease her.

Tilting her chin, she pointed her pretty nose at him. "My family needs that match."

"What about you, Lady Gabriella?" Raphe quietly asked. "Is it what *you* need? What *you* want?" He knew his questions were daring—could practically feel Richardson's disapproval crashing over him. But he wasn't expected to behave like a gentleman, and decided therefore to take advantage. Besides, in his estimation, the Earl of Fielding was a fool. He didn't deserve to be seen with the lovely woman who presently stood across from him.

Her eyes widened with indignation. "My wants and needs are none of your concern," she told him hotly.

Ah, but they could be.

"Very well," he acquiesced. "No dancin' then." Stepping around the desk, he crossed to the door, his shoulder lightly brushing hers as he did so. The effect was immediate; heat rushed through his torso and limbs, accelerating his heart and tightening his stomach until he felt his chest contract and his breath hitch.

With a deliberate cough, he concealed the unbidden reaction, reached for the door handle and turned to face her, his hands going instantly clammy the moment he did so. For there she stood, bewilderment shimmering in the depths of her pale blue eyes—eyes he sensed might swallow him up if he stared at them too long. Her cheeks were flushed, and her lips slightly parted as if on a gasp, and he knew then that the spark he'd just felt had been felt by her too.

"Thank ye-*ou* for comin' and for offerin' to help," he said as he opened the door, suddenly desperate for her to leave so he could get his body under control. He had no business panting after her like a dog. No business at all. "Richardson will show you out."

With a nod, she stepped toward the door. "Thank you for the tea."

"Ye're welcome," he said.

And then she was gone, allowing Raphe to finally sink back into his chair and wonder about what the hell had just happened. He really didn't have time for emotional nonsense, or physical attraction, or anything else that might have him chasing after a woman who was not only destined to marry another, but who most assuredly would never agree to marry *him*. Not that he would consider marriage. Which he wouldn't. Not under any circumstance. It was utterly and irrevocably out of the question. Which meant that he must learn to restrain himself when in Lady Gabriella's presence.

"Your Grace?"

Startled by Richardson's voice, Raphe looked up to find the man standing in the doorway with a grave expression. "Yes?" he inquired.

"If I may offer my opinion, I'd take Lady Gabriella's warning to heart, Your Grace."

Raphe straightened himself with a noncommittal grunt while his secretary quietly returned to the chair he'd been occupying earlier. "It's the same warning as yers, isn't it?"

"Yes," Richardson agreed. He crossed his legs before saying, "But perhaps you'll be more inclined to listen to her than to me."

"An' miss out on the opportunity to impress me peers?"

Richardson groaned and, from the looks of it, appeared to be trying very hard not to roll his eyes.

Raphe frowned. "Ye don't think I'm capable," he remarked with the same degree of flatness he felt.

"I did not say that, Your Grace."

"Ye didn't 'ave to!"

"*Have* to, Your Grace. *Have* to." Richardson sighed, his shoulders slumping slightly beneath the weight of what Raphe assumed to be reluctant resignation. "I would be remiss in my duties toward you *and* your sisters if I were to let you attend such an event before you are ready."

"Then I suggest that we do what we can to ensure me readiness, Richardson, because I'm goin' to that dinner." *Especially if Fielding was hoping to make a laughingstock of him.* "I'll prove meself capable. Mark me word!" Richardson didn't look the least bit convinced, but Raphe could see no other way around it. "To send me regrets would just signify *their* victory and *my* defeat. An' just so ye know, I like to win."

"Doesn't everyone?" When Raphe didn't respond, Richardson blew out a deep breath and eventually nodded. "Well, in that case, I suggest we get started. There's a lot for us to accomplish within the next few days, so I'll summon Humphreys and Pierson right away." He didn't need to say that they would need all the help they could get. That thought was heavily implied.

Chapter 8

Flipping through a recently purchased book about centipedes, Gabriella waited for her mother and her aunt to leave the house the following morning.

"Are you sure you don't want to join us?" Her mother asked, eyeing Gabriella's book with a twitch of her nose.

"No, Mama. Poetry readings have never interested me very much."

"More the pity," her mother murmured.

"Oh for heaven's sake," Aunt Caroline said, "it doesn't interest us either. We're only going because it was *your* idea to host the event, Portia."

"With good reason, Caro," Gabriella's mother shot back. "It's an excellent way for me to raise money for the hospital."

And since nobody wanted to argue the importance of a charitable event, Gabriella simply wished her mother and aunt a good day, listening carefully for the sound of the front door closing behind them.

Expelling a deep breath, she took another sip of her tea and glanced at the clock that stood on top of a large cabinet. The hands ticked merrily along, bringing her closer to her next encounter with her neighbors. A touch of excitement slithered through her belly. How thrilling this would be—what a challenge! She'd come up with several ideas on how to proceed since her interview with Huntley the previous day. None of which would include the man himself.

Which was how it should be—how it *had* to be. After all, she could not allow him to continue doing whatever it was he'd been doing to her yesterday. The way she'd responded to him had felt . . . strange and unfamiliar . . . indecent and . . .

Stop it!

Tearing her mind away from the duke, she forced herself to focus on his sisters as she went in search of Anna. *They* were the ones she'd be helping, not Huntley. She'd even managed to find the etiquette book she'd been given for her twelfth birthday: *A Lady's Guide to Proper Comportment and Social Skill.* That ought to help.

"We will go through the garden today," Gabriella told her maid, deciding to take advantage of the fact that Warwick House backed up to Green Park, with a wrought-iron gate offering easy access to the footpath. If any of her servants went looking for her, they would simply assume that she'd gone for a stroll.

"Yes, my lady," Anna dutifully replied as they set out together.

Turning toward her, Gabriella said, "Anna, you have every right to refuse coming with me, you know. Especially since there is a good chance that my parents will find a way to punish you if they ever discover that you agreed to join me—that you did not do everything in your power to prevent me from visiting this house. All I can do is promise you that I will tell them you tried to change my mind and that, failing to do so, decided to remain at my side for the sake of propriety."

"Thank you, my lady, but I would never think

of abandoning you." They made their way along a footpath. "In fact, I think it's wonderful what you're doing for those girls."

Touched by her kindness, Gabriella offered Anna her thanks and hurried onward, entering the Huntley garden through a narrow opening in the fence—a remnant from years gone by when Gabriella and her sister had played with Shirring and Lord John as children. Crossing the springy grass of the lawn, they approached the stairs leading up to the terrace and knocked on the glass door there.

"The duke's sisters are expecting you," Pierson said in the same dry tone that Simmons employed as he admitted them. "This way, if you please."

Arriving in a brightly lit sunroom with large potted plants in each corner, Gabriella smiled at the sight of the two young women who jumped to their feet with boisterous enthusiasm the moment they saw her. "My lady," one of them burst out in jubilation, "you've come!" She hurried forward and instantly enfolded Gabriella in a tight embrace. "Thank ye." Stepping back, eyes shimmering slightly with emotion, she said again, "Thank ye ever so much!"

"It's my pleasure," Gabriella said, unable to resist a wide smile in response to such forthright elation. She was also pleased to see a bit more color in their cheeks. "You needn't be so formal though. Gabriella will suffice."

"Then ye must call us Amelia an' Juliette," Amelia said, gesturing first to herself and then toward the petite brunette who stood behind her. The girl responded with a timid smile, immediately underscoring the difference between the two sisters. Both had chestnut-colored hair, though Amelia's was slightly curly with a hint of copper, while Juliette's was straight and slightly darker.

"Well, it's a pleasure to see you both again," Gabriella said. She glanced around. "I take it your brother will not be joining us?"

"Probably not. Said 'e'd be takin' lessons with 'is valet an' secretary," Amelia said.

Gabriella breathed a sigh of relief, reassured by the knowledge that her nerves would not be subjected to the duke's dashing looks and charming smiles today. "Well then, let's get started, shall we?" She waited for Amelia and Juliette to sit so she could observe the way in which they moved. Both appeared to lack any semblance of grace as they strode across the floor, plopping down on chairs as though their feet had just been swept out from underneath them.

Gabriella exchanged an uneasy look with Anna, who responded with a teasing grin. "Good luck," she whispered. "I think I'll retreat to that corner over there."

Envying her maid's lack of inclination to participate, Gabriella turned toward her hostesses and quietly said, "We have a great deal of ground to cover before either one of you will be ready to venture out in public. You will have to speak precisely, without cutting your words in half, and you will have to move about gracefully. Additionally, we shall have to discuss a few subjects of importance, so that your conversational skills can be improved." Setting her reticule aside on a small table, she offered them the book she'd brought. "I think this will be a useful reference guide."

"Ye brought us a book?" Amelia asked, accepting the gift and turning it back and forth as she studied the gold-embossed leather cover.

A thought struck Gabriella and she suddenly asked, "You do read?" She hadn't even considered the possibility that they might not until this moment.

But then the girls smiled, appeasing any concern she might have on that score. "Yes," Juliette said. "Raphe taught us."

"Raphe?"

"Our brother," Amelia explained. "The duke?"

Gabriella felt her heart skitter a little.

Raphe.

What a perfectly suitable . . .

She gave herself a mental kick. "Lesson number one: you must always refer to a peer by his or her title when in polite society. Whenever you speak of your brother in the future, you should say 'Huntley,' or 'the duke.'"

The sisters stared at her in dismay.

Gabriella sighed. "Perhaps I ought to begin by teaching you how to walk properly. She faced them with both hands at her sides. "Watch me carefully as I move toward that sofa over there. My back is straight with my head held high. As I walk, I step slowly, as though I have all the time in the world. A lady never rushes, you see, and now that I am here, I lower myself as though I am gradually sinking into a warm bath. Fluid movements, that is the key."

Their eyes widened. "You look so weightless," Amelia said. "Like a butterfly flittin' about the room on a stream of air."

Gabriella chuckled. "Thank you, but as easy as it may look, I can assure you that such grace took many hours of practice for me to perfect." Endless hours, in fact, and with her mother constantly correcting her every move. "So I don't want either of you to be discouraged by the length of time it might take for you to learn such skill." She nodded toward Amelia. "Now you try. Go to the bellpull and ring for a maid to bring us refreshments—lemonade will do."

Pressing her lips together, Amelia rose from her

seat with exaggerated slowness, her body occasionally jerking from the strained effort. Once she was upright, she walked stiffly toward the bellpull. Her pace was decent enough, but her chin was too high and rather than give the velvet rope a gentle tug, she pulled on it as though she were ringing a church bell. "How did I do?" she asked Gabriella with inquisitive hopefulness.

"Err—" Unwilling to crush her spirits, Gabriella said, "That was a good start, but there is still a great deal of room for improvement." She looked toward Juliette. "Let me see you try."

As it turned out, Juliette was much more capable of elegant movement than her sister. Her diffidence, it seemed, served her well in that regard. But whenever she spoke, it was with a mumble that was virtually impossible to understand, her gaze never quite meeting Gabriella's. A maid arrived to take their order of lemonade before departing once more with quick efficiency.

"Tell me more about your schooling," Gabriella said once Juliette had resumed her seat. Knowing exactly what the girls had learned over the years would be useful since it would help form a picture of their level of education.

Amelia stared back at Gabriella for a moment, then eventually said, "We lived quite far from the nearest school, so we learned what we could at 'ome. Our brother taught us our letters, ye know. He always insisted we educate ourselves as much as possible so we'd 'ave a better chance at a proper future."

Realizing she must be gaping at her, Gabriella sank back against the sofa, unsure of what to make of this puzzling bit of information. There was also something curious about the two sisters' account. At no point did either of them mention the people with whom they'd allegedly lived. They only spoke of their brother and the influence he'd had on their education.

Recalling the duke's own muddled version of his childhood and the vague mention of some distant relation somewhere close to the Scottish boarder, Gabriella decided that there was a good chance that the Duke of Huntley and his sisters were not at all what they seemed.

The maid returned, setting down a tray containing a glass decanter and three glasses before departing once more.

Deciding not to quiz the two women anymore, since they were beginning to look ill at ease, she got to her feet and asked them to do the same. "Let's practice your walk again. We can take a turn of the room together and then I will show you how to pour a drink."

For the next two hours, Gabriella applied herself to teaching Amelia and Juliette how to comport themselves as young ladies ought. She corrected their English whenever they spoke incorrectly, while they proved themselves to be better students than expected, both making conscious efforts to heed her advice, no matter how trying it must have been for them at times.

"You know, I'm quite impressed by your progress today," she told them later as they took a small reprieve for luncheon, which consisted of sandwiches brought into the sunroom for the sake of expediency. It was the truth. What these two women had accomplished today during their first lesson was quite impressive, to say the least. Gabriella was confident that as long as they kept it up, they would be sure to turn a few heads once they made their debut in another couple of weeks or so.

"We have you to thank, Gabriella," Juliette said

as she bit into a sandwich. The effort left a blob of butter attached to the corner of her mouth. Instinctively, she stuck out her tongue with the intention of licking it away, but then she saw Gabriella's frown, considered her options, and reached for her napkin instead.

Gabriella gave her a nod of approval and an encouraging smile. Finishing her own food, she studied each of the sisters in turn. They were both quite pretty, she noted, and they were looking a little healthier than when she'd seen them last, although Juliette appeared more fragile than her sister. Thankfully, their maids had been of some use with regard to their attire, for both had acquired flattering gowns cut in the most fashionable styles. "When you meet Queen Charlotte for the first time, you will be required to execute impeccable curtsies," Gabriella told them.

"Do you really think we'll be invited to the royal drawing room?" Juliette quietly asked.

"Without question," Gabriella said. Seeing the troubled look in her eyes, she added, "Not to worry, though. I'm going to make sure that you're ready once the invitation arrives. And when you do go there, I shall come with you."

"Really?" Amelia sounded both happy and relieved.

"Well of course!" Gabriella frowned. "Your brother didn't mention it?"

"He told us not to expect anything beyond a little advice," Juliette said.

Gabriella understood Huntley's reasoning immediately. "He didn't want you to get your hopes up in case I changed my mind." His consideration toward his sisters was touching—a vulnerable side of himself that he otherwise hid beneath honed muscles and a serious expression.

"He's very protective of us," Juliette said. She bit her lip as her expression grew distant. "*Too* protective, at times."

Chuckling as though to alleviate her sister's maudlin mood, Amelia got to her feet with a start, almost overturning her glass of lemonade in the process. "Gabriella doesn't want to hear about that, Julie. Come, let's show her our curtsies instead."

And so they did, while Gabriella corrected their postures and movement of limbs. The idea that Huntley had a compelling reason to shelter his sisters, and that it might stretch beyond the obvious one regarding the *ton*, had lodged itself securely in her mind, however. She wondered about it, increasingly distracted by the many possibilities. She had no business being curious, but she couldn't seem to stop herself. For reasons unknown, she wanted to know more about Huntley and his sisters.

They were not like any aristocrats she'd met before, and her parents would probably lock her away in the attic for daring to speak with them, let alone spend the entire morning in their company. But they were interesting, and . . . enjoyable. A breath of fresh air in an otherwise stale environment.

She was just pondering the notion that one should never judge a person before getting to know them when the nape of her neck suddenly buzzed with acute awareness. Turning with a start, she saw Huntley leaning against the doorway with arms crossed, eyes dark as night, and with a coy smile trailing along his lips. "Am I intruding?"

Chapter 9

Gabriella stared. How utterly unfair of him to look like that, his posture stretching and bunching his perfectly tailored jacket in a way that accentuated the width of his chest and the breadth of his shoulders, his body exuding physical strength while the chiseled sweep of his nose and jawline accentuated the soft curve of his lips. Feeling parched, Gabriella struggled against the dryness in her throat until she finally managed to utter a gravelly, "No." She should have said yes, she reflected, and sent him away. Instead, he pushed himself away from the doorway and strode toward her with the distinct presence of a man who never allowed the opinions of others to affect him.

Knowing he had no choice but to bow to social norms now—to change everything about himself for the sake of appearances—had to be frustrating. His candid dislike of the aristocracy meant that he probably had to deny a great many principles in order to embrace a life among them. That he would do so for his sisters was extraordinarily noble.

"Amelia and Juliette are making excellent progress," Gabriella said, her voice a little sharper than she would have liked.

Pausing, he looked down at her. His features were more relaxed today, his eyes radiating a startling degree of warmth that seemed to spill over her. The slightest dimple appeared at the edge of his lips, in perfect accordance with her escalating heartbeat. In one easy move, he claimed the seat beside her, his sudden closeness disrupting her trained control in a trice. Pushing the palm of her hand into the seat cushion beneath her, Gabriella sought to reacquire some measure of stability in the midst of the strange storm that tore its way through her.

"Then you must be an excellent teacher," he murmured, his words somehow managing to linger between them like unspoken promises.

What was she thinking? He was being perfectly cordial. There was no reason at all for her to suppose this bizarre attraction . . . She drew a breath. *No.* She couldn't possibly be attracted to him, a man she'd met only days before on the pavement in front of his home when she'd mistaken him for a servant. And yet . . . no other man had ever affected her in such an uncomfortable way. It had to be his unusualness that made her react so. *Yes. That was it.* She simply wasn't accustomed to dealing with a man who was so . . . *different* from the other gentlemen of her acquaintance.

And then, while his sisters proclaimed that indeed she was the best teacher in the world and proceeded to praise her to the heavens, Huntley reached for her hand, the unexpected touch stealing through her with fiery sparks of awareness. It was all Gabriella could do not to forget to breathe, her dazed mind barely registering the gentle scrape of a callused thumb against her soft skin as he raised the hand slowly to his lips.

She could not look at him, but neither could she look away, which presented something of a conundrum. The kiss was airy—scarcely a touch at all. Nevertheless, it sent heat rushing through her veins, scorching her from the inside out while her heart beat in concert with her ragged exhalations of breath.

Aware of the crimson that surely blanketed her cheeks and temples, Gabriella closed her eyes just briefly enough to regain what little composure she had left. "Thank you, Your Grace. It has been a pleasure getting to know them better." With a gentle tug, she drew her hand away from his and willed the sensations he'd stirred in her to abate. This was wrong. She ought to feel this way about Fielding, for whom she'd hardly spared a thought since her arrival here. Sobered by guilt, she managed a cooler tone when she spoke again. "You'll be pleased to know that they've applied themselves diligently the entire morning."

His gaze drifted to the table where Amelia had placed the book that Gabriella had brought with her. His eyebrows rose as he reached for it, studied it and set it back down. "My secretary gave me somethin' similar: *The Gentleman Instructed, In the Conduct of a Virtuous and 'appy Life.*" Leaning back, he stretched out his legs in a casual pose of relaxation. "If I do as it suggests, my days will be filled with nothin' but social visits. Frankly, I don't know 'ow gentlemen get anythin' practical done when they 'ave—*have*—to call on any friend who has recently returned from a journey, who requires an expression of joy or sympathy, upon 'is *host* at any party immediately followin' the event, upon any lady who's accepted 'is escort . . . the list goes on."

"I suppose that's why gentlemen value their secretaries so much," Gabriella said with a teasing smirk.

"They obviously need someone to manage their busy schedules."

His eyes caught hers, twinkling in response to her comment—just long enough to convey his appreciation of her sarcasm. But then he sighed and shook his head, dislodging a lock that settled across his brow. "It's not very efficient, is it?" He grinned then. "If it were up to me I'd let the calls accumulate and then put everyone together in one room, say whatever needed to be said, offer a bit of tea, and be done with it in 'alf an hour or less."

Gabriella laughed. "How enterprising of you!"

"But," he added, all traces of humor fading, "I don't suppose I should worry too much since I 'ave no friends to call on yet."

"You will, I believe," Gabriella assured him. "Eventually."

"Because I'm a duke and everyone will wish to know me?"

"There is that," she agreed, "but there's also the man you are without the title—your character and your personality. You needn't change either just because you're learning to speak and conduct yourself differently. In fact, I think it would be a shame if you did."

His eyes stayed on her for a long moment, and then he suddenly turned toward his sisters, who'd fallen into their own conversation. "May I see what Lady Gabriella has taught ye?"

Gabriella flinched, startled by the sudden change of mood, but she quickly recovered, straightened her back and smiled at the two sisters. "Juliette. Why don't you begin?"

Rising with great hesitation, Juliette's confidence seemed to grow increasingly fragile as she moved about the room. Clearly, Huntley's perusal was making her too self-conscious. "Just relax," Gabriella told her gently. "You're doing very well."

"Shouldn't she hold her head a bit higher?" Huntley asked.

Juliette faltered, her body jerking slightly as she turned with a strained expression that conveyed deep concentration with an underlying hint of defeat. Gabriella's lips thinned. She turned to Huntley, who was clearly the cause of his sister's distress, most likely because she'd hoped to impress him and wasn't self-assured enough to bear his comment as anything other than a criticism aimed at her. "I suppose you think you can do better?" Gabriella asked.

The duke started just enough for Gabriella to appreciate his discomfort. His expression tightened, producing a slight strain in his jawline. "Probably not," he admitted.

"Oh?" She gave him a frank stare. "Perhaps you shouldn't comment on the progress of others unless you have something positive to say, then?"

"I'm sorry, Julie," Huntley told his sister with a touching degree of sincerity. "I didn't mean to sound critical. Please," he moved his chin in his sister's direction, "do continue."

For the next fifteen minutes, the sisters showed their brother everything Gabriella had taught them that morning, including how to pour drinks for guests. No other mistakes were made, which led to an impressive smile of appreciation from Huntley as soon as the demonstration was over. He clapped his hands. "Well done!"

His enthusiastic praise lifted Gabriella's spirits in a way nothing else ever had. She felt a strong sense of accomplishment, even though she knew this was only the beginning. "There is still a lot of ground for us to cover before you're ready, but if your dedication doesn't change, I suspect you will both obtain the admiration you deserve."

"What about me?" Huntley asked. "Do ye think I'll receive the admiration *I* deserve?"

Swallowing, Gabriella tried to keep her expression as bland as possible. "If you apply yourself as well as Juliette and Amelia, then I'm sure you will."

He rolled his eyes in an unapologetic way. "Richardson expects me to learn about opera an' some famous composer called Beathoevan."

"It's pronounced *Batehoven*, Your Grace, and Richardson is correct. There are certain subjects that you will be expected to be familiar with in order to converse with the ladies and gentlemen you meet."

"Can't I just talk about current events? I've been readin' the papers fer as long as I can remember, keepin' up to date on politics an' such. T'would make fer a more interestin' debate."

"I'm sure it would," Gabriella agreed, "But discussing politics in public is considered vulgar for precisely that reason, which is why gentlemen tend to address these matters in the privacy of their clubs."

"Sounds stupid."

Gabriella couldn't resist laughing. "Perhaps it does, but it prevents tempers from rising on account of differing views."

"Hmm." He didn't seem to agree. "Is there anythin' else that I should avoid talkin' about?"

"Religion," she said. "As with politics, this is an area that can easily rile and offend. Instead, I would suggest focusing on books you've read or the arts—even the weather will do if you can think of nothing else."

"If ye take a look at the paintings ye own," Juliette suggested, "ye can talk about that. I've noticed a couple of De Latours upstairs as well as a Rubens in the library."

"Yes," Gabriella agreed with a few rapid blinks. She was somewhat surprised by Juliette's unexpected knowledge about painters. "Your library is an excellent resource in general. I suggest you make good use of it."

"Thank you," Huntley said, his voice a deep and honest conveyance of gratitude.

Fearing her own voice might betray her, Gabriella nodded her response with a smile. "Well then," she said, determined to remove herself from Huntley's presence before her legs grew too weak to walk. "I really must—"

"Tell me somethin', me lady," Huntley said, interrupting her without further ado.

Gabriella drew a fortifying breath. "Yes?

"What does someone like ye do fer sport?"

She blinked at that. "For sport?"

"I mean, ye don't work, which surely gives ye a great deal of time to fill." He gave her a lopsided grin before adding, "When ye're not busy with social calls, that is."

"Oh." She sat back, noting the looks of interest on all three faces. "Well, most young ladies like to paint or play an instrument and are generally very accomplished at needlework. Some might pass an entire day selecting the gown for their next social event, visiting the modiste and going for rides or walks in the park."

"But that doesn't answer the question. What I wish to know is what ye—*you*," he amended, "like to do."

Gabriella bit her lip. She rarely spoke of her hobby with anyone. People simply didn't understand her fascination with insects and since they tended to respond with shock instead of interest, she generally chose to avoid the subject unless she felt a need to press it, which was what had happened the other day with Fielding.

But the thought of possibly sharing her greatest passion with someone and not feel so alone . . . "Entomology."

Silence.

They stared at her, all three. Gabriella felt the heat of censure creep up her spine. She cleared her throat. "It's the study of—"

"Insects," Juliette supplied.

"That's what you enjoy doing?" The question was asked by Amelia.

Gabriella gave her a tiny nod. "Yes."

"Well, I'll be," Huntley said. His eyes sparked with renewed interest. "I'd never 'ave thought it, but ye might just be the most interestin' contradiction I've ever 'ad the pleasure of meetin'."

And just like that, Gabriella's heart melted. She was doomed, she realized as she got to her feet with a sudden desperation to quit his company. All because he'd given her the nicest and most meaningful compliment she'd ever received. "I really must go," she said as panic tightened its hold on her, squeezing until she could scarcely breathe.

This must have been how her sister had been lured away from Bellmore, with pretty words and a devilish smile that made her feel things that no young lady had any business feeling. Gabriella began backing away, adding distance, almost stumbling into a side table in her sudden haste to get away. "We can resume your lessons tomorrow," she told the sisters. "Will the same time do?"

"Yes. That'll be fine," Amelia said while Juliette nodded. Both were watching her desperate departure with wide-eyed curiosity, while Huntley himself . . .

Gabriella averted her gaze from him and focused on reaching Anna, who was waiting for her by the door.

"Me lady," Huntley said, drawing Gabriella's attention back to him with great reluctance. "Thank ye again fer doin' this—fer wantin' to help. We're most appreciative."

His sincerity was almost too much to bear. Oh, if he'd only been rude and unpleasant. But he wasn't. Quite the contrary. He was charming and funny. Which meant that she had no choice but to like him, no matter how much she feared doing so. His sisters were safe, but Huntley . . . he was the furthest thing from safe that she'd ever experienced. "You're welcome," she managed, her voice a little raspy.

Reaching the door, she paused just long enough to bid them all a good day. And then she fled without a backward glance.

Chapter 10

"**I** need a break," Raphe said as he stood up and strode toward the parlor window. It was Wednesday morning, with only two days to spare before the infernal dinner party at Fielding House, but by God he would go mad if he had to practice his *heiches* and *dees* for one more second. Not to mention that there was a right and a wrong spoon depending on the meal being served. *Idiotic*. A spoon was a spoon. It served the same purpose regardless of shape and size.

Apparently not.

"Very well," Richardson said while Pierson looked on with concern. "Will one hour do?"

Raphe glared at him.

"We're only trying to help," Humphreys explained as though speaking to a stubborn child.

"Fine," Raphe agreed. "We'll reconvene here in one hour."

The servants filed out of the room, leaving Raphe alone. He considered the table that had been set up for him to practice at. There were five dishes, four of which were piled on top of each other while one—the bread plate, as they called it—stood to one side.

Raphe stared at it. Who would ever have thought to make a special plate just for bread? Seemed strange.

Stranger still was the need for different glasses. There were four of these too, depending on what one was drinking. And all of this was surrounded by an army of silverware. Ten pieces to be exact, including the fish fork, the salad fork and the dinner fork, each with an accompanying knife to go with it. Picking up the dessert fork, he studied the piece for a moment and eventually shook his head. A grown man should not have to use such a tool. It was far too flimsy and feminine looking.

Grimacing, Raphe turned his back on the nightmarish place setting and strode from the room. With little time to spare before his lessons resumed, he'd be happy to catch some fresh air. But as he neared the doors leading out to the garden, he paused upon hearing a bit of laughter from one of the closest rooms. His sisters', he recognized, but there was another more feminine sound, so pretty in its cadence that he simply had to see . . .

Approaching, he reached for the door handle to the room, and then paused again. Aware of the distress he'd caused Lady Gabriella the last time he'd seen her, he'd deliberately stayed away from her since, allowing her to tutor his sisters in private. But that didn't mean he hadn't thought of her or been aware of her presence in his house.

Discovering that she studied insects had certainly been intriguing. And her willingness to risk her reputation on account of people she barely knew had also raised her appeal to a whole new level. He thought of her sense of humor—there was an openness to it that he definitely liked. And the way in which she reacted to him . . . It obviously terrified her, but still, there could be no denying that it was there—a very elemental awareness always simmering beneath the surface when they were in the same room.

Another bit of laughter flew toward him.

Oh, to hell with it.

He pushed the handle down and the door swung open, revealing a scene that put him momentarily off his guard. Because there on the floor, with her bottom sticking up in the air while she reached for something under a table, was Lady Gabriella—the very image of feminine comportment in a state of absolute disarray.

His sisters, Raphe noted, were lying flat on their bellies, both trying to help her with whatever it was they were hoping to accomplish. Holding himself perfectly still, he stared, aware that a gentleman ought to announce his arrival. But he couldn't seem to bring himself to do it—could not deny himself the pleasure of admiring a part of Lady Gabriella that was otherwise hidden from view. Yes—it was only the contour of her bottom, but it was enough for him to measure its size and shape. And then, heaven help him, she wriggled it, and Raphe almost let out a groan. Instead, he clasped the door frame for support, took a second to compose himself, and finally said, "Might I ask what you're looking for?"

His sisters squealed at the sound of his voice, both jumping back while Lady Gabriella went instantly still. A second passed. He heard the clock tick and wondered if she might remain underneath the table forever after, her embarrassment too great for her to come out. But then she slowly scooted back and gracefully rose to her feet, her cheeks as pink as blossoms in bloom. "There . . ." she cleared her throat and straightened her spine a bit. "I found an interesting spider." And then she did the most unexpected thing. Stepping closer to him, she held out her closed hand and carefully opened it to reveal a black creature with long spindly legs. "See?"

Raphe stared down at the thing, unsure of how to react without causing offense. He raised his eyes to her face, seeing the stiffness there, the slight trembling of her lower lip as she held herself rigid, the puckering between her brows. She was nervous, but with the spider in her hand she made no effort to retreat as she had done before. Perhaps the creature gave her comfort, as strange as that thought seemed. "Yes," he told her softly. "I see."

Her eyes, swimming with uncertainty, met his. Impossible to resist. And he found himself not thinking. Instead he said the first thing that came to mind, "Would you like to take it home with you?"

She beamed then, a brilliant smile as dazzling as any star. "If you don't mind."

Raphe chuckled slightly, amused by their odd conversation. "I'm sure we can manage without him."

She laughed as well then, her demeanor more relaxed than he'd ever seen it before. "I believe it might be a *her*, Your Grace."

He wasn't about to ask her how she might know—not now when they were once again enjoying an easy bit of conversation, devoid of the usual tension that whirled between them. So he crossed to the bell-pull instead. "I'll ask a maid to bring a small box for it then."

"Eleanor," Lady Gabriella announced.

Raphe glanced back over his shoulder at her. "What?"

"I think I will call my new spider Eleanor. What do you think?" But she wasn't looking at Raphe any longer, she was addressing his sisters.

A spark of something—something Raphe didn't care for at all—squeezed at his chest with unbidden force. He gave the bellpull a disgruntled yank and crossed his arms.

"I think it suits her," Juliette said.

"It's the perfect name," Amelia agreed. She took a seat in one of the armchairs and Raphe couldn't help but notice that she did so with a bit more elegance than usual. "Do you 'ave a very large collection of insects?"

"*Have*," Juliette reminded her sister.

"I like to think so," Lady Gabriella said as though commenting on a painting she might have made. There was pride in her voice, and a sort of intensity about it that conveyed great passion for her hobby. "I've been gathering samples since I was seven and . . ." She bit her lip, shook her head and eventually shrugged a shoulder. "Never mind."

Curious.

"Do you go out into nature often then?" Juliette asked. "With a net?"

Lady Gabriella chuckled. "Well I—"

"What about your friends? Do they ever go with you?" Amelia inquired. "I think it would be a wonderful way for us to make their acquaintance. Much better over tea and cake. It'd be less formal, see? That is, if you'd like for us to meet your friends." She paused for a second and Raphe watched as his sister's smile slipped from her animated face. "Or perhaps you'd rather we don't meet them. I mean, we'd hate to impose."

Frowning, Raphe moved so he could get a better glimpse of Lady Gabriella, surprised by how stunned she looked. But it wasn't just that. There was that touch of fear again. "My lady?" he asked. He didn't want to force an explanation, but he wouldn't let her hurt his sisters either, by allowing them to think that they weren't good enough to meet her friends.

"I err . . ." Lady Gabriella looked at them each in turn, her hands still clasping the spider.

Where in God's name was the maid?

"To be perfectly honest, I have none."

Juliette and Amelia both frowned at that while Raphe instantly bristled. The least she could do was be honest, but to lie to them . . . The door opened at that moment and a maid entered. Raphe asked her to bring a small box, then turned back to face Lady Gabriella. "A word, if you will." He waited for her to join him at the other side of the room, his voice a low whisper when he spoke once more. "They've taken a liking to you. Don't ruin it with falsehoods. They might lack your upbringing, but they're not stupid, Lady Gabriella, so as long as you're in this house, ye'll treat them with respect." *Damn it*. He'd let the last *you* get him.

Her eyes had gone wide, her lips parting as she stood there staring up at him. And then she took a breath and managed to say, "I would never lie to them about such a thing. If I had any friends, which I do not—"

"I don't believe you," he said. She blinked, averted her gaze, blinked some more. He saw her throat work as though she was finding it difficult to breathe. So he bowed his head, moving it closer to hers and asked her gently, "How can a pretty society lady with a kind disposition, such as *your*self, possibly be without friends? It makes no sense."

Twisting her mouth until a web of fine lines began distorting the feature, she stood as though he'd just asked her to make an impossible choice. Indecision warred behind those pale blue eyes of hers, so clear and liquid now, like a pair of water-droplets just waiting to spill over.

But they didn't. Instead, she found a safe point of focus, somewhere just to the right of his shoulder. "First of all," she told him quietly, "I am not pretty, I am—"

"Daft," he murmured. "If you truly believe that."

Her mouth opened, closed again. She turned more fully toward him, her brow now puckering while her eyes—oh those innocently tempting eyes—implored and chastised while her hands balled tightly into fists at her side. "No, I am not, but I do own a mirror, Your Grace, and I am also aware of what others have said about me."

He drew back, almost as though she'd struck him. His eyes widened, allowing her to spot another nuance to their coloring. Not just brown with flecks of gold. No, there was a subtle ring of amber toward the edge—a gradual transition toward the darker tones at the center. They held her now until she felt like squirming. He prepared to say something, but she wouldn't let him, would not allow him to try and convince her that she was something that she wasn't. "I know that I am strange and peculiar. I am keenly aware that everyone thought my sister would be the one to . . . to . . . ." She took a gulp of air. *Enough.* She'd said enough. "I did not lie to them, Your Grace."

When he said nothing in response, she turned away briskly and walked back to where Amelia and Juliette were still sitting, resuming their lesson by asking each of them to take turns reading from the *Mayfair Chronicle*. Patiently, she corrected their pronunciations while doing her best to ignore the large man who stood like a looming shadow to one side. Eventually, she heard his feet move across the floor, and then the clicking of the door handle as he made his exit. She breathed a sigh of relief, her hands still trembling from their encounter.

Put him from your mind, Gabriella.

Focus.

As wise as her own advice was, however, she had to concede that she was only human and that the Duke of Huntley represented every craving she'd ever wished to indulge in.

Chapter 11

"**S**o if a gentleman asks me to dance I 'ave to accept? Even if I don't like 'im?" Amelia asked the following day.

"Unless you have a very good excuse," Gabriella told her, "like another offer from a different gentleman or a sprained ankle, though this would likely remove you from the dance floor altogether."

Amelia shook her head. "What daft rules."

"There are many more, but I suppose the point is that a lady should always be polite and treat other people with respect. Don't make the mistake of supposing that a gentleman is incapable of feeling slighted or hurt by your disinterest in him."

A sudden crash in the hallway made Gabriella jump. She glanced toward the door, which stood ajar, but saw nothing. And then, "No more," was bellowed with such force that the windows in the parlor almost rattled.

Huntley.

"I'm done with this nonsense—this imbecilic madness." His voice was steady and clipped. "Don't do this an' don't do that. Not to mention all the useless information ye keep pilin' onto me brain. *My* brain. God damn it!"

"Your Grace," Richardson spoke with endless degrees of patience. "Perhaps we should try again."

Eyeing Amelia and Juliette who were sitting completely still, eyes wide and lips pressed together, Gabriella got to her feet and crossed to the door. She peeked out and saw the duke standing in a wide stance with his hands on his hips as he faced his secretary. The remains of what appeared to be a vase lay at his feet.

"No," Huntley said. "Not as long as you expect me to treat a teacup as if it's a precious relic. I refuse to hold it the way *you* want me to, Richardson."

"Is everything all right?" Gabriella asked, even though it clearly wasn't.

Huntley turned to her with a glower while Richardson hastily bowed, "My lady," he said. "I am simply trying to educate His Grace in taking tea correctly."

"To be precise," the duke grumbled, "Richardson thinks I'm some effeminate creature with a delicate touch when I actually 'appen"—he winced—"*h*appen . . . to be a rather large man."

"Really?" Gabriella murmured, hoping to lighten the mood while ignoring the increased beat of her pulse. "I hadn't noticed."

Richardson coughed while the duke's eyes darkened. He turned more fully toward her and crossed his arms while shards of porcelain crunched beneath his feet. The edge of his mouth kicked up, and then he allowed his gaze to drift over her with a slowness that sent ripples down her spine. "Is that so, my lady?"

Shifting, Gabriella drew herself up to her full height. She was still upset by the accusation he'd made yesterday about deceiving his sisters, and although she wished to address the issue and defend herself more fully, she'd no desire to do so with Richardson present. So she called upon her most affected tone and said, "What I see is a brutish individual who just wrecked an antique vase."

He dropped his gaze to his feet and studied the mess there. "It was an accident," he said. "I didn't knock it over on purpose."

Gabriella raised an eyebrow. "Well, your frustration with Richardson's teaching methods has just cost you five hundred pounds by my estimation."

His head whipped up, eyes widening with incredulity. "Five hundred pounds?"

"Six, actually," Richardson said. "I'll call for a maid to clean it up."

"In the meantime, perhaps Your Grace will allow me to show you how to hold that infernal teacup that has you so overwrought?" Gabriella suggested as she gestured toward the parlor where his sisters sat waiting.

Huntley eyed her with suspicion, but then relented with a nod, though he did not look the least bit pleased. "Very well."

"Is everything all right?" Juliette asked when Gabriella returned with Huntley on her heels.

"Quite," Gabriella assured her. She smiled as she resumed her seat. "Your brother is simply having a bit of difficulty handling the china."

Muttering something inaudible, the duke took a seat next to Gabriella, which prompted her to look at him. To her surprise, he didn't look the least bit annoyed but rather . . . amused. Pleased by his reaction to her dry sense of humor, she struggled to refrain from smiling too broadly herself. Instead, she tried to set her mind on the task at hand, which was to teach Huntley the art of taking tea with the innate skill of a true Englishman. Lacking a spare cup and saucer, she offered him her own, setting it down before him with as much professional poise as she could manage.

I am a rather large man.

She willed her thoughts to remain sensible by sitting back stiffly with her chin held high and her hands neatly folded in her lap. Meanwhile, the duke stared at the delicate cup and saucer like some might stare at a venomous snake. "Go ahead," Gabriella urged. "Pick it up in whichever way you find most comfortable."

He leaned forward hesitantly, frowned a bit and then placed one hand on either side of the cup, lifting it as though it were a bowl. Mission accomplished, he raised his eyes and looked at Gabriella with a hopeful expression and a lopsided grin. "This feels right."

"Hmm," she tried to think of how best to help him. "Keep holding on to the cup's ear with your right hand, and let go completely with your left."

He did as she asked, two fingers curled through the ear, braced against his thumb, while another two fingers rested beneath the cup, propping it up. "Like this?"

"Not quite. Perhaps if you could . . ." she gestured toward him in an effort to show how his fingers ought to be placed, but he wasn't getting it.

Knowing what had to be done, she got up and walked around to his other side. "Like this," she said as she proceeded to maneuver his fingers into the correct positions.

Her ability to think straight immediately faltered at the feel of his warm skin beneath her fingertips, and although she stood at his shoulder with some measure of distance between them and both his sisters present, she became instantly aware of his masculinity. It flowed toward her, compounded by an earthy scent of leather and sandalwood, until she found herself surrounded and overwhelmed.

So she drew away and took a hasty step back. "Like that," she said, surprised by the gravelly tone of her voice. "That will do."

Tilting his chin, he raised his gaze to hers. A crease formed on the bridge of his nose. "But Richardson said that I was supposed to straighten the ring finger and pinky." He tried to do as the secretary had advised, but the cup simply slipped from between his fingers, thudded against the carpet and rolled beneath the table. The tea that had been inside it went flying in every direction.

The duke's jaw hardened as he looked down at the spillage, his mouth drew tight, and he suddenly looked as though he might slam his fist against something in pure frustration. Until Gabriella hastily distracted him by saying, "Never mind what Richardson told you about how to hold a teacup. I've seen several gentlemen struggle with this particular exercise over the years."

"Really?" Juliette sounded fascinated.

"It is understandable considering the superior size of a man's fingers when compared to those of a woman's." Returning to her seat, Gabriella told Huntley, "The way you held it before—as I showed you—is good enough. Nobody will fault you for it."

"Well, that's a relief," Huntley said as he reached beneath the table and retrieved the fallen teacup. "I'd hate to be judged on the proper position of my fingers alone."

"Then you needn't fret," Gabriella told him frankly, "for I can assure you that you will be judged on a great deal more than that."

By the time Friday afternoon arrived, bringing with it the delivery of fresh evening attire, Raphe began having second thoughts about his stubborn determination to show up the *ton*.

Perhaps he ought to send an excuse?

"So a viscountess, countess and marchioness are addressed as, 'Your Ladyship' or Lady title," Humphreys was saying, while Raphe buttoned his cuffs. "Their husbands would naturally be, 'Your Lordship' or 'My Lord,' or simply their title, while their daughters would be 'Lady' plus first name."

Sighing, Raphe took a seat on the brocade-clad chair that stood in his bedchamber and reached for one of his shoes. "Yes, Humphreys. I remember."

"What about their eldest sons?"

Having pushed his feet inside the shoes, Raphe began doing up the laces. "Lord honorary title," he said with the confidence of a man who'd spent the last week cramming his head full of what he considered to be the stupidest details in the world.

"And their youngest sons?"

"They would be Mr. last name."

Humphreys nodded. A spark lit in his eyes. "And the youngest son of a duke or a marquess?"

Raphe stilled. A second passed, and then he got to his feet. "Also Mr. last name."

Humphreys groaned. "I knew you weren't ready!"

"Don't be ridiculous," Raphe said as he grabbed his cravat and began winding it around his throat. "Of course I am."

"Not when you don't know that the younger son of a duke or a marquess should be addressed with, 'Lord first name.'" He looked about ready to throw up his hands with exasperation. "How many times have we been over this?"

"Too many to count," Raphe told him dryly. And then, "Don't worry. It will be fine."

Humphreys stared at him. "How can you say that when your cravat looks like something a laundry woman just rung out?"

Muttering an oath, Raphe stepped away from the mirror and faced his valet. "Can you help?"

A bright smile stretched its way across Humphreys's face. "I'd be delighted to."

One hour later, following a few thorough reminders on etiquette from Pierson, Humphreys, and Richardson, Raphe climbed into the Huntley phaeton and began the short ten-minute drive that would take him to Fielding House. His sisters, whom he'd seen before leaving home, had assured him that he looked more handsome than any other man they'd ever seen, their eyes shining with admiration when he'd demonstrated his newly acquired bow to each of them in turn.

"You look like a bloomin' prince, Raphe," Amelia had declared.

While Juliette, the quieter of the two sisters, had smiled prettily before saying, "I barely recognize you." Both had managed to drop their ye's and replace them with you's.

"It's your turn next," he'd told them with a wink.

The carriage swayed slightly as it turned out onto Piccadilly, the springs easing the uneven rhythm of the cobblestones below. Tugging gently at his cravat, Raphe silently cursed Humphreys for tying it so tightly. Hell, he'd be lucky if he'd be able to swallow his food and drink, considering how restrictive the bloody thing felt.

Another five minutes brought the carriage to a

gradual stop in front of a mansion that stood secluded on the fringe of what appeared to be a large
park. Reaching for the tiny brass knob beside him,
Raphe prepared to open the door, when it swung
open, almost causing him to fall out. Halting his
progress, he stared down at the footman who stood
at attention and quietly cursed himself for forgetting
that he was expected to depend on servants to see to
his every need now, no matter how much that bothered him.

Alighting, he took a moment to straighten himself before facing the footman, still holding the door.
"Thank you," he told him with the swift authoritative
precision that he'd been practicing with Pierson.

The man's eyes widened just enough to convey
how shocked he was to have been addressed at all. A
moment of awkward silence passed until the footman
eventually allowed himself to respond with a brief
nod. Turning away from him, Raphe strode forward,
conscious of keeping his chin up and his eyes trained
on the doorway before him as he started up the front
steps toward the spot where another servant stood
waiting.

"Welcome to Fielding House, Your Grace," the
man said, upon reading the invitation Raphe handed
to him. "Right this way." He directed Raphe toward
the foyer, where another servant stood ready to escort
Raphe through to a large parlor that appeared to have
been adorned by a gathering of finely clad ladies and
gentlemen. They stood and sat in clusters throughout, gems sparkling beneath the brightly illuminated
chandeliers overhead. Their clothes were rich, their
postures regal, regardless of age, and their mannerisms seemed to convey the sort of superiority that was
owned, not acquired.

"The Duke of Huntley," the servant intoned as soon as Raphe stepped over the threshold.

All conversation drew to an immediate halt. And then, as if commanded by the servant's voice, each pair of eyes within the room turned to give Raphe their full attention. Stiffly, he remained where he was, uncertain of what was expected of him at this moment. He glanced about, inadvertently searching the curious faces for one in particular, only to discover that *she* wasn't there. His heart slowed to a heavy beat.

"Your Grace," a shrill voice cried. Turning toward it, Raphe saw that it belonged to a petite woman with silver hair. Her face was long and slim, her eyes sharp with predatory arrogance. Coming to a halt before him, she allowed a smile, the pink slash of her lips pulling tightly at her pale skin. "We are so delighted to finally meet you. Allow me to introduce myself. I am Lady Fielding, your hostess for the evening."

"A pleasure," Raphe said. He paused for a second. Richardson had told him to bow before his hostess, but that scenario had involved Raphe approaching her and not the other way around. Additionally, he'd been told to bow before speaking. Too late to change that now, though the question still remained—*should he bow before her now, or not?* Unsure, he attempted something a little less formal than what he'd initially had in mind, just a slight tilt of his torso.

Straightening himself, he tried to assess Lady Fielding's response, but gave up on doing so when her expression failed to convey any kind of emotion. Instead, she raised her head slightly, her eyebrows arching into two sharp points. "Shall I introduce you to the rest of the guests?"

Raphe nodded. "Thank you. I'd appreciate that."

She stared at him with considerable scrutiny until Raphe began to wonder if he might have said or done something to displease her. He could think of nothing, until she stepped toward him, turned and raised her hand, as though it was meant to be resting on something.

Giving himself a mental kick, Raphe quickly offered her his arm. *Christ!* How many times had Humphreys reminded him to do so? Apparently, he was incapable of remembering the simplest things, which did not bode well for the rest of the evening.

They started forward. Raphe made a deliberate effort to keep his pace slow and his stride half as long as usual in order to avoid dragging his hostess. "You have a lovely home," he told her.

She glanced up at him. "It is in the Greek style."

"I see."

Arriving before a small group of ladies and gentlemen, Lady Fielding said, "May I introduce Baron Hawthorne and his wife, Lady Hawthorne, the Duke of Coventry and his mother, the Dowager Duchess of Coventry. And my son, the Earl of Fielding, with whom, I believe, you are already acquainted."

Raphe greeted everyone with a bow and a general, "Pleased to meet you." Eventually, his gaze met Fielding's. Seeing no hint of malice, he decided to be polite. "You look well."

The edge of Fielding's mouth drew upward into a smirk. "And you look remarkably better than when I last saw you."

Recognizing the barb, Raphe prepared to respond with an equally veiled insult when the dowager duchess said, "Sounds intriguing. Would you care to elaborate?"

The smirk lit Fielding's eyes. Raphe felt his jaw

tighten. He drew his fingers into fists. "I met Huntley when he first arrived," Fielding explained. "Lady Gabriella and I were returning from a lovely drive in the park and, as you know, her house is right next door to Huntley's."

"Oh, yes. So it is," Lord Hawthorne said.

"Frankly, I had no idea who he was at the time," Fielding continued. "So I daresay I made quite a fool of myself when I went to introduce myself."

"But you are the very model of propriety, my lord," Lady Hawthorne said. "You could never say anything inappropriate."

"Alas, I fear that isn't true," Fielding told her with a highly exaggerated tone of regret that rankled Raphe to the bone. "For indeed, I made the unforgiveable error of presuming that he was a *servant*."

Unified gasps and wide-eyed disbelief followed. The effect drew other guests closer—the promise of scandal and gossip surely too great to be ignored.

Raphe bristled. "An understandable mistake," he told his host sharply, "under the circumstances."

"But why on earth would you presume such a thing?" someone asked from behind Raphe.

Fielding shrugged, a casual gesture that made Raphe feel like punching him. "His clothes were— simple, unsophisticated and cheap." Murmurs began weaving their way through the crowd. "And when he spoke—well"—he gave Raphe a deliberate once-over, accompanied by a look of pity—"suffice it to say that I would never have guessed you attended Eton, Your Grace."

Silence fell like heavy flakes of plump snow, filling the room until it threatened to bury them all. "Perhaps because I didn't," Raphe told him. He spoke slowly, paying great attention to his choice of words and pronunciation. "But . . ." he added, unwilling to let the unpleasant man get away with his insult, "in spite of your fine education, I still outrank you, Lord Fielding." He allowed a deliberate smile. "Frustrating, isn't it?"

A flood of crimson colored Fielding's cheeks like an ugly rash. He glared at Raphe. "You . . . you . . ." he sputtered while his chest pumped up and down with ever-increasing fury. The man looked just about ready to explode.

"Yes?" Raphe inquired, unable to hide the fact that he was enjoying this.

"Cad."

Raphe stared at him. Feeling his lips begin to tremble, he pressed them together and did his damnedest not to laugh, then told his adversary frankly, "I've received many insults over the years, all of them far worse than that. So if you're looking to offend me, you'll have to do better. *Much* better." Leaning closer, he added, "Put that Eton brain of yours to good use, man."

"Simpleton," Fielding told him.

Raphe winced, embarrassed for the fellow. "Sorry, Fielding, but I'm not impressed."

Fielding's mouth dropped open.

"I suggest you leave it alone," Hawthorne interjected while everyone else nodded.

"I'm not done," Fielding protested. "Can't you see that he doesn't belong here?"

"What I see," Coventry, said, "is a man handing you a spade and asking you to dig."

Raphe smirked. He liked that analogy. And he quite liked Hawthorne and Coventry too for backing him up. Perhaps the *ton* wasn't all bad. Lady Gabriella certainly wasn't. And with that thought came the awful reminder that she was supposed to marry the arrogant earl with whom he was presently sparring. The idea was so unjust it made Raphe's hands go all clammy. His cravat felt suddenly tighter—less comfortable, if such a thing were possible. He narrowed his gaze on Fielding, deciding he was very similar to Guthrie in his abuse of power. If only there were a way to save the world from men like them.

"The Earl and Countess of Warwick," a servant announced, dislodging his thoughts. "And their daughter, Lady Gabriella."

Raphe felt his pulse rise in response to her name. Turning, he sought her with his eyes, a sigh of pleasure cascading through him the moment he saw her. She was wearing a pale blue gown trimmed with silver, displaying a figure that ought to bring every mortal man to his knees. Raphe's throat went dry. *He shouldn't want her, but by God . . .*

"I suggest you look elsewhere," a tight voice murmured in Raphe's ear. *Fielding.* "She is not for the likes of you."

"Would you care to bet on that?" Raphe asked, unable to let the comment go.

Fielding scoffed. "I think not."

And then the earl brushed his way past him, crossing the room with the elegance of a panther until he stood before the woman who'd somehow—*inexplicably*—begun occupying far too much of Raphe's mind.

He watched the pair for a moment; the way Fielding bowed and smiled . . . Lady Gabriella's timid response. It looked so rehearsed and so frustratingly false. They were like actors in a bad play, each trying to play the part that was expected of them rather than one that conveyed any ounce of true emotion. His pulse returned to normal, their interaction reassuring him that Fielding and Lady Gabriella shared a weaker connection with each other than he did with her. It seemed unlikely that they'd even kissed, though Raphe could not for the life of him comprehend Fielding's restraint.

But he was thankful for it.

Indeed, his certainty of the matter filled him with jubilation. *Ridiculous*. It wasn't as though he wanted to win her himself. Except, of course he did—ever since she'd wriggled her bottom at him. What man could possibly forget such a thing? What man could resist it?

But it was more than that. Much more. It was her kindness, her vulnerability, her pain. He wanted to taste it all on her pretty lips, bathe in her light and soothe away her fears.

A slow and tortured breath poured out of him. Wincing, he shook his head. He had no right thinking of her as anything other than his neighbor. She would marry Fielding, while he would ensure that his sisters made the best matches they could possibly achieve. And then, once they were properly settled, he would decide what to do with his own life.

Chapter 12

Smiling at Fielding, who'd just come to greet her, Gabriella remained keenly aware of Huntley's presence across the room. It was impossible for her not to, considering his size; looming just beyond her direct line of sight, he portrayed an intense mixture of pure masculinity and raw power. A fleeting glance in his direction was all she'd allowed herself upon arriving. And it had been enough to send a swarm of fluttering sensations straight to her stomach. So she kept her gaze on the man she meant to marry, determined to will away the strange pull that would draw her to Huntley the moment she let down her guard.

Although their interaction had been amicable when she'd helped him with the teacup, she could not forget that he'd accused her of lying to his sisters. Words. That was all they'd been, but they'd hurt, damn him. The fact that he would think her capable of such deceit, of treating his sisters so carelessly, simply meant that he didn't know her at all. Which was why she'd given herself a very firm talking to after returning home yesterday. "Gabriella," she'd said, applying her mother's tone, "you will keep your thoughts on point and quit all romantic imaginings of the duke. He is *not* the man you're going to marry."

It was a reprimand that had worked quite well since she'd had Eleanor to occupy her mind instead—the task of setting up a home for her in a vacant glass box a welcome distraction. Until she'd gone to bed and sleep had claimed her, filling her mind with dreams of lips pressing fully against hers, of strong fingers reaching, touching, stroking . . .

She'd awoken in a fever, her chest rising and falling with heavy beats and her nightgown hiked up around her hips.

"My lady?" Fielding said, reminding her of time and place. "Would you like some more champagne?"

She studied him for a moment, wondering if he might have caught a glimpse of her scandalous recollections by simply looking at her face. *No.* He did not look the least bit suspicious. So she gave him a nod. "Yes. Thank you."

His absence allowed her another glimpse at the most unlikely duke in British history. He was even handsomer tonight than when she'd last seen him. He'd filled out since arriving in Mayfair, for which he had his cook to thank. The slim fit of his evening attire now enhanced the breadth of his shoulders and the firm planes of his chest. In the past, Gabriella had never spent any time pondering the shape of a man's legs, but as she hastily regarded Huntley from head to toe, it was impossible for her not to notice how long and sturdy his legs appeared to be beneath the fine black wool of his perfectly tailored trousers.

His eyes met hers, intense and unyielding. Daring, almost. And then the edge of his mouth tilted into something that wasn't precisely pleasant. It was rather . . . She struggled to find the right word while awareness took over, heating her in all the wrong places until she felt herself fighting for control. It was awful. *He* was awful, standing there so casually while she struggled to remain upright.

His cravat was beautifully tied this evening, his dark hair neatly styled, while his jaw appeared to be more freshly shaved than she'd ever seen it. Oddly, to her complete consternation, she found that she missed the faint hint of stubble that usually shadowed the sides of his face. The notion struck her as one of the most preposterous things to ever have entered her head. A man *ought* to be well groomed and presentable. To be seen by others—especially by ladies—with day-old whiskers bristling forth from beneath his skin, was unseemly.

Why, then, did the memory of him without a cravat, his hair ruffled as though he'd just stepped out of bed, and with his face roughened by unshaven whiskers, form a molten ball of lava in the pit of her belly?

Fear crept in, prompting her to look away just as Fielding returned with her glass. She took a sip, drowning the urge to revert to the impulsive girl she'd once been. She'd already gone far enough by choosing to help Huntley's sisters. Allowing the duke himself to tempt her would only lead to severe unhappiness.

"Would you like to greet the other guests?" Fielding asked, scattering her thoughts. He offered his arm with perfect poise.

"Of course," Gabriella replied with a polite smile that felt as though it had been glued to her face.

Slowly, they made a tour of the room, speaking briefly to those whom they passed along the way until they came within a few paces of Huntley. He was speaking to her father now, Gabriella noticed. "Suffice it to say," Huntley murmured in low, even tones, his face reflecting the cool expression of a marble statue, "that I did not have the time, the funds, or the opportunity."

Warwick flattened his mouth before speaking with cutting solemnity. "If everything you say is true, then I'd suggest you stop pretending to be someone you're not, and go back to wherever it is you came from."

Gabriella's chest tightened. She knew her parents could be critical of others and blatantly protective of their stations in life, but to publically denounce a duke, was shocking even to her. "Papa," she heard herself say as she reached her father's side, "Huntley is the rightful heir. His title demands our respect." She decided not to mention that he outranked them all, since everyone in the room would be quite aware of the fact.

Swiveling his head in her direction, her father leveled her with a patient look that conveyed a willingness to humor what he no doubt considered a frivolous female notion without substance. "Gabriella," he told her, "your kindness is commendable, truly it is, but we must face facts." He smiled with lukewarm sympathy. "Huntley does not have the necessary upbringing that the peerage requires of a duke."

"And you have come to this conclusion in the space of five minutes?" Gabriella asked, annoyed by her father's accusation.

"All I can say is that a man—any man—who holds a noble title, must be deserving of its power, and the vast responsibility it embodies."

The words were as sharp as a newly forged sword— a deliberate attack on Huntley's worth and one that her father would never have dared use had he been speaking to someone else. Unable to help herself, Gabriella's eyes flew to Huntley's, the dangerous blackness of his gaze forcing her back a step. His jaw was clenched so tightly that slashes of white appeared to slice across his temples. Knowing that a verbal attack was no doubt forming in his mind, Gabriella shook her head and prayed for him to resist. Nothing good could possibly come of it.

She turned to Fielding. "My lord," her voice beseeched him to say something—to do as a host was expected to do when emotions ran higher than what was seemly, and to attempt to diffuse the situation with decorum.

Instead, Fielding eyed Huntley with the sort of fleeting glance he might offer a stray dog, or a beggar. "Your father is right, my lady. The aristocracy is a very old institution to which many aspire, but few belong."

Her mouth went dry. They hadn't even sat down to supper yet and already Huntley was being dismissed as an inferior person, unworthy of their attention. She could scarcely believe it. They were snubbing a duke—a man whom they would have had the greatest respect for—feared, even—if only he'd had better diction. And for some reason, that thought alone was enough to make Gabriella's spine stiffen. "You have invited him here," she told Fielding sharply. When his eyes widened a fraction, she deliberately calmed her voice. "Please be polite."

"Don't you think that Huntley would be more comfortable elsewhere?" her father asked with a sigh.

The tightly held control with which Gabriella had been comporting herself for the past ten minutes began to snap. "I'm sure he would, Papa. Especially considering *your* hostility." Tugging her arm away from Fielding's, she met Huntley's gaze once more. "Your Grace. If I may, I should like to apologize to you on behalf of us all. Unfortunately, good manners appear to be in short supply this evening."

Silence settled around them. Gabriella held her breath. Slowly, like the sun rising over the horizon, Huntley's eyes filled with deep curiosity and the sort of admiration that Gabriella had never before been subjected to from anyone. He stared at her a moment before quietly saying, "It must be the weather."

A sigh of relief swept through her. "Yes, it must be." She gave Warwick and Fielding a pointed look. "Don't you agree?"

They reluctantly nodded, though their guards clearly remained in place, secured like impenetrable walls of steel. They didn't trust Huntley in the least; that much was clear. And they didn't like the fact that he'd come here from out of nowhere, without the pedigree to commend him for the position.

A sudden dislike rose through her throat, tingeing her tongue with a bitter taste. It made her want to leave this place and the people it contained with uncanny speed. And yet, as much as she disliked it, it was the life to which she'd been born, the life to which she was beholden. To simply turn her back on it now when her parents depended on her . . .

A bell sounded, signaling that it was time to go in to the dining room. Fielding offered her his arm once more, and she dutifully accepted. But as she did so, her gaze landed on one of the windows, and on the reflection captured within. It was of a blonde-haired woman, her eyes filled with resigned sorrow, affording her the look of a sacrificial lamb being led to the slaughter.

"I have to say that I found your behavior this evening baffling, Gabriella," her father told her later during their drive home. Shadowed against the opposite side of the carriage, her parents' expressions were impossible to read, but Gabriella had heard the tightening of her father's voice, a reminder of his trained control. Her mother's silence, on the other hand, was like a living, breathing thing that filled the space between them, to the point of suffocation.

"*My* behavior?" Gabriella dared, her hands curling into the diaphanous silk of her skirts.

Not once, in all her years, had she ever questioned her parents' behavior or argued against them. It wasn't done. *Was it?* Children were taught to respect their elders. Her father's word had always been law, and her mother's advice had been meant to be followed.

Gabriella stared at them now—at the faceless silhouettes that bobbed in time to the carriage's movement. Occasionally, the glow from a streetlight would steel through the window, brightening the tips of their noses for one flickering second.

"That *is* what we are discussing," Warwick grumbled.

Nails digging against the sides of her thighs and her heart drumming wildly against her chest, Gabriella shoved aside the temptation to smooth things over with platitudes and chose honesty instead. "You were unforgivably rude to Huntley," she murmured.

Her mother gasped, but said nothing further. Warwick, however, leaned forward with the slow precision of a predator. His face emerged from the darkness, shrouded by dull shades of gray that no doubt softened the furious glint in his eyes. "He may have a title, Gabriella, but he is *not* one of us."

"He is common," Gabriella's mother pointed out, as if she sensed that Gabriella needed reminding.

"And he speaks as though he's struggling to pronounce the words," Warwick added, "not to mention his lack of education. For heaven's sake, Gabriella, the man has had no proper schooling. He admitted as much himself. And he is a peer! A man we're meant to consider our equal! Forgive me, but I don't believe I have ever heard of anything more absurd!"

Fearing that her parents might become suspicious of her concern, Gabriella chose to retreat, saying simply, "It was no reason for you to be cruel." As much as she'd always loved her parents, she had seen a side of them in recent days that she intensely disliked. It was a certain sense of superiority that she'd never really noticed before, perhaps because there had never been occasion for them to show it so clearly. But it was out in full force now with Huntley's arrival, and Gabriella found herself, for the first time ever, questioning her station in life.

"Cruel?" Her father laughed. "I did the man a favor by informing him that he is never going to be welcome among our set. If he's wise, he'll stop wasting his time trying."

Oh blast. She could *not* let that statement go without comment. "Like it or not, Papa, he is the Duke of Huntley. I really think you ought to resign yourself to the fact."

"The most unsuitable duke I've ever seen. And his sisters!" Gabriella's mother shuddered. "I'll trust you to remember that we have forbidden you from socializing with any of them in any capacity."

"The last thing we need is for Fielding to withdraw his interest on account of any poor judgment on your part," Warwick said.

"Oh heavens," Lady Warwick exclaimed with her hand on her chest, "you must not squander the opportunity you have of becoming Lady Fielding."

A prospect that hadn't really concerned Gabriella one way or the other, until recently. Now, after witnessing how unfeeling he could be, she couldn't help but wonder if it was the right choice for her, no matter the stakes at play. Marriage was, after all, quite permanent.

"Would you still love me if I didn't want to marry him?"

She'd spoken without thinking, and found herself completely surprised by the thought she'd just voiced, and quite unsure of where it had come from.

A lengthy moment of silence passed, as though her parents were having some difficulty processing her words themselves. Eventually, her mother chuckled. "What a silly idea," she said with a smiling voice. "Of course we would."

"You don't seem to approve of Victoria's choice, and she chose love above everything else," Gabriella said with a strange sense of envy that she'd never felt before.

"Your sister broke a brilliant engagement in order to marry a tradesman," Warwick clipped with unconcealed vehemence. "That doesn't mean we don't love her anymore, it just means that we would be forced to move in different circles if she were still in England, which, as you know, she is not."

"But all of that is beside the point, is it not?" Gabriella's mother asked as she placed a calming hand on her husband's arm. "After all, Fielding will eventually propose, and when he does, Gabriella will accept. That's all there is to it. She will *not* make her sister's mistake."

"But will I be happy?" Gabriella asked, choosing to ignore her mother's note of warning.

"Of course you will," Warwick insisted. "Fielding will make an excellent husband. You will want for nothing."

"What about love?"

Heavens, it was as though a lifetime of unanswered questions were spilling out of her. Questions she'd never dared think about, let alone ask. Her future had been pre-ordained since the day she'd been born. Or at least, that was how it had always felt. Because although her parents had always placed their highest hopes on Victoria, they'd still expected Gabriella to make them proud. To consider straying from that path had seemed increasingly impossible as her mother had helped her prepare for her debut, desperate to turn her strange and awkward daughter into a diamond of the first water.

But there had been no need to worry. Gabriella's dowry had drawn great attention and Fielding had claimed the first dance. Her parents had been giddy with joy. Gabriella hadn't really cared one way or the other. She was simply fulfilling her purpose, indifferent to her choices since none of the gentlemen she'd met that evening had made much of an impression on her. Apart from differing looks, they were all quite similar. So then, why shouldn't she have aimed for the best in the end, as her mother had advised? It would have been silly of her not to.

But then a dark-haired man so unlike the rest—a man whose masculinity oozed from every fiber of his virile body—had moved in next door, upsetting every thought she'd ever had, on pretty much every topic.

"Love will come," her mother said smoothly.

"Will it?"

"Yes," her parents spoke in unison, just as the carriage pulled to a jostling halt outside their home.

"It did for us," Warwick added, as if that assurance would ease away Gabriella's concerns.

"Really?" She couldn't help but ask. She also couldn't help but wonder if their idea of love was equal to hers, for she could not recall ever witnessing any signs of affection between them.

"Of course," her mother said, bringing the conversation to a close.

Alighting, Gabriella followed her parents inside, where she bid them both good night before retiring to her bedchamber. Sleep would not come quickly this evening, she realized.

There was far too much for her to think about.

By the time she descended to breakfast the following day, Gabriella found only her aunt waiting for her. Apparently, her mother had decided to go shopping with one of her friends, while her father had chosen to visit one of his investments. Breathing a sigh of relief, Gabriella pulled out a chair and sank into it. She reached for the teapot and poured.

"How was dinner last night?" Aunt Caroline asked from across the table.

Looking up, Gabriella saw the inquisitive glow in her eyes. "Worse than expected," she said as she set the teapot aside and pulled a slice of toast onto her plate. "Papa made it very clear to Huntley that he doesn't belong in our midst."

Aunt Caroline's lips curved just enough to convey her lack of surprise. "But you disagree?"

Sipping her tea, Gabriella schooled her features before saying, "I disagree with the way in which Papa treated him. It was horribly impolite."

"I wonder if anyone else considered it so, besides you and Huntley."

Buttering her toast, Gabriella eyed her aunt. "Nobody said anything." With a shake of her head, she dropped her gaze to her plate before setting her knife aside and picking up the toast. She bit into it with a decided *crunch*. "You know how it is. It only takes one person to deem someone unworthy. The rest will follow like sheep." She knew, from personal experience. "And unfortunately, in this case, Huntley's expensive clothes were not enough to distract them from his unsophisticated speech and mannerisms."

A lengthy pause followed while Gabriella ate the rest of her toast. Eventually, her aunt said, "I know you don't understand or agree with your father's reasoning, but you ought to know that he is a man of strong principles, and that he has never dealt well with change."

"That does not excuse his arrogance." Allowing her finger to trace the delicate edge of her saucer, Gabriella said, "You should have seen him. He was so angry at me for questioning him. And Mama was no better. She still insists that I must have nothing to do with Huntley, or his sisters." The thought of them discovering her disobedience prompted her to reach for her teacup once more. She took a fortifying sip.

Aunt Caroline sighed. "They are both very protective of you, Gabriella. All they want is what's best—especially after your sister's hasty marriage to a man of inferior social standing."

"He is a wealthy businessman, and Victoria loves him! Shouldn't they be happy for her, rather than fretting over the fact that he's not an aristocrat?"

"I'd say it's a bit more complicated than that, Gabriella. Even *I* find her broken engagement to Bellmore hard to accept, and I'm a lot more open-minded than my brother." A smile crept across her lips. "Look at it this way. If your father were to take you to Tattersall to purchase a horse, don't you think he would buy the most expensive champion available?"

"Of course he would," Gabriella murmured, her fingers tapping impatiently on the table.

"Because he wants what is best for you, even if that may differ from what you believe to be best for yourself. You see, it's not just the scandal that needs fixing."

"Whatever do you mean?"

"Well, I think your father feels as though he failed Victoria. He blames himself for what happened, and he's determined to do better by you, Gabriella."

"What if I don't want Papa's version of what's better?" The words were out before she could think.

A gentle frown puckered her aunt's brow. "I never cared much for Fielding myself, but you have always seemed pleased by his attentions. Are you saying that this has changed?"

"I don't know." Biting her lip, Gabriella tried to untangle her emotions so she could figure out what she was feeling, but it was proving difficult. "I don't approve of the way in which Fielding treated Huntley last night. It makes me think that he's not a nice person." But was that enough reason for her to push Fielding away? Perhaps not, but then again, it wasn't just about that, was it? It was also about the way Huntley made her feel—interesting and attractive—unfamiliar sensations that sparked a hope for something more. Something . . .

"You want *love*!"

Jolting, her hand almost knocked over her teacup. "No. Don't be absurd."

"You just went all dreamy-eyed, Gabriella."

"That's ridiculous."

"Really?" Her aunt gave her a dubious stare.

"I have no expectations of marrying for love, Aunt. I never have. But harmony would be nice. And frankly, Fielding and I have nothing to talk about, besides the mundane."

Leaning forward slightly, Aunt Caroline pushed her plate aside so she could rest her elbows on the table. "Love is a wonderful thing, Gabriella. If you think you have a chance at it, then I would advise you to take it."

"I am not in love!" She shook her head, regretting having said anything at all.

"Marriages within the aristocracy are much like business arrangements. Mine certainly was, and as a result, I gave up on love in favor of marrying for duty. I ended up living with a man with whom I hardly spent any time at all. We were partners in a deal our parents had struck, but our hearts were never in it. He loved another, and so did I. The most painful thing of all was watching those whom we cared for end up just as we had—married to the wrong people."

"I'm so sorry," Gabriella whispered. "I never knew." And what a different story from the one her parents had told her last night when they'd adamantly insisted that she would eventually find love with Fielding.

"You had no reason to, until now." Staring firmly at her, Aunt Caroline said, "The point is, marriage cannot be undone, so you must be absolutely certain that you say your vows to the right person."

"What if that person doesn't exist? What if Fielding would be best for me, and I ruin my chance with him on account of some misguided uncertainty?" The fear that she would make a mistake that could not be fixed—the sort of mistake her sister had made—weighed heavily upon her shoulders.

"Perhaps if we go over all of your options, we'll arrive at the right one," Aunt Caroline suggested. "What are your thoughts on Lord Rothgate?"

"I suppose he's pleasant enough, but Fielding is handsomer, I think."

"How about Lord Barkley, then?"

Gabriella frowned. "Too shy for my taste, and not nearly as well liked as Fielding."

Several more bachelors were mentioned, including a couple of well-known scoundrels. The mention of their names made Gabriella laugh. "Papa would have an apoplectic fit if I married either of them. He would never approve, and frankly, neither would I."

"*Hmm . . .*" Aunt Caroline gave her a shrewd look. "Shall we consider Huntley, instead?"

The mention of the duke's name brought an unbidden flash of heat to Gabriella's cheeks. She glanced away, unable to meet her aunt's gaze. "No. Papa would never give us his blessing."

"But what if he did? Would you seriously consider him then?"

"Don't be absurd," Gabriella said, her voice much higher than she'd intended. "I barely know the man. It—it would never work."

Aunt Caroline seemed to consider that for a moment before shrugging slightly and saying, "You're probably right. For such a match to happen, you would have to go against your parents' wishes and the expectations that everyone has for your future." She nodded pensively. "Yes, you would be a duchess, but would you still maintain your social standing? Probably not, considering the *ton's* response to Huntley. And since you're not the rebellious sort, Fielding does seem like the safest choice for you."

Pressing her lips together, Gabriella stared back at her aunt. "Stop trying to influence me."

Aunt Caroline leaned back with a snort. "Forgive me if that is how you see it. My only intention is to give you a fresh perspective so you can determine your own wants—something that must be difficult to do after constantly having to listen to everyone else's." Pushing away from the table, she stood up. "Now, I do believe I shall go for a walk. Will you join me?"

"No, thank you," Gabriella murmured. Her mind was filled with so many conflicting thoughts and emotions, it seemed impossible to think straight. "I think I'm going to see if there are any ladybirds about."

Leaving the dining room a short while later, Gabriella headed out into the garden. The weather was cooler today, prompting her to wrap her arms about herself as she descended the stone steps leading down to a paved path on the right side of the terrace. A small gathering of birds took flight the moment they heard her approach, their cacophonous calls accompanying her as she went.

Reaching the rose beds, Gabriella admired the fresh little buds. Another week or so and they would start to open, permeating the air with their thick aroma and luring bees and butterflies to them. A sigh escaped her. If Fielding proposed as expected, she would probably be planning her wedding once these roses were in full bloom.

If she accepted.

A loud grunt drew her attention. Tilting her head, she stilled to listen, her breath coming sharply when she heard it again. A succession of other exclamations had her staring at the wall that separated her garden from the courtyard that sat between her house and Huntley's. There was a large wooden door in it that was meant to provide the gardener with easy access—a door she'd never really considered before since she'd had no use for it. It loomed before her now, drawing her closer with each resounding utterance rising from the opposite side.

Reaching the door, Gabriella studied the coarse grain and the iron handle for what felt like an eternity. She knew where it led—to the stable courtyard that stood between her house and Huntley's. Both had access to it. Another few grunts. *Ugh. Hmpf. Augh.* Gabriella wrinkled her nose at the door. She should not venture through it. She ought to move on—continue with her ladybird search and ignore whatever was going on in the courtyard. That would be the proper thing to do. But as yet another grunt was hurled up into the air, she couldn't help but push down the handle and ease the door open, just enough to appease her curiosity.

Instead, she came face-to-face with a brick wall that rose before her a few feet away—the back of the stables. So she opened the door a bit more and leaned slightly forward. She still saw nothing. Whoever was making that sound of exertion was hidden from view. It came again, and then once more. Frowning, Gabriella glanced back over her shoulder to ensure that no one had seen her. She then stepped all the way through the doorway and into a narrow alleyway that ran between the garden wall and the Warwick stables. Closing the door behind her, she inhaled sharply. A knot had formed in her belly, and her heart was leaping so rapidly against her chest that it ached.

Swallowing, she started forward with hesitant steps in the direction of the courtyard—a short distance of less than ten yards that seemed terribly far in the nervous state she was currently in. Another grunt hit her ears, this one louder than the previous ones.

Oomph! Her pace quickened, and she finally reached the end of the stables.

Easing her head forward, she peered around the sharp corner, and almost expired from shock.

There, hunched over in the middle of the courtyard was Huntley, his legs firmly planted in a wide stance and his knees slightly bent for ease of movement. Arms raised with fisted hands, he bobbed slightly on the balls of his feet. Heat washed over Gabriella, flushing her skin as she took in the scene, her mouth going dry at the stark realization that he wasn't wearing any clothes, besides a pair of scandalously tight breeches.

She'd never seen a man's bare chest before, and could not help but stare at the rippling muscles that were drawn tight, like the grooves of a washboard, across his abdomen. Everything about him screamed masculine strength, from the bunching and flexing of his toned biceps to the powerful punches he threw at the canvas bag that was strung up before him.

Fleetingly, Gabriella wondered if Fielding might look like that as well beneath his starched shirts and crisp jackets. *No*, she decided, dismissing the thought. *Nobody else could possibly look like this*—as though he were capable of felling a dozen men with his bare hands. And the way he moved . . . his agility was nothing short of impressive.

With her blood simmering in her veins, Gabriella flattened her hand against the stable wall, steadying herself. She ought to look away and return to the safety of her garden before her weakened knees gave way beneath her. Yet she remained transfixed, her body refusing to listen to her brain—as though the two had become disconnected from the moment she'd laid eyes on him.

Another punch split the sack, and flour poured out onto the ground in a fine, powdery stream. Huntley stepped back and straightened himself. Hands on hips, he watched as the flour spilled through the tear in the canvas, his back heaving slightly with his heavy intakes of breath. Fielding did *not* look like this, Gabriella decided as her gaze slid over Huntley's sharply defined contours. In fact, she very much doubted that anyone else of her acquaintance did, considering how much effort it probably took to develop such a mouthwatering physique.

Feeling the tips of her fingers tingle with a sudden desire to touch him, she stepped back hastily with the intention of fleeing at once. But then he turned, alerted no doubt by the scrape of her feet against the gravel. His eyes met hers, capturing her with intense awareness and freezing her in place. She'd intruded, spied on him, and she could not for the life of her get the necessary apology past her lips. Not when he was now striding toward her with swift precision, his sweat-dampened hair a chaotic mess that clung to his forehead and temples. Gabriella's throat tightened. Dear God, she could see his nipples and his naval—a dusting of fine, dark hair disappearing beneath the waistband of his breeches . . .

With flaming cheeks, she averted her gaze, fixing it on a spot somewhere to the right of his shoulder. And then he was before her, so close she could smell him—the pungent scent of his labor mingling with underlying hints of musk and sandalwood. It ought to make her stomach roil. Instead, it made her pulse beat faster.

"Lady Gabriella," he said, his voice a gruff rumble that stirred her senses even more.

"F—forgive me," she managed, in spite of her protesting tongue and a mind that felt far too muddled for any coherent thought. "I—"

"Were ye watchin' me?" Gone was the perfect diction with which he'd spoken last night.

The unexpected question brought her eyes to his with surprising swiftness. Her chest squeezed as she faced the dark gleam of his gaze. There was curiosity there, but there was also something more—something hot and tempting, and very, very dangerous. "I heard a sound and came to investigate," she told him honestly. "It was not my intention to pry."

"So yes, ye were watchin' me?" he asked again with a mischievous lilt. Annoyed by his insistence to increase her discomfort, she flattened her lips and tried to glare at him. "It was difficult not to when you were right there, for the entire world to see."

"*Hmm* . . ." He nodded. "Even so, ye probably should have turned away. Or at least made yer—*your* presence known."

He was right, of course. "Sorry." And then, because she felt as though she ought to explain herself, she said, "I was surprised by what I saw and found it difficult to look away. I've never seen anyone box before." She took a step back, adding distance, and then repeated, "I'm sorry."

"Well, I wouldn't exactly call this boxing." His tone changed and he was speaking properly once more, with greater effort. "I was just doing some training—trying to keep fit."

Shifting restlessly beneath his gaze, she fought the many responses that formed in answer to *that* comment, and said, "Most gentlemen would ride or duel with swords, and if they were to box, as I know many of them do at Gentleman Jackson's, they would do so properly attired."

He responded with a mischievous chuckle—a contradiction to his otherwise serious façade—which produced a pair of charming dimples, while his eyes maintained their wicked appeal. The combined effect was so potent that Gabriella felt herself caught in a net of desire so intense it became quite painful to breathe. He pierced her with his gaze. "As your father mentioned last night, I am *not* a gentleman."

The harsh rebuke made her wince. "He did not say that."

"He might as well have," Huntley replied. His eyes hardened, burying the welcoming look he'd given her earlier. "I was judged and deemed unworthy of my title."

"I tried to warn you." She could no longer look at him directly. The shame of her father's harsh dismissal of Huntley the previous evening, and Fielding's blatant dislike of him, was too acute. "The aristocracy does not favor outsiders. Least of all when they come from questionable backgrounds."

Huntley's eyes darkened. "My background is far from questionable. I am the rightful heir!"

"Perhaps," she conceded. "But you are too different— too common." *Oh dear. That was not the right word.*

He responded with a gruff snort. "I should have known that my expensive clothes would make no difference. I should have listened to you and to Richardson, Humphreys and Pierson, but I was too bloody stubborn—too bloody intent on putting Fielding and his ilk in their damned places!" Gabriella's eyes widened, but he did not apologize for the expletive. Instead, he just tempered his voice, before saying, "Thank you for speaking up on my behalf." He expelled a breath. "Your kindness did not go unnoticed."

"Think nothing of it," she said with a lightness she did not feel. "It seemed like the right thing to do."

He nodded once before saying, "I hope it doesn't complicate things for you." His features softened around the edges, and then something awful resembling pity seeped into his eyes.

It was more than she could bear. And yet, hearing the sincerity with which he spoke—as though he actually cared—she could not seem to fault him for it. So rather than the clipped retort that initially formed on the tip of her tongue, she spoke from her heart, saying simply, "So do I." Deciding that it was time to leave, Gabriella straightened her spine and prepared to retreat. "I," she began weakly.

It was at the same moment as he said, "My—"

Befuddled by their overlap, Gabriella allowed a helpless smile, and then tried again. "I should probably go."

"Of course."

She turned away, ignoring her heart's wish to stay.

"You look very pretty today," he called after her. His voice was shallow, the compliment so unexpected that she couldn't help but look back at him. His eyes caught hers and the edge of his mouth lifted. "Beautiful."

"I . . ." She shook her head. "You don't have to say that." She couldn't bear the thought of him making her believe that she was anything but plain.

He shrugged one shoulder. "I know. But I thought it was time for me to tell you that I quite like looking at you."

I quite like looking at you. The words vibrated through her.

She stepped back further, suddenly more afraid than she'd ever been before in her life. Because here stood a man—the most incredible specimen she'd ever seen—and he was telling her that he thought she was beautiful. That he quite liked looking at her. And she was tempted—tempted to let herself wish for something she'd never allowed herself to wish for before— tempted to bask in the joy of his appreciation—tempted to turn her back on her responsibilities just as her sister had done.

Dear God. What was she thinking? It was just a compliment, for heaven's sake. Nothing more. "Th . . . thank you," she said, then added, "My eyes are too big and my mouth too wide." Other girls had made her aware of her flaws years ago.

He nodded. "A strange combination and yet so lovely."

Was he mocking her?

"Are you mocking me?" She had to know.

"No." The word rumbled out from somewhere deep inside his chest. "I was just making fun."

"Of my appearance?" Of course he was. So many others had done. Why would he be any different?

"Oh no, love, not of something so perfect. Just . . . your nerves seem a bit frayed, so I thought to ease the tension. I'm sorry if I offended you." He puffed out a breath. Scratched the back of his head. Eyed her carefully.

She stood completely still now, unable to move or to gather her thoughts. What had he said? That her looks were perfect?

Something like that.

It seemed impossible. Incomprehensible. It made her feel like laughing.

Instead she simply smiled.

He kept on looking at her until he was smiling as well—grinning almost. "Do you know how tempted I am to kiss you right now?"

The question was so astonishing it landed like a punch to Gabriella's senses. She almost stumbled from the shock of it. "You . . . you . . ." Oh God, she didn't know what to say, except, *Yes please. I think I'd like that.* And then what? Break her engagement to Fielding just as her sister had broken hers to Bellmore? Add fuel to the scandal her sister had started? Disappoint her parents? Marry Huntley? Heavens, he said he wanted to kiss her, not marry her. What was she thinking?

"I . . . I . . ." She retreated a few steps. "I have to go."

He didn't comment, simply watched her with curious eyes as she moved closer to the door leading back to her garden.

Reaching it, she gave Huntley one last glance and then flung it open. Hurrying back to her house as fast as her feet could carry her, she dared not contemplate the feelings the Duke of Huntley had stirred in her as he'd stood before her just now, bare chested, and with thoughts of kissing. To do so would be dangerous territory indeed.

Chapter 13

Returning upstairs to his bedroom with a brisk stride that made his boots click sharply against the marble floor, Raphe waited for the footmen and maids preparing his bath to leave before shedding his breeches and smalls. *Christ, what a morning.* And it wasn't over yet. Lady Gabriella would be back soon to tutor his sisters.

He thought of her as he sank into the warm water. Yes, she was dazzling and yes, she was tempting, her luscious lips inviting him to imagine all sorts of naughtiness. But it was more than that. It wasn't all physical. His attraction was also based on her stalwart determination to defy her parents in the name of something that mattered more to her than their censure—namely doing what she believed to be right. Her kindness toward his sisters and her willingness to face all kinds of disaster on their behalf exceeded anything he'd ever experienced or witnessed before. Selfless. That's what she was. And then there were her quirks—her peculiar fondness for insects. He couldn't help but smile. Most women would prefer a puppy or a kitten. Not Lady Gabriella though.

Lathering himself with soap, he pondered her reaction to his complimenting her looks. She'd doubted his sincerity. That much had been obvious. The question was why? Why didn't Lady Gabriella realize how gorgeous she was? Her face was delicately shaped but with strong features, her body slim and lithe, perfectly proportioned—her breasts, he'd noticed, not too big or too small. And her bottom . . . for heaven's sake, he could not shake the vision he'd had of it. Could not stop himself from wondering what it might look like without several layers of fabric draped over it.

Indecent.

That was what he was. He set the soap aside and lowered himself further into the water, washing away the suds. What if some man were having such lewd contemplations about one of his sisters?

"What then, Raphe?" he asked himself.

The only response was the sloshing sound of water as he stood up. He knew the answer of course. He'd bloody murder the blighter, that's what.

And yet . . . Christ, the way she made him feel. It was as if the air came alive around him whenever she was near. And that hint of pain in her eyes when she'd explained that she had no friends. It had made him want to take her in his arms, soothe away the hurt and reassure her of her worth. Instead he'd let her go, watching as she'd beat a hasty retreat, like a mistreated kitten who no longer trusted the world around it. He hated thinking of her like that, hated whoever had made her feel that way.

Drying off, he considered his options. There were two: leave her the hell alone, or pursue her until he got what he wanted. If he picked the first, he could go out and sate his desires elsewhere. It wouldn't be the same, granted, but it would rid him of the itch that had been building since . . . well, since the first time he'd laid his eyes on her.

Or, he could try and convince her that he was better than Fielding. He'd certainly give her greater pleasure. Of that much he was certain. Smiling wickedly in response to that thought, he started to dress, making use of the clothes that Humphreys had laid out on the bed. But bedding a lady like her would require marriage.

Could he do that? Marry a woman he barely knew just to satisfy a craving? It seemed like an awfully high price to pay. He flung his shirt over his head and stuck his arms through the sleeves. Forget her then? He could not. The very idea of it seemed more impossible somehow than pledging his life to an institution he didn't believe in. There was also his responsibility toward his title to consider. He'd dismissed the notion at first on account of his aversion to marriage, but perhaps he ought to re-think this position if it involved Lady Gabriella. He put on his smalls, acutely aware of the frustrated fool he'd turned into because of a woman. Not just any woman though but the most intriguing one he'd ever met.

Making his decision, he finished dressing and went downstairs. "I need you to find an excuse to leave me alone with her," he told his sisters without preamble as soon as he'd located them in the music room. Amelia was banging away at the piano while Juliette danced along to the arrhythmic tune.

Both went completely still. The music ceased. They stared at him as though his head had fallen off on his way in. Perhaps it had. He certainly wasn't using it.

"What?" Amelia asked.

"Lady Gabriella," he clarified. "I want to be able to talk to her without the two of you there."

"She's a lady, Raphe," Juliette said as though he might not have realized that much.

Amelia narrowed her gaze on him and stood up. She crossed her arms, standing as though she were blocking his path. "Don't think we haven't seen the way you look at her—the way you're always trying to be close to her. It unnerves her, you know."

"I just . . ." He looked at each of them in turn. Was he really having this discussion with his sisters? "I like her, all right?"

"No," Amelia told him sharply. "It's not all right." She shook her head. "We know you, Raphe, you're a good man, a kind man, but you've never been with a woman for anything other than a bit of sport."

"Amelia . . ." He put a hard edge into his tone, hoping to stop her right there.

She didn't listen. "Lady Gabriella is not a plaything, Raphe. She's a gently bred woman—a lamb to your wolf. I won't allow you to chase after her just because it's been a while since you—"

"Stop!" He gave Juliette a hasty glance. Bringing the subject to his sisters' attention had been a colossal mistake. *Jesus.* He was practically blushing because of it.

Except Amelia had set her mind on having her say. "You'll leave Lady Gabriella alone. She deserves better."

Raphe gaped at her. He tried not to feel offended by that. It was no use. "What if I marry her?"

That seemed to silence Amelia. She opened her mouth as if to say something, except nothing came out. She was mute. Dumbfounded even, judging by her expression.

"I'd be in favor of that idea," Juliette said after a bit of hesitation. "She'd be a wonderful sister-in-law."

Amelia's mouth opened and closed a few more times before she finally managed to ask the one thing Raphe had wanted to ignore. "Isn't she supposed to marry Fielding?"

"She's not engaged to him yet," Raphe told her, "which means that there's still a chance I might win her."

"Do you care for her then?" Juliette asked.

"I . . ." He wasn't quite sure how to answer. Eventually he said, "Having seen her with Fielding, I think it's fair to say that *he* certainly doesn't." Whatever that meant to any of them.

"Well," Amelia said. She uncrossed her arms.

"Lady Gabriella has arrived," Pierson said, materializing in the doorway. "Shall I show her in?"

Raphe glanced at his sisters, raising his eyebrows in question. Amelia looked to Juliette, a silent exchange appearing to pass between the two. Eventually they nodded. "But if you hurt her in any way," Amelia said as soon as Pierson was gone, "I'll make you regret your decision."

He knew she meant it as he watched her go, hurrying away to another part of the house with Juliette trailing behind. It was touching, how fond his sisters had become of Lady Gabriella—how much they liked her. Juliette was right. She'd make a fine addition to their family, and in the meantime, he'd enjoy getting better acquainted with her.

Following Pierson toward the music room, Gabriella did her best to rid her mind of her earlier encounter with Huntley. *Naked*. The word had been taunting her for the past two hours. Not completely, but enough to make her wonder about the rest. She hadn't wanted to contemplate it, but it was as if she'd lost control, unable to halt the assault of unbidden images—images that made her all fidgety and stupid. *So inappropriate*, she chastised herself as she and Pierson arrived at their destination. *So unladylike*.

Pierson announced her arrival and stepped aside, granting her entry. Her senses sprang to awareness, skin pricking against the fine muslin of her gown while her chest suddenly seemed constricted against her stays. For there he was, casually leaning against the piano, his eyes following her into the room, watching as she surveyed the space. "Where are your sisters?" she asked while looking anywhere but at him.

"They got delayed. Thought I'd keep you company until they arrive." Straightening, he came toward her, closing the distance until she fairly trembled with alertness. He touched her elbow, and she practically leapt away, only staying in place out of sheer force of will. "Please . . ." He guided her forward toward the sofa. "Have a seat."

She did, relieved that she no longer had to rely on her legs. "Will they be long?" She glanced at the door once more.

"I can't say," he replied as he lowered himself into an adjacent armchair. Tea had already been brought in, but she didn't trust herself to pour without spilling. Thankfully, she didn't have to since he did it for her—an unusual task for a man but one that he didn't seem to mind, as though he was quite accustomed to making himself useful. "It's hot," he said as he set her cup before her. "Mind you don't burn yerself."

"Thank you." She took a careful sip. *Aaah*. Much better.

Leaning back against his chair, he crossed his legs,

considered her for a second and finally said, "I'd like to apologize to you."

This, she had not expected. With no effort to hide her surprise, she raised her gaze toward his. "Whatever for?"

"I think you know." When she didn't respond, he said, "It was terribly wrong of me to engage you in conversation earlier, given the state I was in."

A feverish flush flared from Gabriella's chest all the way up to the edge of her hairline. She hadn't wanted to address the issue—had hoped it would simply be forgotten or ignored by both of them. Since that was no longer possible, she did her best to school her features before saying, "While you could certainly have done with more clothes, I intruded upon *you*, Your Grace, not the other way around." She averted her gaze, training it on a vase. "I should have left the moment I spotted you."

"Why didn't you?" There was an almost abrasive touch to his voice. It suited his rugged style, accentuating a virile masculinity that was rare to Mayfair, where the leisurely lives of gentlemen resulted in slighter frames. Compared to Fielding, for instance, whose body was slim and elegant, Huntley looked like a hardened fighter. And, though she was loath to admit it, there was something elementally attractive about that.

"I was surprised and intrigued. Do you box like that often?" Her attempt to steer the conversation toward a more concrete subject was deliberate. It was safer that way, and would hopefully make her blush less.

"The exercise is satisfying," he told her evenly. "I enjoy it."

Not a direct answer, but certainly one that explained the physical shape he was in. "I'm sorry I watched," she said with honesty.

"I'll forgive you if you forgive me," he told her wryly.

She didn't dare tell him that there was nothing to forgive, so she gave him a smile. "You have a deal."

"Very good." He smiled as well for a moment, but then turned pensive. "We grew up in the slums, you know."

The suddenness with which he said it completely threw her. If she had to guess, she'd say it took a full minute for her brain to absorb the comment before she was ready to respond. "How can that be?"

His jaw tightened, just enough to inform her that he didn't enjoy sharing this part of himself. And yet he was sitting there offering the information to her as though her knowing about it mattered. "My father took his own life when I was eight."

Oh God! She hadn't known. "I'm—"

"Don't say it. Please. It's in the past and as awful as it was, my sisters and I managed to go on without him."

"What about your mother?"

Something dark crossed his face. He frowned, his eyes growing distant. "She left us shortly before—ran away with another man as far as I recall."

"But . . ." She shook her head, unable to fathom the struggle of losing both parents at such a young age.

"There was a debt and no one to pay it—no one to take us in." He drummed his fingers against the armrest, then halted the action. "I was worried that we'd be separated, sent into care with different families, so I ran."

"With your sisters . . . they can't have been more than five and seven," she said, doing the math.

He gave a quick nod. "It wasn't easy." A humorless

laugh escaped him. "In fact, I'd say it's a miracle we survived."

It seemed an impossible struggle for such young children to go through, a hardship that no one should have to endure. She met his gaze, his dark eyes gleaming like rich drops of honey. "Why are you telling me this?"

"Because it's important," he told her simply. "And because friends don't lie to each other."

Her mouth went dry. "Friends?" Such a foreign concept.

He nodded. "If you like."

She did. Very much so. But then his words sank in and she realized that she would have to be just as candid. She bit her lip, fidgeted with the skirt of her gown. Honesty in exchange for friendship. "I didn't lie about not having any. Friends, that is."

"I know," he told her gently. "I'm sorry I didn't believe you."

"But you do now?" She realized then that his trusting her mattered.

"Yes."

She expelled a sigh of relief, then thought to ask, "Why?"

"Because kind people aren't generally deceitful. And because of your eyes. The pain in them when I accused you . . ." He shook his head. "I'm sorry."

His apology made her feel lighter somehow, more relaxed and at ease. Perhaps because it showed a more sensitive side to him, a side that she was infinitely more comfortable with than the roguish charmer who made her feel as though there were worms wriggling about inside her belly. "I appreciate that." They stared at each other a moment.

Drawing a breath, she willed herself to take courage, to be as honest with him as he'd been with her.

For the sake of friendship. Nothing more. "When I was six," she began, "I saw a group of boys crowded together in the park. They were laughing at something that I couldn't see. So I approached without thinking, abandoning my governess with an impulsive need to know what they were about." She hesitated, realizing all of a sudden how silly her story would probably sound. He'd been a boy too after all. "Pushing between them, I looked down, trying to find the object of their amusement. And then I did." She took a staggering breath, hating the transparency of her emotions. "They'd trapped a bumblebee, pulled off its wings, and were poking it with twigs so it spun on its back, round and round while they stood there laughing at how ridiculous it looked."

"It upset you to see an innocent creature tortured." He watched her closely. Too closely.

Gabriella shifted, unable to remain still beneath such scrutiny. "I don't believe I've ever been so cross in my life," she said. "I snapped. Like a twig giving way to great strain I just . . ." What was it her mother had called it when she'd heard of the incident. *Oh yes.* She winced. "I'm afraid I went mad for a second, shouting at them to stop and then hitting them when they refused." She looked away, embarrassed by how she'd behaved. "Word got around of course. It always does. My parents had to send apologies to the other families."

"What about the bumblebee?"

Gabriella blinked. Nobody had ever asked, not even her sister. He was the first. "It survived. For a bit. I brought it home in my hand."

A chuckle rose from his throat, released into the room with a smile. He shook his head. "Of course you did."

Of course. That was all he said, and Gabriella felt her heart melt in response to his tone of understanding. "That bumblebee led to my fascination with insects. It gave me something to do when all the other children ignored me. When my hobby eventually became known . . . well . . . whatever chance I'd ever had of becoming acceptable company dwindled. I was labeled strange—an eccentric girl who ought to be avoided. After that, there was nothing about me that they did not mock."

"Including your appearance."

She nodded. "Yes."

He was quiet a moment. "It hurt," he eventually said, echoing her memories.

"Yes." She tried to smile and almost succeeded. "So I faded away between the shadows, avoiding all attention while Victoria thrived in it. She was a perfect lady; well spoken, accomplished, beautiful and clever. My parents chose not to worry about my future. They had her, after all, a daughter who was going to marry a marquess."

"Except she didn't."

"No. She did not."

"Why?"

A question that Gabriella had asked herself countless times since. "I like to think she fell in love." When he stayed silent, she stalwartly added. "It happens."

"Yes. I suppose it does." Rising, he moved toward the door. "If you'll excuse me, I think I'll go and see what's keeping my sisters."

And then he was gone, out the door with a swiftness that unsettled Gabriella more than his presence had done. In fact, it hadn't bothered her much at all this time.

Speaking with him of more personal matters had

been rather nice, she decided. A pity he didn't return with his sisters, but he'd apparently gone off to practice his dancing. The instructor, according to Amelia, was an old Italian fellow who didn't believe in allowing partners until they'd mastered the steps, which meant that Huntley and his sisters took separate lessons, since these were not the same for men and women.

Do ye like to dance?

The question he'd asked when she'd first come to offer his sisters assistance drifted through her mind like a tendril of smoke, curling, twisting, reminding her of his daring. He'd been so different ten minutes earlier, siting right there in the chair that Juliette now occupied. And he'd listened to her. Attentively. As though he'd genuinely cared about her past and the scars it had dealt her.

Friends. That's what they'd become—in the strangest and most unusual of ways. And as she walked home later with Anna by her side, she couldn't help but wonder if she would ever have the courage to wish for more than that.

Chapter 14

When Gabriella awoke the following morning, she lay staring up at the ceiling for a long while after, trying to come to terms with yet another dream. It had been even more provocative than the last. Her pulse still raced in time with her sharp inhalations, the sheet tangled chaotically around her legs. *Dear God!* She'd dreamt of Huntley's naked body pressed against hers—of her fingers creeping gently across his broad shoulders.

Closing her eyes, she remembered more, her face flushing with the memory of his hands moving over *her*, caressing her in the most inappropriate ways possible. With a groan, she pushed the sheet aside and sat up, her skin still quivering lightly with the recollection of what had happened. Except it *hadn't* happened.

It wasn't real, she told herself later while her maid placed pearl-tipped pins in her hair. But it had *felt* real, and because of that, Gabriella knew that today would be more difficult to get through than any of the ones that had come before.

By the time she descended for breakfast, her stomach had tied itself into knots over the thought of having to face Huntley again. Heaven help her, she would not be able to look at him without remembering what he'd looked like yesterday without his shirt, and how her brain had chosen to put that image of him to use in the most outrageous way possible.

God help her.

"Would you like me to act as chaperone when Fielding arrives?" her mother asked from the opposite side of the table.

Gabriella jolted. "What?"

"He'll be here within the hour." Her mother pushed a note toward her. "Haven't you been listening to what I've been saying?"

Gathering her thoughts, Gabriella read the note before telling her mother, "Anna can easily act as chaperone if you have other things to attend to."

"Well. If you're sure . . ."

Gabriella gave her mother a definite nod. "Enjoy your day." She waited for her to leave before scribbling a note to Amelia and Juliette, informing them of her unexpected delay and asked Anna to deliver it. Then, walking through to the drawing room, she proceeded to read her favorite book—a well-used copy of Kirby and Spence's *Introduction to entomology or elements of the natural history of insects.*

When Fielding arrived half an hour later, he brought roses. "You look as lovely as always, my lady—my apologies for not calling on you sooner." He took a step in her direction. "I should have called on you yesterday after my mother's dinner party, but I feared I might have upset you. I was not as hospitable to Huntley as I ought to have been, and with your gentle nature in mind, I'm sure you must have thought me a scoundrel."

Gesturing to the sofa, Gabriella asked, "Shall we

sit?" He inclined his head and waited for her to lower herself before claiming the spot beside her. "The truth is that I thought both you and my father quite rude. He and I quarreled all the way home in the carriage."

"I am sorry to hear it," Fielding said. Reaching out, he took her hand, enfolding it in his. "While I cannot speak on his behalf, I should like to explain the reasons for my less than cordial behavior that night." He took a deep breath. Expelled it. "The fact of the matter is that I was jealous."

Gabriella's lower jaw almost hit the carpet. "Jealous? Of Huntley?"

With an awkward shrug, Fielding slid his gaze to a point beyond Gabriella's left shoulder. "He's very handsome, fit and without a doubt wealthy. His title far outranks my own. So when I found him looking at you as though . . ." The thought faded. He shook his head.

"As though what?" Gabriella prompted.

"It was wrong of me to behave as I did," he said, not answering her question. "Can you forgive me?"

She pressed her lips together. He'd owned his mistake, asked for her forgiveness in a very polite way. She gave a little nod. "Of course."

He expelled a breath. "Good." He produced a smile. "I spoke to your father at the club last night about drawing up a marriage settlement and what that would entail."

"Oh?" Gabriella felt her stomach shift. With everything that had been going on, she'd completely forgotten to tell her father of the stipulations that she wished to make. She would have to remember to do so soon. Before Fielding proposed.

"It was a very productive discussion, so you needn't

worry. Everything is going to turn out precisely as expected."

Nodding numbly, Gabriella resigned herself to the conversation that followed—a mundane discussion about bridles and saddles and how well his looked when compared to so many others. She, on the other hand, was given no chance to speak of her own interests. Whenever she tried bringing it up, he would simply go on with his own line of thought as if she'd said nothing at all. It was both annoying and exhausting—her patience stretched to the limit by the time he departed again.

With a hasty glance at the clock, Gabriella turned to Anna. "We don't have much time today. Mama is due back in an hour."

"Then we'd best be on our way," the maid suggested. She was quickly putting away the mending that she'd been doing in a corner during Fielding's visit.

"Might I be honest with you, my lady?" she asked as they walked toward the back of the house and exited onto the terrace.

"Of course." Not wanting to waste another minute, Gabriella quickened her step.

"It would pain me to see you marry the earl. He'll crush your spirit."

"Thank you, Anna, but I'm afraid that I don't have much choice."

"Are you sure about that?"

"There's nobody else."

Her maid did not respond to that, for which Gabriella was grateful. Especially since she knew she was lying, not only to Anna, but to herself. Because the truth . . . the real truth, was a terrifying thing to face, her options impossibly difficult to consider. And

Huntley . . . he was a friend, nothing more. Their acquaintance had been brief. To even consider marrying him, with all the consequences that might follow, would be mad.

More mad than marrying a man whom you don't even like?

Already, in little more than one week, she felt a greater connection to Huntley than she'd ever done to Fielding. Huntley had actually listened to her, shown an interest, *and* been intrigued by her curious passion for insects.

She stepped through the parting in the hedge, distracted by all the worries that crowded her mind. Could she break her connection to Fielding? Did she dare to? She had no other plan than him. And her parents would never allow her to marry Huntley. Provided he asked, of course, which was rather unlikely since he had so much else to think about at the moment than acquiring a wife.

A movement at the edge of her vision halted her thoughts on the matter. She instinctively turned toward it, almost stumbling the moment she spotted him.

"Goodness," Anna murmured.

Indeed, Gabriella thought, for there was the duke sprawled out on the grass, eyes closed, and with a very satisfied smile upon his lips. The pose was one of complete relaxation, no hint of tension about him at all.

"Wait here," Gabriella whispered to Anna as she took a step closer, studying him as she approached—appreciating the opportunity to see him at rest. But out here? On the grass? It was most unusual. Her gaze dropped to one of his hands, palm down in the grass, the fingers gently moving as though caressing the ground. The movement produced a flexing of tendons, a tightening of skin across reddened knuckles. He'd been boxing again.

And just like that, the image of him standing before her, bare chested while sweat ran down the sides of his face, flew to the front of her mind. She gasped. He opened his eyes, staring straight up into her face. His mouth tilted, and then he smiled. "You're watching me again."

Heat rushed to her face, burning her until she feared she might combust. "I . . ." What on earth had she been thinking not to make her presence known? "I didn't want to disturb you." A silly excuse. She'd wanted to get a good look at him—a *private* look at him.

He held her gaze just long enough to make her cringe with embarrassment. "You should rise," she suddenly blurted. "A gentleman doesn't remain seated or . . ." she waved her hand "lying down, when a lady arrives. He stands up and greets her properly."

He seemed to consider this and for a second she thought he would follow her advice, but then he said, "How about you come down here instead?"

"What?" She gaped at him.

He patted the grass by his side, then raised a challenging eyebrow. "I think you'll like it."

She didn't doubt it for a second. But she was a grown woman, for heaven's sake. Such things weren't done, no matter how prone one might be to spontaneity. "Your sisters will be expecting me. I ought to go and find them."

"They're having embroidery lessons," Huntley said, rising onto his elbows. "Richardson arranged for Mrs. Bryant, our housekeeper, to teach them."

"Oh. Well." Disappointment suddenly filled her. "I'll come back tomorrow then."

He tilted his head. She didn't move, torn between doing the right thing and just letting go. He patted the grass once more and she glanced back at Anna, who seemed to be giving a potted plant a great deal of attention.

"If you join me, I'll show you the beetle I found."

She allowed herself to give in. "Very well, but just for a moment."

He offered his hand to help her down and she accepted, the contact sending ripples of energy up her arm and into her chest. She caught her breath and lowered herself to the ground while little shivers raced down her spine at the gentle squeeze of his hand. He did not let go right away as he ought, holding her for a second longer than what was deemed proper. "You're so soft." The whisper breezed against her cheek, accompanied by the scraping of a callused thumb against her palm.

"I . . ." The word was more of a croak than anything else. He let her hand go, allowing her to win back some of her composure. She tried again. "I shouldn't be here like this. With you, I mean. It's not the least bit appropriate."

"Your maid is here too," he pointed out. "You're at no risk of being ravished."

The smile that followed was filled with so much cheekiness that it was impossible for Gabriella to refrain from laughing. "I should hope not."

"Unless of course you'd like to be." He waggled his eyebrows.

"Your Grace." He was making her uncomfortable again, the worst part being that she actually felt like he'd already done what he now suggested, her dream a memory based on her own imaginings, her desires . . . She licked her lips, then realized he'd followed the movement, his pupils dilating slightly as he watched. "A gentleman doesn't say such things," she told him sternly. If only they could find a way to revert to the conversational friendship they'd shared the day before.

He drew back a bit, his expression changing to something more debonair. "You're bound by too many rules. If you're not careful, you'll just be another Society lady one day, no different from the next."

"But . . ." She stopped herself. Perhaps he had a point? She considered the ways in which her life had changed since Victoria's marriage. Her parents had given her more attention than ever before, and she'd faced daily reminders of how to speak and behave. "You must learn to restrain yourself," her mother had said as she'd brought up the bumblebee incident from Gabriella's childhood. "You must make them forget that you ever behaved so poorly." Lessons in etiquette had followed. She'd been schooled in how to walk and how to sit, how to stand and even how to listen. And although she hadn't thought it possible to begin with, she'd changed. Rules had become a significant part of her life—a structure that would lead her to her destination without incident. But where was the joy in that? She'd allowed herself to be molded into a creature she no longer recognized—a woman who'd forgotten how to live.

What a momentous bit of insight that was.

She glanced at Huntley and found him watching her with interest. *You want more than this.* Perhaps running from it was the wrong idea. Perhaps facing it would be better. "I don't know what to do." She hadn't meant to speak the words aloud, and yet she had.

"What would you like to do?" He tilted his head. Curious.

She pressed her hand into the grass, loving the feel

of each straw between her fingers. "This," she said, and then she lay back, just as he had been doing earlier, and stared up at the sky. She could see it through between the branches and leaves of a nearby oak, a light blue color with shifting tones and worn-out clouds. *Aaah*. She sighed with contentment.

"There you are," he quietly murmured. "I've finally found you."

She knew what he meant. It was as though she'd rediscovered herself—the girl who'd been lost for a year had returned. But she wasn't quite ready to talk or think of what that might mean for her future. So she caught hold of a different thought instead and said, "You impress me, Huntley."

She sensed him shift a bit as he lay down beside her. "In what sense?"

She turned her head, her eyes meeting his across a small stretch of grass dotted by clover. It wasn't precisely scandalous, but it certainly wasn't proper either. Gabriella found that she no longer cared, too caught up in the intimacy—the connection she'd formed to another person. It filled a need—a craving—that had likely been there for most of her life. "The way you managed to make a life for yourself after losing your parents, the way you saved your sisters and—"

"Only Amelia and Juliette," he said. A sheen of moisture appeared at the edge of his eyes. "I lost one. Couldn't save her."

Gabriella's chest contracted, squeezing until her heart ached with pain. Without thinking, she reached for his hand. "I'm sorry. So terribly sorry."

"It happened suddenly. I wasn't prepared and I couldn't . . ." He swallowed hard, but he didn't look away, holding her gaze with unyielding resolve. "She was only seven when it happened. I was twelve."

"A child with far too great a burden to carry." She squeezed his hand in sympathy, then moved to pull away.

He held her fast. "You should reconnect with your sister."

"I have written to her more than once, but she never responds."

"Were you close?"

Gabriella tried to shrug, which was difficult, given her position. "I always thought so. But then she did what she did without a word of warning. She only left me a short note."

"I'm not surprised."

Gabriella stared at him. "Why?"

"You were her little sister and your opinion of her mattered. That's why she didn't say good-bye to you in person. She just couldn't face you."

She considered that for a second and finally nodded. "Very well, I'll accept that. But she could have mentioned Connolly to me before she chose to elope with him. She should have said that she planned to break her engagement with Bellmore."

He watched her a moment, his expression signifying deep contemplation. "Let's pretend the roles were reversed."

"I don't see—"

"Let's pretend that you got engaged first. To Fielding. A fine match to everyone's liking. But then one day, you meet someone else. A dockyard worker who reminds you what it's like to chase your own dream, fulfill your own wants and desires."

She stared at him, enthralled by the image he'd painted, and by him. "You were a dockyard worker?"

"I had to make my way somehow." The air grew still between them, and then he suddenly grinned, sweeping aside the tension that had materialized out of nowhere. "Anyway, imagine that, and then imagine telling your sister that you've changed your mind about the earl and that you'd rather have the dockyard worker instead."

Gabriella's heart pounded against her chest. "I wouldn't have trusted her to understand the way I feel." She barely got the words out, their breathiness like a puff of air pushed toward him.

"Gabriella." He spoke her name softly, abandoning the honorific for the very first time. "What do you want?"

A question—the most important question she'd ever been asked. Not Fielding. Never Fielding. But then what? She met his gaze. *You. Possibly you.* She couldn't say that, so she sat up instead and looked for Anna. "I should probably go. Mama will be home soon." She rose to her feet and he got up as well, brushing off leaves and bits of grass. "Please tell your sisters that I will return tomorrow. Ten o' clock."

He crossed to the terrace step and retrieved a small wooden box that he promptly handed to her. "This is for you."

Unable to hide her surprise, she accepted the offering and peaked inside, instantly smiling at the sight of a shimmering green mint beetle. "Remarkable."

"Do you like it?" It was touching how shy he suddenly sounded, this man who was always so strong and confident. He cared about her opinion now. That much was clear.

"Yes. They're usually smaller than this one. Where on earth did you find it?"

"In the herb garden." He pointed to a low wall that jotted out from the other side of the house. "I was investigating my property and spotted the fellow. Made me think of you."

It was suddenly impossible for her to speak, the

emotions he stirred in her threatening to tip her over. So she stood completely still and stared down at the beetle, afraid of meeting Huntley's gaze—afraid she might cry. "He's . . ." She cleared her throat. "Thank you."

"It's nothing."

He might as well have pushed her. Her head jolted back as she sucked in some air. "How wrong you are." She snapped the box shut and pressed it to her chest. "There is no better gift than this." Calling for Anna she spun on her heel and hurried away, chased by the feeling of imminent change.

Chapter 15

"**Y**ou would be fortunate to win her," Richardson said, his voice breaking the silence and making Raphe wince. He hadn't noticed his secretary's arrival.

"What makes you think I've an interest?"

With a chuckle, Richardson came to stand beside him. "One look at you right now is all it takes."

Shoving his hands into his pockets, Raphe turned to face his secretary—a man whom he'd come to consider a friend more than employee. The same could be said of Humphreys, although not Pierson. "I have more important things on my mind than considering a courtship."

"I suppose that explains why you've asked your sisters to make themselves scarce whenever Lady Gabriella comes to call?"

That got Raphe's attention. "How did you know?"

"All it takes is a pair of eyes and a bit of common sense."

Raphe pressed his lips together. "I just want to get to know her better. That's all." He would never reveal the effect Gabriella had started to have on him—her pink lips as tempting as ripe fruit on a summer's day, her porcelain skin a bloody torture device, inciting the most deplorable contemplations. Hell, he'd had a difficult time sleeping last night, his body tight with the memory of how she'd looked at him in the courtyard, as though she hadn't known whether to devour him or run.

"Really?" Richardson sounded entirely too skeptical for Raphe's liking.

"Of course it is!"

Liar.

"A pity," Richardson told him. "I personally think she would make you an excellent wife. And there is no doubt in my mind that you would be better for her than that fop Fielding."

Raphe almost choked on a laugh. "Surely, you jest."

Arching a brow, Richardson met Raphe's gaze. "You don't give yourself enough credit, Huntley. You're a good man with a sense of normalcy that the *ton* lacks. Lady Gabriella—"

"Would run screaming in the other direction if she knew all there is to know about my past." Raphe inhaled deeply. "Besides, her parents would never give their approval. It would be a wasted effort to even consider the possibility."

"So you've told her part of it then? About your past?"

"Yes. Most of it really, just not the part about Guthrie."

"Hmm. And how did she react? Was she horrified? Appalled?"

"No." He recalled the sensitive look in her eyes when he'd told her, the pain there when he'd mentioned Bethany. "Far from it."

Nodding, Richardson said, "I'd recommend focusing on that then. Trust her to understand the rest of it." When Raphe said nothing, he added, "In the meantime, I thought I'd suggest an outing tomorrow afternoon. You and your sisters have not been out much since your arrival here. We can go for a bit of shopping on Bond Street, and then for an ice at Gunther's?"

Raphe eyed him with hesitation. "I don't know . . ."

His caution prompted Richardson to ask, "Do you really wish to hide away in this house?"

"No. Not really. It is just—" *Oh, how could he possibly explain?* "What if something bad comes of it?"

Richardson stared at him in surprise. "Something bad? From an excursion in Mayfair?" He looked dubious. "I don't see any threat, as long as we venture out together. Your sisters will have our protection, if that is your concern."

Pushing aside his fear, Raphe allowed a faint smile. *Did Richardson not realize that there existed threats beyond anyone's protection?* "I worry about Juliette's health," he admitted.

"Really? She doesn't look sickly to me."

"No. But she has been quite susceptible to illness in the past."

Richardson nodded with understanding. "It was just a suggestion, Your Grace. If you think it best for your sisters to remain at home, I completely understand."

Inhaling deeply, Raphe expelled a lengthy breath. Richardson was right. They had spent far too much time indoors—a pity, considering all there was to see in this part of town. In St. Giles it had been easier. Juliette had happily remained at home with the few books he'd managed to acquire, but she'd also been younger when he'd initially demanded she stay indoors after barely recovering from the same sickness that had claimed Bethany. Terrified of losing her and unable to afford a good doctor, Raphe had insisted she stay at home, away from possible infection.

But now they were here, in a place where people would never think to bring their illnesses out into public. The risk of her getting sick was small. And besides, she would have to venture out soon if she was to make her debut. Forcing himself to consider her wants and needs, he told Richardson, "Thank you for your suggestion. I think we would all enjoy getting out of the house."

A slight drizzle dampened the air the following morning, but that did not deter Raphe and his sisters from setting out with Richardson. Seated across from his sisters in the phaeton, Raphe couldn't stop from smiling in response to their giddy expressions. They'd talked of little else since he'd brought the subject up last night during supper, their endless comments and questions prompting him to retire early after claiming a headache. But the truth of the matter was that he was thrilled to bring some happiness to their lives, even by such simple means.

"You mustn't forget yourselves," Richardson warned in a jovial tone when the carriage finally drew to a halt and Amelia jolted forward. "Remember what Lady Gabriella has taught you. Today's outing will be good practice."

"For all of us," Raphe said, amused by Amelia's eagerness to escape the carriage so she could explore the shops. He reached for the door, opening it. "Allow me to alight first so that I may help you down."

Swinging himself through the low doorway while taking care not to bump his head, Raphe stepped down onto the street below and held the door open for his sister. Although she appeared to move with a conscious attempt at decorum, managing the heavy folds of her skirt while balancing on the narrow step of the carriage proved too much of a challenge for Amelia. With a shriek, she stumbled forward, legs caught in billowing lengths of twisting fabric.

Catching her about the waist, Raphe stopped her immediate fall, the momentum of her body driving him back a step. Juliette didn't fare much better, which prompted Richardson to mutter beneath his breath, "Another area where there's room for improvement."

Dastardly fellow.

Knowing he meant well, Raphe let the remark slide without comment, but it did make him wonder if going out in public like this had been a wise decision. After all, they would be seen, and then they would be judged. Aware that one misstep could ruin everything, Raphe tried to determine if Amelia and Juliette's inelegant descents from the carriage had drawn attention.

Relief seized him with immediate force at the realization that it hadn't. In fact, nobody seemed to pay them any notice at all. It appeared as though everyone was too caught up in their own errands, or too busy talking to their companions to pay Raphe and his sisters any mind.

"There's a milliner just over there, right next to one of the finest cobblers in London," Richardson said as he led the way forward. "If you'd like to—"

"Look at that," Juliette gasped, her hand settling against Raphe's upper arm to stay his progress.

Glancing at the spot to which she pointed, he saw a large glass façade on the opposite side of the street.

Above the impressive double doors leading into the building was a sign that read: *The Book Company, est. 1805.*

Of course.

It didn't matter that they now owned an enviable library. Books had gotten them through the most difficult years of their lives, inspiring them, educating them and offering brief moments of escape from their daily toil. Feeling the same pull as Juliette, Raphe called to Richardson, who'd moved ahead of them on the pavement.

"One can never have enough books," Amelia said as she spotted the object of Raphe's admiration. "Shall we explore?"

"Oh, let's do," Juliette exclaimed. She gave Raphe's arm a gentle tug.

"But the milliner," Richardson began when he was close enough to hear what they were saying.

"Can wait another hour," Amelia told him firmly.

Smothering what sounded like a deep sigh of resignation, Richardson proceeded to guide Raphe's sisters to the opposite side of the street. He then opened the bookshop door for them, holding it while they hurried past him.

Bringing up the rear of their small party, Richardson spoke to Raphe in a conspiratorial tone, "Favoring books over pretty ribbons and lace—I do believe there are some gentlemen who would find that quite refreshing."

A bell jingled, announcing their arrival to the shopkeeper—a young man who quickly appeared from behind a section of shelves to inquire if they needed help finding something in particular.

"No thank you," Amelia told him, "we're just having a browse."

The shopkeeper's face fell a bit. "Oh. All right then. Well, let me know if you change your minds."

"Actually," Raphe said, an idea springing to mind, "Do you have any books about insects?"

His sisters turned to look at him with raised eyebrows. He ignored them, his attention fixed on the shopkeeper, who instantly smiled. "Oh yes," he said. "Right this way."

Raphe followed him down a narrow aisle.

"You can't give her a book," Amelia hissed from somewhere behind him. "It's not proper."

He frowned at that. "How would you know?"

"Because Gabriella confirmed it after I read about it in that etiquette book she provided. You cannot give her a gift unless you're engaged to be married. It simply isn't done."

"That's just plain idiotic."

Amelia expelled an exasperated breath behind him, and then Juliette's voice carried across the shop, "I think it's very romantic."

Raphe pushed back a bit of laughter while the shopkeeper came to a halt, his hands going straight for a burgundy spine. He pulled the volume out and offered it to Raphe. "This was published last year in Philadelphia. We just received it a couple of weeks ago."

"*American Entomology*, by Thomas Say." Raphe flipped the book open and took a sharp breath. The book was filled not only with names of insects and their descriptions, but with vividly colored drawings. "I'll take it."

The shopkeeper beamed. He took the book from Raphe and went to wrap it up. Amelia held her brother back. "Are you sure about this?"

"It will make her happy," he told her simply. "That's all that matters to me."

"You care for her." She searched his face and suddenly flung her arms around him in a tight embrace that almost knocked him over. "I'm so happy for you, Raphe. So very happy indeed."

"Amelia." He peeled her off of him. "I like her well enough. Let's stick with that, shall we?"

"You're buying her a book about insects." He walked away from her as she spoke but she happily followed. "It's obvious that you've been paying attention to her interests."

"It's been difficult not to, considering the fact that she went crawling about the floor of our parlor in pursuit of a spider."

"Oh, come off it, Raphe. You're not the sort of man who'd pursue a woman for anything less than love, much less think of marrying her, as you suggested doing."

"You don't know that," he muttered.

"I'm pretty sure I do," she countered.

"I need some air." All this talk of love and romance was putting him off. So he left Richardson to take care of his purchase and stepped out onto the pavement.

"Matthews?"

Halted by the familiar use of his name, Raphe turned toward the man who'd spoken and immediately stiffened. "MacNeil."

The Scotsman stared at Raphe with interest. "Ye disappeared withou' a trace, ye did."

"I had a family matter to see to." Which was true. *In a way.*

"Guthrie's been lookin' fer ye." Crossing his arms over his massive chest, MacNeil studied Raphe's appearance with shrewd eyes. "Looks like ye've come into some blunt."

"I paid my debt to Guthrie," Raphe said, not wanting to offer a more detailed explanation.

The Scotsman nodded. "Aye. So ye did. But if ye think that's made 'im ferget yer bargain, yer're mistaken." The door to the bookshop swung open again and Raphe's sisters, accompanied by Richardson, stepped out. A distasteful smirk pulled at MacNeil's lips. "I'll leave ye with that thought. 'Ave a good day, Matthews!"

"Who was that?" Richardson asked as Raphe watched MacNeil disappear down the street, blood thundering in his ears while shards of pain threatened to split his skull.

"An old friend," Raphe ground out. He could feel his muscles bunched tightly together in his shoulders, and realized that he'd been poised to fight the man if the need had arisen. Thankfully, it had not.

"Do you think he'll be trouble?"

Expelling a ragged breath, Raphe turned his attention more fully on his secretary. "I don't know. MacNeil works for Guthrie." Glancing at his sisters, he added, "Perhaps we can discuss this further once we get home. Let's enjoy the rest of the day, shall we?"

With a stiff nod, Richardson abandoned the issue. Still, it seemed to hover over them like a dark cloud while they drifted from shop to shop, purchasing handkerchiefs, fans and bonnets. It was three in the afternoon by the time they arrived home after enjoying delicious ices at Gunther's. Amelia and Juliette were in excellent moods, completely oblivious to the heavy thoughts that weighed on Raphe's mind.

"Brandy?" Raphe offered Richardson once the two of them had removed themselves to Raphe's study.

"I take it this conversation will warrant it," came Richardson's dry response.

Filling two tumblers, Raphe handed one to his friend. "There's something I haven't told you—something that could very well bring scandal to my doorstep if Guthrie's in the mood to follow up on it."

Richardson paled, but his expression remained firm. "Tell me."

"A couple of hours before receiving word of my inheritance, I struck a deal with Guthrie, one that I chose to walk away from. Given my new situation, I knew following through with it would have been impossible without tarnishing my sisters' and my own reputation. We would have lost our chance at the future I wished to give them by claiming the title. But Guthrie wouldn't have seen it that way. He would have forced me to make good on my promise, so I ran, hoping he'd never suspect where to find me."

Taking a long sip of his drink, Richardson set his tumbler aside and calmly asked, "What was the nature of the deal?"

Inhaling deeply, Raphe forced the words out. "I was to fight the world champion title holder—a man known as the Bull, in return for my freedom."

"But you've already bought your freedom." Richardson had dropped the money off at Guthrie's house himself, disguised as a messenger. "More than that even. So then—"

"It's a prestigious fight that's going to bring in a fortune. Guthrie knows I'm his only chance at winning. My freedom was my incentive, but the real prize is the money he stands to make off of me. I don't think he's going to walk away from this so easily."

"I take it you shook on it?"

Raphe nodded.

"Jesus!" Shoving his hand through his neatly combed hair, Richardson disturbed the locks, producing a wild look of dishevelment. "It's a matter of honor then. Extricating yourself won't be easy." He was quiet for a moment before saying, "We can hope he won't know where to find you, and if he does, we can try paying him off—as much money as necessary. One thing is for certain, however. You cannot engage in that fight."

Agreeing, Raphe tossed back his drink, hoping this mess would soon be forgotten.

Chapter 16

Lying in bed that night, Gabriella stared up at the ceiling unable to sleep. She simply couldn't stop thinking about the present that Anna had brought to her room after supper—a book about insects. *North American insects.* A copy she'd yet to acquire. She'd read it until her mind had boggled with all the information that clung to the pages. And the drawings! She let out a sigh. She knew precisely who the giver was, however inappropriate that might be. But she didn't care. She was too pleased to care, too thrilled with this new acquisition and too besotted with the man who'd known how much this and the beetle would mean to her.

Which led to a great deal of trouble. She knew that. Oh yes. She'd seen her sister's plight, had been keenly aware of Society's reaction to it and of the shame her parents had suffered. But Huntley was right. There had to be more to life than that. There had to be happiness beyond all else.

Impulsively, she got out of bed and put on her robe. Sleep felt like ages away. It would never claim her. Not when she constantly tossed and turned, restless for to-morrow to come just so she could see him again and thank him for his kindness.

Sliding both feet into her slippers, she headed downstairs and out into the garden, careful to close the door firmly behind her. On a deep inhalation of breath, she captured the crisp night air, sucking it deep into her lungs before expelling it again with a misty puff. Feeling slightly chilly, she wrapped her arms around herself and gazed up at the shimmering stars.

Crickets called from somewhere close by—*drrrr, drrr drrr*—a musical sound as lovely to her ears as any orchestra. But there was something else too. She strained to listen. Silence passed for a number of seconds, and then it began again. *Whistling*. She could hear it distinctly now.

Stepping down from the terrace, Gabriella moved toward it, no more able to stay away than a moth might be of avoiding a flame. It was coming from Huntley's garden, a bit louder now and with greater certainty, as though the whistler had finally settled on the right tune.

Intrigued, Gabriella continued walking, not stopping until she reached the gap in the hedge. There she paused, unsure about crossing the boundary without invitation. It was night, after all. She shouldn't be out here. Except she couldn't really help herself. More important, she no longer wanted to—not now that she'd acknowledged how awful the past year had been, pretending to be someone she wasn't. She'd no desire to live the rest of her life like that.

So she stepped forward, her stomach buzzing with excitement, her curiosity eager to be sated. The whistling came from her left, drawing nearer until a figure emerged from the darkness; tall, broad and utterly perfect.

Huntley.

"There you are," he whispered, as though he'd

been expecting her. He stood before her now, so close she could lean against him if she wished. Shadows played across his face, obscuring his eyes and casting the bridge of his nose and his upper lip into stark relief.

"I couldn't sleep, so I came outside. You were whistling."

A low chuckle escaped him. It made the air around her rumble, made her feel as though he was touching her, even though he wasn't. She shivered slightly in response.

"I sometimes do. It relaxes me." He tilted his head, allowing a beam of moonlight to sweep across his face. "What kept you awake?"

She shifted, uncomfortable with the question. *You did.* She couldn't possibly confess that much. So she said instead, "*American Entomology.* I couldn't stop reading it."

"Ah." There was a sigh to his pronunciation. He nodded. "So you like it?"

"You knew I would. And yes, I do. Very much so."

"Amelia said it would be inappropriate." He stepped back a bit, back into darkness—away from the moonlight. "I chose to ignore her."

"And I'm glad you did, for it is without question," she drew a deep breath, forced herself to be honest with him, no matter how difficult that might be, "the most incredible gift I have ever received—besides the beetle, of course. Thank you, Huntley."

"Raphe." There was a raspy sound to the name as he spoke it. "I'd like you to call me Raphe."

Gabriella felt her skin tighten around her. A flush of heat broke out across her chest. It cascaded through her, teasing and tempting and daring. "Raphe," she said, abandoning what was left of propriety.

He made some sort of noise. Something that almost sounded like a groan—rough and guttural—an elemental response that filled her not only with heat but with a sudden restlessness, a neediness, she didn't quite understand. The air had somehow come alive between them and she . . . she didn't know what to do.

"Gabriella." He spoke her name with so much longing that it almost made her weep.

There was so much emotion that she found herself overcome by it—frightened almost. For she wasn't sure she understood what he wanted, or if she'd be able to meet his demands, so she pulled back a bit, and chose to reach for safety. "Did you have to leave many friends behind in order to come here?"

He didn't answer at first, no doubt startled by the sudden change in mood. But then he said, "Just a few, but only one that really mattered. I think of him often, actually, wondering how he's doing and if he and his family will be all right."

"Have you considered going back for a visit?"

There was a grunt. Silence. And then, "I can't take the risk of anyone knowing about my past. The *ton* would never accept my sisters into their midst if they knew."

"And yet you confided in me. Why?"

He was suddenly before her, so close she could feel his breath upon her forehead. "Because I didn't want to deceive you. I didn't want to . . ." He tilted her chin with his hand, the warmth of his touch seeping deep beneath the surface. "Jesus, Gabriella. Do you have any idea what you do to me?"

She shook her head, unable to fathom the intensity of the moment, of his touch—so gentle and yet so acute. It was dizzying. He'd asked her an impossible question—one she could not answer. So she reverted to the conversation. "When I was younger—once it became clear to me that none of the other girls liked me—I used to wish my life was simpler."

"The way we lived, Gabriella . . . it might have been simpler, but it was also a hell of a lot harder."

"I know that, but at the time I just wanted a different life for myself. I just . . . I've never felt as though I belonged in this world, where speaking my mind is frowned upon, where one restriction follows another until I feel as though my hands are tied behind my back." She uttered a sigh. "I'd never had a real connection to anyone outside my own family until I met you and your sisters. You're different. You like me the way I am."

"You're perfect the way you are," he told her softly. "I wouldn't change a thing."

"Not even my birthright?" She tried to say it jovially, but there was no denying the underlying seriousness of the question. It was one that had been niggling her since the day they'd met. "I know you dislike the aristocracy, Raphe."

"As a group," he explained. "Not you as an individual. Never you, Gabriella. But . . ." She heard him take a breath, exhale it again—a strenuous sound. "My mother was a viscount's daughter, and although I don't remember her well, I remember enough to tell you that she was a deplorable woman. All she cared about was wealth, pretty things, the chance to outdo her friends and to show off. She placed objects and tea parties before her own children. I spent more time with the servants during the early years of my childhood than I did with either of my parents."

"It's actually not uncommon for gentry children to be raised by governesses and tutors."

He laughed grimly. "I'm not talking about that," he said. "I'm talking about being raised by the maid and the cook in the kitchen. Yes, there may have been a governess once, but I don't remember her. By the time I was six or seven there were only three servants. Years later, I was told that my father struggled to support my mother's extravagant lifestyle. He was a second son—a vicar with a modest income. But he didn't have the strength to say no to her. Got him into a massive debt until one day, there was no way out. She left him for another man and the following day, my father killed himself. I found his body."

"Good God!" What a terrible thing for a child to endure. "I'm so sorry."

"Neither deserved to have children." His voice was bitter now. "They shaped my impression of the aristocracy, and although I always knew I might be wrong—that my parents might have been exceptionally awful—my experience at Fielding House has convinced me of the contrary."

She couldn't blame him. He'd been treated abominably by most of those present, including her own parents. Cringing at the recollection, she asked, "Who was it—the person who told you about your parents' financial troubles?"

"One of my father's creditors."

Gabriella frowned as she tried to make sense of it. "I don't understand. When would a creditor have had the opportunity to speak to you about that? You said yourself that you ran away and that—"

"It was a long time ago." There was a sense of finality about the way he said it that told her this conversation was over. He no longer wanted to talk about it.

She understood.

She didn't want to talk about her own bad experiences anymore either. So she asked the first question that came to mind. "How are your dance lessons coming along?"

He closed the distance between them with one step, then bowed his head to whisper in her ear, "I can show you, if you like." He didn't wait for her to respond or for the quivers he'd stirred in her belly to cease. Instead, he grabbed her by the hand and pulled her into a waltz, guiding her across the lawn, her feet occasionally sliding against the slippery dew. But he held her upright, his palm spread against her lower back, the heat of it burning its way through her thin robe and nightgown, while the other hand held hers.

He danced with surprising elegance for a man who was new to this sort of thing, his movements agile and smooth, just as they'd been when he'd stood in the courtyard hitting a bag of flour. Her mind went still, narrowing to a point where only that image of him existed.

She felt him shift. "Are you all right?" Just a murmur, but it was enough to make her entire body shudder with pleasure.

"Yes," she said, her nightgown twirling about her legs as he led her around, closer to the park fence, further from the house—a place so dark it grew difficult to see.

"You gasped."

"Did I?" She hadn't realized.

His movements slowed. "Tell me how you feel."

"I can't." She could barely speak now, they were standing so still, their bodies gently swaying to a silent tune.

A slight, almost imperceptible press of his hand against her back—that was all it took to bring her up against him. She tried to breathe normally, but it was almost impossible. All she could do was feel the hard planes of his chest rising and falling against her own, the steady beat of his heart against her breast. He was all solid strength and raw power, the perfect complement to her softer feminine curves.

"God help me," he murmured. "I cannot seem to resist you."

His honesty broke its way through her, instilling a sense of beauty she'd never experienced before. Her mouth went dry and her limbs went weak and all she could do was cling to him as he moved his hands, holding her more securely about her waist—holding her closer—so close that their thighs touched. Heavens, it felt delicious.

His breaths began coming deeper, vibrating through her until she burned with a need for more. This wasn't enough.

"Shh . . ." he whispered. "Easy now."

"I feel . . ." The answer to his question. "Wanted."

"And so you are." Reaching up, he drew his fingers along the edge of her cheek, tenderly caressing. "Gabriella, I'd like to kiss you now. If I may?"

She nodded once. That was all it took. His lips were on hers before she could blink, gently pressing, moving, exploring, while his hands . . . they roamed lower, his fingers spreading across her bottom to provoke the most wanton sensations she'd ever felt. Lord, the man was wicked in his seduction, and she was savoring every moment of it, reveling in his desire for her—the strange girl who, until recently, had only been able to lure suitors with the help of her dowry.

"Open your mouth," he instructed in low sensual tones that whispered across her lips.

She did, and he took advantage, deepening the kiss, exploring and guiding until she matched his every move with a desperation unlike any she'd ever known before. It was as if he'd taken her out of a quiet pond and tossed her into a stormy ocean. Her senses were drowning—overwhelmed by the experience—but she was learning how to swim. And for the first time in her life, Gabriella knew what it meant to be truly alive. No going back now. It was much too late for that.

Except he was now drawing back, ending the kiss and stepping out of her arms. "You need to leave."

"What?" She felt bewildered—abandoned—and really, really cold now.

"This wasn't meant to happen. I've overstepped—demanded too much of you too soon. I just . . ." He pushed his fingers through his hair and then said, "You're a bloody dream come true, Gabriella. I couldn't stop myself, but if we don't end this now there'll be no stopping at all. Do you understand?"

She shook her head, too confused to absorb what he was saying. Except the part about her being a dream. She rather liked that.

He muttered an oath. "When a man wants a woman the way I want you, he'll do whatever he can to have her. Which means . . ." He was gritting his teeth. "If you don't run from me right now, I'll have that transparent nightgown of yours up around your waist in a trice while I—"

"I understand," she said already backing away. She pulled her robe around her, cheeks heating from what he'd just said. Had he really seen . . . oh God, how mortifying that was.

"Good night, Gabriella," he told her hoarsely.

"Good night." A swift response before she bolted, running as fast as she could away from the man she wanted. Just not like this—not how he'd described. They both deserved better than that, and it was apparently up to her to save them.

Chapter 17

When Gabriella came to call the following day, she was wearing a lavender-colored gown that revealed a delicious amount of skin, not that it mattered much to Raphe. She could have been wearing a high-necked gown with long sleeves and he still would have been able to recall what she'd looked like last night. His stomach tightened. Dressed in no more than a thin nightgown and a robe that had slipped out of place more than once, he'd been offered a stunning view of her body.

"Good afternoon," she was now saying, addressing Raphe's sisters before allowing a brief glance in his direction. A flush of pink rose to her cheeks as their eyes met. "Your Grace."

With her hair pinned back in a loose coiffure that allowed stray locks to curl against the sides of her face, she looked more lovely than Raphe had ever seen her—as though she'd just tumbled out of bed, dressed with haste and hurried on over. Eager to see him, perhaps? He could only hope.

Unable to resist, he crossed the room to bow before her. "Lady Gabriella. Always a pleasure." He then offered her his arm—a superfluous gesture, considering the short distance she needed to travel—but one that would ensure a touch of intimacy between them.

A brief hesitation brought her gloved hand to rest upon his arm, the delicate touch causing his muscles to strain beneath the wool of his jacket. He glanced at her, aware of the charged energy between them, but unsure of how to deal with it since they were not alone. And although he'd spent a restless night with vivid imaginings of all the ways in which he'd like to claim her, he had no wish to cause her any embarrassment. So he chose to remain silent for now while discreetly caressing her wrist to remind her of his regard.

When they arrived at the sofa, he released her, allowing her to take her seat across from Amelia and Juliette. Tea was brought, along with a plate of madeleines, and the sisters took turns pouring, their expressions softening in response to the praise they received from Gabriella.

"Have you received an invitation to the Duke of Coventry's ball on Saturday?" Gabriella asked.

"Yes," Raphe told her while doing his best not to think of the kiss they'd shared. He could still taste her—rosy and sweet. "It arrived yesterday, much to my surprise. I would have thought that word of my unsuitable company would have spread since the dinner at Fielding House."

Inclining her head, Gabriella said, "Not inviting you would have been frowned upon, considering your station. And besides, Coventry is different from the rest—more agreeable. I've always liked him."

Reflecting on how pleasant the duke had seemed when he'd first met him at Fielding House, Raphe nodded his head. "Perhaps you're right. But he won't be the only peer there, and I'm just not sure that I want to meet any others. Not until I know that I'm capable of making a good impression."

"While I'm inclined to agree with you, my fear is that since you've already ventured out into public, people will wonder why you've suddenly chosen to retreat from social events, allowing the negative gossip to grow deeper roots until you'll stop receiving invitations altogether. Considering your aspirations for your sisters, I don't believe that would be in your best interest," Gabriella concluded.

"I quite agree," Amelia said. "If we are to marry well, we must prove ourselves worthy. And connections must be made so you will know which gentlemen to introduce us to once we make our debuts, Raphe."

"She is right," Juliette said. "Hiding away is unwise."

"I feel as though you're conspiring against me," Raphe grumbled.

"What I propose," Gabriella continued, ignoring Raphe's remark, "is that we work on your conversational skills and help you polish up on a few more areas so you can make fools of anyone who may have spoken against you."

"Including Fielding and your father?" Raphe asked, surprised by her eagerness to go against them. When she nodded, he couldn't help but ask, "Why?"

Folding her hands neatly in her lap, Gabriella looked at each of them in turn. "Because I believe my father, and Fielding, and whoever else was present that evening at Fielding House have greatly misjudged you. Having gotten to know the three of you better . . ." She paused then, her composure failing her as she turned a bright shade of crimson. She glanced at the ceiling, then at the floor—anywhere but at Raphe. Eventually, she straightened her back, took a deep breath and somehow managed to collect herself in a way that Raphe found absolutely astonishing. He watched with open admiration as she seriously told them, "I think you can all become respectable members of Society."

Gabriella drew a breath. Miraculously, she'd stopped herself from melting under the heat of Raphe's presence. Good heavens. Had he really kissed her in the garden last night, under a blanket of darkness? It seemed inconceivable. And yet, she knew from the scorching look in his eyes that it had been very real indeed.

She averted her gaze, determined not to lose focus. "Let's come up with a plan then. If you agree, that is?"

As reluctant as he looked, Raphe gave her a firm nod. "Very well."

"Good." She drummed her fingers against her seat cushion, caught herself and stopped. She thought of what would be required of him and asked, "How many dances have you learned so far?"

The edge of his mouth twitched. "I'm quite familiar with the waltz." The intensity of his gaze as he said it pierced her to the core until she felt her lungs restrict against the tightening of her chest.

The man was impossible!

"Well." She glanced at his sisters, who appeared to be watching her with great interest. "Some young ladies will not be allowed to dance that particular dance. Not until they've been given permission. So, you'll have to learn the quadrille and the minuet, at the very least."

He produced an immediate scowl. "I don't like those dances. They make me look stupid."

"Oh? So you have attempted them?" He didn't answer, which prompted her to say, "Your sisters will depend on your ability to adhere to protocol. It's just for one evening, Your Grace, and then you can stand on the sidelines forever after, if that is what you wish to do."

He gave her a wary look. "I will think on it," he finally told her noncommittally. "In the meantime, perhaps there are other more useful things you can teach us?"

"Of course," Gabriella said. Forcing a smile, she faced Amelia and Juliette, not daring to look at Huntley for fear that he would see the disappointment she'd felt in response to his adamant refusal to do as she advised. Because although she knew that Fielding would be her obligatory partner for the waltz until she told him their courtship was over, she'd had the silly idea of partnering with Raphe for one of the other dances. She shook her head, unsure of herself once more. He'd made no promises. . . . Realizing everyone was staring at her, she pasted a smile on her face and addressed Raphe's sisters. "Have you been practicing your walks and your curtsies?"

"That, as well as sitting and pouring tea," Amelia told her proudly.

"Excellent," Gabriella said. "Let me see."

For the next half hour, Amelia and Juliette took turns improving their poise and elegance. For Juliette it seemed to come naturally, while Amelia continued to struggle with her posture and ease of movement. Her steps were often too hasty. "You are certainly doing much better than when you started," Gabriella remarked before taking a sip of the tea that had recently been requested. "But how will you fare on the arm of a gentleman?" She gave Huntley a shrewd look. His presence continued to unsettle her, leaving her composure in tatters while he sat carelessly by her side. It wouldn't hurt to add some distance between them, or to make him suffer a little under her tutelage. So, quelling her fluttering nerves, she asked him sweetly, "Will Your Grace please oblige?"

The narrow-eyed look he gave her reflected the sort of mistrust one might feel when suspecting that a prank was about to be carried out at one's expense. She paid him no mind as she gestured toward Amelia, who presently stood waiting.

"Very well," he muttered as he straightened himself and rose to his feet.

Pleased with herself for managing to bother him just a little, Gabriella watched as he and Amelia took a turn about the room. "Slow your pace, Huntley. There's no hurry," she called.

He glared at her, but there was a hint of amusement about his eyes, the effect producing a devastating culmination of heat in the pit of Gabriella's stomach. *Lord, the man had a maddening effect on her!* Schooling her features in the hope that he wouldn't see her discomfort, she waited for him to return to the starting point, where Juliette now stood, her posture the perfect image of a well-bred lady.

Reaching her, Huntley drew his arm away from Amelia's and turned to face his youngest sister. "You must excuse yourself to Amelia first," Gabriella chastised. "She is not a rag for you to toss aside." Huntley's jaw hardened. His eyes darkened. Gabriella refused to let the effect of it keep her from her purpose. "Thank Amelia first, step back and bow, then turn toward Juliette and ask her politely if she would care to accompany you on a tour of the room."

A brief hesitation followed until he eventually did

as Gabriella asked, allowing her to tutor his sisters in their responses. Huntley then tucked Juliette's hand against the crook of his elbow and proceeded to walk with her, speaking to her in low, inaudible tones as they went.

"He makes a dashing duke, don't you think?" Amelia asked as she lowered herself to the spot on the sofa that Huntley had recently vacated. "Quite imperious."

Watching his progress, Gabriella couldn't help but agree, even though she didn't dare voice such thoughts. Instead she said, "You have all improved significantly since your arrival. It has been an honor helping you with that."

"And it has been our honor getting to know you," Amelia said. "Our situation would have been quite hopeless without your help, you know."

Gabriella chuckled. "I'm sure you would have found a way to manage, though it might have taken a bit longer."

"Perhaps, but then we would have missed out on a new friendship."

The impulsive response warmed Gabriella's heart. "Thank you," she said, while wondering if Amelia realized how much her words meant to her.

A smile passed between them and then Amelia said, "Oh look, they're back."

Returning her attention to Raphe and Juliette, Gabriella regarded the way in which they parted ways, observing how well Huntley applied the advice she'd given him earlier. *But there was still one thing . . .* "When you wish to extricate yourself from a lady, Huntley, it is important that you take her hand and gently remove it from your arm first, rather than immediately pulling away."

"Why?" He looked as though he was trying not to roll his eyes or sigh with belligerence.

"Because the last thing you want to do is to accidentally drag a lady after you as you turn away. *That* would cause a scene, which would hardly be to your advantage."

Studying her with the intensity of a marksman, he quietly murmured, "No, I don't suppose it would." The way he looked, a few stray strands of hair falling against his brow and that infernal cravat of his missing as usual, was almost piratical.

Her heart made a funny little leap inside her chest, while tingling heat crept across her skin. *Good heavens!*

She watched in amazement as his lips rose with mischief, as if he knew precisely what he was doing to her—how unsettled he was making her feel. "Perhaps you ought to demonstrate," he said. Stepping toward her, he extended his hand. "Please allow me to escort you about the room."

Hesitating, she eyed Amelia and Juliette, wondering if they might have noticed that their brother's proposition meant more than a simple request for tutelage. But the sisters seemed oblivious to the charged atmosphere that threatened to unravel Gabriella at any moment. Instead, they urged her to do as Huntley asked, claiming an interest in seeing how a real lady ought to walk with a gentleman.

Inhaling sharply, Gabriella felt her throat constrict as her gaze dropped to Huntley's upturned palm. Of course he wasn't wearing gloves—he was at home, for heaven's sake. Not that it made much difference, since he probably wouldn't have worn them even if he'd been out. And oh, just looking at that hand, she recalled what it had felt like last night, clasped against her own. Could she really endure such exquisite torture again? Now, with his sisters present? For she'd removed her own gloves in order to eat the madeleines the maid had brought with the tea. Eyeing the lengths of fabric that lay draped across the armrest, she considered putting them back on for the duration of this exercise. It would be the proper thing to do—the *safe* thing to do.

Her decision came a second too late as Huntley leaned forward, his large hand closing about hers before pulling her to her feet. "Huntley!"

"I grew weary of watching you ponder your options," he said, facing her with a stormy expression that made her wonder if her legs would carry her the necessary distance. It only got worse when he scraped his callused thumb across the edge of her hand, producing a scorching collection of sparks against her bare skin. *Lord help her.*

"Your Grace, I—"

"Raphe," he amended, raising an eyebrow. "Just let me guide you." Turning sideways, he lifted her hand, arranging it neatly against the crook of his arm.

A muscle flexed beneath his jacket as she curled her fingers over him, and she realized then with startling awareness that in spite of his nonchalant manner, he was just as affected by her as she was by him. Her heart took flight, scattering her composure like the seeds of a dandelion blown away by a gust of wind. As a result, it was something of a miracle that she managed to step forward without tripping, her posture as rigid as a slab of granite.

"I've missed you," he murmured when they'd gone a few paces.

Unable to be anything but honest, she said, "I've missed you too." Just a few hours, that was all it had been, but it had felt like an eternity.

"Will you dance with Fielding at the ball?"

"It is expected," Gabriella replied, her breath hitching slightly when he placed his opposite hand over hers, trapping it against his arm.

"I don't like it, Gabriella. I can't stand the thought of him holding you in his arms the way I did last night."

Swallowing, she did her best to remain calm. "Oh, I can assure you that it will be nothing like that." They continued for a bit before she had the courage to say, "Fielding has been courting me for two months. He is by all accounts an excellent match. But then I met you and everything changed."

"How?" His muscles strained beneath his sleeve, flexing and tightening to match his voice.

Glancing sideways, she met his dark brown eyes, more vulnerable now than she'd ever seen them before. They compelled her to say what was in her heart. "I fell for you, Raphe, and I fear there's no getting up."

They'd reached the windows. Stopping, they paused for a moment, pretending to admire the thick foliage of rhododendron in the garden.

"I'll ask your father for permission to court you. This thing between you and Fielding, it cannot continue."

Her heart gave a happy bounce. The possessiveness with which he spoke was thrilling. Unfortunately, it wouldn't solve all their problems. "My father will never allow it. He doesn't approve of you, Raphe, and with Victoria's mistake in mind, I'm afraid he'll see my attachment to you as a repetition of the past."

"There has to be a solution." He gave her hand a gentle squeeze as if to say, *We're in this together, you and I. We'll find a way.* Out loud, he said, "One thing is for certain—I will not stand idly by and watch Fielding make you his wife."

Chapter 18

He needed time. *They* needed time. Time in which to explore this relentless pull between them—time for them to fall in love. It was the only way any of this would ever work, he realized. Because in spite of his protestations, Amelia had been right: he would never marry for anything less. "Tell me what I need to do," he told Gabriella, almost desperately.

Sighing heavily, she said, "You must prove yourself worthy—a superior match to Fielding."

"He may be an earl, but I am a duke."

"Yes," she agreed, "but it's more than that. Your reputation needs to be impeccable." She was silent a moment before saying, "The ball will be your best opportunity to alter my parents' opinion of you. If you can gain the high regard of other respectable members of Society, perhaps then you will stand a chance. And—"

"Yes?" He held his breath.

"One whisper of scandal attached to your name and we'll lose our chance. They cannot discover your past."

Reminded of St. Giles and of his recent encounter with MacNeil, Raphe felt his lungs constrict. His heart thudded painfully against his chest. To win her hand would be impossible. He'd known it since the moment the notion had entered his head. Stubborn fool that he was, he would try, anyway—he would turn his back on his deep-rooted fear of marital misery, on the knowledge that he came not only from gentry, but from the shameful slums of London, and on the fact that he was as undeserving of her as a beggar would be of a princess.

"And there's something else," she added. "Something that might work in our favor."

"What is it?"

Lifting her chin, Gabriella glanced up at him, meeting his stormy expression. "My father has a particular fondness for Rubens. He's been especially interested in acquiring *The Three Graces*—a painting that you just happen to have in your library." She'd noticed it the first time she'd come to call.

He was silent for a moment, lips firmly set in contemplation. "I don't like the idea of trying to buy you with a painting, Gabriella, and I doubt your father will either." Drawing her away from the window, he led her further about the room at a moderate pace.

"You wouldn't be trying to buy *me*. Just permission to court me. There's a difference."

"None that I can see."

"And besides," she added, trying to make him see reason, "it's not so terrible a thing when I'm the one suggesting it and we're both in agreement."

"Your father won't know about that. He'll just see me as a mercenary, and frankly, I don't blame him."

It was true. She knew he was probably right, but she also knew that if there was one thing that might tempt her father to comply with their wishes, it was that painting. "I can think of no other way—not if we're going to stop sneaking around. For that to happen, we'll need my father's permission."

"And you'll need to stop seeing Fielding."

Yes, she would. But doing so would not be easy, and her parents' reactions . . . Her stomach was already rolling over, agitated by the thought of what was to come. But if it meant having Huntley instead, then it would surely be worth every struggle she'd have to endure.

Over the course of the next few days, Gabriella continued tutoring Amelia and Juliette in preparation for their debuts. Her encounters with Raphe became fleeting, but she knew that he was keeping busy with his own lessons—a necessity if they were to have any chance of ever being together.

"I am completely devoted to this endeavor," he told her one day in passing when she told him how much she missed him. "I am completely devoted to you."

Her heart swam with joy and the possibility of a brighter future filled her vision.

When she returned home on Saturday, Gabriella was met by her aunt. "You look as though you had a healthy walk," Aunt Caroline said. "I can't recall ever seeing you so flushed before. Mind that your dear mama doesn't see you like that, or she will reprimand you for overexerting yourself."

Rolling her eyes, Gabriella untied the bow of her bonnet and set it on a nearby table. "Mama puts too much weight on appearances."

Aunt Caroline's eyebrows went up. "Does she really?"

"Yes," Gabriella told her decisively.

"You sound rather mutinous," Aunt Caroline said. A smile slid into place. "I quite like it. Might I ask about the cause of this startling transformation?"

"Oh, I am not so terribly transformed, Aunt. My views have always differed from my mother's. I just wasn't aware of how much until recently."

"How interesting. I cannot help but wonder if this newfound clarity might have something to do with our handsome neighbor." Leaning slightly forward, Aunt Caroline narrowed her gaze on Gabriella. "Tell me, where exactly did this walk of yours take you?"

"To the garden, and—and beyond," Gabriella told her irritably. "Anna was with me."

"Yes, I can see that," she said with a nod. "And in case you're wondering, I don't disapprove."

"You don't?" Gabriella thought for certain that her aunt would at the very least have advised her not to repeat the outing—that it would be her duty to inform Gabriella's parents so that any future efforts to see Huntley could be thwarted.

"Of course not." Aunt Caroline waved her hand dismissively. "I'm surprised you would think otherwise, or have I not made my position on Fielding clear to you?"

"Well yes, but that doesn't mean you might encourage me to seek out Huntley instead."

"Ah, so you *were* rendezvousing with him!"

"I'm helping his sisters prepare for their presentations at court."

"Of course you are, dear." Aunt Caroline's eyes twinkled. "Frankly, I think Huntley is quite a catch, but then again, I'm a widow, so my view on the matter is going to be quite different from your parents'. They want the best of the best for you, however misguided their idea of what that is might be. Which reminds me—Fielding is waiting for you in the parlor."

Air *whooshed* from Gabriella's lungs. "And Mama and Papa?"

"They have not yet returned from their respective outings." Studying Gabriella, Aunt Caroline quietly asked, "Would you like for me to come with you?"

"No," Gabriella said. "That won't be necessary." After all, she'd been alone with Fielding several times before. But that had been before she'd decided not to marry him—before Huntley had kissed her. *Would Fielding see the betrayal on her face? Would he even care?*

Numbly, she approached the parlor and entered. He was standing by the window, perfectly straight and with his hands folded neatly behind his back. "My lord. What a surprise."

Turning, he regarded her with restrained appreciation. "I know you weren't expecting me today. I'm sorry if I've upset your plans."

"No, no." Crossing to the sofa, she tried to calm the quaking of her nerves as she lowered herself onto it. She addressed Fielding. "Won't you have a seat?"

"Of course." He claimed the spot beside her so quickly it almost made her head spin. She tried to smile, and almost managed it until he said, "I think it is time for us to announce our engagement."

A squeak was all Gabriella could manage. She'd known this moment would come, and yet it still caught her by surprise. Blinking, she tried to meet his gaze. "Did you just propose?"

With a wince, he shifted closer. "Forgive me." He took a series of breaths before saying, "I have always striven to excel at every task. When I decided to choose a bride, I never considered anyone but you. Nobody else is as . . ."

He seemed to struggle a bit, so she added dryly, "Rich?"

"No!" He had the decency to look a bit embarrassed. "I was going to say, 'Exceptional.'"

She had to admire the smoothness with which he delivered such a compliment. Had it come from Raphe, she'd have believed him, but Fielding? Not a chance. The man was only interested in one thing.

"With you by my side," he continued, "I shall be—" *Able to buy all the horses in England*, Gabriella imagined him thinking. "Truly happy," he said. "Will you do me the honor of becoming my wife?"

"I—" Gabriella's mind whirled. She wasn't prepared, but she knew it was time for her to break her attachment to Fielding.

A crooked smile emerged in the confines of her mind, accompanied by dark, piercing eyes.

Raphe.

A man who, in the space of two weeks, had managed to make her doubt every aspect of her life—of the person she was, and more important, of the person she wanted to be. He'd blown into her life like a thunderstorm, stirring the very foundations of everything she'd ever known. She cared for him, and she believed he cared for her too. It might not be love, but it was more than what Fielding was able to offer. And in that moment, Gabriella finally understood how Victoria must have felt. It wasn't easy, swimming upstream instead of flowing with the current. And Raphe was the Duke of Huntley—rich and powerful, no matter how one chose to look at it. She'd want for nothing except perhaps Society's approval—an artificial attainment that she'd learned to live without years ago.

As for her parents, Gabriella knew they would likely resent her, but she'd already decided that she would accept that when she'd spoken to Raphe earlier. After all, they'd had their chance to live their lives. It was her turn now, and to marry a man she didn't even like when the one she cared for was ready to take his place, would be monumentally stupid.

With this in mind, she gave Fielding her full attention. "You are exceptionally kind, my lord, but I fear that I must refuse your offer, as much as it pains me to do so."

He sat back with a jolt. "I beg your pardon?"

"I cannot marry you," she clarified. Seeing his lips thin as he clenched his jaw, she hastily added, "You deserve a wife who shares your interests. A woman you can grow to love and who—"

"Love?" He stared at her. Incredulous. "Marrying has nothing to do with love, my lady. It is a business transaction that I have every intention of following through to the end."

"But—"

"What's happened? What's changed?" He studied her as she drew back a bit, not liking his tone in the least. "It's *him*, isn't it? You've gone and lost your head over that rotten scoundrel who lives next door to you."

She shook her head, frightened now by his anger. "He's a duke," she tried.

"He's not fit to clean your shoes, and you want to cast *me* aside for *him*?" He scoffed at her as if he thought her a pathetic imbecile. "If you imagine that I'm just walking away without a fight—that I will allow him to encroach on what is mine—then you don't know me at all."

"But . . ." Her heart was beating frantically against her chest while she fought to find the right words—a solution to this mess she'd created. "You cannot *force* me to marry you."

He rose then, standing over her like a threatening shadow. "We'll just have to see about that, won't we?"

And then, without the slightest warning, he swooped down and kissed her, hard and angrily, and with no consideration for her feelings.

Stepping back, he glared at her a moment, then executed a swift bow and left. Gabriella remained where she was for a long while after, unable to move. Tears burned at the backs of her eyes, the violation of Fielding's advance and the cruelty with which he'd executed it tightening her throat and making her tremble.

His message was clear. He was not a man who liked to lose, and he did not take kindly to sharing what he believed to be his. Raphe had intruded on Fielding's "property."

Gabriella winced. She knew now that this was how Fielding saw her. Which meant that he would do everything in his power to keep her. She considered her options and immediately decided to tell her parents. If they discovered how calculating Fielding actually was, then they might just change their minds about him.

But when they eventually returned home that afternoon it was already late in the day and with little time left to prepare for the Coventry ball. Both of her parents were in a rush to bathe and dress, insisting she tell them whatever was on her mind later. Agreeing, Gabriella succumbed herself to waiting for a more appropriate time, even if that meant having to dance with a man whom she now detested.

Lord help her, she was in trouble!

Chapter 19

Standing to one side of the Coventry ballroom, Raphe snatched a glass of champagne from the tray of a passing footman and took a sip. He was not oblivious to the whispers or the inconspicuous glances being sent his way, but as tempting as it was to do something shocking for the sake of provoking all these pompous nobs, he refrained, staying on his best behavior just as Gabriella had advised.

While she'd been preparing his sisters for their presentation at court, which was due to take place in only one week, according to the invitation that had arrived two days earlier, he'd shut himself away with Richardson, Pierson and Humphreys. The three trusty servants had applied themselves to teaching Raphe everything he needed to know in order to make the right impression at the ball. Hell, he'd even allowed that silly little Italian man who called himself a dance instructor to teach him the quadrille and minuet just as Gabriella had suggested. The memory made him shudder. But, nothing was going to deter him from the chance he had of winning her for himself.

So, when he saw her arrive with her parents and

aunt, he set his glass aside with purpose, straightened his back, squared his shoulders and began making his way through the crowd. "Lord Warwick," he said, drawing the man's attention. "What a pleasure it is to see you again. And Lady Warwick." Executing an impeccable bow that had taken no small amount of exasperation to perfect, he reached for the woman's hand and raised it to his lips. Straightening, he then said softly, "I can see where your daughter has gotten her beauty from." Addressing Gabriella, who was quietly gaping at him as though he'd just fallen off the back of a carriage and hit his head, and her aunt, who was eyeing him with a smirk, he simply said, "Ladies. The evening is saved with your arrival."

A solid moment of silence passed between them, during which Raphe congratulated himself for not gagging on his overly affected words. And then Warwick finally spoke up. "I thought I made my opinion of you quite clear when last we met. You are not—"

"I may not have attended Eton, my lord, but will you honestly judge me on that alone?" Raphe leaned toward him. "I am a duke, you know. My influence might serve you well one day."

Warwick stared. Lady Warwick's eyes bulged. Lady Gabriella's mouth dropped open and her aunt . . . well, that lady surprised Raphe the most by actually laughing out loud.

"Your influence?" Warwick said as though Raphe were suggesting they fly to the moon.

"Precisely," Raphe said without blinking, "Let's put our differences behind us, my lord. I'd much rather hear your opinion on the Rubens that's hanging in my library."

Raphe knew the second the words were out that he'd hit his mark, just as Gabriella had predicted. He'd never seen a man go quite so still, his eyes hungry and his mouth set with the eagerness of a thief who'd just discovered an unlocked jewelry shop.

"I, err—" Lord Warwick began. Turning toward his wife, he spoke with a joviality that Raphe had not presumed him capable of. "Why don't you go and mingle with the other ladies, my dear. Take my sister and Gabriella with you. Apparently, His Grace and I have something to discuss."

Lady Warwick looked uncertain. She stared at her husband, then at Raphe, then back at her husband once more. "But—"

"Let us adjourn to one of the salons," Warwick told Raphe. "If you'll excuse us, ladies."

Lady Warwick appeared as though she might start sputtering in response to her husband's dismissal. Raphe's gaze drifted across to Gabriella, whose cheeks immediately darkened the moment their eyes met. A smile captured his lips, which seemed to make her blush even more. He loved it when she blushed. He loved knowing how easily he affected her. It was mutual, of course. He'd never met a woman who made his fingers itch with such desperate need to touch her, the way Gabriella did.

Regretting that he would have to forego her company for a while, Raphe hastily whispered in her ear as he passed her, "Save a dance for me." Without pausing to check her reaction, he followed Lord Warwick to the salon he'd mentioned. It was a cozy room swathed in red hues and with two seating arrangements at each end. "Care for a drink?" Warwick asked as he crossed to the side table.

"No, thank you," Raphe said, uncomfortable with the idea of helping himself to Coventry's private selection of liquor without asking permission first. So he took a seat in one of the armchairs instead and waited for Warwick to join him.

"Tell me about the Rubens," Warwick said a moment later as he lowered himself to the opposite seat and took a sip of the brandy he'd poured himself.

Leaning back into a comfortable position, Raphe began, "I understand that you're an art collector, my lord, and that you would like to add *The Three Graces* to your collection."

The sparkle in Warwick's eyes confirmed that this was indeed the case. "I offered your predecessor a handsome sum for it once, but he refused me."

"Fifty thousand pounds, from what I understand," Raphe murmured. He drummed his fingers lightly against the armrest.

Shifting, Warwick's mouth twisted as though he'd just bit into a lemon. "It was more than the painting is worth."

Raphe was aware of this too. He inclined his head in agreement. "Which can only mean that you want it a great deal."

"It would complete the mythological theme that I've been putting together in the north gallery of Warwick House."

With a nod of understanding, Raphe asked, "What if I told you that I'm willing to part with it?"

For a second, it looked as though Warwick would either leap from his chair with joy, or tumble to the floor in dismay. "That—" He cleared his throat and took another sip of his drink. "I would certainly welcome such a prospect." He appeared to process the idea for a while before saying, "I suppose you'll want the fifty thousand for it?"

"No," Raphe said, amused by Warwick's stunned expression. "In fact, I don't want any sum of money in return."

"No money?" he sounded incredulous. "But—surely you don't mean to give it to me for free? Especially knowing how I feel about you and your family and considering how unaccepting I've been of you."

"An incident that I will be willing to forget, in exchange for an apology." When Warwick's jaw tightened in protest, Raphe leaned forward, elbows on his knees. "Look, I know I'm not what you imagined I'd be, but I am the Duke of Huntley, and I will not continue to allow you or anyone else to treat me with less respect than I deserve." He paused for emphasis before spreading his hands and saying, "But, if you're too proud to admit your faults, then perhaps I ought to hold on to the Rubens after all . . ."

"No. You are right," Warwick spoke with haste. "You have improved yourself greatly since our first encounter—impressively so, in fact. And—and, I apologize for the things I've said to you. It was badly done."

"Thank you, Warwick. I appreciate that."

Looking like a dog with his tail between his legs, Warwick averted his gaze and took yet another sip of his drink. "So then the only question is, what do you want in return for the painting?"

Savoring the power that he knew he now held over the earl, Raphe took a second to answer. He laced his fingers together and did his best to hold still, in spite of his straining heart and the blood that thundered through his veins. "Permission to court your daughter."

"What?" Warwick's face went white.

Raphe smiled sardonically. "I believe you heard me."

"You—and Lady Gabriella?" When Raphe nodded, Warwick's expression tightened, his eyes narrowing with piercing intensity. "No," he said with the swipe of a hand. "Absolutely not."

Praying that Gabriella was right about her father's obsession with *The Three Graces*, Raphe shrugged with a casualness he did not feel, and began to rise. "I wish you luck in completing your Greek theme then, Warwick. A pity I wasn't able to help you with that." It was the oldest bargaining trick in the book. One he'd witnessed more times than he could count on the streets of St. Giles, applied by vendors and buyers alike. *Just walk away*, he told himself. He turned to leave.

"Wait!"

Stopping, Raphe schooled his features before looking back at Warwick, eyebrows raised in question.

"Fielding came to see me earlier today. He formally asked for my permission to marry her, and I have given it," Warwick said. He almost sounded apologetic.

The comment was like a punch to his gut. "Does she not have a say in the matter?" Raphe felt his blood begin to boil. Whatever agreement Fielding and Warwick had come to, Raphe was certain that Gabriella knew nothing about it. Which made him wary.

"The match will be good. The best, in fact."

"And marrying me instead would be bad?" When Warwick didn't answer, Raphe said, "My rank trumps everyone else's, except for the Regent's. Are you really telling me that the prejudice you have for me on account of my inferior upbringing is going to deny your daughter the chance of becoming a duchess?"

An infernal length of time followed before Warwick formed a response. "I don't like mystery," he eventually said. "And where you are concerned, there are too many unanswered questions. Like which relative it was, exactly, who took you in after your parents died. I knew your mother's family well enough to say with certainty that they did not have any relatives near the Scottish border. As for your father's side, I've looked into his relations since meeting you, and have come up with no verifiable facts. Which makes me wonder if you really are who you claim to be."

"I can assure you—"

"Don't bother," Warwick clipped. "I've dealt with imposters before, and I suspect that I am dealing with one right now."

"I am *not* an imposter," Raphe said, his voice dangerously low.

"Then tell me where you've really been for the past fifteen years."

Glaring at him, Raphe felt whatever hope he'd had of winning Gabriella for himself slipping away like sand through an hourglass. Confiding the truth would not help. On the contrary, he stood to lose so much more than just Gabriella if he did that. So he said the only thing he could say. "I cannot."

A long, drawn-out silence settled between them, and then Warwick finally rose from his chair to face Raphe. He stood completely still, eyes boring into his. "Keep the painting," he finally said with cool disdain. "And stay away from my daughter."

Raphe watched him walk away with mixed emotions. As much as he hated the man for denying him the chance he'd requested, he also admired him for putting his daughter's best interests—no matter how misguided Raphe and Gabriella both believed them to be—first.

I've dealt with imposters before.

Briefly closing his eyes, he hoped the earl would not investigate him any further. Perhaps coming here this evening had been a mistake. Perhaps enlisting Gabriella's help had been selfish. If her parents discovered the extent of their relationship with each other, they would never forgive her. Worse than that, she risked a respectable future with a respectable man—a man whom she'd been dreaming of marrying until *he'd* come along and ruined that dream.

Christ, what a mess!

Inhaling deeply, he made his decision and strode forward with purpose. Gabriella was funny, intriguing, beautiful and kind, and by God, if she didn't make him want things he'd never wanted before. He liked her more and more every day and could not imagine losing her to someone else.

So he returned to the ballroom with the intention of seeking her out. He'd have his dance, and then he'd tell her what her father had said. Perhaps together, they could find another solution.

He spotted her almost immediately, her expression serene and with a perfect Society smile adorning her lovely face like a piece of jewelry she'd put on to match the rest of her ensemble. She was standing with her parents and Fielding, listening to whatever it was he was saying with polite attentiveness. And then, as if she sensed he was watching her, she turned her head, and her face lit up, eyes sparkling as her trained smile transformed into a more natural one of pure happiness.

Unable to look away, he smiled back. Oh, how he longed to go to her, to have her in his arms again—to trace his lips along the delicate curve of her neck. He wanted to run his hands over every part of her, feel her tremble and sigh in response to his touch and . . .

Fielding, as if registering Gabriella's sudden lack of interest in him, looked his way as well. His eyes darkened with uninhibited rage. Gabriella, however, didn't seem to notice, her gaze never straying from

Raphe's, her body turning as though she meant to come to him.

Fielding's mouth twisted, and in that moment—in a split second—Raphe knew that something awful was about to happen. He wasn't sure what, but he knew that somehow, he had to prevent it. So he started forward, intent on reaching her side.

One step.

That was all he managed before Fielding reached his arm around Gabriella's shoulders, pulling her back to him and kissing her, right there in the middle of the Coventry ballroom, for everyone to see. All conversation ceased, not even a whisper could be heard. And then, finally, after what felt like a decade of inexplicable torture, Fielding stepped back and, speaking to the assembled guests, said the one thing that would ruin Raphe's chances forever. "Lady Gabriella has just agreed to be my wife. You may congratulate us both."

Chapter 20

Raphe had taken his fair share of punches before, but none had ever hit him as hard as this. Whether or not Gabriella had really accepted Fielding's offer was inconsequential. She would not be able to refute it now without scandal.

Cheers and applause swept through the ballroom as the partygoers began closing in on the newly betrothed couple. Raphe wished he could just see her face—wished he'd be able to see the truth in her eyes. Instead, his gaze found Fielding's. There was an arrogant flicker about it that caused Raphe to clench his fists, nails digging against the palms of his hands. And then the bastard winked! The crowd closed around him and Gabriella, and Raphe, cursing the day he'd met the earl, turned on his heel and strode away.

"I'll walk," he snapped at his coachman. He didn't care that it was raining—a steady downpour that soaked his greatcoat and dripped from the brim of his hat. The gray wetness suited his mood, the beat it played against the shimmering cobblestones matching the furious beat of his heart.

He shouldn't care, he told himself. *She was just a*

woman. A woman he'd known for a very short time. But the thought of having lost her was gut-wrenching, no matter how he looked at it.

Pulling his hat further down on his forehead, Raphe crossed Piccadilly, his shoes sloshing through a stream of water that flowed toward the gutter. By the time he reached his front door, he looked as though he'd just been for a swim in the Thames.

"Your Grace," Pierson said, his expression a little perplexed as Raphe handed him his soggy hat and greatcoat. "Did something happen to your carriage?"

"No," Raphe clipped. "Is the fire lit in my study?"

"Ye—yes. Yes of course."

With a nod of approval and the anticipation of having a very large glass of brandy, Raphe stepped past his butler.

"Err—Your Grace," Pierson called after him, halting him in mid stride. "You should know that there's a man waiting to see you."

Raphe spun back to face him, annoyed that he would not be allowed to wallow in peace. "At this hour?"

"I told him you'd be late in the hope that he'd return at a more decent time, but he insisted on waiting for you—said you would want to meet with him."

Expelling a breath, Raphe thanked Pierson for the information before resuming his progress. He wasn't sure who the man could possibly be—he didn't think he knew anyone who'd be rude enough to call on someone after ten o'clock at night. But when he reached his study and stepped inside, he realized that unfortunately, he did. "Guthrie," Raphe growled.

"Good to see ye," Guthrie said before setting the crystal tumbler he held to his lips and taking a long sip. He didn't bother to rise from the chair on which he slouched. But he did extend one hand and make a gesture that seemed to encompass the whole room. "Nice place ye 'ave 'ere."

"What do you want, Guthrie?" Raphe asked. Perhaps if they got straight to the point, he could get rid of him again soon.

Guthrie chuckled. "Per'aps I just wanted to stop by. See 'ow ye're doin'."

"I don't believe that for a moment," Raphe said. Picking up the carafe that stood on a tray on his desk, he poured himself a brandy, downed it and refilled the glass.

"Rough night?" Guthrie asked.

"None o' yer business," he said, falling back into the old dialect. "Now tell me what ye're doin' 'ere. I've paid off the debt plus some, so the way I see it, I don't owe ye a damn thing."

"Is that so?" Guthrie's eyes narrowed. "We 'ad an agreement, you an' I. Did ye honestly think I'd let it go fer a couple o' pennies?"

Raphe froze. His muscles went taught. "I paid ye a hell o' a lot more than that."

"Nevertheless. I ain't lettin' it go."

Raphe glared at him. "That arrangement was made so I could buy me freedom, Guthrie. I've done that now, with *interest*, if I may remind ye. So go find someone else who can fight fer ye."

Guthrie nodded, and for a long, wonderful moment, Raphe thought he'd managed the situation to his own advantage. But then Guthrie set his glass aside and smiled the smile that Raphe had seen a thousand times before. On the surface it looked pleasant enough, but Raphe knew better. He braced himself for what was to come.

"It's not just about yer freedom, laddy. It's also about winnin'. An' I can't think of anyone else who's capable of winnin' against the Bull." His smile widened. "He's the reignin' world champion. People will pay twice—nay, *thrice* as much as usual. An' if *ye* win . . ." He gave a low whistle.

"How about if I match the expected winnin's meself," Raphe suggested, "for yer trouble?"

Guthrie snorted. "Ye really want out, don't ye?" Raphe nodded. Guthrie studied him a moment, and then shrugged. "Like I said, it ain't just about the blunt. And besides, ye owe me."

Raphe's eyebrows shot up. "How do ye figure that?"

"Because," Guthrie said, "ordinarily, when a man doesn't make good on 'is word, I'd find a way to punish 'im. But—considerin' our 'istory, I'm only goin' to ask for the fight." He appeared to consider his nails. "I won't even mention the fact that ye're a duke, if that'll ease the deal fer ye."

"An' if I refuse?"

Guthrie pinned him with an unforgiving glare. "After everythin' I've done fer ye? Or 'ave ye forgotten that I was the one who provided ye an' yer sisters with food an' a place to sleep at night after ye lost yer 'ome? Ye'd be dead in the street if it weren't fer me, laddy, or worse, yer sisters would be gettin' paid to lie on their backs."

"Bastard!"

"That I ain't," Guthrie said, "but I do take care o' me own." He leaned forward in his seat. "Everythin' trickles down, ye know. St. Giles depends on me an' on the protection I offer. If the Bull wins that fight, it's a win fer Bartholomew too. 'e'll take over—toss me out, an' then where will we be?"

Raphe stared at Guthrie in shock. There was so much more at risk than he'd ever realized. "Ye're playin' with people's lives."

Guthrie shrugged. "Seemed a safe bet as long as I 'ad ye in me corner."

"Christ." Raphe slumped his shoulders, ran both hands through his hair. "There's never a guarantee. Even if I were to fight, what if I lose?"

"Ye won't."

"How can ye be so sure?"

"Because if ye do, Bartholomew takes me place." His expression hardened. "I might 'ave dabbled in gamblin', contraband an' a bit o' gin distillin' 'ere an' there, but I'd never force women an' children into sellin' themselves against their will the way 'e would."

Just the thought of it made Raphe's stomach churn with disgust. "Then why'd ye make a deal with the devil, Guthrie? Ye knew the risk."

Guthrie nodded, slowly and with a degree of sadness that conveyed more than words ever would. "All ye need to know is that ye ain't the only one with their back against the wall." Rising, he went to the door. "I'll be in touch—let ye know when an' where to show up. Once the fight's over, I'll let ye off the 'ook."

Raphe stayed where he was for a long while after Guthrie's departure, unable to move. *How the hell had everything gone so horribly wrong during just one evening?* It didn't seem possible, and yet it was.

Feeling as though his life was being torn apart before his eyes, Raphe eventually managed to get himself to bed, collapsing fully clothed on top of the mattress. But when he woke the following morning, he soon realized that Gabriella and Guthrie were by far the least of his troubles.

Chapter 21

When Gabriella rose the morning after the Coventry ball, she got dressed and made her way downstairs with one sole purpose—to tell her parents that she meant to call off the engagement. Lord help her, she'd never been so furious with another person as she was with Fielding right now. *How dare he do what he did?*

Arriving in the dining room, she didn't even bother wishing her parents and her aunt a good morning, saying instead, "I will not marry him."

A rustling of paper and a clattering of china brought everyone's attention to where she stood, cross-armed and rigid. "I beg your pardon?" her father asked.

"I said," Gabriella bit out, "that I will not marry him."

"Nonsense, dear," her mother said, waving her hand dismissively. "Of course you will."

Aunt Caroline gave Gabriella a sympathetic smile. "Perhaps she's changed her mind."

"Don't be foolish," Warwick growled. Folding up his paper, he set it aside. "Fielding is an excellent match, Gabriella. The very best match. You ought to be thrilled that he even bothered looking in your direction."

Stepping further into the room, Gabriella glared at her father. "He forced my hand, Papa, announcing an engagement that I never agreed to."

"A minor detail, since you would have done so eventually," Lady Warwick said. She took a sip of her tea. "Now, if you'll stop complaining about being the luckiest girl in London for just one second, I would like to discuss our plans for today. There are arrangements to be made now, after all. I thought we might—"

"No," Gabriella snapped. "I am not going to plan for a wedding that isn't going to take place."

A hush fell over the room, and then Warwick slowly pointed to one of the empty chairs and said, "Sit. Down."

His tone was hard—more terrifying than Gabriella had ever heard it. So although she didn't feel like complying, she did. Albeit, with great reluctance. "Marriage is forever, Papa," Gabriella tried, hoping to talk some sense into him. "Do you really want me to spend forever with the wrong man?"

The moment the words were out, she knew she'd said the wrong thing. Her father's face tightened, reddening until it looked as though it might explode, and then he quite unexpectedly slammed his fist against the table, rattling the china and making his family jump. "I am tired of dealing with spoiled women!" Warwick narrowed his gaze on Gabriella. "First your sister, and now you."

"Victoria married the man she loved," Gabriella shot back.

"And almost ruined this family's reputation in the process."

"Mr. Connolly is a successful businessman who—"

"I know precisely the sort of man he is, Gabriella,

but that doesn't make him appropriate marriage material for an earl's daughter. And it doesn't excuse your sister from breaking her engagement to Bellmore just so she could run off and do as she pleased." Shaking his head, Warwick expelled a tired breath. "If it's Huntley who's making you hesitant about marrying Fielding, then you ought to know that he isn't who you think he is. I've had him investigated."

"You've what?" Gabriella couldn't hide her shock.

"What I have discovered so far is that he has *not* been living with relatives close to the Scottish border as he says."

"I know," Gabriella said. "He's told me so himself."

That seemed to shut everyone up. But only for a second.

"When?" Her mother asked.

"At Fielding House," Gabriella blurted, thinking up an acceptable explanation as fast as she could. "When we went for dinner."

Her father looked confused. "Why lie to the rest of us then? What possible reason can he have unless the answer is something completely unacceptable? If you know the truth about him, Gabriella, then I must insist you tell me what it is for all of our sakes. We cannot—"

"He is a *duke*, Papa!" She could feel a tension growing inside her, building up and threatening her control. It was the bumblebee all over again. "Isn't that enough?"

"Not to me," Warwick told her seriously. "Are you also aware that he has ties to Carlton Guthrie?"

A chill swept down Gabriella's spine. Carlton Guthrie—an immigrant worker from Ireland whose accumulation of wealth could not be explained—was reputed to run all kinds of illegal operations, though he'd yet to be charged with any crime. She'd read about him in the *Mayfair Chronicle*, though the articles had been nothing more than speculation. Witnesses had apparently been hard to come by. People either denied knowing him, or disappeared before they could testify against him. If Raphe was involved with him somehow . . . She shook her head, unwilling to believe it.

Her father didn't wait for her to answer. "My fear is that you will end up losing your chance with Fielding over this, only to be disappointed by Huntley."

"Your father does have a point," Aunt Caroline said, speaking up for the first time. "Tell me, do you think you've fallen in love with Huntley? Is that why you're insisting on him?"

The question made Gabriella's cheeks burn. She shook her head. *No. She was not in love with him. Was she?* "I like him a great deal."

"And you've decided this after only a couple of brief encounters with the man?" her mother asked with marked disbelief.

Not daring to look at her aunt for fear that her parents would see the truth in her eyes—the fact that she'd spent more time with Huntley than her parents were aware of—Gabriella dropped her gaze to the table. "I will speak with him." She would ask him to confirm or deny her father's claim and hope that by doing so, she would discover the truth.

"You will do no such thing," her mother warned.

Gabriella's gaze snapped up, meeting her mother's. "What will you do to stop me? Lock me in my bedchamber?"

"If need be," her mother railed. "You obviously don't know how to protect yourself or this family from scandal."

"Enough," Warwick said. "Nobody is locking Gabriella away. But, I would like to think that you have enough common sense in your head to do what is right," he told her.

"Which is why I must speak to Huntley, if for no other reason than to know what my options truly are." And to explain to Huntley that Fielding had trapped her with his announcement last night. Hopefully, he'd believe her when she told him this was not at all what she wanted.

Warwick stared at her for a moment as though considering the pros and cons. Eventually, he nodded, though with great reluctance. "Very well."

"**A**re Lady Juliette and Lady Amelia at home?" Gabriella asked Pierson a couple of hours later. Standing on the front step with Anna by her side, she'd chosen a more direct path than usual.

The butler eyed her with a wariness that immediately caught her attention. "No, my lady, I'm afraid not."

"You do not understand," Gabriella insisted. "The matter I wish to discuss with them"—or their brother, rather, since it was him she was really there to see even though it would be improper of her to say so directly— "is of great . . ." Her voice faded to the sound of footsteps descending the stairs. A dark-haired man who appeared to be in his thirties, with troubled eyes and a rigid jawline, came into view. She recognized him immediately. "Dr. Florian? What are you doing here?"

He responded with a tight smile, but refused to answer her question. Instead, he addressed Pierson. "Have the cook prepare a strong chicken soup with plenty of onions and garlic in it. And chamomile tea with honey for when she's not eating. I'll be back to check on her tomorrow afternoon." He then gave Gabriella a courteous nod, accompanied by a polite greeting before hurrying past her.

Gabriella blinked. "Pierson. Will you please tell me what's going on?"

"It's best if you stay away at the moment," the butler replied. He began closing the door.

Placing her palm against it, Gabriella held it open. "Maybe I can help? Maybe—"

"Gabriella!" It was Amelia who drifted into view with a silent tread. "Please, do come in."

Pierson gave her a look that clearly indicated some breach in protocol, but Gabriella decided not to question it. Instead, she stepped inside the grand foyer of Huntley House and asked Anna to wait for her there before following Amelia through to the parlor. "Is everything all right?" she asked the moment they were alone. It was then that she noticed the tight lines on Amelia's face.

"It's Juliette," Amelia said. "She retired last night with a headache, but this morning when her maid went to tend to her, she found her flushed with fever."

"Oh no. I'm so sorry!" Seeing the anxious look in Amelia's eyes, Gabriella quietly asked, "Is there any indication of what might be causing it?"

"Florian mentioned influenza, but he says it's too soon to be certain." Amelia wrung her hands in her lap. "Of course Raphe blames himself."

"But it's not his fault," Gabriella told her adamantly.

"He allowed the outing that probably subjected us to the illness in the first place. We can think of no other time when it might have happened." She shook her head with a bleak sense of hopelessness. "We lost Bethany like this. If we lose Juliette as well, Raphe will never forgive himself."

Feeling her bones turn to ice, Gabriella asked. "Is he with her right now?"

When Amelia nodded, Gabriella told her firmly, "Then take me to her room. Let me see her." The thought of Raphe having to deal with Juliette's illness alone was distressing. It was the sort of burden that required support.

"He won't let you in," Amelia said. "He's too afraid of contagion."

"Nevertheless, I would like to try."

Choosing not to argue with her, Amelia showed Gabriella upstairs in spite of the protestations made by Pierson, Humphreys and Richardson, whom they passed along the way. "He'll have our heads, my lady," Pierson begged.

"Not if I have anything to say about it," Gabriella promised him. Hurrying after Amelia, she allowed her friend to lead her down a long hallway.

"This is her room." Amelia said when they reached the third door on the left.

Gabriella instinctively raised her hand to knock, caught herself, and lowered it again. She stared at the door, then looked at Amelia. "You should return downstairs. Let me handle your brother."

Amelia hesitated. "Are you sure?"

"He told you to stay away from Juliette's room, didn't he?"

Amelia nodded. "He doesn't want to risk my health."

"Then let's respect his wishes."

A look of uncertainty crossed Amelia's face, but then she nodded and stepped back. "Good luck," she whispered before leaving Gabriella alone in the hallway.

Facing the door, Gabriella drew a breath. Knocking would be the polite thing to do, but it would also warn Raphe of her arrival, and give him the chance to send her away before she even made it inside. She dropped her gaze to the door handle. *Would it be locked or not?* There was only one way to find out.

Placing her hand on the handle, she carefully pushed down. The door gave way, opening to a dimly lit room. Without pausing, Gabriella stepped inside and closed the door behind her.

"What the—" Before she could manage to get her bearings straight, he was there, towering over her, with murder in his eyes. "What the hell are you doing here?"

It was difficult to stay calm when faced with that much anger—except it was more than anger. Anger would be too simple a word to describe the emotion that filled Raphe's face. There was also pain and fear and the worst kind of hopelessness Gabriella had ever seen. "I came to see you," she told him simply.

His jaw tightened. "Get. Out!"

"No. I will not let you deal with this on your own." He'd done so before, had lost a sister doing so.

For a second, she saw appreciation, but it was quickly gone again. "Fielding won't like that," he spat. "And if you get sick, I'll never forgive myself."

"We'll get to Fielding later, but, the way I see it, you have been carrying too much responsibility on your shoulders for far too long. You shouldn't have to carry this too. Not on your own."

His entire body seemed to strain beneath that statement. "I have to save her." His voice broke and he averted his gaze. A dark strand of hair fell haphazardly across his brow.

Reaching up, Gabriella placed her hand carefully on his arm. "I know," she whispered. "Please let me help you."

Silently, he turned away from her and walked across to the four-poster bed where his sister was lying, propped up against thick pillows. "The doctor says it's probably influenza," Huntley said as he carefully touched his fingers to Juliette's cheek.

Following him over to the bed, Gabriella looked at the sleeping face of the young woman she'd come to know. She appeared so frail and delicate. No wonder Raphe was worried. Gabriella was too, seeing her like this, her breath rasping past her lips with each inhalation she took. Steeling herself for Raphe's sake, Gabriella asked, "Shall we see if her compress needs changing?" With a fever, it would probably have to be done often.

Nodding solemnly, he carefully gathered the piece of linen from Juliette's forehead. "It's warm." He moved toward the washbasin and proceeded to soak it with cool water. "I just changed it before you arrived."

"I'll prepare another," Gabriella said. She was determined not to let Juliette's dangerously high fever deter her from her task. The last thing Raphe needed was for her to show signs of distress. She must be strong and practical now. "That way we'll be able to switch them without leaving her without one."

Raphe didn't respond, which Gabriella took to be a sign of approval. So when he went back to Juliette, she began preparing another compress. They exchanged the two until a maid arrived with the chicken soup the doctor had ordered, and then for a long while after, until a knock eventually sounded at the door.

Muttering an oath that Gabriella had never heard before, Raphe went to the door and opened it just enough to speak with whoever happened to be on the other side. "I thought I asked not to be disturbed." His voice was cool and tight with restrained anger. "What is it?"

"There's a message from the Earl and Countess of Warwick." Gabriella recognized Pierson's voice. "They demand to know what you have done with their daughter."

Although she could not see Raphe's expression, Gabriella knew from his sudden change in posture that he was about to explode. She stepped hastily forward and nudged him aside so she could speak to Pierson directly. "Bring me some writing equipment and I shall prepare a note for them." She should have done so earlier when she'd decided to stay, she reflected, but the urgency of Juliette's illness had made Gabriella forget about everything else.

"Perhaps you ought to return home," Raphe said once Pierson had gone to do her bidding.

"I will not leave you," Gabriella told him stubbornly. Glancing toward Juliette, she shook her head with increased determination. "Not like this." It didn't matter that her actions were just about as inappropriate as they could possibly be for a young unmarried woman who'd just gotten engaged to someone other than the man whose company she was choosing to keep. She could not bring herself to abandon Juliette or her brother, for any reason. Not until she was absolutely certain that they would both be well. If incurring her parents' wrath would be the price she'd have to pay, then so be it.

Which was precisely what she wrote in her missive to her parents after Pierson returned with paper and quill a short while later. Handing the letter over to him, she closed the door once more. A dry cough resonated through the room, drawing Gabriella's attention. Turning, she saw that Juliette's eyes had opened, and that Raphe was standing over her.

"How are you feeling?" he asked as he gently placed his hand against Juliette's cheek.

"Like I'm—" Juliette coughed again, the effort shaking her slim body with a violent tremor. "Like I'm burnin' up."

"Do you think you might be able to eat something?" Gabriella asked, moving closer.

Another cough wracked Juliette, and then another, and another. "Maybe later," she eventually managed. Her eyes fluttered as if she was struggling to keep them open. "Thirsty—"

Grabbing the pitcher that stood on the bedside table, Gabriella poured a glass of water and held it to Juliette's lips. "She needs handkerchiefs," she told Raphe. "Her nose is runny."

He was back with a stack of handkerchiefs before Juliette had finished drinking. Unfolding one, he handed it to his sister and helped her sit. "Thank you," Juliette told them both a short while later. Her smile trembled and her eyes were red.

"Please try to eat something," Gabriella urged. Picking up the bowl of soup, she perched herself on the edge of the bed and dipped the spoon into the broth. "You need the nourishment."

Coughing between each spoonful, Juliette managed to eat a third of the soup before eventually slumping back against the pillows. She looked exhausted. "Perhaps you should try and sleep some more," Gabriella suggested. Without thinking, she reached down to brush Juliette's hair away from the side of her face, and stilled.

"What is it?" Raphe asked from the opposite side of the bed.

Gabriella stared down at Juliette's face where blotches of pink were beginning to spread. "I don't think this is influenza," she said. Setting the soup aside, she spoke with greater insistence. "Help me. Hold her upright so I can get a better look."

"I don't—"

"Stop arguing, would you?" The note of authority with which she spoke seemed to do the trick. Raphe didn't question her any further. Instead he brought Juliette into a sitting position, holding her steady while Gabriella pulled at her chemise. She brought it up until Juliette's back had been completely exposed. Raphe gasped.

"What is it?" Juliette asked, her voice weak with sickness.

"This looks like measles to me," Gabriella said. "Which means I can't get sick from it. What about you?"

"I had measles when I was a lad," Raphe replied. "Same time Amelia had it. Before Juliette was born."

Nodding in understanding, Gabriella lowered Juliette's chemise back down so Raphe could help her get settled. A moment later, she was fast asleep once more. "This is my fault," he said. "I should have taken better care of her—protected her more."

"And deny her any freedom?" Gabriella quietly asked. She felt for him, but she was also fairly certain that his solution would make his sister miserable. "People get sick, Raphe, and then they get better. She will get through this."

His face twisted with too much misery for Gabriella to bear. Rising from the bed, she went to where he was standing. Uncertain of what to do but knowing she had to do *something*, she came to a halt before him. Tentatively, she extended her hand toward his, her fingers carefully requesting permission. Their eyes met, and Gabriella's breath caught, freezing her in place. There was so much agony to be found there, but there was also a desperate plea for comfort that very nearly broke her heart. Nobody should have to feel as alone as he did at that moment.

So rather than take his hand in hers as she'd initially intended, she flung her arms around his neck and pulled him to her in a tight embrace. It was unplanned— completely inappropriate by most standards—but it also felt right. A moment of startled silence followed, and then he hugged her back, his arms tight about her waist while his head pressed against the curve of her neck.

He was just as solid as she remembered—a perfect fit for her softer curves. And the way he smelled . . . there was something so familiar, so heartwarmingly welcoming that she already mourned the moment when she'd have to step back and let him go.

It came sooner than she'd wanted, but this was a sickroom. Juliette needed their attention. She should not be thinking of being held by the Duke of Huntley, or of how wonderful it had felt. Her treacherous mind would not let her forget it, though. Nor would it deny her the thought of what it had been like to feel his lips upon hers. Oh, how she longed to be kissed by him again.

She moved to turn away, to add some distance, but he caught her by the wrist and held her fast. "Thank you," he murmured. His hand loosened, and his fingers trailed a slow path up and down her arm. Gabriella shivered, but not from cold. Her chest rose and fell with unsteady movements. And then she felt his fingers against her cheek—a tender caress that made heat fan out across her skin, while her heart made a funny little leap and her tummy seemed to fold itself into a fizzing mess of nerves.

He dropped his hand and took a step back, breaking the moment. Gabriella flinched, then hurried over to Juliette to check on the compress. Anything to keep her jumbled mind from turning her into a stuttering fool.

They didn't speak anymore. Not until much later, when Juliette had woken again, eaten some soup and fallen back to sleep. "I should probably return home," Gabriella said as she checked the time. It was past supper now, and staying overnight would really be pushing the boundaries of propriety. "And you should get some rest, Raphe. Now that we know what it is, Amelia can help watch her for a while."

He looked dubious. "I don't want to leave her. What if—"

"You look exhausted, and you won't be any good to her if you're asleep when she wakes."

Conceding her point, he gave a reluctant nod. "Very well. I'll ring for someone to fetch Amelia."

Gabriella stayed until Amelia arrived so she could help explain the situation. She then bid them all a good night and prepared to leave.

"Wait a moment," Raphe said. He muttered something to Amelia that Gabriella couldn't hear before joining her at the door. "Have a drink with me first."

The request caught her completely unawares. Her mouth dropped open. She wanted to but knew she shouldn't. "I . . . I don't—"

"Please."

The honest plea in his eyes achieved what words could not. Gabriella nodded. "Very well, but then I really must be on my way."

"Agreed."

He led the way back downstairs where Gabriella found Anna still waiting for her in the hall. "My lady," she said, rising to greet her. "Is Lady Juliette all right?"

"She will be," Gabriella said, appreciating her concern. "We can return home shortly, Anna. The duke just wishes to have a quick word with me before I leave."

"Should I wait for you here then, or—"

Gabriella silently thanked Anna for allowing her to make her own decision. "Yes," she said, aware of how scandalous it would be for her to be completely alone with Raphe—of what being alone with him would imply. But she'd been alone with him before, and longed to be so again. "I won't be long."

And then she turned away, following Raphe through to the parlor, not saying a word as he shut the door firmly behind them.

Chapter 22

A thrill of something forbidden darted its way along her nerves, producing a light tremor at the base of her neck as he strode past her, brushing her gently with the edge of his jacket. "Brandy?" he inquired, reaching for a decanter.

"I've never tried it," she confessed as she lowered herself to the sofa.

He returned with two glasses and handed her one before claiming the vacant spot beside her. She took a sip, winced, then tried it again. Raphe gave her a lopsided grin before taking a sip of his own. "It's pretty strong stuff, but it'll do wonders in any number of situations."

Gabriella set the glass aside. "I like the warming effect, but the taste will take some getting used to."

A comfortable silence settled between them for a while, during which Gabriella became increasingly aware of how close he was to her. He could have taken one of the chairs, but he hadn't. Instead, his large frame occupied most of the sofa, allowing for only a symbolic amount of space to fall between them. If he moved an inch, his thigh would come into contact with hers. Unless she moved, scooting further back against the armrest.

But she did not. *Would* not. Not when she craved the closeness.

"Why did you come here today?" he quietly asked, breaking through the myriad of indecent thoughts she was now having, specifically of the ways in which he might ruin her right here, right now, on this very sofa.

Unbalanced by the question, she picked up her glass and took another sip of brandy, which gave her a couple of extra seconds to ponder her response. She could take the cowardly route and say that she'd come to discuss Amelia and Juliette's presentations at court—the work that still remained to be done. Or she could be brave and tell him the truth. "I didn't want you to think that I agreed to marry Fielding. Especially not after you made your own intentions toward me clear and I promised to help find a way for us to be together."

"So he forced your hand?"

She nodded. "He did."

"I thought so."

"You should know that he came to see me yesterday though. Before the ball." His eyes hardened and she glanced away.

"Why are you telling me this?" he asked, when she failed to continue.

Her eyes flew to his. "Because I don't want to keep anything from you."

"Then tell me what happened, Gabriella."

She drew a deep breath. "He proposed and I declined. But he refused to listen, and then . . ." she swallowed, forcing herself to get the words out. "He kissed me."

Raphe's jaw tightened. His shoulders seemed to strain as if holding back some invisible force. Bracing his elbows against his knees, he stared into the glass he held between his hands. "Will you marry him then?"

How could he possible think so? "Not if I can help it. I already told my parents that I intend to call off the engagement. They were hardly thrilled."

Straightening, he set his glass aside and turned in the seat so he faced her. "And with good reason, I suspect. Whatever his shortcomings may be in my eyes, Fielding is a good match for a lady like you. He's a *respectable* match."

Stunned by his words, she carefully asked, "What are you saying?" She shook her head. "I thought—"

"And you thought correctly, but the fact of the matter is that however attracted I may be to you and—vice versa—you and I are an ill-suited pair."

His gaze met hers with a smoldering heat that brought her close to melting. "You don't believe that. Not unless—" She had to focus. She had to discover the truth. "Papa told me this morning that he's discovered a connection between you and Carlton Guthrie." Hating herself for not having enough faith to dismiss her father's words completely, she asked, "Is it true?"

Reaching out, he removed her glass from between her hands and placed it next to his own. He then took her hand in his, encasing her with a warmth that swiftly stole up her arm and fanned out across her chest. Gabriella's pulse quickened. "Partly," he said, his unapologetic gaze holding hers. "Guthrie was one of my father's creditors. He took me and my sisters in when we were left with nothing and had no one else to turn to."

"So, you're saying that everyone's wrong about him? That he's a kind man?" It seemed unfathomable.

"No." He shook his head sadly. "He considers

himself a businessman of sorts, and he wasn't willing to forgive Papa's debt when I was there to repay it on his behalf."

"But you were just a boy," Gabriella said. The thought that some horrid man had taken advantage of him after everything else he'd been through was insupportable. She edged closer to him, needing to offer what comfort she could.

Huntley scoffed. "Such men don't care about age. Guthrie just wanted his blunt, and he saw an opportunity to get it. When I was old enough, I began fighting for him, paying back everything my father had owed along with whatever Guthrie had spent on me and my sisters."

"Fighting?" She couldn't help herself from recalling the way he'd looked when she'd spied him in the courtyard, bare chested with rippling muscles and a sheen of masculine sweat upon his brow. A blush crept over her, and she instinctively dropped her gaze, fearful of what he might see in her eyes.

"Boxing," he amended. His tone was a little rougher than before. "I'm a bare-knuckle boxer, Gabriella. Or at least I was before I became a duke. During the day, I worked at the docks as a common laborer and in the evening, I fought the men Guthrie told me to fight. Not exactly marriage material for a well-bred Society lady such as yourself. Especially not now that you know who I was boxing for."

"And yet . . ." *And yet I can think of no one else I'd rather be with, no one who makes me feel the way you do.*

"I would hate to ruin your chances for the sort of life you've always dreamed of," he said, pulling his hand away and letting her go. "You deserve better than anything I can possibly offer."

"So you think Fielding would be *better*?" she asked, feeling more alone than she'd ever felt before. And with that feeling, came anger—unbridled and real. "I have lived my entire life knowing that my choices would be limited by my parents' demands, that I was unlikely to have a passionate marriage or even a tolerable one for that matter. But then I met you and I discovered that I didn't know anything at all. I didn't have any idea of who I really was, or of what I really wanted until the moment you walked into my life. And then I knew, without doubt, that the very last thing I wanted to do was to tie myself to a man like Fielding. You've reminded me of who I am, Raphe. You've made me feel alive again, and the truth of the matter is, that even if Society decides to shun me for it, the only man I want to be with is you. So if you feel the same way about me—and I hope you do, or I'll never get over the embarrassment of this conversation—then—"

She didn't manage another word as his mouth crashed over hers, claiming her with more possessiveness than she'd ever thought possible. This was not the gentle exploration they'd shared in the garden days earlier. This was hungry . . . demanding . . . utterly delicious. This was a need to break boundaries, to explore the irresistible yearning they shared for each other . . . to uncover its meaning. So she held nothing back, clutching him to her just as desperately as he clutched her—as if they'd been drifting through time, two souls with one shared destination: here and now.

"Raphe," she had to speak his name, even if it was just a bare whisper of air.

He rewarded her with a low, guttural growl, his fingers digging against her back as if he hoped to somehow burrow his way inside her. His lips parted over hers, their breaths mingling in a hot burst of desire that filled Gabriella with restless need. She wanted him to touch her. *Everywhere*. In the most intimate way possible. *Did that make her wanton?* She didn't know and she didn't care, could barely think when he was doing such wonderful, mind-numbing things with his mouth.

But then he drew back, breaths coming just as fast and irregularly as hers. "My God." He lowered his head again, this time to the curve of her neck, and it was all Gabriella could do to keep herself from whimpering in response to the hot embers he placed there. So she held on tight, her fingers tunneling through his hair and over his shoulders, touching him just as he touched her, with a need for increased closeness . . . to know him as well as she knew herself.

"You cannot imagine how much I want you, Gabriella," he murmured against the flushed surface of her chest. Another kiss, more tentative than the last, sent a fiery longing spiraling through her. *Oh yes.* "I'll never get enough of you."

"Nor I of you," she said, her fingers creeping beneath his waistcoat to tug at his shirt.

He caught her wrist, stopping her progress, and inhaled sharply. "We should stop." He blinked, focused his gaze more intently on hers. "We *must* stop."

"But . . ." The memory of his naked chest danced before her eyes, and her fingers itched for permission to touch it.

"There's something else I must tell you first."

The seriousness with which he spoke gave her pause. Her hands stilled. "What is it?"

He hesitated for a moment, then rose to his feet and started pacing about the room. "Guthrie came to see me last night." Halting by the fireplace, he stared into its gaping emptiness. "He reminded me of a deal that he and I made before I became a duke."

Straightening herself, she watched him with increasing unease. "What sort of a deal?"

Turning, he eyed her carefully for a moment before saying, "I am to fight for the world championship."

She sank back against the sofa. "A public boxing match?" He gave a curt nod, to which she said, "I don't suppose there's any hope of it being the respectable kind that a gentleman of your rank might engage in without inviting scandal?"

"It will probably be in a field somewhere with enough space to accommodate a large crowd."

A gasp of air escaped her. "Your reputation will suffer."

"As will yours. Unless we break off our acquaintance."

A knot began to form in her throat. "What about your sisters? Their presentations are next week."

"And you can still assist them with that, provided Juliette is well enough by then. But as far as you and I are concerned, I think you need to consider what it would mean for you if anyone were to find out that you broke off your engagement with Fielding in order to allow the attentions of a man like me."

"I would be proud to be associated with you. Don't you know that?"

Stilling, he looked at her as though he longed to encourage her to be reckless, but didn't have the scruples to allow it. "But it's not just your reputation at risk, Gabriella. It's your entire family's. Are you really willing to drag them all down with you? Now that you know how likely I am to do that?"

Feeling her eyes begin to burn, she got to her feet and faced him. "Then we'll just have to fight this.

You're a duke, Raphe, a powerful peer with a trust-worthy secretary and capable solicitors at your command. Surely, there has to be a way to stop Guthrie from holding you to a deal you made under very different circumstances from which you presently face. You could—"

"No. I will not back away from this."

"But—"

"If I renege, the people of St. Giles could face a terrible fate. I can't have that on my conscience. And besides, I have always prided myself on being honorable. Guthrie is right. We have a deal, and I intend to make good on that deal."

"What about your sisters?" she asked again, her voice trembling with the desperate need to make him see reason. "They'll be ruined by association. People will surely discover that you are one of the opponents, even if you try to prevent them from doing so. Gossip will follow, and Amelia and Juliette will lose the good chance they have to make suitable matches for themselves."

For a second, she thought she might have reached him, but then he shook his head. "My sisters' well-being has always been my first priority, but I will not ignore my moral compass, not even for them."

"Then there really is no hope for us. Is there?" Because once word got out about the fight, it would probably just be a matter of time before everyone discovered that the Duke of Huntley had not only risen from the slums of London to the elegance of Mayfair, but that he was also involved with Carlton Guthrie. Questions would be asked and rumors would spread before dawn the next day. Raphe's character would be called into question to such a degree that he and everyone associated with him would become social outcasts. "I don't know," he said. His hand found her cheek, his calloused fingers scraping against her soft skin until heat began to bloom there.

Stepping forward, she touched her lips to his, kissing him with the fear of finality, with the need to imprint the feeling of him on her mind. She knew he would do what he could to find a way for them to be together, but she didn't know how—could not see a clear way forward. There were simply too many obstacles in their path, and since his title wouldn't even be enough to persuade her father to let her marry him, Gabriella wasn't sure what would. If anything even could.

"You told your maid that you would just be a moment," Raphe told her gruffly, drawing her attention back to the present. "It is late. Your parents will be expecting you and I would like to return to Juliette's bedside."

All excellent reasons to stop what they were doing and part ways, however much Gabriella regretted having to do so. "I will call on you tomorrow, to see how Juliette is doing."

He nodded in response. "Please do." And then, in a whisper that brushed the edge of her ear to produce a soft shiver, "I'll look forward to it with great anticipation."

Chapter 23

"**A** letter, from the Duke of Coventry, has just arrived," Richardson said as he strode into Raphe's study a week later. Juliette had made a full recovery from her bout with measles, and was now busily preparing herself for her presentation at court, which was set to take place in just a couple of hours.

Accepting the missive that Richardson handed him, Raphe tore open the seal and read quickly. "He's inviting me to join him at his club this evening."

"Excellent," Richardson said as he lowered himself to a vacant chair. "It's about time you make friends with other high-ranking members of Society."

"As amiable as the duke seems, I'm sure there's another reason for why he wants to meet."

"Must you be so cynical?"

"Considering the fine reception I received when I first arrived, I find cynicism difficult to avoid."

Richardson's face remained blank. "Point taken," he said as he reached for one of the ledgers. "Shall we discuss the repairs required at your estate in Gloucester?"

"Absolutely."

Discussing *her* was out of the question. Richardson, Humphreys and Pierson all knew this. She'd visited Juliette and Amelia every day as promised, even though her visits had resulted in a few angry letters from her father. Apparently, Lord Warwick was under the impression that Raphe had more authority over his daughter than he did. A touching thought since the truth of the matter was that Gabriella was proving to be the most stubborn woman that Raphe had ever encountered in his life. She simply refused to listen to reason, so unless Warwick meant to lock her in her room, Raphe wasn't sure of what to do with her.

Not entirely true.

He knew what to do with her, he just knew better than to act on those baser urges. Which only denied him the kisses he longed for, leading to restless nights that were, more often than not, haunted by dreams of her skin against his in an intimate tangle of limbs that left him aching for more.

Pushing her from his mind as best as he could, he focused on what Richardson was saying about drafty windows and rotted fencing. "There's also a need for a new caretaker. Mr. Elliot is getting on in years—the work required of him is too taxing."

"Perhaps we can find a way to reward him for his years of service," Raphe suggested. "Ensure that he's able to enjoy his dotage."

Richardson agreed, and a little over an hour later, they'd decided how much money to allocate toward the repairs and drawn up a plan to help Mr. Elliot afford a comfortable retirement. They had also agreed that Raphe would soon have to visit his other estates so he could become properly acquainted with them. "Getting out of the city will be a welcome change," he told Richardson. "Will you join me?"

"If you wish it," Richardson replied.

"I think I'd enjoy the company." A knock sounded at the door. "Enter!"

Amelia peeked inside. "Lady Gabriella has arrived. We are almost ready to depart."

Rising, Raphe followed his sister out into the hallway, where Gabriella was busily admiring Juliette's gown. Hearing him approach, she turned to face him, a pretty blush rising to her cheeks the moment their eyes met. Raphe's chest tightened. "My lady. It is a pleasure to see you again."

A timid smile captured her lips, and he was instantly reminded of what it had felt like to kiss her there. Lord, what he wouldn't give to kiss her there again. But he mustn't. Not if he cared for her. Not until he knew beyond any shadow of a doubt that they stood a real chance of being together. So he schooled his features and refrained from showing any sign of emotion.

"Likewise," she said, her smile slipping in response to his cool detachment. She gave her attention to Amelia and Juliette. "Your sisters look lovely. I have every confidence that they will make a fine impression today."

"I don't understand the need for such—voluminous gowns," Raphe muttered as he regarded the wide-hooped skirts that seemed more of an impairment than a benefit of any kind.

"It is the queen's preference," Gabriella replied. "It is what is worn at court."

A silly fancy so typical of the elite in its utter lack of practicality. But Raphe couldn't deny that his sisters did look rather fetching. "Good luck to you both," he said. "I'll expect a full report upon your return."

They left without further ado, piling into the carriage while Gabriella and one of the footmen helped arrange their massive skirts. Raphe watched from the doorway. "Do you suppose they will be all right?" he asked Richardson, who stood by his side.

"Of course. Lady Gabriella is with them. She will make sure that everything turns out well for them." They waved as the carriage pulled away, and then went back inside the house. "May I say something, Your Grace? As your friend?"

"Only if you cease with all the 'Your Grace' business and start calling me Raphe or Huntley."

Richardson grinned. "Very well then, Huntley." They strolled toward the back of the house. "I think Lady Gabriella would make a fine match for you."

Raphe almost tripped as his foot came down a touch too quickly behind the other. "She deserves better."

"I see. And you think Fielding would be better? Because, let's face it, that is who she will marry unless you decide to offer her another option."

They arrived at the French doors overlooking the terrace. "If she and I were to become attached, she would suffer social suicide. My reputation is questionable enough already. Just think of what will happen once I fight the Bull. And Warwick knows that I lied about where I was living before moving into this house. It will only be a matter of time before someone finds out that the Duke of Huntley is nothing more than a fraud—possibly a criminal—and completely unworthy of the title and of Lady Gabriella's hand."

"I think you are treating yourself unfairly. You are an honorable man, Huntley. It isn't your fault that you ended up indebted to Guthrie. Considering all that you have done for your sisters, the sacrifices you have made on their behalf . . ."

"Circumstance demanded it of me. Anyone else would have done the same."

Richardson laughed. "If you truly believe that, then you're not very familiar with human nature, or how the world works."

"It doesn't matter. I still won't be able to win the *ton's* approval, and without that, Lady Gabriella will remain as unattainable as a star in the night sky."

"Does she share your opinion?"

"What?"

Facing Raphe, Richardson eyed him sharply. "From what I gather, Lady Gabriella has few friends among the aristocracy. Her sister and closest confidant left England to marry an American entrepreneur. She isn't close with either of her parents, though she will do her duty if that is all that is left for her to do, simply because that is what she has been *taught* to do. But, if you ask me, I think she'll be horribly unhappy with such an outcome—more unhappy than she would be with you, scandal or no."

"You don't know that for certain," Raphe muttered. "And you weren't there when I told her of my decision to honor my agreement with Guthrie. She pleaded with me to find a way out of it."

Richardson shook his head. "Your stubbornness in this—and I don't just mean yours, but hers as well—will see you living unhappy lives, apart from each other." He sighed heavily before turning more fully toward Raphe. "Look, nobody can know anything for certain, but I will wager that if you don't fight for her, you will regret it for the rest of your life."

"You may very well be right. I just don't see how I'll ever convince her father to agree, and without his approval, we stand no chance at all. I will not ask her to elope with me."

"No. That would be a terrible idea. But I've seen the way you look at each other. There's real emotion there. Perhaps, if you let yourself explore your feelings for her a bit more, you'll find the answer you seek."

"**H**ow did it go?" Raphe asked as he and Richardson rose from their chess game to greet the women a couple of hours later.

"It was easier than expected," Amelia said, "though I did almost knock down a vase with my skirt."

With a grimace, Raphe hid the smile that threatened. "The queen didn't notice?"

"I caught it just in time," Gabriella said. "No damage done."

"So you are now officially out," Richardson said, directing a courteous bow at Amelia and Juliette. "Congratulations."

"Thank you." They spoke in unison before displaying the perfect curtsies they'd been practicing for so long.

"We couldn't have done this without you," Raphe told Gabriella. "Your assistance has truly been invaluable."

"Think nothing of it."

The lightness with which she spoke held a dismissive tone that seemed to add distance between them. Raphe felt his heart begin to ache. "Will you stay for a celebratory glass of champagne?" he asked.

"I should probably return home," she said. She turned toward Juliette and Amelia. "Please let me know when you receive your first invitations. I would love to help you prepare for your debut."

No mention of seeing him again then, Raphe

mused. He knew he shouldn't envy his sisters, but he just couldn't help it. Feeling irritable, he offered to escort Gabriella to the front door—a gesture she could not refuse without being rude, and one that he therefore decided to take advantage of. "My dancing is progressing," he said as he guided her along the corridor that led to the entryway. "Perhaps you'll do me the honor of adding me to your dance card at the next ball?"

"I think doing so would be unwise." She didn't look at him, which only made Raphe's heart hurt so much more.

"Why?"

"You know why, Your Grace." She was silent for a moment before saying stiffly, "Marrying Fielding will be difficult enough after what happened between us, so unless you can guarantee a shared future for you and me, then there cannot possibly be anything more. It would simply kill me."

Resisting the urge to pull her closer, to dip his head and kiss her, Raphe led her to the front door where Pierson stood waiting, and released her arm. "If there's a way, then I will find it," he told her.

A flicker of hope shimmered in her eyes, fading as quickly as it had formed. "Good day, Your Grace." A politely trained smile was all she gave him before turning away and exiting his house.

Returning home, Gabriella paused in the hallway before turning to Simmons. "Is my aunt at home?"

"Yes, my lady. I believe she is on the terrace."

Thanking him, Gabriella went in search of her and found her sitting in a folding chair with a canvas in her lap, her hair concealed by a lime green silk turban. A low table stood at her side with paints and brushes spread out upon it. Registering Gabriella's approach, Aunt Caroline looked up from her painting, a slim brush elegantly poised between her fingers. "I was trying to capture a swallow earlier, but the dratted bird refused to stay still and finally flew away before I could finish it. So I've decided to punish him by covering him up with hydrangeas." She returned her attention to her artwork.

"May I join you for a bit?" Gabriella asked as she came to stand beside her. Looking down, she studied the painting in progress.

"That depends on what you think about my masterpiece."

Gabriella's mouth twitched. "Well, I—opinions are rather subjective, don't you think?"

Her aunt laughed. "How diplomatic of you. Don't worry, I know how blotchy it looks."

"Oh. I was going to say innovative."

Aunt Caroline looked up once more. Her eyes were dancing. "I like that, Gabriella. Thank you." She waved toward another chair that stood a few paces away. "Why don't you have a seat? There's clearly something you wish to discuss."

"Is there?"

Her aunt's expression turned skeptical. "Would you have sought me out otherwise?"

"Perhaps I just want company."

Shaking her head, Aunt Caroline dipped her paintbrush into a blob of purple paint and began applying the color to a blotch that was meant to depict a flower. "This will be so much easier if you tell me what's troubling you."

Unnerved by her aunt's uncanny ability to see inside her head, Gabriella fetched the vacant chair and sat down next to her. "It's Huntley," she said after a lengthy stretch of time. "I've been thinking about what you said about marrying for the right reasons—for love, that is."

"And?" Setting her paintbrush aside, Aunt Caroline turned her head toward Gabriella. "Do you love him?"

"I—" She considered the man she'd gotten to know in recent weeks. *Raphe.* He was everything a man should be: protective of those he cared about, willing to make the necessary sacrifices on their behalf, kind but unwavering in his principles. Considerate. Thoughtful. Honest.

Yes, he'd initially lied to her about where he'd grown up, but he hadn't owed her the truth back then. As soon as that had changed, he'd volunteered everything, holding nothing back about who he really was. More than that, he'd shown a real interest in her. With his support, she now felt more comfortable with who she was than she ever had before.

She stared at her aunt. "I—" *Dear God.* She loved him. Quite desperately, really. *How could she not have realized this sooner?* It was as if she'd been walking around with blinders on, and now they had finally been removed, allowing her to see.

"You?" her aunt prompted with a curious twinkle in her eyes.

"Yes. I do. I love Huntley, Aunt Caroline. I love him so very much I think my heart might explode with it." A grin slipped past her lips. "Oh dear. What do I do? I think I should probably tell him, don't you? But then of course I run the risk of him not reciprocating my feelings and then—Oh dear, oh dear, oh dear. I think I might be sick."

Aunt Caroline placed one hand over Gabriella's.

"Calm yourself, my dear. Take a deep breath." When Gabriella did so, her aunt met her gaze with a kind smile. "Yes, I think you should tell him, and then I think you should do whatever it takes to get yourself disengaged from Fielding so you and Huntley can be happy together. You deserve happiness, Gabriella."

"Mama and Papa will be furious."

"Yes. They will be, which leaves you with a choice. You can either run from conflict and live a passive life, married to Fielding, or you can fight for more."

"They'll never forgive me."

"They will eventually, Gabriella, I'm sure of it, but even if they don't . . ." Her aunt drew a breath and raised her gaze to the sky. "They would kill me if they heard me encouraging you like this, but the time has come for you to think of your future. Who do you want to live your life for, Gabriella? Your parents, or yourself?"

The question had only one answer. "Myself."

"So then?"

"I want to marry Huntley more than anything else in the world." Saying the words out loud felt empowering. It filled her with immense satisfaction, a feeling that followed Gabriella upstairs as she went to find some paper and a quill. She would send Raphe a note and ask him to meet her that evening in the garden. And then she would tell him. She would open her heart and reveal the depth of her feelings for him.

A smile played upon her lips as she entered her bedroom, where Eleanor had been laboring over an intricate web inside her glass case. She would set her free again soon she decided as she carefully lifted the lid and dropped a couple of flies inside. No insect ever stayed with her too long—just enough for her to study their behavior and make a few sketches. Crossing to the windowsill, she tore a few leaves from a potted mint she'd recently acquired and dropped the greenery into the box where the beetle Raphe had given her now lived.

Satisfied that the creature was well taken care of, she took a seat at her desk, pulled out a clean sheet of paper and was just about to set the tip of her quill to it when there was a soft knock at the door. Anna entered upon her command. "This just arrived for you, my lady. I think it might be from your sister. It looks like her penmanship."

Taking the letter, Gabriella tore open the seal and read with haste, her eyes flying across the words. And as she absorbed the message, her heart plummeted, crumpling like the piece of paper she held, scrunched in the palm of her hand.

Chapter 24

"**I** must confess that I was surprised to hear from you, more so to receive an invitation to this fine establishment," Raphe told Coventry when he met him at White's that evening. He was of a similar height to Raphe, with sand-colored hair and a welcoming expression, though perhaps a few years older.

"You haven't been here before?" A waiter arrived to take their orders, returning shortly after with two glasses of brandy.

"I don't get out much due to my unpopularity."

Sipping his drink, Coventry leaned back against the leather armchair he occupied, crossed his legs, and studied Raphe with a sly smile. "You're different from the norm, I'll give you that. Unlike most aristocrats, I find that intriguing, rather than horrifying."

Raphe raised a questioning eyebrow. "I don't belong to any clubs, scholastic or otherwise."

"I know. It makes your story—this sudden acquisition of a duke's title and wealth—even more fascinating." He must have seen Raphe clench his muscles, for he immediately waved his hand dismissively and added, "I don't judge. In fact, I'm sure you're more deserving of it than anyone else."

"You have me at a loss." He couldn't possibly be serious.

Coventry carelessly shrugged his shoulders. "The fact that you've put Society on edge is telling. I quite admire it, in fact—especially since I'm of the opinion that it could do with a bit of a shake." He flicked a piece of invisible lint from his trousers. "I'm sorry I wasn't able to speak with you at greater length the other evening during the ball, but my attention was in high demand and—well, here we are."

"I'm still not sure of why you invited me to join you," Raphe said. *There had to be an angle.* "Surely, a man like you doesn't lack company."

"True. But it's the quality of the company that's important." He sounded bored. "The men and women of my acquaintance are mostly the same—paper cutouts who shop at the same shops, exchange the same gossip, and think the same thoughts. They're completely unoriginal."

"So—" Raphe took a second to ponder this new piece of information. "You seek a change of pace, and you hope that I might provide that?"

"Partly." He tilted his head. "For starters, I'd like to know more about where you grew up, because rumor has it that it wasn't where you claim it was."

Raphe stilled, his eyes pinned on Coventry's. "How do I know I can trust you?"

"Because if you do, I'll help you end the engagement between Lady Gabriella and Fielding." With a grin, he tossed back the rest of his drink and refilled his glass. "I hear you've some interest there."

"You certainly hear a lot," Raphe murmured.

The duke shrugged. "Word gets around."

"What I don't understand is how cordial you were with Fielding when you were last at his house for dinner. I mean, if you dislike him so much that you wish to ruin his engagement . . . it just seems a bit odd."

"Perhaps, but then again one does have a greater advantage over one's enemies when they remain unaware of one's true feelings. I plan to catch Fielding by surprise, you see, but I also intend to take something from him—something he values." He gave a crooked smile. "Your desire to win Lady Gabriella for yourself is something of an opportunity."

Still hesitant, but increasingly intrigued, Raphe leaned forward and set his half-empty glass on the table. "I'm not a simpleton, Coventry. Don't think you can take advantage of me."

"I wouldn't dream of it." He studied Raphe for a moment. "Why don't you start by telling me a bit more about yourself. You said you've never received formal schooling, but you didn't claim to lack an education."

"I'm self-taught," Raphe explained before listing the subjects of his interest and telling Coventry how he'd traded old books for new ones in order to learn as much as possible.

"That's very determined of you. I must say I'm quite impressed."

"Thank you," Raphe muttered. "Nobody else seems to be." Which wasn't entirely true, he reflected, considering Gabriella.

"They're idiots," Coventry said. "Or rather, their way of thinking is idiotic. You might find this hard to believe, but I would welcome the opportunity to remove myself from the pack and try something different—expand my horizons, so to speak."

"Without inviting scandal, I'd imagine," Raphe

said, still unsure of what to make of the odd contradiction of the man who sat before him.

"I have my reputation to uphold." Coventry stated simply. "There's a limit to what I can allow myself to do."

"Perhaps you should try boxing," Raphe suggested. "It can be wonderfully rewarding to fight an opponent—your strength against his—the harnessing and releasing of energy."

"You speak as though from experience." Coventry hesitated a moment, his eyes lingering on Raphe's before asking, "Have you heard of Gentleman Jackson's Boxing Academy, over on Bond Street? I know a few men who go there for sport, but I've always had the impression that it's mostly for show—that they're all too polite to actually hit each other properly. So I never bothered with it myself."

Raphe took a sip of his drink and considered the idea that sprang to mind. He'd liked Coventry from the moment he'd met him. He hadn't sneered or judged. Instead, he offered friendship. Raphe knew he'd be a fool not to welcome it, so he set his glass down and said, "Well, if you're interested, we can visit the place together. I could actually do with a sparring partner, so if you're willing . . ."

"Thank you, Huntley. I think that sounds like an excellent idea indeed—finally something real for me to sink my teeth into."

"As for Lady Gabriella," Raphe said, "I would like to ask that you refrain from interfering."

"Are you certain?"

Raphe gave him a decisive nod. "Absolutely." As amicable as Coventry seemed, he didn't know him well enough to let him interfere with his affairs. If there was a way for him and Gabriella to be together, Raphe would find it on his own.

Boxing with Coventry the next day turned out to be precisely what Raphe needed in order to expel some of the frustration he felt about Gabriella.

"You need to learn how to harness your anger," he told Coventry as they took a break to catch their breaths. "Otherwise, you're just hitting with a repetitiveness that'll tire you out before giving you the result you crave." He'd then shown the duke a variety of different punches for him to practice, while others looked on with interest. Coventry had been right in his assumptions about the club. Most of the gentlemen here just stood in one spot while loosely hitting a small leather bag. They'd have little success against a real opponent.

"Can we call it a day?" Coventry asked an hour later. "I'm not accustomed to this much exertion. Not that I don't like it. I have to admit that I haven't had this much fun in ages, but I think I need to build my stamina slowly."

"You're right," Raphe told him. "I forget that I'm more used to such vigorous exercise than most people."

"Yes. It does appear as though you are." They made their way toward the changing room so they could freshen up and put on clean shirts. "Why is that?"

Raphe hesitated, then decided to risk a bit of the truth. "I lost my parents when I was eight and grew up poor. When I got older, I started boxing for a living."

"Well, I'll be," Coventry murmured. He gave Raphe a broad grin. "I knew you were interesting, Huntley, but this is better than I'd ever expected." Removing his sweaty shirt, Coventry reached for his clean one and pulled it over his head. "Why don't you come by my house for a drink. It'll give us a chance to talk and get to know each other better."

Raphe hesitated. "Will you tell me why you offered to help me ruin things for Fielding?" He'd been curious about that ever since Coventry brought it up.

The duke's eyes darkened. "I'm afraid that's a secret I cannot share since there are other people involved. Suffice it to say that the man crossed me once, and that I've never forgiven him for it."

When Raphe returned home that afternoon, he was greeted by a pale-faced Pierson. "What is it?" Raphe instantly asked, fearing for his sisters.

Pierson stepped hastily back, ushering him inside. "Lady Gabriella is here. She's waiting for you in the parlor. Has been here for the past couple of hours."

Frowning, Raphe handed over his hat and satchel containing his dirty clothes, and went in search of his guest. Pierson wasn't usually one to look frazzled, which naturally stirred a whole string of questions in Raphe's head. Finding the room, he stepped inside and shut the door. Propriety be damned—as usual.

And then he saw her, and his heart sank. She was sitting on the sofa—right where she'd been when he'd kissed her. Except she looked very different now, her body hunched over as if in pain while she clutched a piece of paper between her hands. Hearing him enter, she raised her head to display a pair of red-rimmed eyes and a quivering smile. "I didn't know who else to turn to," she said, her voice trembling as she spoke.

And in that moment, Raphe felt his heart expand and break at the same exact moment. Because here she was, placing her faith in him, with the conviction that somehow, whatever her troubles might be, he'd be able to fix them for her. But at the same time, he could not bear to see her so distraught without a hint of the laughing eyes he'd grown so fond of. He stepped toward the spot where she was sitting, lowered himself beside her, and pulled her gently into his arms. "*Shh . . .*" he whispered against the top of her head. "Just tell me what happened, and I'll see what I can do to help."

A moment passed before she drew a shuddering breath and leaned back. "I received a letter from my sister, Victoria, today." She raised the piece of paper she was holding. "My maid delivered it to me in secret."

"I take it the news wasn't good?"

Wincing, Gabriella shook her head. "It is the worst possible news I could have received." With a sob, she put her hand to her mouth, as if to hold back the torrent of emotion that consumed her. "Mr. Connolly, the businessman who married her, abandoned her almost a year ago. Apparently, he took her dowry and fled the country, leaving her not only penniless, but alone with child."

It was indeed a terrible scenario. Determined to hide his anger for Gabriella's sake, Raphe calmly asked, "Where is your sister now? Did she give you an address? Some means by which to contact her?"

"Yes—there is a street name here, with directions." She pointed to a spot on the paper.

Taking it from her, Raphe studied the elegant script and then grimaced. "I know this place. It's in St. Giles." Not an appropriate place for an earl's daughter by any stretch of the imagination. "We have to get her out of there. Have you spoken to your father?"

"No! Of course not, or I would not be here asking for your assistance." She dropped her gaze. "Victoria asked that I not mention this to him. I've decided to respect her wishes until I know exactly what happened to leave her in such a dreadful state."

"Very well then," Raphe told her firmly. "I will set out immediately in order to find her, and once I do, I shall bring her here so that you may speak with her."

Raising her head, her eyes met his with a remarkable degree of strength for a cultured lady of breeding. Whatever fear or misgiving had been there before, it had swiftly been replaced by steel. "If you think I will sit here and passively wait for your return, then you are mistaken." She rose. "I am coming with you."

"Absolutely not," he said as he got to his feet as well. "St. Giles is no place for a lady. It's bad enough that yer sister is there, but yer father will murder me, and rightfully so, if 'e finds out that I allowed 'is daughter to go traipsin' through that part of town." *God damn it!* She'd riled him to such a degree that his roughened tongue was running away with him again.

"She's my sister!" She jabbed a finger at his chest.

"An' ye came to me fer 'elp. So let me do me job an' bring 'er back safe."

Crossing her arms, she glared at him with menace in her eyes, which to his consternation, Raphe found strangely arousing. "If you refuse to take me with you in your carriage, I shall find the place by myself. Is that what you want?"

"Christ, woman!" He wanted to grab her, shake her, talk some sense into her. Arguing with her was impossible, though. She was simply too bloody stubborn. "Ye'll do as I say, an' ye'll stay by me side. Is that clear?"

"Perfectly, Raphe." Her expression eased—a calm after the storm—and then she stepped forward and touched her lips to his, setting off a series of sparks with that simple gesture. "Thank you. I will never forget your kindness."

Chapter 25

Comfortably seated in the ducal carriage, Gabriella waited for Huntley to issue instructions to his coachman before climbing in and claiming the opposite seat. "I fear this will prove to be a very bad idea," he murmured.

"You don't have to come with me if you don't want to," she told him sharply, annoyed by his comment.

His dark eyes pinned her to the plushly upholstered squabs. "Have you ever visited that part of town before?"

"No." Her parents had always restricted her outings to Mayfair proper. Even when they left London for the country, they travelled north past Regents Park, avoiding any travel through the less favorable parts of the city.

"Then ye've no idea what to expect," he said with no effort to speak in a cultured tone. "Ye did the right thing, comin' to me. Ye'll see that soon enough."

Knowing that he was probably right, she turned her head away and stared out of the window as the carriage started along. She didn't like being difficult or sounding ungrateful, especially since he could easily have refused to help her. He didn't owe her, after all, and considering what she knew of him, it might not be easy for him to return to a place that probably held bad memories for him. But the fear she felt for Victoria, the shock of discovering that she was living in squalor, abandoned by her husband, filled her with such anxiety that she found herself turning into an impossible person to deal with.

Raphe didn't deserve that. His kindness and sympathy and concern for her safety demanded her appreciation. So she took a breath and let it out slowly, feeling some of her tension dissipate. "I apologize," she told him softly. Turning her head away from the window, she looked at him. His expression was tightly drawn, his mouth set in a strict line. "I'm grateful to you for agreeing to help, and for letting me come along with you."

"You gave me little choice." His voice was hard.

"She's my sister," Gabriella said. She could feel that awful tightening of her throat again as her eyes began to burn. "Please try to understand."

"Of course I understand!" Leaning forward, he grasped her hand. "Understanding is not the issue. Don't ye see?"

She shook her head, unable to look away from the depth of his gaze.

"Just as ye fear for her, I fear for *ye*. If word of this little expedition gets out, the consequences will be dire."

She studied his face; that dear face that filled her thoughts whenever she wasn't with him. His eyes were overflowing with aching emotion, making her wonder . . . would he welcome the declaration of love she planned on making? Did he perhaps feel the same way? Her heart stuttered slightly in response to that thought, her nerves drawing tight. *I have to tell him what's in my heart.* "I—"

The carriage rolled to a sharp halt and Raphe looked out. "We're here," he announced. Removing his hat, he set it on the bench beside him and then removed his cravat to reveal the bare skin that dipped toward his collarbone.

Gabriella swallowed, the tips of her fingers already itching to reach out and touch him. "What are you doing?"

"Blending in as best as I can, considerin' me well-tailored clothes," he said as he reached up to scuff his hair, creating an untidy mess of haphazard locks.

Gabriella's mouth went dry. There was no denying the appeal he exuded when he tossed aside his gentlemanly appearance in favor of a more rugged one. As far as masculinity went, Raphe topped the list, his solid build and virility so potent it made Gabriella feel small and fragile by comparison. "Well, you, err— seem to be doing a good job of it." *Lord, she sounded like a nitwit!*

He gave her a curious look. "Stay here," he ordered before opening the carriage door and stepping out into the shadowy alley beyond.

Gabriella breathed a sigh of relief. As desperate as she was to find her sister and discover what had happened to her, she also needed a reprieve from Raphe, however brief. Leaning back against the squabs, she closed her eyes and tried to focus on bringing her racing heart under control. They were here to see Victoria—to figure out what had happened to her. Now was not the time to be letting her feelings for Raphe distract her. She had to stay calm, for her sister's sake. The carriage door opened again, bringing Raphe's face into view. "I have found her." The sympathy in his eyes was no comfort. He held up his hand. "Come. Let me take you to her."

Discarding her internal struggles for now, Gabriella placed her hand in his and allowed him to help her alight, the acrid stench in the air immediately assaulting her senses and making her flinch. "Dear God," she murmured, her feet slipping slightly against the greasy cobblestones.

"Here," Huntley said. He offered her a handkerchief with one hand while steadying her with the other.

Thanking him, she placed the pristine piece of linen to her nose, savoring the sweet scent of lavender trapped among the threads. They started forward, his arm protectively at her waist as he steered her toward a crooked building with blotchy walls. A couple of scraggly women, one carrying a wailing infant, stopped to stare as they passed. Raphe offered them each a coin while Gabriella gave them a smile. She only received dejected grimaces in return.

"Don't take it personally," Raphe said as he pulled her away from the women and toward the building's door. "They belong to a harsh world." He rapped twice on the door before opening it and ushering her inside.

Gabriella blinked, her eyes adjusting to the gray interior. This place was like a deep well, absorbing all light that fell into it. A second passed, and then she saw her. Standing to one side, Victoria looked like a wraith—a mere shadow of the woman she'd once been—and Gabriella's heart broke, her eyes stinging at the sight of her beautiful sister looking just as disheveled and drawn as the women she'd just seen on the street. Rushing toward her, she flung her arms about her and pulled her close, embracing her with equal measures of love and pity. Dear God, this was so much worse than she'd ever imagined. *How on earth had it come to this?* She felt so scrawny, so devoid of the sparkling happiness that had always defined her.

"What happened?" Gabriella asked as she took a step back and looked into Victoria's eyes. They were so horribly bleak.

"Let us sit," Victoria said, her voice achingly frail as she gestured toward the plain table and the two chairs that stood on either side of it. "I can make some tea if you like."

Gabriella shook her head. "Thank you, but there's really no need." Averting her gaze, she took a moment to compose herself, not wanting to add to her sister's troubles by starting to cry for all that she'd lost. Her chest was heavy, making breathing difficult. Briefly, she eyed Raphe, who gave her a discreet nod of encouragement. Moving to one of the chairs, she sat down, while Victoria claimed the other.

"I'm sorry to involve you like this," Victoria began after a brief moment of silence, "but I didn't know what else to do." Her voice broke and she looked away, eyes cast toward the floor.

Reaching out, Gabriella took her hand and gave it a light squeeze. "You did the right thing, Vicky. I just wish you would have done it sooner."

A quivering breath escaped Victoria's hunched over frame. "I was such a fool, Gabby." She shook her head. "Connolly—" She laughed grimly. "I don't even know if that was his real name."

"What do you mean?" A chill had driven its way to her bones. Gabriella shuddered, only slightly comforted by the light pressure of Raphe's reassuring hand against her shoulder.

"He wasn't the man we thought him to be, but by the time Papa discovered the truth about him, it was too late. Connolly and I had already been discovered in a compromising position at the Marsden ball." Victoria's lips trembled as she clasped Gabriella's hand. "He said he loved me—promised to give me the world. Except he wasn't the rich entrepreneur he claimed to be."

Realization struck Gabriella with the force of a battering ram. "He tricked you." She shook her head, disgusted that such a thing had happened to someone as good as Victoria. But it was that goodness that Connolly had prayed upon. "He tricked us all." The man had been so likeable, so charming and flattering and . . . perfect. Everyone had liked him.

"It was all very deliberate," Victoria went on. "After my ruination, Connolly met with Papa and demanded he pay him fifty thousand pounds in order to make him marry me. Naturally, Papa was furious with me for putting him in such a difficult situation, but he saw no other way around it."

"Oh, Vicky!" Fifty thousand was more than twice the amount of Victoria's dowry—an astronomical sum.

"Naturally, Papa attended the wedding so he could make sure that it took place. But he didn't count on Connolly's deceitful nature. The despicable man left me at the inn where we spent our wedding night. When I woke the following morning, I found a measly five pounds on the nightstand, along with a note that read, *Good luck*. I realized later that day that the ship we were supposed to take together had departed earlier than he'd told me it would. He went to America without me, Gabby."

It was all too awful to contemplate—a gently bred lady, forced to endure a life of poverty. "Why didn't you come home?"

"I think you know the answer to that," Victoria told her mildly. "Papa would have thrown me right back out. My pride could not allow that to happen. So I took a job at the inn I just mentioned. A few weeks later, I realized that I was with child—married, abandoned, and pregnant. It felt as though I was drowning, but at least my wages allowed me to afford this place. Unfortunately, I haven't been able to work since Lucy was born, and with no income at all to sustain us—" A sob shook her rigid shoulders. "I'm sorry, Gabby. I never wanted to drag you into this mess, but I simply didn't know what else to do."

Appalled by the fact that their elevated lives had made it so impossible for her sister to return home—the idea that her parents would reject her because they cared more for appearances than for their daughter—filled Gabriella with an unquestionable amount of anger. She made a conscious effort to calm herself for Victoria's sake and forced a smile that she did not feel. "Where is Lucy now?" she asked, deliberately drawing attention to the only positive outcome in all of this. "Can I meet her?"

"She's sleeping just over here," Victoria said as she rose and stepped toward a sheet that hung from the ceiling, dividing the room into two sections. She drew the sheet aside and gestured for Gabriella to approach.

Moving to stand beside her sister, Gabriella spotted the tiny bundle that lay swaddled in a wooden box on the bed. She felt her heart clench. No child should have to grow up in a place such as this. "Here. Take this," she said, handing Victoria her reticule. "Make sure you eat well so you can feed her properly. I will speak with Papa, and—"

"No." Victoria's eyes widened with fear. "You cannot tell him about this. Please, Gabby, promise me that you will keep this between us."

"I—" Gabriella cast a wary gaze in Raphe's direction before looking back at Victoria. "You cannot remain here, and with your daughter in mind, there is a good chance that Mama and Papa will welcome your return. Surely they will want to know their first grandchild."

"You didn't see how furious Papa was when we parted. I've never seen him like that, Gabby." Victoria practically trembled.

"Perhaps I can help," Raphe said before Gabriella could comment.

"I cannot possibly ask that of you," Gabriella said, unwilling to involve him any further.

"You helped my sisters," he said, ignoring her comment. "Allow me to help yours."

"It is good of you to offer, Your Grace," Victoria said, "but my sister is right. It would be wrong of me to rely on your generosity, especially since I have little hope of ever repaying such kindness. I wouldn't be comfortable with it."

Raphe bowed his head to her and Gabriella saw the respect that loomed in his eyes. "What if I were to think of something that wouldn't make you feel beholden?"

Uncertain of what he had in mind, Gabriella exchanged a look with Victoria, who looked ready to ask about the details of such an offer when a knock sounded at the door. "Excuse me a moment," she said as she went to open it. She exchanged a few words with whoever had come to call, glanced hesitantly over her shoulder at Gabriella, and then opened the door wide enough for the visitor to enter. "This is Mr. Thompson," she said as a man with striking red hair stepped into the home. "Mr. Thompson, I'd like you to meet my sister, Lady Gabriella, and her friend—"

"Raphe?" Mr. Thompson said, his stance frozen just inside the doorway as he stared at Huntley with a look of disbelief.

Gabriella blinked. She looked at Huntley, whose expression had gone slack with emotion. He nodded once. "It's good to see ye again, Ben."

Mr. Thompson stared back at him for a long moment, as if wondering how to react. Eventually, he set the canvas bag he was carrying on the table and addressed Victoria. "There's carrots an' turnips, an onion an' a loaf of bread in 'ere. I couldn't manage any meat this time." He sounded truly apologetic.

"That's quite all right," Victoria said. "I'm very grateful for whatever you're able to bring."

He gave her a curt nod and then turned back to Huntley, his expression a great deal harder than it had been a moment earlier. "Ye owe me an explanation, Raphe." Gone was the familiarity with which he'd spoken before. "What the 'ell 'appened to ye?"

Chapter 26

Raphe bristled. He'd known the risk of coming here, but he hadn't for the life of him imagined running into his old friend, Benjamin Thompson, in Lady Victoria's home. Feeling Gabriella's gaze on him, he forced himself not to look at her, directing all of his attention at Ben. He was right after all. He *did* deserve an explanation. "My life took an unexpected turn," Raphe began. "I received a letter, informin' me about an inheritance."

Ben crossed his arms. "Go on."

Guilt gnawed at Raphe's insides. He felt his stomach roil with the queasy distaste of it. Turning his back on Ben and his family had been a difficult decision, but he'd made it in order to ensure that his sisters got the chance they deserved. "I knew yer thoughts about the aristocracy," he said.

"Were they any different from yer own?" Ben asked. His gaze went fleetingly to the two women, who stood to one side, before returning to Raphe.

"No. Which is why I feared tellin' ye the truth." Inhaling sharply, Raphe braced himself for Ben's reaction. "My mother was a viscount's daughter, Ben." He then went on to explain what had happened to his parents, how he and his sisters had ended up in St. Giles, and how a twist of fate had landed him a duke's title.

Ben stared back at him in disbelief. "Ye should have told me."

"I know, but I was young back then—just a lad, if ye'll recall—an' I desperately wanted to fit in. So when ye started rantin' about yer distaste of the aristocracy, I chose to keep quiet. As time went on an' our friendship deepened, tellin' ye got increasingly harder. Besides, I didn't think there was any need to say anythin'. I thought I'd left that life behind me fer good."

"An' then ye became a duke." Ben assessed him a moment before saying, "Ye look pretty grand, to be sure, but I ain't goin' to address ye by anythin' other than yer name, Raphe."

The comment eased Raphe's nerves a little. He managed a smile. "I wouldn't expect anythin' else from ye, Ben."

A curt nod told Raphe that Ben understood his motivation, even though he didn't approve of his choice. It also said that although he was still angry with Raphe for leaving without explanation, he would get over it in time. Eventually, they would be friends again, perhaps sooner than expected if Raphe suggested the idea that had just presented itself to him. He glanced toward Lady Victoria. Ben wouldn't visit her on a regular basis without good reason. He took a step closer to his friend and lowered his voice so only he could hear. "How long have ye been comin' here?"

Something awkward flickered in Ben's eyes. "Ye wish to know my intentions?"

"It's not me place," Raphe admitted. "But she's the Earl of Warwick's daughter, an' I promised her sister that I'd help get 'er out of this mess."

"Do ye know all that 'appened to 'er?" Ben asked through gritted teeth. An angry shadow slashed its way across his face, hardening his features.

Raphe nodded. "Yes." They stared at each other for a long, silent moment until Raphe knew that their thoughts matched. He might be an aristocrat, but he didn't care for the higher echelons of society any more than Ben did.

"We met when she was still workin' at the *Hounds Tooth Inn*. We're friends."

Raphe watched him, assessing. "Do ye think there's a chance ye might be more than that?"

Though he didn't avert his gaze, Raphe sensed a distinct air of protectiveness that could only be caused by deep emotion. "Per'aps," Ben quietly whispered. He shrugged then, as if to dispel the comment.

"Then let me try to help. Let me try to make things better."

Caution filled Ben's eyes. "What do ye 'ave in mind?"

"A life for the two of ye far away from 'ere, in a place where she'll be safe an' well cared for." He placed a hand on Ben's shoulder. "She 'as a child, Ben. If ye love 'er—"

"Ye're suggestin' bigamy? *That's* yer plan?"

It sounded awful. Still, there had to be a solution. "She doesn't deserve what 'appened to 'er, or to suffer for it for the rest of 'er life. An' considerin' that 'er husband lied about his identity, an annulment should be possible."

"Ye're certain of that?"

Raphe shook his head. "No, but I 'ave a competent secretary and solicitors who can find out."

Ben did not look convinced, but he nodded anyway. "Very well." His gaze drifted toward the ladies. "If she agrees."

Turning, Raphe found Gabriella and her sister watching them with marked curiosity. "I have a suggestion," he said.

"Go on," Gabriella urged when her sister failed to respond.

Raphe squared his shoulders. "I've a property in Gloucester that's in need of a caretaker. The position comes with a two-bedroom cottage, the wages are decent, an' I can promise ye that none of my staff will question who ye are or 'ow ye arrived there. I'll make certain of that."

"You're suggesting that I move there with Ben?" Lady Victoria hesitantly asked.

Raphe nodded. "I'm also going to see if I can get your marriage to Connolly annulled."

"I'll do it anyway," Lady Victoria whispered with tears in her eyes. "Anything to get away from here and to—" Her eyes shifted to Ben. "Would you really be willing to move across the country for me?"

With a light grin he stepped toward her, taking her hand in his. "It's not like there's much of a life for me 'ere in St. Giles. I'll miss me family, to be sure, but what Raphe is offerin' is a rare opportunity, so if ye're amicable to the idea, then so am I."

Rolling his eyes at his friend's idiocy, Raphe went to whisper in his ear. "Tell 'er how ye feel, man!"

Leaning forward, Ben placed an awkward kiss on Lady Victoria's cheek. "I believe I forgot to mention that it's mostly because I love ye."

A sob broke from between Lady Victoria's lips as she flung her arms about Ben. Speechless for only a moment, Gabriella sought Raphe's eyes and silently mouthed the words *thank you*, her gaze bright with emotion and happiness and something powerful that Raphe hoped signified a deeper attachment between them.

"I'll send a note tomorrow," he told Ben and Lady Victoria. "Let you know what I find out."

Thanking him, Ben gave Lady Victoria an almost shy embrace and took his leave. "We ought to get going as well," Raphe told Gabriella. "The streets of St. Giles are no place for a lady after dark."

Gabriella's lips parted. She looked to her sister with grave concern.

"He's right," Lady Victoria said before Gabriella could voice a protest. She reached for her sister's hand and gave it a squeeze. "You should go."

Pressing her lips together, Gabriella gave a hasty nod, as though prolonging the moment would make her weep. "I will see you again soon, Vicky. I promise."

Stepping out into the dimming light, Raphe offered Gabriella his arm and began leading her back toward the awaiting carriage. "Everything will be all right," he murmured, sensing that she needed the reassurance. "I will do all that I can in order to help your sister. You must believe that."

"You are too kind." She spoke in a hushed whisper. "And I cannot thank you enough." She hesitated a moment before adding, "Encountering Mr. Thompson cannot have been easy for you."

"He helped me carve out a place for myself when I moved here all those years ago," Raphe explained. "We became good friends and eventually ended up working together."

They reached the carriage and he helped her inside. Climbing in as well, he sat down across from her and knocked for the driver to set off. Silence settled between them, accentuated by the gentle sway of the carriage, until she finally said, "You had no responsibility toward Vicky, but you chose to help her anyway."

He shrugged one shoulder. "I can't let your sister

stay in a place like that. Even if things don't work out for her and Ben, I'll find a way to ensure a better life for her."

"But—" She gave him a questioning look. "Why? You don't owe her anything."

"I owe Ben," he said. "He was like a brother to me, always there whenever I needed him, and I lied to him—abandoned him without explanation."

"Oh." She slumped back against the squabs and nodded as though that made perfect sense. "I understand."

But the tone of her voice suggested that perhaps she didn't. Or perhaps she'd hoped for a different explanation. Raphe could only wonder. He wanted her in his life—indeed, he wanted her to be the most central part of his life—but not unless she was willing to accept the ramifications of what that would mean without any regret. "I especially did it for you," he found himself saying. The confession went against his better judgment. He didn't want to manipulate her with grand gestures. He wanted her final decision to come from her heart. But he couldn't help himself from being selfish, either—from wanting her to know that he cared, and to win the appreciation such knowledge would bring.

Her eyes widened. And then her lips parted as though she meant to say something but couldn't quite think of what, and it was all he could do not to leap across to the other side of the carriage and pull her into his arms. With everything that had happened today, he needed to feel the warmth of her touch.

As it turned out, he didn't have to. She was beside him in an instant, her thigh brushing his as she reached for his hand. Raphe forced back a groan in response to the sudden contact. It assaulted his senses, his entire body clamoring for more.

"Explain yourself," she demanded. She shook her head as though trying to focus. "You cannot say such a thing without doing so."

He took a deep breath, determined to dampen the hot desire that her touch had evoked. God, she drove him to distraction with her delicate fingers clasping his, her face so close that if he but turned to look at her, their lips would likely touch. A tremor shook him at the thought of such pleasure—the instant reminder of how it had been between them before when they'd given in to abandon. "I don't know what I feel for you," he said, telling her the truth. "I know that I care for you, and I know that I want—I want . . ." *Christ, he could not say it.* Not to a woman of her breeding—of her perfection. She'd think him a beast if she ever discovered the visions he'd had of her as he lay in bed at night, his mind tormented with the possibility of her there with him, of what it would be like for them to touch each other in the most intimate ways possible.

Shifting, he moved to pull away, determined to add some measure of distance, lest he act out his fantasies within the confines of this very carriage. She was a lady, after all. She did not deserve to be treated so coarsely.

"*So do I,*" she whispered.

Blinking, he tried to recall the last thing he'd said to her, and then blinked again the moment he did. "What are you talking about?" His voice was gruff with restraint.

Raising his hand, she pressed it to her chest, allowing him to feel her heart. It was beating a frantic tattoo. "I want it all," she whispered. "But only with you." Her eyes shimmered, sparkling like stars in the night sky. "I—I . . ."

He wanted to press his mouth to hers, to silence whatever thought that was stopping her from acting on the words she'd just spoken. But the caution with which she spoke made him hesitant. Whatever it was, it seemed to be very important. "You?"

"I love you, Raphe." She blurted the words with complete lack of finesse, as though they'd been building up inside her just waiting to burst free. "My life changed the moment I met you. You taught me how to live again—you made me rediscover my true self— and you showed me that I can be so much more than I ever expected to be as long as I have the courage to try. I love how you make me feel and I love that you find me interesting rather than strange. I love your smile and the way in which you make *me* smile. You're an impressive man; considerate, kind, honorable and . . . You are everything to me, Raphe. When we're apart, I can think of nothing but you—of being with you again—and I . . . I'm sorry if I ever doubted our chance of being together. I was stupid, and afraid, but I refuse to be so anymore. I refuse to marry a man I don't love when I can marry the one that I do. As long as you'll have me, that is."

She barely managed to speak the last words before he was kissing her, pulling her closer, his arms tight about her waist and shoulders, too impatient to wait a moment longer to embrace her softness and taste her sweetness.

She reciprocated with an eagerness that wrought a groan from his throat, her desperation for closeness equal to his. Fingers splayed across his back, she matched his movements, following his lead as he deepened the kiss, exploring and sharing an unspoken wave of emotion. He hadn't reciprocated her declaration, and would not do so until he was certain he felt the same way. She deserved the honesty—not the deception that came from hastily casting words about. And while he knew that he liked her and cared for her, he had to know that this burning need to be with her was more than just a passing fancy or a haunting obsession.

He'd learned that from his parents. "*I thought I loved her,*" his father had told Raphe shortly before taking his own life. "*I realize now that the passion I felt was anything but. The constant craving she instilled within me wasn't love. It was a sickness—a compulsive need to possess her.*" He'd looked so tired and worn out as he'd spoken, his only confidant, an eight-year-old boy who should never have witnessed such emotional outpouring from his father. "*I should have known that I'd never make her happy. She didn't love me either, you see.*"

It was a tragedy that Raphe had sworn to avoid, yet here he was, kissing Gabriella as though his life depended on it—reveling in her love for him. He pulled back, adoring the hazy look in her eyes, her puffy lips and her rosy cheeks. Swiping away a stray strand of hair from her cheek with his fingers, he quietly asked, "How do you know?"

She stared up at him, cheeks darkening with the burn of his question. "I just do."

"You just do?" It was the most unsatisfactory answer he'd ever received. It didn't help him at all.

She nodded with conviction and he found himself envying her certainty. "I've never felt this way about anyone else before," she whispered shyly.

Neither had he, but that didn't mean that he loved her. *Did it?* He watched as she lowered her lashes, and he realized then that too much time had passed between them—time in which she'd probably hoped for him to match her courage. So he did the only thing he could think to do and kissed her again, long and deep and with an openness that would hopefully ease her mind a little.

When the carriage rolled into the courtyard between their two houses, he took her hands between his own and gave them a gentle squeeze. "I'm going to ask Richardson to investigate your sister's marriage immediately. I'll send you a note as soon as I know if there's a chance for an annulment."

She nodded demurely. "Thank you." When he moved to alight, she caught him by the elbow, holding him back. "Just so you know, I plan to end my engagement with Fielding."

Her directness shook him for a second, due to the implication. She'd said she loved him, and now she planned to prove it by casting aside the man her parents had chosen for her to marry—the safe choice that would ensure a respectable place of admiration amid the *ton*.

"If you need help, I'd be happy to oblige."

"Thank you, but I would prefer to do this on my own."

"**Y**ou want to do *what*?" Richardson asked with unfeigned dismay.

Taking a moment to convey the details surrounding Lady Victoria's marriage and her current situation, Raphe faced his friend and secretary. "Do you think it's possible?" he asked.

Richardson ran both hands through his hair as though the mere suggestion was too disturbing to contemplate. "What about Warwick?"

"What about him?"

Richardson gave him a look of exasperation. "Does he know?"

"Of course not." The comment did little to appease Richardson, who was looking increasingly uncomfortable. "His daughter determined her own future when she got herself married to a man that Warwick had not approved of."

"It looks as though his other daughter might be heading down that same path," Richardson grumbled.

"I thought you were in favor of a match between Lady Gabriella and I," Raphe said, crossing his arms.

"Of course I am." Richardson blew out a breath. "I just wish there wasn't so much scandal attached." He eyed Raphe for a second before saying, "She really means to end things with Fielding?"

"That's what she told me."

"One has to admire her courage. Warwick is bound to be furious once he finds out." He shook his head. "As for her sister, if she married a man under false pretenses—a man who claimed to be someone he wasn't—an annulment ought to be possible. I'll call a meeting with your solicitor, Mr. Fischer, who will probably turn to the chief magistrate. It may take time to settle."

Raphe nodded. "Please keep me apprised of the progress."

"Of course." Richardson paused on his way out the door. "Any news about the fight yet?"

"No. But I doubt it'll be long before there is. A day or two at most."

"Well," Richardson said, his eyes softening as he spoke. "When scandal arrives it seems to do so in droves."

An unfortunate truth that Raphe could not deny.

Chapter 27

Pacing restlessly back and forth in the parlor, Raphe listened with increased frustration to his sisters' complaints about the lack of activity in their lives. It was only a day since he'd seen Gabriella last, but he'd been in an agitated state ever since and knew that he wouldn't relax until he found out if she'd been successful or not in her attempt to break her engagement with Fielding.

"Is there no invitation that you can accept?" Amelia asked. "We're out now. Surely we ought to be seen!"

"Not until you've perfected the quadrille and the cotillion," he told her gruffly.

"What about the waltz?" Juliette asked. "Mr. Humphreys says—"

Raphe's eyebrows shot up. "You will *not* be waltzing."

Amelia glared at him. "Do you want us to find husbands or not?"

"Of course I do. And you will," he assured her, "but not by waltzing."

Both sisters huffed out a breath and rolled their eyes, their ladylike manners momentarily forgotten.

"You're too overbearing sometimes," Juliette complained.

"He's overbearing *all* of the time," Amelia grumbled.

Raphe stopped pacing and faced them. "Must I remind you that Juliette has recently been quite ill? How do you think she contracted the measles in the first place? By going out in public, *that's* how."

"Then lock us in our rooms and throw away the key," Amelia told him petulantly.

"You needn't be so dramatic," he told her. "But I'm your older brother. I worry about you and feel responsible for you. What if—" The reminder of loss, of holding his sister's lifeless body in his arms, of watching her being placed on a cart and carried off to the cemetery, would always haunt him.

"You have to let us grow up eventually, Raphe," Amelia quietly whispered. "You have to let us go so we can live our own lives."

"I'm terrified of losing you." His voice broke and he turned away, facing the window.

"We know," Juliette said. "We feel that fear every moment of the day. You're so protective of us, so frightened of letting us out of your sight. And yet, you did all of this *for* us." She gestured to the space around them. "So that we can have the future you wish for us to have."

"An impossibility, unless you set us free," Amelia said. She waited a second and then suggested, "What if we do something here? At the house?"

Considering such a possibility—the chance for his sisters to socialize in a controlled environment— Raphe slowly nodded. "We can host a ball." He began warming to the idea. "We'll invite everyone— let them see that we're deserving of their high regard."

Coventry would be able to help with that. Raphe was certain of it.

"I think that sounds splendid," Amelia told him. "Thank you."

The door to the parlor opened at that moment, admitting Gabriella, who brushed past Pierson before he was able to announce her. "I'm sorry, Your Grace," the butler blustered.

"It's quite all right," Raphe told him, pleased by the sight of the woman who'd captured so much of his attention lately. Addressing her, he said, "I'm so glad you're here so I can share the good news." He waited for the door to close behind her before saying, "My solicitors are meeting with the chief magistrate today. I expect to hear from them by this time tomorrow, but in the meantime, you ought to know that I've invited your sister to stay with me until everything has been resolved."

Gabriella's eyes grew to the size of saucers. "Vicky and Lucy are here?"

He nodded. "They've been given one of the spare bedchambers."

"When?" She looked dumbfounded. "I mean—"

"I couldn't knowingly leave them in that place, so I returned for them yesterday evening."

Tears pooled against her lashes. "Thank you." Her voice was small, and he realized then how distressed she looked. "What's the matter?" he asked.

"He won't let me do it," she said, almost gasping for breath. "I've met with Fielding and he refuses to break our engagement." Her eyes darted about the room as though hoping to find a hidden solution to her troubles in one of the corners of the parlor. "He's always prided himself on winning, and now—he's quite determined for the two of us to marry."

Raphe stiffened, his mind already plotting and planning. He addressed his sisters, whose welcoming smiles had faded in response to Gabriella's unsettled tone. "I believe your studies await you in the library," he told them pointedly.

They didn't linger, both offering Gabriella a brief acknowledgement as they hastily took their leave. The door clicked shut behind them. "Let me help," Raphe said while repressing the vehement anger he felt toward Fielding.

"How?" The pain with which she spoke made his heart shudder. He hated that she felt so helpless. Hated Fielding and her parents and all of Society for being the cause of it.

Considering his options, he met her gaze. "I think he and I need to talk."

"What?"

"Fielding's a greedy bastard who needs to be put in his place."

Gabriella's eyes went wide. "How? I mean, what exactly do you—"

"I'm the Duke of Huntley, Gabriella, and I will be damned if I'm going to let him get the better of me when I have the power to crush him like the gnat he is."

"Oh!" She bit her lip, eyes sliding over him until he felt the blazing heat of her gaze as though it were the sun itself. It burned him to the core.

"Gabriella?"

"Hmm?"

"Come here." His tone was authoritative—ducal—commanding.

She slid into his arms a second later, melting against his hardness for a smoldering kiss that completely undid him with its honesty. It stripped him of every shield he held until he was left with no choice but to whisper the truth that had pounded through his veins since she'd bared herself to him yesterday. "I love you too, Gabriella. With all my heart. I love you."

She went completely still, leaning back so she could get a proper look at him. Her eyes trembling with emotion, her lips parting until a question drifted toward him. "Really?"

Lifting his hand, he stroked it over her hair, brushing aside a stray lock before continuing down across her jaw. With a nod, he told her simply, "You've conquered my heart." He dipped his head and kissed her gently—a soft pressing of lips as he whispered against her, "I am yours."

His arms went around her, holding her close in a silent exchange of emotion. For a brief moment their troubles vanished and it was just the two of them— him holding her, the woman he loved.

But it couldn't last forever. Not if they were to have what they wanted. So he eased away from her and said, "You should spend the afternoon with your sister. I'll take care of Fielding."

"But—"

"Don't fight me on this, Gabriella."

She hesitated a moment and then nodded. "Just promise me that you won't hurt him."

Raphe felt his jaw tighten and his fists clench. "I'll promise not to engage him in any way. Unless he asks me to."

"What does that mean?"

She followed him out into the hallway "Pierson," he said, locating the butler, "can you please tell Lady Victoria that her sister is here to see her?"

The butler hurried away, leaving him alone with Gabriella once more.

"Raphe?" She asked with urgency in her voice. "What are you planning to do?"

"Nothing that the earl doesn't want. I'm going to let *him* decide how to end this."

Reaching out, she placed her hand against his arm. "Please be careful."

Her concern for him was heartwarming. "Of course." He heard Pierson's footsteps approach. "Now go to your sister. I'm sure the two of you have much to talk about."

Gabriella swept into her sister's arms a few minutes later, embracing her as though she feared this might be a dream that was destined to fade. She had no words for what Raphe had done. He'd saved Victoria, and now he would try to save her as well. Love was perhaps too mild an emotion for the way in which she felt about him. Soul-deep adoration was more precise.

"Is Lucy sleeping?" Gabriella asked Victoria as she pulled away from her.

"Why don't you come and see for yourself?" her sister asked. Moving aside, she gestured for her to step further into the bedchamber.

Lucy was lying on a thick quilt that had been spread out on the floor, her chubby fingers grasping a rattle while her legs kicked at the air. "She looks so much like you," Gabriella said as she crouched down next to Lucy. The girl chortled, one hand thrusting out toward Gabriella, who instinctively offered her finger. "And her grip is quite firm." She laughed, unable to contain the fondness she already felt for this tiny little human.

"She's the most important part of my life now,"

Victoria said, joining her on the floor. "I never knew it was possible to love another person so much. Which just goes to show how wrong and foolish I was regarding Connolly. What I felt for him doesn't come close to this." She lowered her head and placed a tender kiss against Lucy's forehead.

"What about Ben?" Gabriella asked. "How do you feel about *him*?"

A wry smile captured Victoria's lips. "I'll tell you as soon as you tell me what is going on between you and Huntley."

Tugging her finger away from Lucy's hand, Gabriella looked into her sister's curious eyes and told her the truth. "I love him, Vicky. It's that simple, really, even if the reality of it is far more complicated than I ever would have believed possible."

"That's wonderful news, Gabby. I'm so happy for you." When Gabriella failed to elaborate, she puckered her brow. "Does he not feel the same way about you?"

"Oh no," Gabriella hastily shook her head. "It's not that. It's all the obstacles we face. I'm worried that things won't turn out the way we want them to—that we won't be able to be together."

"It's my fault. If I'd stayed and married Bellmore the way I was supposed to, you would have had more freedom to marry Huntley." She shook her head. "I'm so sorry, Gabby. I made a terrible mistake."

"You thought yourself in love."

"No. I didn't, Gabby. Not really—not now that I know what love is supposed to feel like. It was just a meaningless attraction and I allowed it to win against my better judgment."

"At least you have Lucy and Ben now," Gabriella said, hoping to offer comfort.

"Yes. I've no regrets there. Ben is a good man. I'm sure we'll be very happy together. But it was a struggle getting here—to this point. There were times when I lost hope—when I was certain that I would die poor, unhappy and forgotten. So don't lose hope, Gabby. Huntley's a wealthy duke and the two of you love each other. You've already got a lot more than I had when Connolly left me."

Encouraged by her words, Gabriella made a deliberate effort to set her concerns aside and enjoy her sister's company until Raphe returned.

Arriving at Fielding House, Raphe waited for a footman to open the carriage door before stepping down. Today he would play the role of duke to perfection with the intention of letting Fielding understand that he was not to be trifled with. Least of all when it came to Gabriella. So he climbed down and ascended the front steps with a brisk no-nonsense stride.

"The Duke of Huntley," he told the butler in greeting. Raphe handed him his card. "I'm here to see the earl."

A pair of bushy eyebrows drew together. "Please come in," the butler said. He closed the door behind Raphe. "I'll see if his lordship's at home."

"He'd better be," Raphe murmured under his breath.

The butler either didn't hear him or pretended not to as he strode away, returning only moments later with a strained expression. "My apologies, Your Grace, but the earl is apparently out."

Raphe felt his jacket draw tight across his back as the muscles in his shoulders tensed. "Then I'll wait for him to return."

"I, err . . . ah . . . of course." He looked around uncertainly. "Perhaps you'd care to have a seat in the parlor? I can have some tea brought up for you."

"Thank you." He allowed the servant to show him through to a pretty room with spindly furniture that looked too fragile to hold a man of his size. So he positioned himself by the fireplace instead and waited for the butler to leave.

Three seconds later, Raphe was back in the hallway and striding toward the part of the house where he'd seen the butler go earlier. Popping his head into every room that he passed along the way, he eventually found his quarry in the library.

Seated in an armchair, the earl looked up from the newspaper he was reading as Raphe stepped into the room. "What the—"

"So you're also a liar then, telling me you're out when you're actually not." He took a seat across from Fielding. "Worse than that, you made your butler lie on your behalf." Leaning forward, he glared across at his adversary. "Rather cowardly, wouldn't you say?"

Fielding set his paper aside and narrowed his gaze on Raphe. The top of his lip began to curl in an unattractive snarl that proved his lack of restraint. "I ought to call you out for your insolence. How dare you come into my home without invitation?"

A rapid clicking of heels announced the butler's arrival. "My lord," he gasped as he spotted Raphe. "I'm so sorry. I showed His Grace into the parlor but—"

"Don't trouble yourself, Norton. I am aware of the duke's shortcomings. Unfortunately they're difficult to ignore." He waved toward the servant in a dismissive manner. "You may leave us now."

Raphe watched as the flustered butler backed away, apologizing one more time before shutting the door behind him. With a shake of his head, Raphe turned his attention back to Fielding. "You're an arrogant bastard. Do you know that?"

Fielding's eyes narrowed. "Which do you favor? Pistols or swords?"

"Neither."

"Now who's being a coward?" But Fielding didn't wait for Raphe to answer. He added swiftly, "My education and upbringing are superior to yours, Huntley. That's not arrogance—that's plain fact."

"And yet, I outrank you." Raphe allowed a smirk. "Funny, don't you think?"

"Hilarious."

Raphe studied him a second. Oh, how he'd love to knock that haughty expression from the blighter's face. He grit his teeth in preparation for battle. "Break off the engagement to Lady Gabriella."

"So you can have her instead?" Fielding scoffed, leaned back, and crossed his legs. "That's never going to happen."

"No?" Raphe held himself in check. "Not even if I tell the world that you tricked her? What would people say if they discovered that she never agreed to marry you and that you're holding her hostage—using her fear of scandal and her family's misfortune against her in your greedy attempt to acquire her fortune?"

A muscle twitched at the edge of Fielding's mouth. "It would be your word against mine."

"True. But are you really willing to take that risk?"

"I repeat: pistols or swords? We'll meet at dawn. The winner gets Lady Gabriella."

"You seem fairly confident of the outcome."

"I'm aware of my skill with both weapons." His mouth twisted with disdain. "You'll lose."

Tilting his head, Raphe finally smiled. "Arrogance, Fielding. It'll be your downfall." The earl's face darkened to a shade of uncomely red. He opened his mouth as if to say something, but Raphe went on. "The worst mistake you can ever make in a fight is to underestimate your opponent. But the truth is that I have the advantage."

"How?"

"*You* challenged *me*, Fielding. That means that I decide how we go about this. But we won't be firing pistols or dueling with swords. We'll be using our fists."

"What? That's preposterous, Huntley. Nobody duels with their fists!"

"There's a first time for everything, Fielding." Raphe's smile spread until he was practically grinning. He'd suspected that goading the earl would lead to this, and so it had. But the earl no longer looked as self-assured as he had a moment earlier. "And since you're the one challenging me, I get to choose the terms, and I choose fists, tonight at Gentleman Jackson's. Unless of course you wish to renege."

"Renege?" Fielding's eyes had taken on a look of distinct panic.

"Think about it, Fielding. I'm taller and broader than you are. I train on a daily basis in order to keep myself physically fit while you look like the sort of man whose idea of sport is going for a ride in the park. I've fought against hardened laborers, men who wanted to knock my head off my shoulders, and I've won—every time. Don't make the mistake of facing me in the ring on account of pride." Leaning back, he held Fielding's gaze. "Either way, you lose Lady Gabriella, but you can choose to avoid the humiliation of losing to me in front of a crowd by simply walking away."

It took ten more minutes for Raphe to convince Fielding that the odds were too great against him, and for the stubborn earl to finally agree to back down. He didn't shake the hand Raphe offered him, and he didn't respond when Raphe bid him a good day, the glower in his eyes following Raphe like a black shadow until he left Fielding House with the hope of never having to deal with the earl again.

But the pleasure his victory over Fielding had brought was swept aside and replaced by a new concern the moment he returned home and Richardson handed him a letter.

Sighing, Raphe dropped down onto his chair and read the ugly scrawl. He then asked, "Is Lady Gabriella still here?"

"She is in the music room with your sisters and Lady Victoria," Richardson told him.

"I'd like to give her an update on my visit with Fielding. And I'll need to tell her about this." He jabbed the letter with his finger as he leaned back in his seat. "Can you please ask her to come and see me?"

She arrived moments later with a wary smile about her lips. "How did it go?"

Rising to greet her, Raphe strode around his desk and clasped her hands between his own. "You're free of him. He's letting you go."

A whoosh of air escaped her. "How?" She stared at him as though he'd performed a miracle, and he realized that in a way, perhaps he had.

"I insulted him, he challenged me to a duel, and I threatened to give him the thrashing that he deserves."

Her eyes went wide, her lips parted, and then she suddenly laughed as she flung her arms around his neck and pressed a series of kisses to his cheek. As much as he wanted to lose himself in the moment—to close the door to his study and show her what it meant for her to be his—Gabriella needed to know about the news he'd just received. So he pulled back, unraveling her arms from around his neck, and met her joyous gaze.

"There's something you need to know," he said. "The boxing match I told you about will take place in about a week and a half. There's no getting out of it. It's been confirmed."

The reminder of what was at stake made Gabriella stiffen. But only for a second. Burying her fears somewhere deep down inside her, she squared her shoulders, determined to do the right thing and stand by his side. "I'd like to come and watch. If you'll allow it."

Surprise sprang to his eyes. He stared at her. "It will hardly be fitting for a lady to attend such a spectacle. And I would never—as much as I appreciate your support, I would never—"

"Boxing has been a monumental part of your life until recently. I would like to be there, not just for support, but to catch a glimpse of that part of you."

"Your parents will never allow it."

"They needn't know," she told him fiercely. Her love for him—for this man who'd done so much for her—made being there for him the most important thing in the world right now; more important than her parents' opinions, more important than Society's approval, and more important than her own reputation. There was nothing she wouldn't sacrifice for him. She'd even walk through fire if she had to. So she told him firmly, "But even if they were to find out about it, I wouldn't care. This is a large part of who you are, and I refuse to turn my back on that."

He stared at her for a long, drawn-out moment until her legs felt weak and her mind went numb with the worry that she might have said the wrong thing. She'd just begun tracking over all her words when he spoke in a gravelly tone. "Do you have any idea how incredible you are?" Admiration lit up his eyes. But there was something deeper, too; a tender warmth that made her insides melt.

Unable to utter a word, Gabriella kept quiet. The clock ticked loudly on Huntley's desk. He flexed his fingers, his throat working as if to keep some inner turmoil at bay. "It would be too dangerous for you to be there," he finally said. "The crowd can be unpredictable."

"I needn't be in the middle of it. I can stand to one side."

"Gabriella."

Her name was spoken with a gruffness that instantly reminded her of hot kisses and gentle fingers caressing. "Yes?" she asked, aware of her own raspy tone.

He took a breath, his chest straining with the effort. His jaw tightened and then he moved toward her, closing the distance with precise steps. His hands settled against her shoulders, producing a slow burn that weakened her limbs. Instinctively, she sagged forward against his chest, desperate for the closeness and needing the support. He wound his arms around her waist, holding her in a possessive grip that made her feel so incredibly treasured. "If anything were to happen to you," he murmured against the top of her head, "I'd never forgive myself. In fact, it would likely kill me."

Gabriella's throat tightened with emotion, her stomach twisting itself inside out as his words settled in her consciousness. His love for her ran just as deep as hers did for him. Nothing else would compel such concern for her welfare. Nothing else would have made him fight for her with such unrelenting determination. He wanted to keep her safe—protected. But she wouldn't allow him to keep her away. Not when she'd chosen to share the rest of her life with him. "Perhaps Richardson will be there cheering you on? I can go with him."

His hold on her tightened before loosening once more. "Why must you be so stubborn?"

"Because I love you, Raphe, and because I worry for your safety just as you worry for mine. I need to be there to see the match, not sitting at home fretting over the outcome. I'll go mad doing that."

He held her gaze until she felt his love for her pouring through her. And then he nodded. "If Coventry agrees to go as well, so you have two men watching your back, I'll consider it."

"Thank you!" Tilting her head back, she looked up at his handsome face. It was mid-afternoon; hours since his morning shave. His jaw was beginning to show hints of stubble. Reaching up, Gabriella brushed her thumb across it, the abrasiveness sending a thrill of energy straight to her toes. She longed to deepen the bond, between them—to give him everything. No boundaries. But they were presently in his study with a house full of servants and sisters—both his *and* hers.

"I'm not guaranteeing anything," he warned her.

She nodded to ease his concerns. But she now felt confident that she would manage to be there for him when he took on his opponent in a match that would likely go down in history as one of the most memorable ever. She was sure he'd be victorious, and didn't want to miss sharing that with him.

He searched her face. "Gabriella." His hand slipped to the back of her head, supporting her there as he leaned in closer, his scent infusing her awareness with a thrill of anticipation. And then his lips touched hers, his strength and vitality pouring through her as he pressed his hand to her lower back and molded them together. He was all power and pure masculinity, his body firm, his manner rough with a passion she'd never allowed herself to dream of. "You drive me to distraction," he murmured as he kissed his way along her jawline. "You make me want the impossible."

A gasp was all the response she could manage as his teeth grazed her earlobe in a gentle nibble. "We'll make it possible," she promised. With a low growl, he playfully bit into her shoulder as though marking her as his. The thrill was impossible for her to ignore, the fire it lit producing a molten heat in her veins. It stirred to life an unrepentant thirst in her that only he would be able to quench. "I only want you."

"And you *will* be mine now, Gabriella." He spoke the promise with conviction. "But—" Straightening himself, he stared down at her upturned face while his thumb tracked a path across her kiss-swollen lips. "We need to restrain ourselves a little—however difficult that may be."

As if to punctuate the truth in his statement, the door to the study swung wide open at that exact moment. "Oh!" It was Amelia, who'd come in search of her brother. "I—err . . ."

Releasing Gabriella, Raphe stepped away from her to add an appropriate amount of distance. "Yes?" he asked, addressing his sister.

A mischievous grin formed on Amelia's lips. Gabriella blushed. "Please tell me that the two of you have agreed to marry," she said without preamble. "It will make this—" She gestured toward the two of them with her hands. "So much easier."

Raphe darted a look at Gabriella before returning his attention to his sister. "Was there something you wanted?" he asked, ignoring her comment.

"Yes," she said with a little frown of displeasure. "Juliette and I would like to visit the modiste so we can order gowns for the ball you're planning to host."

"You're hosting a ball?" Gabriella asked, looking at Raphe.

"Amelia suggested it and I agreed after she and Juliette had been pestering me about being *out* with nowhere to go," he explained.

"Well," Gabriella said, "I think it's a wonderful idea—the perfect opportunity for all of you to make a new impression on everyone."

"So can we go then?" Amelia asked. "I believe it will take at least a week for the gowns we order to be made."

Pinching the bridge of his nose, Raphe expelled a deep breath. "We've talked about this already. I don't like the idea of Julie going out to places where there's a chance of her catching any number of ailments."

"You're being a blockhead," Amelia told him angrily.

"Am I really?" He shot back. "As I recall, Julie got the measles the last time we went on an outing, and was very sick as a result of it."

"You don't know that she got it then. She might have gotten it in St. Giles before we even moved here. If *you'll* recall, there was a measles outbreak there a couple of months ago. Perhaps the symptoms took time to surface."

"She never ventured outside when we were living there," Raphe said. "So I don't see how she would have caught it."

"Neither do I," Amelia told him grimly. "The point is that you cannot keep her locked up as your prisoner just because you're afraid she might get sick."

"What I'm afraid of," Raphe clipped, his wavering words conveying a vulnerability that shot straight through Gabriella's heart, "is losing her because I failed to protect her. She's not as strong as you, Amelia."

"I know that. Julie knows it, too. Good lord, Raphe, we've been over this a dozen times! At some point you're going to have to give her the freedom to live her own life, no matter the dangers."

"She's right," Gabriella whispered, drawing his attention. "Your sisters are out now. They deserve to be able to go shopping together or to visit museums or enjoy a carriage ride in the park like other young ladies. Being seen will also help with their eligibility, and—your intention is for both of them to secure husbands, is it not?"

For a long moment, he stood there staring at her as though he couldn't quite decide whether to wring her neck for interfering, or break into a grief-stricken state of panic. Eventually, he gave a concise nod. "You're right," he said, turning to Amelia. "I've allowed a tragic experience to guide me. It wasn't your fault, and—" his shoulders slumped with defeat. "It wasn't mine, either." He took a moment to catch his breath before adding, "It just happened. You and Julie have suffered long enough because of it. Especially Julie. So if you wish to have a little outing together, go ahead."

Amelia practically squealed as she flung herself into his arms. "Oh, thank you, Raphe! Thank you so very much!"

"Take the phaeton," he told her, "and ask a maid and a footman to accompany you." He looked at Gabriella. "Am I forgetting anything?"

"You should be home no later than six o'clock," she said, feeling much like the other half of a parent. "And stay on Piccadilly for today. You'll easily find what you need there."

Amelia didn't wait for Raphe to change his mind. She quickly agreed to all the terms and departed with haste. "I'll worry about them until they return," Raphe quietly spoke.

"Yes, but you did the right thing. They're both old enough to escape their leading strings."

He winced at that. "I just—"

"I know," she said as she reached for his hand and gave it a reassuring squeeze. "But Amelia is right. You cannot continue like this. Your sisters have their own lives to live."

Pulling her closer, he lowered his head to hers for a quick kiss. "Thank you for helping me through it."

She smiled up at him. "Thank you for letting me do so."

Chapter 28

"**I**'m hosting a ball in a couple of weeks," Raphe told Coventry a couple of days later as the two of them shared a drink in Coventry's study.

"Yes. I received the invitation. Thank you."

"It's an opportunity for me to prove my worth—to show the *ton* that I'm not an undeserving nobody who just walked in off the street."

"Do any of them claim to know about your past?" Coventry asked with a frown. As Raphe had gotten to know the duke better, he'd gradually revealed his connection to St. Giles and to Guthrie. It had been a risk, but he'd known they'd never be true friends unless he shared this part of himself. And rather than be appalled by it, the duke had applauded Raphe for his "courageous achievements," even going so far as suggesting that Raphe one day show him where he grew up.

"No," Raphe said in answer to his question, "but I'm thinking of being honest with Warwick."

Coventry's eyebrows rose. "That's quite a gamble."

"I know," Raphe agreed. "But he already thinks something's amiss. He accused me of being an imposter, and assured me that he meant to uncover the truth. I think it might be better if I come clean on my own."

The duke tilted his head. "Perhaps."

"I know he cares about Gabriella's wellbeing. If I can convince him of my love for her, I think I may stand a chance."

"And if you don't?" Coventry asked. "Is Scotland an option?"

Sinking back against his chair, Raphe considered the question. "I'm not sure. I think Gabriella deserves better than that."

"**W**hat did you do?" Warwick's posture was more rigid than Gabriella had ever seen it. He'd just burst into the parlor where she was having tea with her mother and aunt, and now stood glaring down at her.

"Wha—what do you mean?" she asked, her teacup rattling slightly against its saucer as she set it aside.

"Fielding just called on me," he practically spat.

"Fielding is here?" Gabriella's mother asked as she looked toward the door.

"He *was* here," Warwick said. "And he informed me that you have cried off your engagement to him, Gabriella, and that he has agreed to honor your wishes. There was nothing I could say to change his mind. Nothing at all."

A rush of relief sailed through her on a wave of elation even as the room was pitched into silence. It was official. Her engagement to Fielding was over. It felt euphoric!

"What. Do. You. Mean?" Lady Warwick clipped with a bite that could snap an adder's neck in half. She turned a frosty look of disapproval on Gabriella.

"It's for the best," Gabriella told her parents, who

looked positively furious now. "I'm tired of being pushed and manipulated into something I do not want, of having my future planned by other people."

"You mean by us?" Warwick asked tightly.

"I've never been allowed to be my own person."

"We are your parents," Lady Warwick told her sharply. "We know what's best for you."

"Do you?" Gabriella asked. "Do you really?"

"Of course we do!" they spoke in unison.

"Is that why I feel like a puppet? Because you know best? For the past year, I've been told what to wear, who to talk to, which parties to attend, and whom to marry. You have influenced everything without ever asking me if it was what *I* wanted."

A nervous laugh escaped Lady Warwick. "Of course it's what you wanted."

"You know that's not true," Gabriella told her seriously. "It's what *you* wanted."

"Yes. It was," Warwick spoke. "We wanted to bury the lingering effects of your sister's stupidity by aligning ourselves with the most respectable family there is. Not just for our sakes, but for yours." His face was set like stone. "And I'll be damned if I'm going to let you run off and marry some good-for-nothing scoundrel instead, because that's what this is about, isn't it, Gabriella? It's that undeserving bounder next door."

"Careful, Papa." Gabriella glared at her father, and as she did so, she saw his eyes widen with what could only be defined as a newfound awareness of her. There was respect there now, perhaps even a little fear, as though he'd suddenly realized that she was capable of more than just being a bargaining chip. The steel in her voice had done that, and it provided her with a sense of assurance she'd never before possessed. It strengthened her resolve and made her feel as though she was capable of taking on anything, if the prize to be won was Raphe.

"You're in love with him," Warwick said. "You're in love with Huntley." His wife gasped, as though this were the most preposterous thing she'd ever heard.

It might well have been, Gabriella decided with no small measure of resentment. "Yes," Gabriella said. She would not deny it. On the contrary, she would shout it from the rooftops, let the whole world know now that she'd found the courage to stand up for what she believed in.

"But do you know him?" Warwick asked. "Has he told you everything there is to know about his past? About him working in the docks as a common laborer?"

"He has told me everything, Papa," Gabriella said.

"So you are aware that he's also made quite a name for himself in St. Giles as a bare-knuckle fighter for Carlton Guthrie?"

"Oh dear," Aunt Caroline murmured. It was the first thing she'd said since Warwick's arrival.

Lady Warwick crossed herself, which was rather odd. She wasn't Catholic, after all.

Gabriella glared at her father with newfound fury. "You've continued with your investigation of him, no doubt hoping that you would find some terrible secret to use against him. Well, I'll have you know that I am perfectly aware of the man he is. I know how difficult his life has been, and if you have any shred of goodness left in you, you'll let this matter rest before it threatens to ruin the most noble and honorable man I've ever known."

"Gabriella—"

"I *will* marry him," she said, cutting off her aunt's

insistent voice. Her hands balled in her lap, her nails digging against her palms. "With or without your blessing."

"Though I do believe we'd both prefer to have it," a deep voice spoke from the doorway.

Elation shot to the surface as Gabriella's head whipped around to face the man who'd stolen her heart. He was standing behind the butler, about to be announced. "Huntley!" Her smile was immediate as she rose to her feet and went to greet him, dismissing the butler as she did so. "What are you doing here?"

"I thought it might be time for your father and I to have a little chat," he said, eyes shining with adoration as he smiled back down at her. His hair was a little disorderly, but it was one of the things she loved about him—his departure from the social norm. "And there is something else," he murmured. "Your sister wishes to make an attempt at reconciliation. For Lucy's sake."

Gabriella stared at him. "How can she be so forgiving?"

The edge of his mouth lifted. "Because the love she feels for her daughter is greater than her pride." He held her gaze. "Would you like to share the news or—"

She shook her head. "I think you should do it, since you're the one who saved her, and since my parents would never have had this second chance with her if it hadn't been for you." When he nodded his agreement, she turned to face her father. "Papa, the Duke of Huntley would like a word with you."

Warwick looked somewhat uncertain. Lady Warwick scowled in an ugly manner that made Gabriella cringe. Her aunt, on the other hand, looked as though she were wishing she was twenty years younger, and available to receive Huntley's ministrations. Gabriella couldn't help but smile. She was well acquainted with his irresistible charm.

"Very well," Warwick finally said. "Let us adjourn to my study."

Chapter 29

"Have a seat," Warwick said as he ushered Raphe into his study and closed the door behind them. Doing so, Raphe watched him go to a narrow table that stood against one wall with a tray full of carafes on it. "I'm guessing this conversation will require fortification?"

"It might," Raphe agreed. "I'll have a brandy, please."

Crossing to his own chair a minute later, Warwick set a tumbler in front of Raphe before sitting down as well. "Are you aware that Gabriella is no longer engaged to Fielding?"

"Yes," Raphe said. He chose not to elaborate, since doing so was unlikely to help his cause. Instead, he said, "With that in mind, I would like to ask you to reconsider your position regarding my request to court her myself."

Leaning back in his chair until the leather squeaked, Warwick regarded Raphe with an assessing look. "I don't trust you," he said after a long drawn-out moment of silence. "According to the man I hired to investigate your circumstances, your last place of residence was somewhere in St. Giles. He also tells me that you have ties to Carlton Guthrie—a man suspected of being behind all manner of crime. Which tells me that you cannot possibly be who you claim to be. No heir to a dukedom could ever have fallen so low."

Unperturbed by Warwick's insistence on finding the truth since he'd been expecting it, Raphe slowly nodded. "I might be equally mistrusting if I were in your position. However, I would ask that you hear me out before making erroneous assumptions."

Warwick's eyebrows flattened themselves as he puckered his forehead. "I've always prided myself on being fair, though I must confess that my daughter has recently cast some doubt in my mind where that is concerned. It appears that she's taken quite a liking to you." Folding his fingers across his stomach, he tilted his head back and pursed his lips. "I'll allow it. For her sake."

Steeling himself, Raphe squared his shoulders and straightened his back. "The information that you've uncovered about me so far is true. I've spent the last fifteen years in the slums, just trying to get by while supporting my sisters."

"Go on," Warwick said, narrowing his gaze.

"My father took his own life when I was eight, leaving behind a massive debt." He went on to tell him how his mother had abandoned them all, how he and his sisters had been forced out of their home, about Guthrie's willingness to help them as long as Raphe paid off his father's debt, and about his sister's untimely death. "I know that my past will always leave a door open to scandal, which is why I concocted the story about growing up secluded in the North. I hoped it would explain our lack of finesse when my sisters and I first arrived at Huntley House.

They both deserve to claim the lives they were born into." Expelling a heavy sigh, he added, "I want you to know that I did the best that I could, under the circumstances."

Warwick's face remained impassive throughout the entirety of Raphe's explanation, except for the occasional twitch at the corner of his mouth. His hard eyes held either admiration or condemnation. Raphe wasn't entirely certain which, until the earl eventually spoke with surprising modesty. "I daresay, I owe you an apology, Your Grace."

"There's no need," Raphe said. "I understand your mistrust of me completely. Especially once I realized that it wasn't just a matter of securing an excellent match for your daughter, but that you were genuinely trying to protect her from harm."

A shadow settled upon Warwick's face, accentuating his age and a weariness brought on by worry and responsibility. "Her sister made an unfortunate match for herself. I wanted to make certain that the same did not happen to Gabriella."

"I understand."

The sympathy with which he spoke seemed to alert Warwick. He gave a snort. "You cannot possibly."

"Which brings us to the second matter that I wish to discuss with you. Your other daughter, Victoria, has suffered a great deal at the hands of the man she married—more than you can possibly imagine."

"How do you—"

"Gabriella received word from her recently."

"I wasn't aware." Warwick's eyes filled with emotion. "Why didn't she tell me?"

"Because she knows how angry you've been and because Victoria asked her not to."

With a tortured breath, Warwick seemed to lose

whatever strength he'd had left. He slumped against his chair and spoke to his desk. "I was heartbroken. And yes, I was furious, though mostly at Connolly. He took advantage of Vicky and of me in the most despicable way possible." He gave a rough shake of his head as he lifted his gaze to meet Raphe's. "I did the only acceptable thing, considering the circumstances. I made certain that they wed."

"He abandoned her, though," Raphe said, watching the color drain from Warwick's face, his lips parting with horror. "He took all the money you gave him and left her to fend for herself, pregnant with his child."

"Dear God." The whispered words sounded like a mournful prayer. "She should have come to me. Why on earth wouldn't she do so?"

"Because of pride and fear, I suspect."

"But I'm her father." Warwick's voice finally cracked. "In spite of everything, I love her. Good Lord! How hard it must have been for her, how terribly difficult and terrifying and—" He got to his feet. "I must go to her. Tell me where she is, please, so I can find her and bring her home."

Raphe stood up as well. "She is safe, my lord. I brought her to my own house."

Warwick's gaze darted to the door with wild emotion. "And the child?"

"Her daughter is naturally with her. But, before you hasten over there to see them, we ought to discuss this matter calmly." When Warwick looked unwilling, Raphe said, "I took the liberty, at her request, of ensuring an annulment of the marriage. It was granted on the basis of Connolly's false pretenses."

"So she is free?"

"Yes."

The tension in Warwick's shoulders dissipated. "I don't know how I can possibly thank you."

"There's no need. And besides, you might want to wait with your thanks until we've discussed Victoria's future. You won't like this, but considering the scandal that her return to Society would likely incur, being an unmarried woman with child, I made her an offer that she has chosen to accept." He then told Warwick about Ben and the caretaker position in Gloucester, complete with the cottage for the two of them to live in.

"This friend of yours is willing to take on the responsibility of being a father to another man's child?"

"He loves her, and she loves him. They would like to have the chance to spend their lives together without the *ton's* scorn."

Warwick sank back down into his chair. He expelled a deep breath. "I don't know what to say. Frankly, I am humbled by the thoughtfulness and the consideration that you have shown toward my family." Raising his gaze to Raphe's, he took a moment to look at him before saying, "If you wish to court Gabriella with the intention of marrying her, you have my blessing."

Joy bloomed in a rush of warmth, filling Raphe to the brim. "Thank you, Warwick." He stuck out his hand as the earl got to his feet once more. They shook on their newfound respect for each other, and drank a toast to the future. Misty eyed, Warwick nodded. "My wife will be speechless when I tell her." He chuckled slightly, then paused. "When can I see Victoria again? And what about Mr. Thompson? I should like to make his acquaintance if he and Victoria are to be husband and wife."

"In an effort to draw the least amount of attention to ourselves, I believe a joint trip to my estate in Gloucester might be the best way forward. There, secluded from the prying eyes of Society, you'll have the privacy that you, and more importantly, *she*, needs. Victoria wants to reconcile, but don't expect her to rush into your arms. There's still a lot of pain and resentment there, and she'll need both patience, understanding, and remorse from you and your wife if you're ever going to repair the relationship that I presume you want to have with her."

"I was a blind fool to put the opinion and high regard of others ahead of my own daughter's happiness. I never should have forced her to marry Connolly once I realized the sort of man he was. I should have found a different way, a better way, without sacrificing Victoria like a pawn in a chess game."

"You should tell her that when you see her again. It's a good beginning."

"Thank you, Huntley," Warwick told him. "I misjudged you when we first met. I'm sorry for that."

"Thank *you*. Again. But I think you might yet change your mind about me."

Warwick knit his brow. "How so?"

"Because I mean to participate in a public boxing match soon, and if word gets out about that, the scandal will be immense. Not just for me, but for anyone associated with me."

"Then you must renege. It's the only sensible—"

"No. I made an agreement with Guthrie."

"You don't owe that man anything, Huntley. Surely you can see that."

"It's a matter of honor, Warwick, and of keeping the people of St. Giles safe from a fate worse than Guthrie. I won't back down."

"Bloody hell!" He gave Raphe a disgruntled look.

"I respect your resolve, but damn it, Huntley, this is a fine mess."

Raphe couldn't disagree. "Perhaps the Rubens will make you feel better?"

Warwick stared. "The Rubens?"

"Consider it a peace offering." The look of astonishment on Warwick's face made Raphe smile. "I insist." He finished off his drink.

"About the fight," Warwick said, "have you told Gabriella about it? Does she understand the consequence?"

"She does." He met Warwick's gaze without hesitation. "At first, she tried to dissuade me, but she has since given me her unwavering support."

"You're certain of this?"

Raphe nodded. He understood Warwick's concern. By forming an attachment with Raphe right after her unsuccessful engagement to Fielding, she ran the risk of becoming a social pariah. "I am. She told me so herself."

"Well, in that case, I'll stand by you as well. You are a duke, after all."

"And yet, that doesn't seem to matter, unless I also have my reputation intact—a reputation that has come under severe scrutiny since my arrival. The fight is unlikely to help."

"I agree, but since your mind's made up and Gabriella's is as well, it's time for me to pick a side too. Perhaps if we can encourage others to see the merit of your character, we can turn this entire debacle around in your favor—make you the hero."

"As unlikely as that is, I appreciate the thought." Raphe stepped out into the hallway. "If it's any comfort, Coventry's with us as well."

"Really? I always took him to be a conformist."

"Not at all. He's rather open-minded, actually."

Warwick snorted as he followed Raphe out. "At any rate, having a likeable duke in your corner can only help."

"Agreed." Raphe gathered his hat and gloves. "Now, if you've no objections, I'd like to take Gabriella for a ride in the park."

"I'll allow it," Warwick told him. "As long as her maid goes with you." Recalling how Gabriella and Fielding had returned unchaperoned from their ride the day Raphe had first met them, Warwick's condition reminded Raphe that he still didn't trust him completely. Hesitating briefly, Raphe considered raising the point, but then decided against it. He'd gotten what he wanted—permission to court Gabriella. If Warwick insisted that her maid accompany them on their outings, then so be it.

Chapter 30

The fortnight that followed was filled with quiet walks, boat rides on the Serpentine and picnics in the park. Raphe and Gabriella even managed a visit to the National Museum. But an evening at Vauxhall Gardens was vetoed. Apparently, Lady Warwick didn't trust the way Gabriella blushed every time she and Raphe were in close proximity of each other. She demanded they only see each other in the light of day, and in as public a setting as possible. "*I will not tolerate any more scandalous behavior*," she'd said, which had made Gabriella wonder if the woman was secretly able to look inside her head and see her most private thoughts. But, as it turned out, she'd been referring to Gabriella's broken engagement. No matter what she said, her mother continued to back Fielding. In her eyes the man was a saint, incapable of doing any wrong.

She did not feel the same way about Raphe, though she had warmed to him a great deal since discovering the lengths he'd gone to on behalf of Victoria. But, that didn't mean she was going to trust him to sit in the parlor and have tea with Gabriella without a chaperone. As it was, the lady almost suffered a fit of the vapors when she discovered that Gabriella had been visiting Huntley House on a regular basis without her knowledge. A fact she'd only been willing to forgive after Gabriella had sworn that Anna had always been there with her, which was technically true, even if the maid hadn't always been in the same room.

So there had been little opportunity to hold hands, and no chance at all for a stolen kiss. Gabriella wasn't pleased in the least. She and Raphe had formed a bond, they'd grown close, and she missed that now. "I hope he proposes tonight," she murmured to herself as she got ready for the ball he was hosting. Planning a wedding would take time. There would be three long weeks of banns, so at the very least, they were probably looking at a month's wait. She sighed, unhappy with the thought of it.

"You look so pretty in that gown," Anna said as she brought her the jewelry box that Gabriella had requested. "Lilac suits you extremely well."

Gabriella smiled. The gown was new, an airy creation of layered chiffon and silk. Opening the jewelry box, she took out the amethyst earrings and matching necklace, the stones a deeper hue than the gown and outlined by specs of shimmering diamonds. "Do you think he'll approve?"

"I think he'd be daft not to," Anna said.

It was only nine o'clock, but Raphe had already decided that he did not enjoy playing host. Receiving a long line of guests was, to put it bluntly, bloody boring. He stuck out his hand again to shake the hand of some earl or marquess, or whoever the man was, who now stood before him. Raphe didn't really care. The only person he was interested in seeing had not yet arrived.

"May we be excused yet?" Amelia whispered at his side.

"No," he told her stiffly. A lady was presented to him, he bowed, she curtsied, and so it continued. "This was your idea. If I'm going to suffer, then so shall you." He pasted a smile on his face and greeted the next individual. Amelia muttered something beneath her breath. He fought the urge to elbow her in the ribs.

"Ah! Huntley!" *Finally, a friendly face.* Raphe greeted Coventry with genuine enthusiasm before presenting him to his sisters. The duke reached for each of their hands in turn, kissing the air above their knuckles. "I'm delighted to make your acquaintances."

Amelia stammered a "Thank you," while Juliette just stood there, gaping openly at the magnificent figure Coventry presented in his perfectly cut evening attire. It took some effort for Raphe not to roll his eyes.

"I'll expect to dance with each of you," Coventry added, punctuating his statement with a brilliant smile before moving on.

Another half hour passed. Amelia was now complaining about her feet aching every five minutes, while Juliette's posture had slipped into a slouch. "Stand up straight," Raphe hissed at her. She just glared at him, which was probably well deserved. He should have known they weren't ready for this. *This* demanded severe training and well-honed discipline.

Hoping it would soon be over so they could retreat to the ballroom and enjoy some refreshment, Raphe turned back toward the entryway. And that was when he saw her. Dressed in some diaphanous concoction that only a Frenchwoman would have been able to produce, Gabriella looked like a dream. Sheer fabric breezed around her, accentuating her figure in all the right places and making him long to just sweep her into his arms and carry her off into the night. She was like a fairy princess, her beauty unparalleled by anyone else, and he could not wait to make her his. *Tonight*, he promised himself, the ring he'd selected securely tucked away in his pocket.

"Lord Warwick," he said, dutifully greeting the earl first. "May I present my sisters, Lady Amelia and Lady Juliette?" He then proceeded to greet Lady Warwick and Lady Everly before Gabriella herself finally stepped forward. "You look enchanting tonight," he told her sincerely, delighting in the soft blush that spread to her cheeks as though mimicking the kisses he could not give her.

"And you look every bit the dashing duke. I'm sure the *ton* is terribly impressed."

Her compliment warmed his heart. "Thank you." Bowing, he said, "I hope you'll save a couple of dances for me."

"If it were up to me," she whispered, "I wouldn't dance with anyone else." With a mischievous smile that made him wish he could simply follow her into the ballroom, she swept after her parents and disappeared from his line of vision.

Muttering a curse, Raphe turned back to face the receiving line. It looked as though it might finally be diminishing. *Thank God!* Just ten more minutes, by his estimation. Which, as it turned out, was off by five. He tried not to look too relieved when the last person stepped forward to greet him. His sisters, however, did not share his tact. He caught Amelia by the wrist and practically forced her into a curtsy.

"Now can we go?" She asked when no other guests remained in the entryway.

Expelling a breath, Raphe gave her a very definite nod. "Yes." He was in dire need of a drink. And of Gabriella's company. The first was easily achieved with the help of a footman, the latter not so much, since Gabriella was already out on the dance floor by the time Raphe entered the ballroom. He studied her partner—some white-haired, dandy-looking fellow.

"She caught everyone's attention the moment she arrived," Coventry said as he came to stand next to him. He looked about. "Where are your lovely sisters?"

Raphe blinked. He'd forgotten all about them in his haste to find Gabriella. "I, err—over there," he said, spotting the top of Amelia's head.

"The competition looks stiff already," Coventry remarked. "I'll have to hurry if I'm to claim those dances I wanted. Back in a moment."

Raphe stared after him, and then focused on the spot where his sisters were standing. They were completely surrounded by the largest assembly of gentlemen Raphe had ever seen. A frown wrinkled his brow. At this rate, they'd both be off to the altar before the end of the Season. And as much as he wanted to see them settled, he wasn't so sure he was ready for it to happen quite so quickly. It was just too much—too many drastic changes in too short a time. He tossed back the glass of champagne he'd been nursing and snatched up a fresh one from a passing tray.

"Lady Juliette has graciously agreed to a country dance with me," Coventry said when he returned to Raphe's side a moment later, "And Lady Amelia has given me the waltz."

Raphe almost choked on his drink. "The waltz? I bloody well told her—" He took a breath and lowered his voice to a murmur. "I thought she needed special permission to dance that."

"You're thinking of Almacks, old chap, but there are many—especially those of higher rank—who don't give a fig about that. Some never even bother to go. And considering her age, which appears to be on the older side of twenty, if I'm not mistaken, and her position as a duke's sister, I seriously doubt that anyone will think ill of her for waltzing without a voucher. Especially since none of Almacks' patronesses appear to be here."

Raphe flexed his fingers. "Nevertheless, I told both of my sisters not to dance that particular dance."

"Then you're fortunate I happened to claim it," Coventry said, "Or it would have gone to Bartham, and *that* would have been a disaster."

Raphe didn't know who the hell Bartham was, but judging from Coventry's tone, he instantly took a dislike to the man. "Then I suppose I ought to thank you?"

"No need," Coventry said with a smile. "I'm happy to oblige."

"What about Lady Juliette?" Raphe cleared his throat so he could get the necessary words out. "Is she waltzing as well?" Against her better judgment and against his approval. She suddenly seemed so young. They both did.

"Yes, but you needn't worry. She'll be partnering with Thimbly, who's perfectly harmless. He'll keep an appropriate amount of distance between them."

With that assurance, Raphe excused himself from Coventry's company and strode forward, moving closer to the dance floor so he'd be able to catch Gabriella's attention when she was through with her dance. She approached him soon after, thanking her partner with a smile that made Raphe want to pummel the man. He held himself in check, reminded that her kindness was one of her best attributes. It was wrong of him to want to monopolize it. "I hope you're still free for two dances," he said as he offered her his glass without thinking.

She hesitated briefly before accepting it and taking a sip, her lips touching the rim where his own had been just a few minutes earlier. His veins thrummed to life with unexpected urgency, increasing the beat of his heart as her eyes met his. They might as well have been kissing each other with mad abandon in the middle of the ballroom for all the difference it made. The effect was certainly incinerating, and as he watched her lower the glass and draw a ragged breath, he knew she felt the same—that exquisite hunger that seemed forever prevalent.

"Of course," she said, her eyes catching the light of the chandelier overhead. "There's the next one—a cotillion."

"And the other?"

She glanced away for a second before returning her gaze to his. "The waltz."

He flexed his fingers. "I can scarcely wait."

A pink blush crept over her skin. "Neither can I," she told him softly. Then, in a more deliberate tone, "You must be pleased with how well this has turned out. I've heard several people praise the grandeur of it, which does suggest that the power behind your title is overshadowing any questions that might exist about your eligibility."

"I suppose the *ton's* shallowness may work in my favor," he said dryly. "Richardson did most of the

planning, which is why I invited him to join us."
Angling his head, he searched the room. "He's over
there with Amelia and her crowd of admirers."

Gabriella chuckled. "I wonder which one she'll
pick."

"Hopefully someone who won't mind her boister-
ousness." The tune to the next song started to play, so
Raphe offered Gabriella his arm and began leading
her back onto the dance floor. "I'd like for both of
my sisters to marry someone who'll accept them for
who they are."

"Would you mind terribly if they didn't marry an
aristocrat?"

"Of course not. I just want them to be happy and
well cared for."

They danced the cotillion without too much trouble, although Raphe did turn the wrong way at least
once, but he quickly recovered, thanks to Gabriella's
swift guidance. He enjoyed the moment with a laugh,
completely oblivious to anyone else's opinion. *Because
really, what did it matter if these people thought he
moved on wooden feet?* The only thing Raphe cared
about was Gabriella, and the joy he found in sharing
the dance with her.

"Would you like to catch a bit of fresh air with me
on the terrace?" he inquired as soon as it was over.

"Certainly." She was breathing a little faster than
usual after their recent exertion.

Making their way through the throng of people
around them, Raphe responded to the compliments
he received along the way. Gabriella was right. His
ball was proving to be a smashing success. With his
hand against her elbow, he guided her through the
French doors and out into the cool night air. "Would
you like my jacket?" he asked as they moved to a spot

where jasmine clung to the balustrade, permeating the air with its sweet aroma.

She shook her head. "It would not be appropriate."

"Are you seriously telling me that it would be more socially acceptable for you to get sick than it would be for you to put my jacket over your shoulders?"

"I know it sounds ridiculous, but—"

"It sounds terribly asinine."

In spite of the dim lighting, there was no mistaking her smile. "I know."

"Just promise me that you'll let me know if you get too cold out here." Oh, how he wished he could simply pull her into his arms and keep her there, warm in his embrace.

"I promise," she said. "But until then, perhaps—"

"Seems pretty sound to me," a gentleman said, his loud voice interrupting Gabriella's as he pushed his way through the French doors and strode toward the opposite side of the terrace with two companions in tow. He was an older, portly fellow with a booming voice designed to carry above all others.

"Who's that?" Raphe asked, unable to recall any of the men's names or titles.

"The one who just spoke is Baron Fullton. The slimmer man on his right is the Earl of Carmel, and the other gentleman you see is the Earl of Prinhurst."

"I've wagered a thousand pounds," Fullton added. In the time it had taken Gabriella to tell Raphe who the men were, the baron had lit a cheroot which he now puffed happily away on.

"On which one?" Carmel asked, his much quieter voice forcing Raphe to strain his ears.

"On the Bull, of course. He's the only fighter I'm familiar with—saw him once about a year ago. He practically obliterated his opponent."

Raphe's eyes slid toward Gabriella's for a second to acknowledge her concern before looking discreetly back at the trio who now held his full attention.

"He's got to be seven feet tall, I reckon," Fullton was saying. "So unless Matthews is bigger or faster, I'd say he's done for."

"I'm starting to regret my wager," Prinhurst said. "I've five hundred pounds on Matthews."

Fullton snorted. "I'd hurry over to White's and place a larger bet on the Bull. It's your only option, at this point."

"You're sure Matthews stands to lose?" Carmel asked.

"Look, there are never any guarantees when it comes to gambling," Fullton said. "But I know the man I'm betting on, and he's a winner if ever I saw one."

"Do you plan on attending this fight yourself?" Prinhurst asked.

"And trudge out into a muddy field?" Fullton sounded affronted. "I'm thinking of sending my secretary or valet." Dropping his cheroot, he put it out with his foot. "Shall we return indoors, gentlemen? I'd like to have a go at cards in the game room, if you don't mind."

"I'll partner you for whist if you like," Carmel said as he and Prinhurst followed Fullton, neither one of them so much as glancing in Raphe and Gabriella's direction.

"I don't like the sound of that," Gabriella said as soon as they were alone again. "What if you lose?"

"Then so be it," he told her dimly. "It wouldn't be the first time."

"I thought you said you were likely to win. Isn't that the whole reason why Guthrie insisted on making you fight?"

Taking her hand in his, he raised it to his lips and placed a tender kiss against the top of it. "Yes. But it's as Fullton said. There are no guarantees." Disliking the angst he saw in her eyes, he forced a smile and said, "Come, let's go and rejoin the festivities."

She held him back, though. "Have you spoken to Coventry and Richardson about escorting me tomorrow?"

"Gabriella—"

"Do *not* tell me to stay away, Raphe! Not now, after what we've just learned."

The fierceness with which she spoke was soul-shattering. His heart ached, both with emotion and concern for her well-being. Still, he could not deny her request. Not when it was made with such force-fulness. "They will accompany you there as long as you agree to stay where they tell you to stay, and to leave if they feel that being there poses a threat to you in any way."

She frowned, just as he'd thought she would, but he refused to budge. Her safety was simply too important to risk on account of anything. "Fine," she said. She accentuated her compliance with a curt nod.

Raphe breathed a sigh of relief. "I think I hear the waltz starting. Shall we go back inside?" The light-ness with which he spoke was deliberately meant to soothe her. There was no doubt that the conversation they'd overheard had put them both on edge, but unlike Gabriella, Raphe knew his own skill. He wasn't too worried. It wouldn't be the first time he met an opponent much larger than himself.

Still, the pleasure of finally holding Gabriella in his arms as they twirled about the dance floor calmed his nerves, distracting him from any concerns he might have for the coming day. Her hand clasped his, warm and certain, her eyes never leaving his until it felt as though it was just the two of them. His heart clenched and he drew her closer, loving the way her lips parted on an airy breath. The way he felt about her . . . it was both wonderful and terrifying, this business of letting another person govern your heart. So he chose not to put too much thought into it, and to simply feel. The ring still lay in his pocket, waiting for just the right moment.

"Gabriella."

He didn't even realize he'd spoken her name until she answered him.

The music slowed, drawing them to a halt and forcing him to release her. Except he found that he did not want to—he would never want to. So he stayed where he was, holding her in place, his eyes trained on hers. A second passed and then another, until he became keenly aware that they were now the center of attention. Everything had gone completely still, save for the whispered murmurs that shifted the air around them. "Gabriella," he said again. Reaching inside his pocket, he pulled out the ring he'd found amidst the Huntley family heirlooms—a brilliant sapphire, surrounded by diamonds. "It would be my greatest honor if—"

"Madam! You mustn't. Not now," several voices spoke in a rush. The whispered murmur increased, accompanied by the rustling of fabric as guests shifted to see what was happening. Raphe stiffened, aware that one of the voices belonged to Pierson, and that he'd spoken in an uncharacteristic state of panic.

And then there was another voice, a voice Raphe had hoped never to hear again. "Darling, it's so good to see you again after all of these years. I'm terribly sorry for my late arrival."

Turning with rigidity, his jaw clenched until he swore his teeth might shatter from the pressure of it. He glared at the woman as she made her approach. She was dressed in a bright red gown that swooshed behind her as she walked, and about her neck she wore the pearls his father had once given her on a whim. Raphe felt his heart begin to pound and his fingers twitch with a sudden urge to tear the necklace away from her. The honorable Delilah Matthews had not just ruined his childhood, but what would have been a brilliant proposal, if she'd allowed him to finish it.

"Mother," he said, deliberately infusing that one singular word with as much loathing as possible. "What the *hell* are you doing here?"

Chapter 31

It took Gabriella a moment to comprehend what was happening—the enormity of the situation. One second she'd known with certainty that she was about to become engaged to Raphe. There had been no doubt in her mind. After all, she was no longer attached to Fielding, her parents had given their approval, and the *ton* even seemed to be somewhat accepting of Raphe as the new Duke of Huntley—at least enough to keep any lingering biases to themselves.

But then Raphe's mother had walked back into his life and ruined the moment with the same degree of selfishness she'd shown when she'd walked out of it. Gabriella's spine stiffened. The mood in the room, so festive and positive just a second before, now leaned in a negative direction, the stares no longer supportive, but rather judging. She had to do something, especially since Raphe seemed incapable of acting with any decorum. Not that she blamed him. She understood the fury now emanating from his entire person. But it wouldn't do his family or hers an ounce of good if he chose to act on it in the middle of the ballroom. Which he might, judging from his clenched fists and his obvious hostility toward the woman who stood before him, her pleasant demeanor displaying not the least bit of remorse for the way in which she'd mistreated him and his sisters.

Unsure of what to say or do, but knowing she had to act quickly, Gabriella stepped forward. A hand on her shoulder drew her back—Coventry's, she realized—and she watched instead as her father presented himself to Mrs. Matthews. "What a delightful surprise," he said as he bowed before her. "I daresay we all feared we'd lost you."

"Lord Warwick," Mrs. Matthews said, looking somewhat perplexed. "I—"

"Need a drink?" he supplied. "By all means, let us adjourn to one of the parlors. This way."

Before Mrs. Matthews could manage a retort, he'd grabbed her by the arm and begun leading her away. She looked ready to protest quite vehemently at first, but then Warwick leaned closer, whispered something in her ear and escorted her toward the nearest exit without further signs of complaint.

Raphe marched after them with his sisters and Gabriella bringing up the rear. "Please do something," she hastily begged of her mother in passing. "Ask the musicians to play something lively—tell Pierson to bring more champagne." This evening would have been perfect! It *should* have been.

Quickening her stride, she hurried after the others. Raphe did not deserve this. Nobody did.

*W*ould *his troubles have no end?* Feeling every sinew of his body stretch to the point of snapping, Raphe faced the woman who'd abandoned her family in search of a better life. "He killed himself because of you." It was the first thought that struck him as she stood there, audaciously smiling back at him.

The smile slipped, but only for a second. "He mismanaged his money until there was nothing left, and then he borrowed—enormous amounts that I knew he'd never be able to pay back. What was I supposed to do? Follow him to debtors' prison?"

"You had children, for God's sake." He could feel himself losing control, the rage rapidly building inside him. If he wasn't careful, he'd do something rash. So he stopped for a moment and took a deep breath, exhaling slowly. "He did it for you, you know. *You* were the one who drove him to it with your demand for a lifestyle he couldn't afford. All he ever wanted was to make you happy."

Snorting, she raised her chin in a regal pose of superiority. "He was always such an optimist."

"That's a terrible thing to say." It was Gabriella who spoke as she stepped closer to Raphe and took him by the hand in a gesture of indisputable solidarity. "And you're a terrible person."

"I assume she's yours," Raphe's mother said to Warwick before addressing Raphe with a smirk. "You've certainly set your sights high. I do commend you for that."

"Nobody cares about your opinion," Raphe told her darkly.

"You might when I tell you why I've come." Glancing at each of them in turn, Raphe's mother paused before saying, "I simply couldn't stay away when I discovered what great heights my son has risen to."

"You're a beast," Amelia said, speaking for the first time.

"And I'd watch that tongue, if I were you," her mother replied. "Gentlemen don't appreciate opinionated women with feisty temperaments. You'll do well to remember that if you want to marry."

"How could you abandon us? Your own children?" Juliette asked in barely a whisper. "What sort of person does that?"

"Taking you with me would not have been possible, and besides, there was no chance of you ending up in debtors' prison. The worst outcome might have been a workhouse for Raphe, but I was confident that someone would step in and save you all if it came to that."

"You. Were. Confident." Raphe stared at her while imagining what it might feel like to wring her neck. "You—" He was finding it difficult to breathe. Gabriella's hand squeezed his. "You are a vile woman."

She didn't even blink. "Do try to understand the situation I was in. My husband stood to lose everything. We were in dire straits, and Captain Tremaine—"

"*That's* who you ran away with?" Raphe gaped at her in shock. He hadn't known. His father had never divulged that much, but it was clear now that the betrayal had been worse than he'd ever imagined. "He and Papa were friends."

His mother shrugged. "He offered escape—the chance to travel the world."

"Did you ruin him, as well?"

Her mouth twisted. "Not exactly."

"Don't tell me." Raphe studied her closely. There was something about her expression—a reluctance to tell him everything. "He left you." If there was any sort of justice in the world, this still wouldn't be enough, but it would be a start.

"In a manner of speaking." She made an odd little wriggling movement, straightening her posture. "The specifics don't matter. What's important is that I'm here now, ready to resume my motherly role."

A hush fell over the room. Raphe became acutely aware that all eyes were on him—Warwick's, Amelia's, Juliette's, and Gabriella's—all seemingly holding their breaths with the expectation of what he might say to that. Pulling himself up to his full height, he squared his shoulders and gave his mother the most deadly glower he could manage. "Are you out of your bloody mind?" His tone would cut steel. "How dare you!"

Shockingly, she did not back down, her righteous posture and upturned nose reminding him of everything he'd ever hated about the aristocracy. But it had always been her. She'd been the source of every negative thought he'd ever had. *Because really, who else had he known as a boy?* He hadn't gone out in high society, had never spoken to another peer. *She'd* set the standard by which he'd measured the entire *ton*, ingraining in him a disdain that had magnified his own negative experience on account of his preconceived certainty that no aristocrat could ever be a decent person.

"Think carefully before you decide to toss me out," she warned. "Consider the scandal."

"It will hardly be any worse than the one you've just caused with your return. Everyone thought you were dead."

"A mistake that was never rectified."

Raphe shook his head. "No. I won't have it. You're not welcome here."

A shrewd look of determination sprang to life in his mother's eyes. "If you prefer, you may offer me a comfortable stipend, in which case I'll happily disappear from public view to live a quiet life in the country. I'm sure you have a lovely estate just waiting to be inhabited."

"I'm not giving you a penny," Raphe told her harshly. "Not after what you've done. You don't deserve it."

"You'll regret that decision," she warned.

"No, he won't," Gabriella told her firmly. "You may think you can threaten him with scandal, but you can't, not as long as he's unafraid to face it."

"And not as long as he has my family's support," Warwick chimed in.

A deep burn clasped at Raphe's chest. Knowing that Warwick was willing to help him in this, that Gabriella would not abandon him because of it all but rather stand by his side, was incredibly moving. "What I will offer," he managed, speaking past the knot in his throat, "is passage to America, with enough to get by on for the next year. After that, you'll have to manage on your own."

"Raphe," she pleaded. "You cannot mean that. I'm your mother, after all, and—"

"My mother left us fifteen years ago. Records show that she died at sea, so as far as I know, you're an imposter trying to take advantage. Unless you can prove your identity without question, I suggest you take the offer and leave before I decide to call the magistrate."

"You're making a grave mistake," she said.

"I don't think so. Now, what will it be? Prison or America?"

"You're detestable!"

"I'm sure I get that from you," he shot back without remorse.

Their eyes held each other in an unwavering glare until she finally relented and gave a nod. "Fine. Have it your way. I never loved you, anyway."

"*That*, madam, is quite apparent." Still, he'd hoped

she wouldn't have driven the knife quite so deep, not so much for his own sake, but for Amelia and Juliette's. Glancing in their direction, he couldn't help but notice the wide-eyed looks of horror on their faces. They shouldn't have been here to see this—he ought to have made certain of that. But he hadn't been thinking clearly. "I'll have a couple of footmen escort you to the docks. They'll wait with you until the next ship sails."

It was a grim parting, but once it had been taken care of and they had returned to the ballroom, where several gentlemen, including Coventry, were waiting to dance with his sisters, Raphe turned to Warwick. "I'm sorry you had to witness that. I cannot possibly thank you enough for your support."

"Think nothing of it. I was more than happy to lend my help." He looked to Gabriella for a moment before saying, "If you'll forgive me, I would not want my daughter to have her for a mother-in-law."

Gabriella's mouth dropped open. "Papa!"

Raphe forced a smile. "Your father is right. I'm glad she's gone."

"I can't imagine how difficult it must have been seeing her again."

"Do you think we can talk about something else?" he asked, hoping to return to the happy state he'd been in earlier that evening. "If I recall, I was about to ask you a very important question before we were interrupted."

"I, err—oh!" She gave her father a hasty look.

"I think I need a drink," Warwick said with a wink before striding away and leaving the two of them alone in a corner.

Raphe gave Gabriella his full attention. The warmth in her eyes made his heart tremble. "I love you, Gabriella." Nothing else mattered. "Please. Tell me you'll marry me. Make me the happiest and most fortunate man in the world."

A nod was her first response as she swiped at her cheeks with the back of her hands. "*Yes*," she whispered, and then nodded again. "I would love nothing more than to be your wife."

The moment she gave her consent, Raphe grabbed her by the hand and led her out of the ballroom at a rapid pace. "Where are we going?" she asked, her heart thrumming with the excitement of their engagement, his declaration of love, and the anticipation of what would come next.

"To seal our agreement," he told her roughly as he ushered her through to the back of the house. Pulling her into the library with an urgency that made her slightly lightheaded, he shut the door behind them and drew her into his arms. "Thank God," he murmured, his warm hands sliding along her back, hugging her to him as though she were precious, as though she mattered, as though he loved her with every fiber of his being.

"Raphe." If only words could describe how she felt about him. But she knew they would never suffice. The only way was to show him. So she pushed her hands up into his hair and dragged his mouth to hers, kissing him as though she'd just crossed the desert and found her oasis, as though her world might fall apart if she stopped. And Lord, if he didn't kiss her back, his arms tightly wound about her torso, crushing her to him with keen desperation.

She gasped for breath and he took advantage, deepening the kiss with a ravenous hunger that dared her to follow. And follow she did, heat surging through her veins, building and burning until she thought she might melt. Her limbs grew weak, her body started to ache. "Raphe," she repeated, the plea for something more passing her lips on a rush of air.

He drew back slightly, kissing her cheek, her jawline, her neck . . . and then he drew back some more, his breath coming hard. "I wish we were already married."

"Why?" she asked, the wanton within overruling the lady.

His chest, so strong and firm, rose and fell with labored movements. "Because then—" Flames burned in the depths of his eyes, heating Gabriella all the way to her soul. "I would take great pleasure in undressing you, laying you bare on that sofa over there, and worshiping your body until your thoughts were of me alone and the pleasure I long to give you."

Her mouth went dry. She couldn't speak. The only thing she could do was think, her mind rapidly seeking a way to make his salacious suggestion possible. *Good lord. What was happening to her?* He was stripping away her reservations without the slightest bit of protest on her part.

"But," he continued, adding a bit more distance between them by taking a small step back, "your innocence is sacred. I will not take it before our wedding night."

Gabriella drew a shuddering breath. As deflated as she suddenly felt, she knew he was right and was glad that one of them had the resolve to do the correct thing. "Thank you."

He pushed a stray strand of hair away from her cheek and swept it behind her ear. "You should." He grinned. "Resisting you right now is no easy feat, but

I'd like our first time together to be special. Not some hasty tumble on a library sofa."

"Three weeks seems like an eternity, though," she couldn't help herself from saying.

He nodded. "It does. But we'll also be very busy during that time. For starters, there's the fight tomorrow, and once that's over I think we ought to arrange the reunion Victoria requested to have with your parents. We can go to Gloucester together and see how she and Ben have gotten themselves settled. After that, there's no reason for us not to spend more time together just as we have been doing during our courtship."

She appreciated his soothing tone—the way in which he tried to lessen her concerns by making light of everything. "I've really enjoyed our outings."

It was true. They'd spoken at great length about a number of different subjects, laughed at jokes, teased each other, and taken pleasure in just being together.

"So have I." His hand came up to cradle her cheek, his thumb lightly stroking. Dipping his head, he gave her a tender kiss before saying, "I think we ought to return to the ballroom now before anyone finds us missing."

Chapter 32

Gabriella studied her mother at breakfast the following day. She looked tired. Drawn. "Did you not sleep well last night?" Gabriella asked.

Plopping a lump of sugar into her tea, Lady Warwick gave her daughter an irritated look. "Of course not, Gabriella. How can I when our entire family risks social suicide?" She shook her head, sipped her tea, and expelled a deep breath. "It's not just Huntley's past, your broken engagement with Fielding, or your current engagement to Huntley. It's also Victoria's annulment, her decision to marry into the lower class and live in a cottage, Mrs. Matthews's arrival at the ball last night, and Huntley's boxing match today. The scandal sheets would enjoy any one of these stories if the truth behind them were ever discovered, but together? It will send the gossip mongers into a frenzy! Our family's reputation will be decimated."

"I know, Mama. I'm sorry it has to be this way. Truly I am."

Her mother pressed her lips together and frowned. "In spite of what you may think of me, I always wanted the best for you and your sister. The situation that you've created seems to be anything but."

"Perhaps to your way of thinking. Because you can't imagine a life apart from Society—a life in which you're not invited to every event there is."

"You're asking me to denounce everything I have ever believed in—the very foundations of my upbringing and—"

"So many rules." Shaking her head, Gabriella reached for her mother's hand, clasping it gently against the white tablecloth. "I have never been popular, Mama. It's always felt like such a struggle for me to do the expected, to fall in line and behave according to a protocol that I didn't always believe in. And yet I was willing to continue doing so for you and Papa as long as I had no other aspirations. But then I fell in love and I realized how meaningless social etiquette is in the grander scheme of things."

Her mother's eyes widened. "You think it meaningless for a lady to behave respectably? To follow her parents' advice with regard to her future?"

"I think a lady ought to have some say, but you gave me none, Mama. Not once."

Her mother's brow wrinkled a bit and then she finally nodded. "I'm sorry." She hesitated a bit before saying, "The thing is that your father and I have been miserable ever since Connolly swindled Victoria into marriage. We were so determined to do better by you that we practically pushed you into Fielding's arms without paying attention to how ill-suited the two of you were. And then Huntley showed up, and our concerns just grew. He came out of nowhere, we knew nothing about him, and so we worried that we would be facing another Connolly all over again. It put a terrible strain on us. We fought often, each of us irritable with the other for no logical reason."

"Is it better now?" Gabriella asked.

Lady Warwick averted her gaze, her cheeks grow-ing suspiciously pink as she proceeded to straighten out her napkin. "We have—reconciled."

"I'd avoid any more questions if I were you," Caro-line said, speaking up for the first time.

Agreeing with her, Gabriella bit her tongue. In-stead, she quietly finished her breakfast and informed her mother and aunt that she was going to call on Raphe so she could wish him luck with the fight.

"You're not thinking of attending it, I hope," Lady Warwick said with a shrewd stare, halting Gabriella's exit from the dining room.

Keeping her expression as tepid as possible, Gabri-ella said, "Actually, I was planning to take tea with his sisters." Which she would do, right before leav-ing for Hackney Meadows with Coventry and Rich-ardson. Thankfully, her mother did not question her any further, making it possible for Gabriella to leave the house without confirming or denying anything. *Technically, she hadn't lied*, she told herself as she knocked on Raphe's front door twenty minutes later. And as long as things went smoothly, there was no reason at all for her parents to ever discover that she had in fact gone to offer Raphe her support.

"**H**ave we told you how thrilled we are with your engagement to Raphe?" Amelia asked as soon as Ga-briella arrived in the parlor, her eager question pre-ceding a customary greeting.

Not minding in the least, Gabriella grinned. "Thank you," she said. She then nodded politely to Coventry and Richardson, who'd risen upon her ar-rival, their felicitations coming in quick succession of each other. Her eyes met Raphe's as he came toward her. "I can assure you that I am quite thrilled as well."

"As am I," he murmured for her ears alone as he offered his arm and escorted her to the sofa. Dressed in a pair of brown wool trousers and a white cotton shirt without waistcoat, jacket or cravat, he looked devilishly roguish.

"Are, err—are you ready for today's event?" she asked as she took her seat and reached for the teapot in a futile attempt to hide her blush. The effect he had on her was surely plain for all to see. Especially when her unsteady hand made the tea spill the moment she started to pour.

"I believe so," Raphe said, sounding amused. Claiming the seat beside her, he made no effort to stop from brushing his shoulder against hers or nudging her with his leg whenever he leaned forward or backward. Taking a sip of his tea he added, "As you know, I've been practicing quite diligently in the courtyard."

Gabriella froze, her cheeks burning with the reference to their scandalous run-in with each other. "Indeed," she said, lowering her gaze to her lap so she didn't have to meet the curious looks she was getting from the rest of those present.

"We leave in fifteen minutes," Raphe continued in a more deliberate tone. "Coventry and Richardson, I expect you to stay by Gabriella's side at all times."

"We won't let her out of our sight," Coventry assured him.

"Keep to the back," Raphe said. "That'll stop you from getting jostled by the crowd."

"But I want to be able to see you properly," Gabriella said. After all, that was the whole point in going.

"And you will. But I'm not going to let you attend unless—"

"I *beg* your pardon," she told him tightly, not liking the proprietary tone he was taking. "You won't *let* me?"

The room went instantly silent. Coventry and Richardson both looked as though they suddenly found the floor and ceiling remarkably interesting, while Amelia and Juliette stared at Gabriella with unfeigned interest, as though they'd never witnessed anything as extraordinary as a woman intent on thwarting their brother's wishes.

"I—" He ran his hand through his hair, sending the dark locks into disarray.

Gabriella's heart rate increased, in spite of her momentary annoyance with him. Apparently, her attraction to him was directly proportional to the degree of dishevelment he happened to be portraying.

"I just want to ensure your safety," he said.

"I know that," she said, taking his hand in hers and lacing their fingers together in a most inappropriate gesture of affection. "But I am tired of being ordered about, of being told what I can and cannot do and of being coddled. What I long for is the freedom to make my own decisions. What I ask is that you trust me to make the right ones, and that I'll know once I'm there if it's safe or not for me to stand closer to you, or if I ought to remain at the back."

He didn't say anything for a long moment, his hand simply clenching hers as he gazed back into her eyes with a slew of warring emotions that threatened to break her heart. But she couldn't allow herself to concede on this point. Not if they were going to have the sort of relationship they both longed for—the sort built on faith and honesty.

"Very well," he eventually said. "As long as you promise to stay with Coventry and Richardson."

"I promise."

It was almost one o'clock by the time they reached Hackney Meadows. A large gathering of people had already formed around the raised platform on which the fight would take place. A variety of vendors set up along the periphery of the field offering food and drink, likening the place to a country fair Gabriella had once visited as a child.

"Can we get some roasted almonds?" she asked, unable to hide her excitement at the sight of two men walking about on stilts, each carrying a sign that advertised the fighters. Insisting on coming had definitely been an excellent decision!

"Go ahead," Raphe said. "I'm off to find Guthrie."

They parted ways, leaving Gabriella to enjoy the next half hour in Coventry and Richardson's company while the crowd of spectators around the platform continued to grow. "I can't believe how many people there are," Gabriella said. She was starting to worry that she would have to stay at the back after all, which presently meant a good twenty yards away from the action.

"Huntley's taking on the world champion," Coventry said. "I'm not the least bit surprised by the turnout."

"Especially not when considering all the bets placed in various Mayfair clubs. I'm sure half the men here were sent by their employers," Richardson said.

"Are either of you familiar with the Bull?" Gabriella asked.

"I read about him in *Boxania* when he took the title last year," Coventry said. "According to the reporter, his opponent didn't stand a chance."

Gabriella winced. "That doesn't sound good."

"Not to worry," Coventry told her cheerfully.

"Huntley's been doing this for years, and if this Guthrie fellow insists that he's the only man capable of besting the Bull, then I'm sure there's got to be something to it."

"His Grace is pretty tough," Richardson said. "I've been helping him train for the past two weeks. Gentleman Jackson's looks like a playground for little girls when compared with what I've seen him do."

As grateful as she was for their attempt to appease her, Gabriella couldn't help but worry about the outcome of the fight. The rules were few, protecting neither man from serious injury, and if Raphe's opponent was bigger and stronger . . .

Nauseated by the thought of him getting hurt, she handed her bag of remaining almonds to Richardson, who put it in his jacket pocket. "Looks like they might be starting soon," he said as a showy man wearing scarlet silk coattails and a matching top hat stepped onto the platform. "Shall we move a bit closer so we can hear what he's saying?"

Glancing about, Coventry nodded. "I don't see why not. Looks pretty civil to me."

"Some people even brought their children along," Gabriella noted, spotting a man with a small boy on his shoulders. "Surely they wouldn't do so if there was any risk of trouble."

"I doubt Huntley would approve of us basing our threat assessment on other people's choices," Richardson said. "But, I have to admit that I've never heard of anyone getting hurt at these events, besides the fighters themselves."

"How reassuring," Gabriella told him dryly.

He gave her a bland look. "You know what I mean."

"Neither have I," Coventry said, "and I've been following the fight reports for years."

"Then you must have read about Huntley's previous fights." When he didn't respond, Gabriella prodded: "As Mr. Matthews?"

"I'm afraid not," Coventry said.

Gabriella's heart deflated. "Oh."

"His fights would not have been reported," Richardson muttered. He gave her a meaningful look before returning his attention to the platform, where the scarlet-clad man was already speaking.

"—So ye're in fer a real treat, ladies 'n' gents!" With a grin, he raised his hands, hushing the crowd. "T'ain't every day we see one of our own take on a brawny Scotsman!"

The crowd cheered, their eagerness for the fight to commence sending them into an excited frenzy.

"Shall I bring the fighters on stage now?"

A roar of approval rippled the air. Nudged from behind, Gabriella shifted. So did the man in front of her, stepping straight back onto her foot. "Ow!"

Coventry caught her by the arm and pulled her back, past the people who'd closed in around them until they were once again standing on the outside of it all. Richardson followed, reclaiming his spot on her right. "Are you all right?" Coventry asked.

Wincing, she gave him a nod. "I'm fine." She would not give either man reason to make her leave, even if her toes were now throbbing with pain.

"Are you sure about that?" Richardson asked. He did not look the least bit convinced. "I saw your expression when that brute stepped back into you."

Gabriella forced a smile. "It barely hurts at all."

Both men gave her a disbelieving frown just as the hulking figure of a long-haired man thudded onto the platform. Gabriella's mouth dropped open. This was no mere mortal, but a veritable Goliath.

"Defending the world champion title, I give you—the Bull!"

The response was a cacophonous blend of chanting and booing, depending on who people had wagered on. Pumping his fists in the air, The Bull expelled a beastly roar that would send any sane man running in the opposite direction. *Not Raphe, though*, Gabriella thought with an odd mixture of pride and fear.

"And now, to challenge his title," the announcer was saying, "straight from the heart of St. Giles—Misterrrr Matthews!"

Shouts, mingling with piercing whistles, burst through the air, increasing in volume as Raphe stepped forward, arms raised as though he'd already been declared the champion. The crowd went wild, chanting his name in a deafening chorus: "Matthews, Matthews, Matthews . . ."

Gabriella didn't even try to speak. *What would be the point?* Her words would just be lost in all the noise. Craning her neck, she tried to get a better look at what was happening on the platform. The Bull appeared to be one head taller than Raphe, which was quite something, since Raphe was without a doubt one of the tallest men she'd ever met.

Gabriella watched as the announcer spoke to each man in turn, too low for anyone to hear. Both seemed to listen closely before nodding and removing their shirts. Gabriella could not help but stare at the indecency.

"I'll 'ave some of that, please," a bawdy woman a few feet further ahead of Gabriella shouted. Laughter broke out, followed by an onslaught of lewd remarks that made Gabriella feel most uncomfortable.

"Do ye suppose they're just as fit below the waistline?" someone else hollered.

Gabriella clenched her jaw.

"Relax," Richardson spoke close enough to her ear for her to hear him above the shouting. "They are just words."

"I know," she told him sharply. Lord help her, her toes were still killing her.

"Then perhaps you'll be kind enough to stop digging your nails into my arm?"

It wasn't until then that she realized she'd grabbed hold of him. She instantly dropped her hand. "Sorry."

"It's quite all right," he told her kindly before straightening once more and turning back to face the platform.

Gabriella did so too, just in time to watch the Bull land the first blow of the fight—a left-handed punch to Raphe's chest. Gabriella gasped, her hands clenched together as she struggled to see, the pain in her foot completely forgotten. It didn't look too severe. Raphe barely appeared shaken as he circled around, blocking another punch before landing a solid one of his own right under the Bull's left eye. Shouts and chants grew to a thunderous roar, not unlike a wave, urging the fighters onward. They exchanged two more blows before going into a clinch, their bodies pushing and shoving until Raphe suddenly stepped aside, throwing the Bull off balance and ending the round.

"How many rounds are there?" Gabriella asked with a shout directed at both her companions.

"As many as it takes," Coventry replied. "They'll fight until one of them either gives up or gets knocked unconscious."

Drawing a staggering breath, she returned her attention to the fight, which had started once more. The Bull charged forward with another left-handed punch that made poor contact, due to Raphe's swifter movement. Shifting sideways, Raphe turned about quickly and attacked with a hit to the Bull's right eyebrow. Gabriella watched in amazement as the larger man staggered backward and Raphe moved in, taking the opportunity to land several more blows until the Bull suddenly pushed back and drove his fist into Raphe's mouth. A spray of scarlet painted the air.

"Oh God!" Gabriella closed her eyes.

"My Lady?" it was Coventry speaking. "Do you wish to leave?"

Her eyes sprang open. "No!" She'd come to support the man she loved, and so she would, no matter how barbaric the sport was turning out to be.

"Let us know if you change your mind," Richardson said.

She would not. Her sensibilities might not be as sturdy as most of those present, but she wasn't about to abandon Raphe to this mob of people who took pleasure in watching two men draw blood from each other. Whatever the outcome, she would be there for him when it was over. No matter how much she longed to sit down and rest her foot. So she stayed, spine straight and eyes staring forward with a new determination to see it all, no matter how difficult this proved at times.

As the fight went on and the fighters began looking equally beaten, one thing became startlingly clear: the Bull might be the larger of the two, but when it came to skill and technique, Raphe was a much better fighter. Watching him, the way he occasionally tricked his opponent into going one way before doubling back and taking advantage, filled Gabriella with a new sort of admiration for him.

But, just as she'd marveled at his ability, she watched him collapse in the next instant as the Bull planted a punch to his face. A hush swept over the crowd, and Gabriella's heart lurched with uncomfortable alarm as she tried to determine if Raphe was all right or not. But then cheers erupted again and he was back on his feet, ready to commence the next round.

He did so by flooring the Bull with a brutal punch of his own.

Gabriella cheered. Somehow he'd managed to rally himself. But it wasn't over yet. The Bull would not be taken out so easily, and was on his feet again soon enough. It continued like this, round after round, the two men punching each other until both looked exhausted. Still, the spectators cheered and whistled in support of their favorite.

By the thirty-ninth round, Raphe was looking so battered that Gabriella had already begun making plans for his recuperation, from bed rest to ice packs, and possibly even a few stitches. If it were up to her, there would have been a stop to this madness half an hour ago, at least. But since there was nothing she could do right now, she tried to think of what she could do after.

The Bull staggered forward, swinging his fist, but Raphe managed to dodge it and land one of his own instead. Two more punches followed, and then the final blow by Raphe, straight to the Scotsman's face. The Bull collapsed like a tree felled by an axe, and the end of the fight was counted off by the man in scarlet.

"We've a new champion!" he declared, grabbing Raphe by the wrist and shoving his hand up into the air. "I declare Mr. Matthews the victor!"

Cheers swept through the air, so loud that Gabriella imagined the sound reaching Mayfair. *Thank God it was finally over.* "Can we go see him now?"

"I—" Coventry began, then stopped with a frown.

"Can you believe it?" a man was saying.

"Bloody hell," Coventry murmured, his eyes following the individual with obvious concern.

"What is it?" Gabriella asked.

"That's Mr. Lewis. From the *Mayfair Chronicle*," Richardson said.

It was right before Gabriella heard the reporter say, "This will make one hell of a headline! The Duke of Huntley fighting for Carlton Guthrie—I can't bloody believe it!"

"Might be worth looking into his background," Lewis's companion was saying as they moved away. "I'm sure there's a juicy story there."

"That's not good," Gabriella heard herself say.

"No, it isn't," Coventry agreed. "Stay with her ladyship, Richardson. I'm going after them."

"Do you think he'll be able to stop them?" Gabriella asked as she and Richardson made their way toward the area where Raphe would be resting.

"I doubt it," Richardson told her grimly. "Reporters don't care about anything other than the next big story, and this one is huge."

"His reputation—"

"Was at risk to begin with, but Huntley knew what coming here today might mean for him and his family. Perhaps you ought to consider what it will mean for you tomorrow, when this story hits the paper."

"I've already done so," Gabriella told him firmly, "and I'm not going anywhere.

Chapter 33

Raphe felt like a broken man. He'd known the moment he'd seen his opponent that the fight would be his most difficult one yet, but bloody hell! His right arm hung limply from his shoulder, his knuckles raw from punching a surface as hard as granite. His face was throbbing in pain. Not to mention his chest. Dear God, there was a very good chance the Scotsman had broken a rib, or at least cracked one. At any rate, his entire body pulsed and ached as though he'd just been stampeded by a runaway herd of cattle.

Raising his fingers to his lower lip, he flinched in response to the sting, his back straining against the movement. He could still taste the blood, fresh on his tongue. It was a tender spot that would take time to heal.

"Let's have a look at you, then," the doctor said after finishing up with the Bull, whose name had been revealed as Thomas MacFrayden. Poor man had to be carried down on the cot that had been prepared for recuperation.

Squinting up at the doctor through partially swollen eyes, Raphe nodded consent. As much as he cursed the day his father had struck a bargain with Guthrie,

Raphe had to thank the man for ensuring that he and MacFrayden were treated properly after the fight.

"I'd say you've seen better days, but I don't think you need to hear that," the doctor said as he took a seat across from Raphe and began looking him over. "You've some nasty contusions, one here on your eyebrow, the other a bit lower, but they ought to go away in about a week." Setting his hand against Raphe's chin, he tilted his head slightly. "The cut at your temple and the one on your lip will have to be stitched up, though. It won't be pretty, and it'll hurt like the devil."

"And if I just leave it alone?" Raphe muttered.

The doctor responded with a shrug. "It may get infected, and then you'll have a whole other level of hell to deal with." Raphe snorted. "Not to mention that your arm appears to have come out of its socket. Shall I pop it in for you? Or would you rather wait and see if it manages to find its own way back?"

Raphe clenched his jaw, ignoring the spark of agony that tiny movement made. "Put it back in its socket and stitch me up."

"Some brandy?" Guthrie asked some time later, offering Raphe a small flask as the doctor put in the final stitch and tied a knot. He'd gone to calculate his profits, but was now back with a wide grin on his face.

Raphe nodded, his ability to speak still lost in the wake of the doctor's rough handling. *Thank God it was finally over.* He tested his arm again, then reached for the bottle and took a long draft. "Thank you," he told the doctor, who gathered his things with a tight smile before moving away.

"Ye fought well," Guthrie said as he claimed the chair the doctor had used. "I'm proud of ye. An' grateful too. In fact, I'll be sorry to let ye go, but a deal's a deal, laddy. Ye've earned yer freedom fair 'n' square."

It felt strange. Raphe took another sip of the brandy before handing the flask back to Guthrie. "Thank ye. I think."

Guthrie grinned. "What'll ye do with yerself now that yer fightin' days are over?"

"Get married. Live a normal life."

"Ye're a duke, Raphe. Yer life won't ever be normal again. But I do wish ye luck. An' if ye're ever passin' through St. Giles, I'll buy ye a beer."

"And I suppose pigs will fly as well, will they?"

Grinning, Guthrie tipped his hat and strode away just as Gabriella burst into the tent. She halted the moment she saw him, her features twisting as her gaze slid over him.

He rose to greet her. "Good heavens." She whispered the words across her rosy lips as she came toward him hesitantly, as though she feared injuring him further.

"I'll be all right in a week or so. Right as rain before the wedding, at least."

For some reason this made her eyes shimmer and her lip tremble and then, without knowing how it had happened, she was in his arms, kissing him as though they weren't surrounded by other people and it weren't the most inappropriate thing in the world. Raphe didn't care. He was grateful for her attention.

"I'm so sorry," she murmured against his mouth. Then, in an even lower whisper, "Reporters from the *Mayfair Chronicle* watched the fight. They recognized you and talked about further investigation. Coventry's trying to stop them, but I doubt he'll succeed."

"I feared as much." Cupping her cheek, he gazed into her clear blue eyes. "Do you think we can brave it?"

She responded with a solid nod. "Of course. We can get through anything together."

Grateful beyond words that she'd come into his life, he kissed her again. Scandal, it would seem, would be inevitable, and it was time for him to accept that instead of constantly trying to prevent it. He was still a wealthy, titled man, after all, so his sisters would manage somehow. And he had Warwick and Coventry on his side too, not to mention the most important person in the world—Gabriella, the woman he loved. Together, they would fight whatever battles might come their way, content with the fact that no matter what, they would always have each other.

Gloucester, three weeks later

Accepting the arm Raphe offered her with a joyous smile, Gabriella left the church with her husband as those nearest and dearest wished them both well. They'd left London two days after Raphe's fight with the intention of visiting Victoria and Ben as planned. But rather than return to London for the wedding as they'd initially intended, they'd decided to remain in Gloucester with Gabriella's parents after the news of the fight spread.

It had all begun with the article that appeared in the *Mayfair Chronicle* titled: *Huntley's Bloody Brawl*. A number of speculations regarding Raphe's relationship to Guthrie and how he'd come to fight for him in the first place had been raised. *Further investigation into this matter will be required*, the author had written, *but the point remains that the Duke of Huntley has a speckled past that defies all comprehension.*

Gabriella's attachment to Huntley also received a lot of attention. *With two daughters breaking off their engagements in quick succession, it is this author's honest opinion that the Earl of Warwick's family may not be as righteous as they would have us all believe.*

Cancellations to Lady Warwick's tea party the following week had begun to pile up within the hour, and by the end of the day, it had become clear that of the two hundred friends or so the Warwicks thought they had, they were fortunate if they had a handful between them.

"Hypocrites," Lady Warwick had said that evening at dinner. "Everyone knows that the Countess of Chester takes many lovers, and that her sons have fathered numerous children out of wedlock. Good Lord! I daresay we could easily find something unforgiveable to say about everyone if we set our minds to it, and yet they treat us as though they conduct themselves with the utmost of virtuosity."

"The difference, my dear," her husband had pointed out, "is that they've had the good fortune to stay out of the scandal sheets, while our family and Huntley's were allotted two full pages, complete with caricatures. That is not the sort of thing that goes unnoticed."

Unable to disagree with that, they'd all agreed that a long sojourn in the country held great appeal, and had departed for Raphe's estate ahead of schedule.

"Happy?" Raphe asked, his voice whispering against Gabriella's ear as he leaned closer to her.

"Very," she replied as he handed her up into the carriage that would take them to the inn where they'd elected to spend their wedding night. Huntley had rented the whole establishment for two days, leaving Amberly Hall to their family and the few friends who'd come to join the celebration. "How about you?" Gabriella asked as he got in beside her, his hand immediately seeking hers.

"Never more so than now." And then he pulled her to him, kissing her as though it would kill him to be apart from her for even one second. With the roof of the carriage pulled back, they made a perfect display of newly wedded bliss, eliciting loud *hurrahs* as the carriage rolled forward along the country road.

Chapter 34

It took five hours of drinking, dining and dancing before the guests finally decided that it was time to retreat. As much as Gabriella had enjoyed their company, she looked forward to being alone with her husband, her arm linked with his as they waved good-bye to her parents.

"I thought they'd never leave," Raphe said the moment their carriage was out of sight. Looking down at Gabriella, he quietly asked, "Are you ready to see our accommodations, Your Grace?"

A delicious thrill of anticipation swept through her at the mention of the room they'd be sharing. Feeling her cheeks warm beneath the heat of his gaze, she gave a slight nod. "By all means, husband, show me the way."

His eyes seemed to darken as he tugged her back inside and led her toward the stairs. "Oh, I intend to." The words, filled with a promise of decadence and sin, enhanced his masculinity in an elemental way that made Gabriella's knees grow weak. His strength emanated from every part of his solid frame as he guided her up toward their destination, his muscles flexing slightly beneath her hand with every step they took.

"Raphe." Her voice stopped him at the top of the stairs.

"Yes?" he inquired.

Turning to face her, his arm slid away from hers until only their fingers connected, the bare touch heightening Gabriella's need for closer contact. She prepared to speak in spite of the nerves that danced inside her, but for some reason, she couldn't seem to align her thoughts. So she just stood there, staring up at him while each exhalation of breath trembled upon her lips.

A moment passed, and then he curled his fingers around hers and raised her hand for a tender kiss. His eyes met hers, full of warmth and sincerity, the hungry desire she'd seen there a second earlier momentarily banked. "You're nervous?" Forcing herself not to look away, she nodded. "Don't be. What you and I are about to experience together will be full of love and devotion. Because of that, it cannot be anything but absolutely incredible."

"But—what if I do something wrong? What if—"

"You won't." He shook his head with absolute certainty. "That just isn't possible."

She dropped her gaze briefly before returning it to his. "I've been told it might hurt."

"Only momentarily." He brought his hand to her forehead, smoothing away her frown before letting his thumb caress her cheek. "I promise to treat you with care, and to make it as enjoyable for you as possible. Trust me, Gabriella, the pain is brief. After that there is nothing but endless pleasure."

"Really?"

He chuckled slightly. "If it were really that awful, women would not be as willing as they are to attract men's attention."

"I suppose that's true."

"Come on," he whispered.

Unable to resist the seductive nudge of his voice, she followed him down a corridor to the room at the end, her lips parting on a gasp as soon as she stepped inside. Rose petals covered the floor, while garlands tied with cream-colored ribbons framed the ceiling. Candles had been placed along the walls, their glow creating an intimate air of subdued lighting. Everything was soft and inviting—an irresistible haven of pure romance. Awestruck, Gabriella uttered a single word. "Beautiful."

The door closed quietly behind her, and then a hand settled carefully against her waist. "I couldn't agree more." He spoke against the nape of her neck.

A shiver curled its way along her spine, leaving nothing but heat in its wake. Gone was the reservation she'd felt in the hallway, now replaced by a sense of calm that soothed her from within. So she settled herself against his strength, reveling in the feel of his hands moving over her. With nimble fingers he undid buttons and ribbons, pulled aside lace and silk, exploring every curve of her body until he'd revealed all of her.

"My God," he rasped, turning her in his arms and taking a step back. "You are so incredibly stunning." His hands went to his neck, tugging off his cravat before shoving his jacket from his broad shoulders. Both items fell to the floor behind him.

Gabriella stared, her own nudity and the self-aware timidity that came with it completely forgotten as she watched him hastily shirk off his waistcoat and shirt. Nothing could make her tear her eyes away from his impressively sculpted torso. Her fingers itched to touch him there—to slide across those hard planes of perfectly carved muscle.

"Go ahead," he murmured, reading her thoughts.

Her eyes flew to his. Drawn by the fire that burned there, she took a hesitant step forward. Then another. And another still. He remained exactly where he was, completely still, save for the rise and fall of his chest. Raising her hand, she placed her palm against his beating heart. A gravelly sound rose from his throat, emboldening her to continue, hands gliding up over his shoulders and down the lengths of his arms, mapping every inch of exposed skin in an effort to sate her curiosity.

"You're killing me," he murmured, even though he still allowed her exploration.

Running her hands across his back, she pressed the tips of her fingers against the tight rows of muscle there. "You're so solid," she said with wonder, "so incredibly hard."

He growled then, moving with a swiftness that would have knocked her over had he not decided to catch her. "You've no idea." And then his mouth was on hers, kissing her with a pent-up passion that burst its way through her, filling her with nothing but thoughts of him and of how good it felt to be back in his arms.

His mouth never left hers as he lifted her off her feet and carried her to the bed like a marauding pirate claiming his treasure. She would later wonder how he managed to remove his shoes and trousers without her noticing. All she knew was that as he lowered himself over her seconds later, she was able to feel every part of him—his warmth and his strength surrounding her in a rich combination of male virility that drove her own desire to new and wondrous heights.

His caresses were careful and gentle, his mouth

hot against her skin as he slid his hands over her. "Gabriella." He whispered her name across her belly on a breath of air that made her sigh with pleasure.

"Yes," she gasped as he kissed his way upward with slow deliberation, her fingers crawling across his back as he moved in closer, their bodies touching in just the right places—her softness against his hard masculinity.

"How do you feel?" he asked as he nestled between her thighs and gazed into her eyes.

Her arms wound their way around his neck. "Incredible."

"And now?" He nudged his hips forward, carefully testing.

She could only sigh, her mind numb with exquisite pleasure. More so when he brought his mouth down over hers in a kiss that shattered her senses. Closing the last bit of distance between them, he bit her lip as their bodies joined, distracting her from any discomfort by sending a hot dart of pleasure straight to her core. And as he kissed her with increased depth, his body moving against hers in a timeless rhythm of shared desire, she followed his lead—touching, tasting, feeling—a beautiful exploration that lifted her up and carried her higher.

"Raphe." His name fell from her lips on a rush of breath as heat spiraled through her. It rushed along her nerves, pushing at her senses until it suddenly burst in a bright crescendo of dazzling light. Clinging to him just as he clung to her Gabriella felt their hearts align as they rode the waves of fulfillment together.

She loved this man—this most unlikely duke—and as he whispered affectionate words in her ear, she placed a smiling kiss on his cheek.

"My love."

He turned on his side and pulled her against him, his arms loosely cradling her body as his lips grazed her temple with soothing tenderness.

"My everything."

Chapter 35

Huntley House, approximately one month later

Balancing on a narrow stub, Amelia reached up into the tree she'd climbed and tried not to look down.

"I don't think this is a good idea," Juliette called from below.

Deciding not to answer, lest she lose her footing in the process, Amelia braced her body against the trunk and carefully maneuvered the nest she held toward a spot where a cluster of branches would provide support. It must have fallen out of the tree overnight, for the wind had been so strong that it had rattled the windows of Amelia's bedchamber, accompanied by the drumming of rain. Miraculously, all the chicks appeared to be safe, their desperate chirping alerting Amelia to their presence the moment she'd walked out onto the terrace for some fresh morning air. After years in St. Giles, she savored having a garden to step out into, and could always be found there before breakfast, as long as the weather allowed.

"Careful!"

Amelia flinched. "Be quiet," she told her sister. She was almost there . . . just a little bit further . . .

the nest came to rest upon the spot that Amelia had selected. Hopefully, the parents would return soon to feed their chicks. She'd seen them flying back and forth between the hedge and the nest earlier, but they'd fled as soon as she'd approached.

Removing her hand, Amelia eased back and began climbing back down, her foot seeking the branch below. One step, then another, and—the branch she'd grabbed hold of snapped, her foot slipped, and before she could manage to regain her balance, Amelia skidded down the length of the trunk, her hands scraping against the bark as she struggled to stop her descent. But before she could do so, she hit the ground, the momentum knocking her back so forcefully that she landed right on her bottom, hands splayed out behind her in the soggy grass. "*Oomph!*"

"Oh my goodness," Juliette exclaimed.

Initially, Amelia thought Juliette had spoken with sympathy, but then she turned her head toward the spot where her sister stood, and immediately froze. Because there, on the terrace, impeccably dressed as always, stood the one man capable of making Amelia's heart flutter: *the Duke of Coventry*. And she, Amelia Matthews, bumbling fool that she was, had yet again proven that she would never make him a suitable duchess, no matter how much she longed to do so.

Acknowledgments

It takes more than an author to grasp an idea and transform it into a book. My name might be on the cover, but there's a whole team of spectacular people behind me, each with their own incredible skills and experience. Their faith in me and in my stories is invaluable, and since they do deserve to be recognized for their work, I'd like to take this opportunity to thank them all for their constant help and support.

To my editor extraordinaire, Erika Tsang, and her wonderful assistant, Elle Keck: your edits and advice have helped this story shine. Thank you so much for your insight and for believing in my ability to pull this off.

To my copyeditor, Ellen Leach; publicists Katie Steinberg, Emily Homonoff, Caroline Perny, Pam Spengler-Jaffee, and Jessie Edwards; and senior director of marketing, Shawn Nicholls, thank you so much for all that you do and for offering guidance and support whenever it was needed.

I would also like to thank the amazing artist who created this book's stunning cover. Chris Cocozza has truly succeeded in capturing the mood of *A Most Unlikely Duke* and the way in which I envisioned both Raphe and Gabriella looking—such a beautiful job!

To my fabulous beta readers, Rhonda Jones and Marla Golladay, whose insight has been tremendously helpful in strengthening the story, thank you so much!

Another big thank-you goes to Nancy Mayer for her assistance. Whenever I'm faced with a question regarding the Regency era that I can't answer on my own, I turn to Nancy for advice. Her help is invaluable.

My family and friends deserve my thanks as well, especially for reminding me to take a break occasionally, to step away from the computer and just unwind—I would be lost without you.

And to you, dear reader—thank you so much for taking the time to read this story. Your support is, as always, hugely appreciated!

Author's Note

Dear Reader,

I hope that you've enjoyed this first installment of my new Diamonds In The Rough series. It has certainly been a joy to write.

Developing Raphe's character was particularly interesting since it took me to the nineteenth-century London slums and also introduced me to the world of Regency boxing. *Boxania*, which is briefly mentioned, was a real periodical at the time, and parts of Raphe's final fight against the Bull were inspired by a fight described therein. Another historical fact of some importance is the way in which Raphe becomes the Duke of Huntley in the first place. The conditions surrounding his inheritance were inspired by William Courtney, the eldest son of the Bishop of Exeter, who inherited his second cousin's title and became the 10th Earl of Devon in 1835.

My intention and hope for this series is to explore class differences during the Regency period by getting the very rich and the very poor to mix and mingle. Right now, I'm writing Amelia's story. She's having a bit of trouble adapting to the many rules of Society, but in spite of her fears, she might just prove to be the perfect match for the Duke of Coventry. We already know that he's bored with aristocratic monotony and that he seeks a change of pace, but I'm not entirely sure that he was planning anything as extreme as being led into St. Giles by a willful hoyden.

I'm having fun with it, and look forward to sharing this new romance with you soon.

*G*ive in to your Impulses!

These unforgettable stories only take a second to buy and give you hours of reading pleasure!

Go to *www.AvonImpulse.com* and see what we have to offer.
Available wherever e-books are sold.

AVONIMPULSE

IMP 0811